Same as God Spoke

JOSEPH WACTOR

Copyright © 2020 Joseph Wactor
All rights reserved
First Edition

PAGE PUBLISHING, INC.
Conneaut Lake, PA

First originally published by Page Publishing 2020

ISBN 978-1-6624-1819-8 (pbk)
ISBN 978-1-6624-1820-4 (digital)

Printed in the United States of America

CONTENTS

Introduction: The Unspeakable 5

1. The Proposition 11
2. From Heaven to Hell...25
3. Seven Down, One to Go 51
4. Same as God Spoke...69
5. Seeing Double...89
6. The Setup 106
7. Don't Come Back without 'Em 122
8. The Roundtable 139
9. The Longest Night 154
10. The Forbidden Touch..167
11. The Offer You Shouldn't Refuse 182
12. Almost Caught..201
13. Dead on the Case 215
14. The Improbable Switch 229
15. The Great Escape 242
16. Compromised 255
17. The Game Plan 271
18. The Takedown 288
19. You'll Never Know 309

INTRODUCTION

The Unspeakable

LJ COULD SCARCELY believe where he was. He found himself lurking in the short darkened passageway of a place he had never been before. Nonetheless, he was all too aware of why he was there. He had been made an offer that he plainly could not refuse!

He stood motionless with his back pressed tightly against the cold bare wall directly behind him. From his vantage point, he could see the murky figures of several men sitting in a conference room. And for some strange reason, they all looked to be wearing Halloween masks. He imagined the glass had to be a two-way mirror, because it was all too obvious that none of them were aware of his presence.

Even as he slow-walked his way across the narrow corridor to his present position of waiting, not one person so much as batted an eye. He also figured this to be the reason that the people on the other side looked so distorted. *Besides, why would anyone be wearing masks in a meeting?* he thought.

As much as he wanted to leave, at that precise moment, he was powerless to do anything other than remain in that dimly lit hallway. With all his might, he wished that he did not have to carry out the absolutely unspeakable act he had been commanded to complete. However, he positively had no say so in the matter.

His orders were clear, they were specific, and most of all, not up for debate. Under the present circumstances, it was the *same as if God spoke*, and he had issued but one commandment! Thou shalt kill!

The last seventy-two hours had been pure hell for LJ. He had been tricked into coming to the God-forsaken resort where he and his family were summarily abducted. And then to top things off, he had been badly beaten because he objected to it all. Then, as icing on the cake, he had been injected with some kind of mind-controlling concoction simply known as the Godspoke. The suitably named drug had rendered him completely submissive, as if a complete servant to God. The only difference was that he served the Good Doctor. Robbed entirely of any free will, his every action was now based on commands given to him by his captor. So for all intents and purposes, when the Good Doctor spoke, it was actually as if God spoke.

Like it or not, he was now at the mercy of the Godspoke drug. The carefully administered alkaloid derivative had but one use. It altered the human mind to render its victim helplessly obedient and compliant. In fact, he could literally do nothing but follow their commands to the letter. And strangely enough, although his handlers had complete influence over his every physical action, they had no power over any of his thoughts.

Be that as it may, his ability to disobey them even in the slightest regard was absolutely nonexistent. He could think anything he wanted, but he could only do as they said, exactly as they said. Literally, the creators of the Godspoke were now his masters! In essence, his freedom of thought became a self-wounding doubled-edged sword.

To this point in his surreal daytime nightmare, LJ had tried everything. Since going under the Godspoke spell, he had been in a constant fight to be free. But, try as he might, the spell was like Teflon. He could not bend it, break it, or budge it. He wondered hard if he would ever regain his free will, and he worried even harder what he would do when and if he ever did.

Truth be told, that's exactly what the mind-altering cocktail was designed to do. The potent concoction was designed to rob the body and slowly melt the mind. Doubting yourself was the first sign that you were fully engaged in this always losing battle. The Godspoke all but forced you to engage in a maddening struggle between accepting the repulsive reality of servitude versus the no-brainer alternative of somehow finding a way to escape! And it worked to perfection!

Still, as dismal as things seemed, right now LJ had an even worse dilemma. Both his mind-altered state, as well as being held captive, paled in comparison to the outright nefarious reason for his being in that very hallway. He was one of the most successful executives on Wall Street, a Harvard graduate, a loving father, and a devoted husband. Yet he had standing instructions to carry out an assassination. That's right. He, of all people, was about to commit capital murder!

The very thought of his circumstance was enough to make him feel sick to the stomach. With great effort, he fought back the nauseated feeling and again challenged himself to break free of the crippling intoxicant. His mind raced at the speed of light, thinking of a way to liberate himself from the Godspoke spell. If anyone could, he reasoned, he was the one that could do it. And that's just what the creators of the Godspoke were counting on—innate human vanity.

Initially, he assumed that the spell would be broken if only he could force himself to act on one of his own commands. Consequently, he intensified his efforts to exercise his free will. First, he tried to raise his arm. Next, he tried to take a step. Failing to move even the slightest bit, he tried in desperation to cough as a means to regain control of his will.

In what seemed like forever, he tried thousands of rapid-fire tactics to break the rock-solid grip of the spell. All the repeated failures left him mentally drained and spiritually demoralized. Just what the creators were counting on. Nothing had worked, even though he had used every trick imaginable, even telling himself that his actions would be a part of his kill mission.

The emotional exhaustion began to exact a heavy toll on him physically; still, he refused to give up. After he got a second mental wind, he tried again. This time he tried to summon, and then act on, his emotions. He first trained his thoughts on his intense feelings of hate, but that was no good. He channeled all the anger he felt for the beating he had suffered at the hands of his captors to the surface. Still nothing!

Finally, he tried to unleash an emotional torrent of rage and pain, coupled with the all-consuming frustration known only to a captive. Surely, that potent mix of emotions would supersede any power that had suppressed his free will, or so he thought. Sadly enough, all his efforts were in vain and to no avail. And once he realized it, his spirit seemed to snap, and that, too, was a part of the creator's forethought.

Up until now, LJ Matthews had lived an unbelievably charmed life. A great many of his experiences were almost too good to be true. This experience was equally surreal, but in the exact opposite manner. *How could this be? Am I hallucinating? What magic elixir have I been given? This is like a dream, yet all too real.*

This implausible nightmare felt like something akin to an out-of-body experience. He almost felt as if he were floating just above the action, watching himself go through those many fruitless exercises. To make matters worse, in his visualization, he impulsively shouted down instructions to this exact replica of himself, but only to have them fall on deaf ears.

As he tried to make sense out of the nonsense, this became all too confusing. At this very minute, he had passed his breaking point. *How*, he thought, *am I able to think my own thoughts, yet I am unable to act on any of them?*

The succubus now had him completely in her grips. The Godspoke had him fighting against himself, second-guessing and re-guessing his every notion. The Godspoke spell was doing exactly what it was concocted to do. It was scientifically amazing yet humanly monstrous!

Suddenly, he snapped back to his present reality and became acutely aware that clinched tightly in the palm of his perspiring left hand was a fully loaded chrome-plated .9 millimeter handgun. At any moment, a complete stranger would walk through the door immediately to his right. And whoever the poor soul was would meet his untimely and ultimate demise. For LJ, the only good thing about the entire affair was that his victim would probably be dead before he knew what killed him.

Pulling the trigger of the shiny semiautomatic weapon would take almost no effort, he thought. Conversely, he knew the very foundation of his manhood would be rocked after the unspeakable act was done. The thought of living with the hands that had taken an innocent human life would be all too devastating.

Just then, a large broad-shouldered man emerged from the meeting room. *Here he comes*, LJ thought. *Doesn't he see me?* LJ wanted to blurt out, "Hey, Mr. Whoever, run. Run fast." He even briefly envisioned that the powerfully built man had seen him, gone on the attack, and disarmed him of his weapon. But none of that was reality; that was more of the Godspoke trickery. The dead man walking was oblivious to his would-be assassin's presence, and thus totally unaware of any danger.

As instructed, LJ took several hurried steps and pulled the trigger when he got close enough. The lethal gunshot struck dead center mass. The large caliber bullet caused blood and brain fragments to splatter everywhere. Despite the mess, this was a clean kill, straight out of the assassin's handbook.

A single bullet to the back of the brain, at point-blank range; it was over in an instant. The blast of the single shot rang out and reverberated throughout the small enclosure. The noise shattered all silence and interrupted the previous calm that had enveloped the small darkened corridor.

After the unspeakable was done, LJ felt nothing. He couldn't cry. He couldn't sob or sigh. He was still not free to act of his own will. His only solace was that the dead man was indeed wearing a mask. It was a mask of Abraham Lincoln. So gladly, he would never have to see the man's actual face. This was as odd as anything that he had witnessed since this whole crazy ordeal had begun, but in all truth, he was thankful for this small bit of strangeness.

As he walked back, LJ again felt the rage of being caged without any bars, and he desperately wanted to be free again. Although, he was starting to believe the chances of that were not especially good. However, he hoped like hell, as he was always taught, that any negative circumstance would be temporary at best. He did not know how temporary, but he knew one thing for certain. If, and when, he was ever able to follow the commands of his own choosing, there was one command that he would execute without any hesitation. That command would be to take his revenge!

His only comfort at that very moment was the thought of the Good Doctor getting what was coming to him. At the right time, he would pay dearly for every single second of misery he had brought to LJ's life and that of his family. He did not know when. He did not even know exactly how, but he was certain that his vengeance would be forthcoming.

LJ was an expert and skilled planner, so he knew that any premeditated scheme that he cooked up would be very detailed. He imagined nothing short of a slow and torturous phase-by-phase punishment for those that he now hated. He nearly smiled thinking about how downright painful it all would be for the Good Doctor and all his associates. Indeed, how sweet it would be to leave an indelible scar on the very soul of the man who introduced the Godspoke to the world!

* * *

LJ awoke in a cold sweat. He had just relived the second worst night of his life. Initially, he thought about trying to go back to sleep. However, the dream had really shaken him. He now felt both weak and impotent. So after only a minute of thought, he got up, got dressed, and headed to the one place that he felt safe and in charge—his office.

CHAPTER 1

THE PROPOSITION

IN ORDER TO shake off the uneasy feelings that he was experiencing, Joseph Matthews snuggled a bit deeper in his handcrafted chair. Right about now, his mind as well as his soul were both in need of some major relief. The chair's lumbar massage feature could soothe like nothing else, at least like nothing else that was immediately available.

And as he sat pondering, he hoped that this quick fix would help him to relax and empty his mind of its many troubling thoughts. Filled to capacity with a scrambled mix of fact and fiction, each competing for supremacy, his mind actually bordered on the brink of breaking, yet again. He desperately needed that relief, and in a hurry!

He grabbed the high-end chair by its arms and quickly sat up, as if suddenly compelled to do so. He could not quite place it before, but now he realized exactly why that dream had shaken him so badly. He had had that dream so many times before and never had this harsh of a reaction. Suddenly, he realized it wasn't just the dream. Today, like no other in a lifetime of memorable events, was *the* anniversary. Unfortunately, this was an anniversary that he wished to God that he could forget. Although unmentionable, it would be quite some time before he would ever fail to remember it.

He could feel that his mind was about to take him to a place that he did not want to go. To a place that was uneasy, a place full of uncertainty...a place of deception, abduction, and murder. Without question, his thoughts were anniversary bound. But knowing himself all too well, it would not first be without a fight.

With one hand stuffed into his pants pocket, he moved several anxious steps over to the fully stocked bar. There, he took the liberty of pouring himself a small shot of top-shelf brown liquor. He downed it and instantly repeated the treatment. The eighty-proof beverage stung the back of his throat as he swallowed hurriedly, but today that would not serve as any serious deterrent. With the assumed goal of slowing down the fierce competition raging in his head, he poured himself a third, but more generous, glass of the aged brandy, and he gulped away.

The effects of the drink had not yet fully taken, and he was still feeling less than his usual confidence. So in desperation, he tried something else. He moved to the center of the room to take a 360 degree survey of his rather large corner office. By any standard, it was filled with high-end everything. Standing midroom, he took careful notice of all the strategically placed symbols of wealth. They were abundant in number and served only to showcase his success as he wooed new clients.

Everything considered, his greatest symbol of success was his present location. His office sat high atop a fifty-story building, located in the heart of the money-making capital of the world, and no less than the renowned Hudson River served as backdrop scenery. Seated once again, he nodded in approval after a final examination of the opulence that completely surrounded him.

Like the deep-tissue chair massage, this was clearly another attempt to create a much-needed distraction. However, this, too, was in vain, because in all truth, he was slowly losing the mental fight to train his thoughts on something other than *it*.

Not giving up just yet, and now sipping slowly, he spun his chair to the left and stood. He arose to view himself in the full-length, handmade, rustic framed mirror just to his left. He looked himself up and then down. He first admired his all-black attire; he then paused to pay visual homage to the very expensive diamond decorated timepiece that donned his wrist.

SAME AS GOD SPOKE

Finding his chair once again, he spun it around so that he was now facing a panoramic view that included Battery Park as well as the lovely Lady Liberty herself. "God, I love my life," he blurted out, as if trying to assure himself that this was all real. He took a long slow sip of the imported elixir contained in the custom-made glass that he now held fragilely between his fingers. Finally, he shut his eyes tightly and let out a Goliath-sized sigh. He said, "Dammit" aloud and gave up the ghost.

Joseph Matthews, LJ to most, then began a slow, strange, and sequenced preparation for the daytime nightmare he was about to experience. Relieved that he no longer had to stave off the haunting feelings that had slowly and stealthily taken up residence in his consciousness, he began to drain his mind of any excess thought. Next, he methodically filled the recesses of his lungs to the point of bursting. Deliberately, he held in this air of comfort for an extended time and then released it. He repeated this deep-lung air-transfer several times over.

This was, in essence, an exercise to help cleanse his mind by way of his lungs. As a finale, he sucked in one more deep rich gulp of the free air that only a former captive can appreciate. He savored it, held it, held it some more, and then savored it still more. Then, with slow deliberation, he opened his tightly shut eyes and exhaled ever so slowly.

Now, prepared to face the impending doom of the Godspoke anniversary, he permitted his thoughts to revisit the life-threatening events of exactly one year ago. For the sake of keeping his own sanity, LJ slowly and gradually allowed his mind to focus exclusively on *it*.

In mere seconds, he was totally consumed with the "who, what, why, and how." He almost lost everything of value to him. More important than his prized symbols of wealth, his wife, children, family, and his freedom were all nearly taken from him forever.

Since *it* had happened, LJ made it a daily ritual to stop and smell the roses, so to speak. Without fail, he made it a point to take time out to salute his wonderful life. This solemn time of reflection, to be both grateful and appreciative, was done the same way, almost every day.

On his way to work, including most weekends, he would tune in to the Weather Channel to catch the forecasted time of sunset. Then and there, he would set his phone to alert him about fifteen minutes ahead of time. When the alarm sounded, he would stop all business, *period*!

No matter what he was doing, he would excuse himself and instantly head to his office, if he was not already there. Each evening possible, his singular aim was to watch the sun slowly set over the majestic Hudson. Minutes before it was time, he would position himself directly in front of the wall-sized tinted glass window.

He would stand silently, looking first toward the heavens to glimpse the fast-changing crimson red sky. Next, he would marvel at the strikingly beautiful shadows that the setting sun cast eerily across the landscape that only the world-renowned Gotham City could provide. The combination of brilliant sun, colorful glowing sky, and the glistening reflection of both atop the almost stilled water of the river made for an awesome spectacle. In his estimation, there was no natural rival to the feeling this moment provided.

He would even observe this ritual on days when he was elsewhere, but nothing compared to that view from his window high atop the world, or so it seemed. In either case, during those quiet minutes of mental solitude, he analyzed and reflected on both the simple as well as the complex. Although precious and few, during those fleeting moments, he would always be thankful for the *now* and would always ponder the *then*. However, and only when he couldn't help it, he reluctantly reflected on the *was*.

The *now* was wonderful, he always thought. He had a thriving business and a beautiful, loving, very successful, and more importantly, an extremely passionate and contented wife. He usually blushed at the thought. He also had two wonderful children. They were well-behaved, smart as whips, and both easily able to con him out of his shirt without even the courtesy of undoing the buttons. The very thought of being taken by the little rascals also made him smile shamelessly.

Moreover, both his parents were still alive and in good health. He even enjoyed the major, major blessing of in-laws who were easy to get along with. He knew all too well that in-laws could be a nightmare, and not just in a metaphorical sense. Firsthand knowledge from his brother Milton, and his daily dealings with his in-laws from hell, was evidence enough of his blessing. "What could be better?" he would always say when contemplating his immediate quality of life. What could be better than *now*? And he would always answer, "Another ten or twenty million dollars" as he laughed aloud.

Once the *now* had been reviewed, he immediately turned his attention to *then*. He would always proclaim with great excitement and anticipation that his *then* would be even better than his *now*. His attention to *then* always focused first on the projected new growth of his company, his baby. In a few months, he and his brother Henry had plans to open up new offices in both Miami and Los Angeles. Additionally, they were perpetually in talks to acquire smaller companies, so business wise, his *then* looked very promising.

Other thoughts concerning *then* centered on the personal side of things. He had overdue plans to expand his family. He and his wife, Mysty, wanted more children, but those plans were put on hold since *it* had happened. However, a year had gone by, and he felt more and more like it was time now, or it would be very soon. All and all, his *then*, his future, looked very, very bright.

The problem for LJ is his *was*. His *was* both haunted and tormented him periodically, but always without warning. His *was* had apparently scarred him for life, but only time would truly tell to what degree. While contemplating his *was*, his mind would not take him back to his sometimes turbulent, although fun-filled, high school years. Equally, he would not even think about his chaotic college days within the hallowed halls of Harvard University. And the thought of starting his business, only to go bankrupt twice over before he ever graduated, never even entered his mind.

His thoughts of *was* had a bizarre and otherwise mind-boggling destination. These particular thoughts always took him back to revisit the all-consuming power that once possessed him and his closest friends. It was the power that forced him to commit an unspeakable and ungodly act, something so atrocious he would surely almost never recover. This power pushed him to the limit; it forced him to do something far worse than murder. The power known simply as the Godspoke!

LJ, which was short for Little Joe, but only to his family and close friends, was a lawyer. In fact, he was one of the brightest. Some say the best in the country, in his particular field of expertise. He, together with his partner and brother Henry, was a mover and shaker in the world of venture capitalism.

He was arguably better at raising money for financially worthwhile projects than almost anyone in the business. He could convince almost anyone with money to invest it with him, and he always seemed to pick the winners. Word on the street was that everyone who did business with LJ made money. Usually, they made lots of it. But more importantly, they made it fast.

Henry Matthews was the exact opposite of LJ. Where Henry was quiet, LJ was boisterous. Henry was the consummate team player. LJ, on the other hand, had to be captain of the team. Although many had varying opinions as to why the venture capital firm of Matthews & Matthews was so successful, most would agree that the divergent but complementary personalities of the two managing partners played an equal part in any final analysis.

The two men worked together like a hand and a glove, like a foot and a sock. But moreover, they complemented each other as well as any world-renowned duo imaginable: Batman and Robin, Ginger Rodgers and Fred Astaire, or Peanut Butter and Jelly, take your pick. They just flat out knew each other, and they knew each other well.

So well, in fact, that one could start a thought and the other could finish it in rhythm. In any negotiation they were involved in, it was always two against one, and that's why they almost always got their way. This tandem made for a very potent, privileged, and powerful combination. And once the prosperity component was factored in…well, who could argue against them? Who would want to?

Three weeks before *it* happened, the four Matthews brothers met to discuss ideas for their upcoming semiannual vacation. In addition to LJ and Henry, also present were Mysty, LJ's beautiful better half of ten years, and Mysty's older sister Beverley, who was married to Henry. Henry always did like older women. However, this situation was tailor-made for an infinite amount of family jokes. The term *robbing the cradle* was tossed around so much by family members that Henry's nickname eventually became Robbie.

Also present was Milton, the eldest of the four, and Greg, the youngest. Rounding out the octet was Greg's fiancée, Pam, not yet a Matthews woman and often reminded of this fact by Hazel, Milton's wife of many years and Pam's chief family nemesis. Most speculate the reason for Hazel's negative attention to Pam probably had more to do with her cultural classification rather than Pam's sometimes less than friendly attitude.

Generally, all the others simply attributed her reserved nature to shyness, together with youthful immaturity, and thus usually overlooked her standoffish ways. However, Hazel reasoned that because Pam was a mulatto, she fancied herself a cut above the rest of her fiancé's family, if not her fiancé himself. This often made for some very interesting verbal and nonverbal exchanges, many of which led to some near catfights.

The group was seated at a large table at Milton's restaurant, and everyone began tossing around suggestions. However, to this point, none were all that well received. Previously, the group had done the Caribbean and spent time in Hawaii. On one occasion, they even vacationed on the Mediterranean coast. On that trip to Nice, in the south of France, LJ purchased his prized handblown glass set.

Hazel, a nurse by profession, suggested that maybe the group should go north this time. She first proffered the idea of visiting Canada. Then she also pointed out that Martha's Vineyard had a quaint small-town feel that everybody in the group seemed to prefer. She then threw in the hard sell, stating that she knew a friend that could get them a great deal on a large cottage rental.

However, neither suggestion got a good deal of traction and almost no feedback, much to her masked disappointment. Conversely, Milton's displeasure was overt, unmasked, and very much on display.

With so many dispassionate suggestions being thrown out, only to die merciless deaths, there was a growing sense of frustration settling in on the group. It was not long before the collective mood began to turn sour. This was especially true for Greg's fiancée, Pam, who finally suggested that each couple should do their own thing this time. She declared that she was tired of the big group ventures, even though she had only been to three.

To which Hazel replied, "Well, you two go on by yourselves." And she added a slightly murmured afterthought. "That is if Greg can stand to be alone with you for that long." Hazel then supplemented her verbal body blow with a hand-on-hips piercing I-wish-you-would glare.

Her stare was immediately returned with a stare of equal intensity but a surprisingly and uncharacteristic silence from Pam. Sensing a win in her battle column, the pediatric nurse spontaneously exchanged a celebratory high-five with Beverley, who was seated to her right.

After several other undesirable suggestions, LJ took charge as he always did. He had been holding a surprise suggestion and wanted to spring it on the group at just the right time. He felt that time was now! He excitedly informed them that he had a great idea. It seemed a client had invited him to visit an upscale resort located in the secluded foothills of the Keystone state.

Taking LJ's cue, Henry chimed in, "Yeah, you mean Mr. Jones, the guy who wanted us to find him some investors."

"Yeah, that's the one," LJ replied. "Apparently," he seductively began once he had everyone's interest, "this guy has opened up some fancy schmancy high-class resort. It's somewhere deep down in the Pennsylvania woods. So remote that he generally describes the location as even behind God's back."

That blasphemous statement got a somewhat nervous round of laughter, but undeterred, LJ continued. "The catch is that he needs a large cash infusion in order to keep his head above water until he builds up his clientele. He had been hounding us for over a year, but with no luck," he added with one of his trademark arrogant hand-and-shoulder gestures.

"A few months ago, he sent me a new brochure detailing all of the new amenities. And I gotta tell you, this place sounds freaking fantastic. I guess he thought that we would have a change of heart once we saw the new improvements. They have everything you could think of in this place. Just name it, go ahead. Anybody, just throw something out and I'll bet you they got it there."

Excited to take the bet, Greg said, "What about Jet Skis?"

LJ shot back, "Got it!"

Mysty blurted out, "What about waterbeds?"

LJ gave her the "you naughty girl" look, then laughingly said with insinuation, "Got it, and we will use it!"

Milton also took on the challenge, but with a very different agenda. He was secretly intent on making the man that he privately called Mr. Perfect look quite imperfect. He said, "Any resort worth something should have party cruises and fishing boats, but what about speedboats? Do they have that?" he said loudly and with a noticeable indication of "gotcha" in his voice.

Without even looking in his older brother's direction, LJ said, "Got it," but in whisper mode, as if to make a special point that he recognized the dark origins of that challenge.

Not to be so easily beaten, Milton shot back, this time drawing on a subject that he knew all too well. "What about the food? Do they have full menu room service twenty-four hours of the day, even at three in the morning? Now," he said with confidence and also in a mocking whisper, "do they have that?"

This time LJ looked directly into the eyes of his sometimes hard to figure elder, who could be a royal pain in the ass when he set his myopic mind to it, and said with even greater emphasis, "*Got it*," almost in a shout.

Henry, sensing the tension between the two, quickly stepped in and continued, "I read the brochure, too, and I am telling you guys, everything that LJ said is right on point. Y'all, this place is the real deal. And I gotta tell you, the hype has me sold. I'm really feeling this place."

Returning to his point position, LJ jumped back into persuasive argument mode and never missed a beat. "Yeah, like I was saying, he had very high hopes that we would take his new brochure into consideration and create a fast-track prospectus. He doesn't care whether the cash is generated by some private financing interest or simply through a public offering. He just wants some money. He wants it badly, and he wants it now.

"He's never gotten so much as a maybe to this point, but it wasn't because he wasn't trying. That man bugged the hell out of both of us, call after call after call. First one, then the other. I have to give him an A, both for dogged persistence and tenacious effort. After so much rejection," LJ began.

"And for so long," Henry added.

"We just couldn't figure out why this guy wouldn't give up," LJ concluded.

"We'd said no in twelve different languages." To which another round of spontaneous laughter broke out. "But to be real, and all kidding aside, we literally had to stop taking his calls."

"So why do we need to know all of this?" Milton cut in out of the blue. "It seems you two big shots are telling us more about how you dissed the man rather than about some vacation that we are supposed to be planning."

"Hold your horses there, big bro," said LJ with a rather dismissive and sarcastic air. "We are getting to that. This all is relevant, if you got a minute, and I think you do. I mean, what's the hurry? No customers are here anyway." Salty, Milton said nothing, even though he really, really wanted to.

"Anyway," LJ continued, after coldly putting his older brother in his place. "After the last time we spoke, I got the impression that he had given up hope and had simply abandoned the idea of any involvement from us. I really thought that we had heard the last of him. But last week, after not hearing from him for a couple of months, he calls out of the blue with this terrific offer.

"As I told you, Henry, after our last hot prospects meeting, I'm still not about to advise any of my people to invest a dime in a business located in a place so desolate, it's described as behind God's back. I don't mean that in a bad way, but I just don't see us investing millions of dollars out there right now.

"What's the name of it again? Uh, let me see? As I remember, its sounds real down-home like. Oh yeah, it is called the Bright

Spot Villas. And get this, it's located in the town of Coulditbe, Pennsylvania."

"Coulditbe? What the hell kind of name is that?" asked Milton abrasively.

"How the hell do I know?" LJ immediately shot back with his own version of abrasiveness, anticipating more of Milton's ulterior motives.

Not wanting the two to reengage in their previous testosterone tug-of-war, Henry intervened once again. "Yeah, I'm cool with that on the investing side, but the whole point of all of this is his latest invitation."

"He just invited us down to take a look and inspect these, and I'm paraphrasing him, top-of-the-line and state-of-the-art badass villas."

"Yeah, that's what I'm getting at," replied LJ, now intentionally dismissing his partner's intervention.

"He made the offer again. And get this, guys. For us, the price is just right. *Free!*"

"I know that's right!" Milton exclaimed, now excited about the possibility of a free vacation. "'Cause if it's free, it's definitely for me."

Greg said, "I'm feeling that."

"Me too," Henry happily joined.

Still not convinced, Mysty said, "Tell me some more about these foothills villas." Hazel and Beverley also agreed that they, too, wanted to know more. However, in character, Pam remained silent.

Feeling more confident than ever, LJ resumed, "Well, ole Jonesy tells me that the place is hidden away in the deepest thickest North American forest this side of the Mississippi. He also says that the Bright Spot has several huge multilevel entertainment complexes. These things are supposed to be so large that you could get lost in there. They are divided into multiple areas of interest. They have gaming, live shows, and indoor sports, including rock climbing and bowling.

"They also boast full-scale indoor tennis and basketball courts. And if that doesn't blow you away, there are also nine very large in-house movie theaters. Plus, speedboats, water tubing, snorkeling, and bareback riding. But most important on the list of group activities is my personal favorite—paintball. Can somebody say gunfights? I'm going to murder someone," he said with a childlike exuberance.

"And," he added with a devilish smile, "I'm told that the gaming complex even has pool tables and air hockey. But here's the kicker. You don't even need money to operate any of the games, or vending machines, for that matter."

Barely able to believe what he was hearing, Greg asked, "Did you say free? I sure am glad, because otherwise that place sounds very, very expensive." Then he asked the best question of the night: "Who gives away free stuff?"

"I don't know," LJ answered. "And to be truthful, I really don't care. But as I said, all of it is free." Then after a slight pause, to give the question some thought, he asked rhetorically, "Anyway, free or not, what's the worst that can happen?" Little did he know that those words would soon come back to haunt him!

"Anyway," he said, now refocused, "back to the story. I said I'd think about it, as usual, and promised to check my schedule and get back to him. He said our stay would be complete with everything we could want, including individual valets, exotic food of every kind and culture, exclusive access to the whole facility, plus, a hundred-dollar gas card when we leave."

"Now how can you beat that?" Henry said excitedly before LJ could get the exact same words out!

Sensing a pique in interest on the part of the women, the master pitchman then moved in for the kill. "Supposedly, the place is huge, resting on over thirty thousand acres of land, which includes a few rivers and two man-made lakes. The brochure says that the guests are pampered beyond belief. It says they definitely strive to provide each guest with the royal treatment."

"Sounds like the bomb to me," cried Milton with a noticeable change of heart.

Before anyone else could respond, Pam rushed in to say, "Everything sounds like the bomb to you, especially since you're always taking one home with you."

"Yeah and ya. Momma helps me," he said jokingly.

"Oops, he got you there. He got you there," said Hazel, and everyone laughed as they nodded in agreement.

Pam gave her usual pouted lip, and predictably, not to mention right on cue, Greg came to her rescue. "Hey, hey…let's leave my baby girl alone and let's get back to focusing on the villas."

"I think I've heard enough," said Henry. "Let's save something for the imagination and something to be surprised about once we get there. That is if we're going."

"Which brings us to a vote," LJ continued. "Raise your hand if you're in favor," LJ inquired, confident in the response.

LJ, Henry, Mysty, Hazel, Milton, and Beverley all immediately raised their hands, and Greg looked as if he wanted to do so as well but waited to see what Pam did. After seeing that all too familiar pleading look in her fiancé's eyes, she reluctantly raised her hand, which was immediately followed by his own.

"All right then, great. An almost free vacation. It doesn't get any better," said Milton.

To which Pam replied, "It would be if certain people were staying behind." She immediately gave Hazel a penetrating stare. Just as abruptly, she turned her eyes skyward so as not to give Hazel the satisfaction of glaring back. Excited and consumed about the trip, Hazel overlooked Pam's comment, together with her glare, even if until the next round.

And so it was agreed that the group would leave in three weeks. LJ would call and finalize the arrangements with Mr. Jones. He'd book a villa large enough to accommodate them all for ten days and nine nights. Over the next three weeks, the four couples busied themselves with vacation arrangements.

Mysty and Beverley, not to be outdone by their successful husbands, jointly owned a health, beauty, and fitness spa. They modeled their one-stop all-inclusive philosophy after Aphrodite, the Greek goddess of love, beauty, and sexual rapture. In America's most famous metropolis, Aphrodite's Garden of Eden was the rave of every socialite. However, as always, the women entrepreneurs of the Matthews clan decided to close for the duration of the trip.

All the children would stay with BJ and Big Momma. BJ was LJ's dad, so of course BJ stood for Big Joe. And Big Momma was just big, so she was called Big Momma. Pam, a hair stylist, gave all her clients' notice that she would be away on vacation and strict orders not to visit anyone else in her absence.

Milton and Hazel left the diner in the capable hands of Willie, the night manager, and arranged for their son James to also stay with BJ and Big Momma. Henry and Beverley did not have any children, but please believe they were working on it. Really, really, really working on it!

CHAPTER 2

FROM HEAVEN TO HELL

ON THE DAY of the trip, the group loaded up LJ and Mysty's Cadillac Escalade and Greg's Lexus LX450. Even though the Escalade was the extended version and had ample seating to accommodate the entire entourage, it went without saying that Greg had to drive. Pam always refused to ride in anyone else's vehicle for fear of being resigned to someone else's control. Control over how fast, what lane, how close to the car in front, when to stop, or even what to listen to.

Both cars gassed up with premium unleaded, and the two-car convoy was on the New Jersey Turnpike rolling along the cars-only southbound lanes at just after 7:00 a.m. Their trip would be a mere two and a half hours if they got lucky. That is to say, if they missed one of the infamous tristate traffic jams, which could quickly turn a thirty-minute turnpike ride into one well over ninety minutes.

As luck would have it, no traffic jams were to be found on this bright and sunny day of about eighty-two degrees. The two cars cruised effortlessly down the highway. Vibrant sounds filled the luxury-laced passenger compartments of both vehicles. Old-school was the music of choice in the Escalade, as LJ and company were all midthirty somethings. They vibed to the sounds of the OJay's, the Temptations, Patti Labelle, and the great one, Mr. Marvin Gaye. Like always, these musical heavyweights were called upon by the elder Matthews brothers to help make the many miles of any trip seem like only a few.

While back in the Lexus, Greg and the twenty-something folks, except for Milton, blasted all the latest hip-hop and R & B tunes. After all, Pam, who was just barely twenty-something, refused to listen to anything that was made before the year 2000. Moreover, Pam's need to establish control was always evident when it came to the radio, as she would often change a song even if the others were enjoying it. Today was no exception.

As the hook was about to play on a track that everyone else seemed to be enjoying, she abruptly changed the CD player. This, of course, started a familiar refrain between Pam and Hazel. Hazel said, "Who died and left you little miss change a song? Put that back. We were listening to it." This was very evident by all the off-note singing that was heard absent the cover music.

She continued, "How the hell you gonna just up and change shit when we were all feeling that song?" She then tried to make eye contact with either one of the two men present. She was looking for some backup, but both wanted nothing more than to stay out of the whole thing. Each had seen this movie play before, and usually the endings were not all that pretty.

"Greg," exclaimed Hazel with all the controlled politeness she could muster. "Can you do something about your woman?" she softly said through clenched teeth in an effort to conceal her growing displeasure, which, if not curbed, would soon grow to be full-blown anger.

But before Greg could speak, Pam responded, "This is my car, my CD, and if I want to change shit, I don't need nobody's permission. I crowned myself little miss change a song, and now you can crown yourself little miss listen to whatever the hell I'm playing or you can close your ears. I don't give a rat's ass what you do as long as you do it back there with your mouth shut." Her remarks were immediately followed by a sudden blast of deafening noise from the state-of-the-art sound system as she cranked the volume up as loud as it would go.

SAME AS GOD SPOKE

Sensing the situation had the potential to get even uglier and out of hand real fast, both Matthews men instantaneously tried their hand at playing peacemaker. Under the cover of the blaring music, Milton quietly asked Hazel to overlook Pam and her immature antics. Assuming his usual manner and permanent posture of always trying to avoid controversy when and wherever he could, Milton touched Hazel gently on the back of her hand in an effort to soothe the growing anger that he well recognized in his wife of many years.

Hazel tried to argue her point, but to no avail. Her husband wasn't having any part of her story and insisted that she remain quiet, at least long enough for the two in the front to work things out. Despite his youth, Milton knew Greg was an experienced negotiator. And if possible, he would work the situation out so that all sides could save face.

Milton sat quietly in the back seat, watching his brilliant theory unfold. However, in the front, Greg had a much more daunting reality. As he well knew, if he pushed too hard, Pam would push back. That only meant that they would end up in a Mexican standoff with neither side giving so much as an inch.

He also knew that Pam was most responsive to nonverbal communication, at least in the presence of others. With that in mind, he gave Pam his "can you please stop embarrassing me in front of my family" look. Right away, he could see the puppy dog look had no effect on the determined lady to his right.

She stared him down with her "are you kidding me, she can't talk to me like that" look. He then tried the "honey, please, I'll make it worth your while later tonight" look. He first squinted his eyes slightly and then proceeded to lick and moisturize his lips slowly. Finally, he raised one eyebrow to expose the dimple in his left cheek that he knew was a romantic weak spot for his long-time girlfriend and recent fiancée.

After what seemed like an eternity, with none of these tactical moves making a dent in Pam's determined posture, he gave her his ultimatum look. Partly out of desperation, but mostly out of disgust. This was the look that said, "If you don't stop it and stop it right now, we will be fighting about this all day and all night, and you will indeed regret your choice." Above all that, this was the look that said, "Sometimes I will let you win, but this is not that time." That look told Pam, "Honey, I love you, but you are wrong, and this right here and right now is my time, so surrender or else suffer some unspeakable consequences."

Sometimes this particular move worked and sometimes it didn't, but Greg was at the end of his proverbial rope, and his tolerance level had been peaked. Besides, that the loud music was killing his ears. Right about then and strangely enough, he thought to himself, *I've got to go back to the stereo shop and have them take some of these loud ass speakers out of here. This is crazy. I'm going to be deaf before I'm thirty.* However, before he could finish his thought, the music was suddenly lowered. Pam had flinched. She had capitulated after all; she even changed the music back to the song that they were all listening to before the big fuss.

Hazel began to blurt out, "Now that's more like it." But seeing the beaten look already on Pam's face, she thought better of the comment. She then softened her voice and changed her original comment to a simple and polite thank you, which she directed to Pam specifically. Pam nodded her acknowledgement, and thereafter, no one spoke a word for the next several minutes.

Meanwhile, in the other vehicle, Henry's familiar baritone voice came forcefully from the rear seat as he said, "Hey, driver, are we almost there yet?"

Everyone enjoyed a brief laugh, and then LJ replied, "We have about another twenty miles, good sir, before we get to the diner where they will give us further directions. At least that's what my GPS is saying."

"So why do we need to stop if you have GPS, LJ?" Henry inquired.

"Yeah, why didn't they just give you the address?" asked Beverley from her rear vantage point.

"That's a good question," added Mysty. "So why do we have to stop for directions?" she said in a familiar accusatory tone.

"Well, according to Jonesy, the place is so cut off from the outside world that it does not even have an address. According to him, it hasn't even been surveyed, so it does not show up on any map yet. Didn't you guys read the brochure? *We are supposed to leave the world behind*," he said in his best imitation of a television announcer. "That's part of their marketing scheme."

"I don't know if I like that being cut off business or not," said Henry flatly.

"Well," Beverley added, "I'll bet you all the tea in China that Ms. Thing in the Lexus back there won't like anywhere that she can't have that precious phone glued to her ear."

Through the symphony of laughter, Mysty shouted, "I know that's right!" And the laughter grew even louder.

Approximately twenty miles later, and as accurately predicted, they arrived at the Smallville diner where the group would stop to grab refreshments and receive further instructions from Nelly, the owner.

"Hey, this is something that we have to talk to Jonesy about. Everybody cannot stop here to get instructions. Some people might think this is a setup to generate more business for the diner. We should look into who really owns this place. Maybe it's Jonesy." Ha! Ha! The laughter went up again.

Laughing and content in the knowledge that most of their journey was behind them, the group moved as a unit toward the entrance doors after they had all had a good "just got of the car after a long trip" kind of stretch. Little did they know that the first sign of trouble was just inside of those beautifully decorated brass doors that they were about to enter.

As they climbed the dinner steps, Milton exclaimed, "Man, I am hungry as hell. Y'all tried to starve a brother to death." But before he could go on, his lips froze in place, as did those of everyone else in the group.

It was almost unthinkable that in the modern-day era of political correctness, racism could be so overt. Although everyone knew it still existed, it was supposed to be a personal dirty little secret. Well, not in the town of Coulditbe. You could actually smell the intolerance in the air. The looks they received were the nearest equivalent to an order to leave. Behind the counter, and staring the hardest, was

Luke, who stood about six feet six inches tall with dirty blond hair. The look of him epitomized the term *redneck*, and next to him was a short stout fat lady.

The sight of the two together made LJ instantly, although silently, think of incest. To him, this extremely odd-looking couple looked as if they were brother and sister by way of brother and sister. From the looks on their faces, everyone else agreed. In fact, stretch and stumpy also looked very unclean and unkempt. The prospect of having either of them prepare something to snack on made everyone lose their appetite. So collectively, they decided to get some bottled beverages, which had to be safe, get some last mile instructions from Big Luke, use the facilities, and hasten to make their leave.

They left the diner knowing that they were just ten and a half miles away from the Bright Spot Villas, the crown jewel of the cozy and quaint village-town of Coulditbe, Pennsylvania. Shortly after they left the parking lot, Greg decided that he wanted to take the lead now that he knew where he was headed. However, LJ had other plans.

Greg struck first, his right foot jammed down, and he nearly mashed the accelerator pedal through the floor. LJ quickly responded in kind. He likewise attempted to make his foot, the gas pedal, and the floorboard as one. The Lexus accelerated rapidly and pinned each of the vehicle's occupants to the rear of their seats. All the four hundred plus horsepower was called upon to rocket the vehicle down the deserted tree-lined two-lane roadway.

As the rpms of the huge eight cylinder climbed higher and higher, everyone could feel an instant adrenaline rush, at least those that enjoyed a good ole-fashioned spontaneous drag race. Milton screamed and urged Greg on. "You got him, man! Hold it. Hold it to the floor!"

Hazel sat up, saying nothing but anxiously looking on to enjoy the action. All the while she was silently wishing that they would prevail, because she knew that LJ would brag if they didn't. LJ always had to brag about everything, even whose car got better gas mileage.

And Pam, in her usual effort to exert some control even when she really had none, chose to play the part of spoiler. As the two vehicles crossed the outrageous speed of 130 miles an hour, she yelled out as if right on cue to spoil everyone's fun. "Boy, if you don't slow this car down, I know what." Undeterred by Pam's effort to assert her well-known will over her sometimes obliging fiancée, Greg ignored her imperative cease and desist order. Matching his stubbornness, Pam continued, "Stop it, stop it, stop it, Greg! Slow this car down!" she screamed. "Slow this car now right now, damnit."

Trying to offset Pam's distraction, Milton, quite out of character, pleaded, "Don't listen to her, man. Get him, get him."

Pam instantly shot back, "That's what's wrong now. He don't listen to me enough, and how the hell are you going to tell him not to listen to me? You are his older brother, but you are acting like some overgrown juvenile delinquent right now, and it's you who should be telling him to quit. Greg, please, I am getting scared now, and so should you if you had any sense or at least any that you cared to use." She urged with a pleading subtlety like she had never before. "We are going entirely too damn fast. Now stop this shit right now!" she said at the top of her lungs, so frantic that she looked as though she would soon burst a blood vessel.

However, Greg was laser focused on winning this battle, a battle with his older brother who always had to win, who always had to come in first. Greg thought, *Not this time, big brother. Not his time.* With that, the two vehicles screamed side by side down the shadowy road with little give and all take, each driver doing everything in their power not to be the one who relented.

About a mile and a half into this impassioned, enthusiastic, and spontaneous drag race, a siren, accompanied by the familiar red and blue flashing lights, blared behind them. The all-out assault on the internal components of both engines, the pavement beneath their tires, and Pam's last nerve was suddenly interrupted.

"Oh no!" shouted Greg. "Shit!" he further exclaimed! "What should I do?" He was fully aware of what he must do. Even then, he reluctantly lifted his right foot, which had been glued to the accelerator up to that point, because he would have to slow down and pull in behind LJ, who, after all was said and done, would still claim victory.

At that exact same moment, Pam was heard to utter with both pride and distain, "I TOLD YOU, DAMN IT! I TOLD YOU. DIDN'T I TELL YOU? NOW SEE WHAT YOU HAVE DONE!" She continued in an unrelenting fashion, having regained the voice she had almost lost just minutes earlier.

At the very same time, Mysty screamed at LJ over the slightly loud music, "Look at what you've done now! You have us out here in the middle of racist West Bubblefuck and you two idiots want to race. I mean really, LJ, now of all times and of all places, so Sheriff Bubba can lock all our black asses up. So no one can ever hear from us again. Damn it, LJ. I cannot believe how reckless you can be at times. You have children at home waiting for you. You do know that, don't you!" she said rhetorically.

LJ looked solemn and apologetic, even without uttering a word, but his arrogance was not about to fail him in a crisis of this small magnitude. After all, he was the managing partner of a Fortune 500 law firm, and he reasoned, if only to himself, that he had been in much tighter jams than this. He watched as the officer passed by Greg's vehicle and headed straight for him. Just as he stepped to the window, LJ took a deep breath and calmed himself.

"Excuse me, sir, could I have your license and registration?" came the very polite request from the tall lanky deputy sheriff of the Coulditbe police department.

"No problem, Officer. And before we go any further, let me say that my actions were inexcusable, and I have no defense." LJ used a matter-of-fact tone but showed no remorse as he fidgeted with his wallet, looking for the requested items.

"You are absolutely right. You have no defense, and neither does your buddy back there. The judge gonna definitely throw the book at you," said the officer with all the sternness he could muster.

"I know, Officer. I know. It's just that drag racing in my blood," said LJ as he went on without pause. "My father took me to my first National Hotrod Association event at the Reading, Pennsylvania, track when it first opened up, and I've never stopped feeling the need for speed since," he said as if to confess.

SAME AS GOD SPOKE

"You say yo daddy took you to the track at Reading?" asked the now curious officer.

"Yeah, my very first taste of drag racing," replied LJ as he handed the officer his credentials.

"You don't say. I was born in Reading, and I almost lived at the track," came the almost happy reply from the officer. "I couldn't always go in," the officer continued sheepishly. "But I was always there. But that's beside the point." He shook off a bad childhood memory. "Now aside from racing on my streets, what y'all doing in these parts?" He was now confident again.

Convinced that he had made a slight connection, LJ turned on the Southern charm that was his forte. "Why hell, we staying down at the Bright Spot Villas for the next ten days," he said with as much Southern drawl as he could without being offensive and mocking.

"Ya don't say," came the gleeful reply. "My momma's cousin owns the Bright Spot. Why didn't y'all say so in the first place? I can't be running away her business now, can I? 'Sides, she'd kill me if she knew I was ticketing her guests," he said as he returned LJ's credentials. "Listen here. I'm gonna let y'all go with a warning this time. Now y'all slow down on my roads, but in the meantime, the Spot, as we call it, is just a ways up the road down yonder. Y'all gonna love it. They just finished fixing it up a whole lot. Now take it easy and welcome to Coulditbe." With that, he walked briskly past Greg and the other anxious passengers of the Lexus and back to his air-conditioned police cruiser.

"Thanks, Officer!" yelled LJ out his still open window. LJ was extremely cautious as he slowly pulled off, at least until he witnessed the cop car make a U-turn, probably on his way back to his well-concealed hiding place. Now content that his smooth talk and quick thinking had spared them all the consequence of something that could have been much worse, he said in his best country hick imitation, "All right, country boy, tell yo daddy hey from LJ next time he at the Reading racetrack." Everyone exploded in some much-needed combustible but still nervous laughter, and each was relieved.

Minutes later, as they eased their way along a beautifully crafted driveway, they appeared to be riding on a surface of the shiniest black onyx one could imagine. Not one of them had ever seen such a sight. In fact, LJ drove even more cautiously, fearing that the shiny surface was as slippery as it looked. His fears were all for naught, as this road was designed to shine and sparkle but also to perform as would any other driving surface. Looking on in awe and wonderment, both cars slowed to what amounted to barely a creep. Each occupant was captivated by the spectacle before them.

Still inside the car, Milton exclaimed, "Aw shit, this place is the bomb!"

Playing off the comment, Greg added, "Oh yeah, it looks like it's all of that and then some."

LJ pulled cautiously up to the main entrance of the largest structure in the whole complex. "*Welcome to heaven*, ladies and gentlemen. And Pam too!" he said with a smirk, which brought mischievous smiles from all the others.

It also brought the comment of "LJ, you're bad" from Mysty, who always loved when he joked.

Standing outside awaiting their arrival, as if on cue, was a well-coordinated greeting party. Each person in the party was individually and enthusiastically greeted by Malcolm, the curator. In a high squeaky voice, which did not at all fit the physical profile of this tall and well-built man, Malcolm was heard to say, "Welcome to the Bright Spot Villas, where our goal is a hundred percent satisfaction." He then proceeded to introduce each of his smartly dressed and uniformly attired staff of twelve.

Having noticed the awestruck reactions to the architectural attractiveness of the place, Malcolm, fittingly, paused to provide some Bright Spot insights. He pointed out that the structures sprawled throughout the vast landscape were all antebellum. He further explained each was similar in design to the elegant plantation homes built in the American South during the thirty years or so preceding the Civil War.

Although varying in size, most of these, he said, were much smaller than their original predecessors. He further informed the group that some of the buildings were designed to accommodate small groups of ten, and others, such as the grand hall, could accommodate sizable groups as large as fifty.

Malcolm then expertly pointed out that the term *antebellum architecture* referred not to a particular house style but rather a time and place in history. He further educated the group about some of the more prominent architectural features eclectically interwoven into the grand scheme of the Bright Spots Villas. The designers included such amenities as high ceilings, front and rear off-center entrances, 360-degree balconies, and many, many pillars.

"Wonderful job, don't you think?" he uttered a question in the form of a statement. He allowed them all another moment to gaze, then he gave the request, "Right this way please." As they entered, they found themselves in a foyer that connected to a grand ballroom just off the main entrance. Led by the tall debonair curator, the group was then shepherded into the grand ballroom, which was breathtaking, to say the least.

Once inside, everyone was again instantly astonished. There was no shortage of fascinated admiration for the majesty that they were now able to behold. The glass ceiling stood some sixty feet high, and it was adorned with chandelier after chandelier, laced with yellow and white gold. You could see yourself in the marble floors; although not mirrored, the shine was so brilliant, the floors actually took on all of the aspects of a true looking glass.

Inside, as they approached a huge conference table situated squarely in the center of the room, each found their names on the back of a reserved seat. Additionally, as a fitting complement, the table was adorned with a matching silver-plated name holder. As they seated themselves, each was then handed a personalized orientation package. Pam whispered to Greg, "Now this is high-class. This is something I could get used to."

Clearing his throat for both attention and dramatic effect, Malcolm, standing at the head of the table, began by saying, "No expense was spared to provide you with a sense of the opulence and extravagance that only a privileged few will ever know." He then directed everyone to look inside of their orientation packets to find a handheld transmitter that resembled a remote control. "This," he continued, "is your direct link to your valet, who will never be more than two minutes away from the time that you depress the call button, which instantly summons your valet to your side."

Seated well off to the side, the cadre of valets was then asked to stand and introduce themselves. Each stated the name of the person they were assigned to and provided some well-reasoned comments about why they loved the service of others. Each valet then made a personal pledge to his or her assigned guest to be responsible for ensuring that their every need and want and desire was met for their entire stay.

"Your valet is your personal concierge. You may ask almost anything of your valet, which helps satisfy your every need. This includes securing a specific type of cologne, body lotion, shampoo, or makeup. At your request, your valet will make appointments for you to meet with our personal trainers, and they can also serve as your workout partner. And last but not least, since each has received extensive training in oriental massage therapy, he or she also doubles as your personal masseuse.

"On the table before you is an exact replica of the telephone system in each of your rooms. In addition to being able to call on any service area including a twenty-four-hour kitchen, you can also communicate with each other without leaving your own. All you need to do is press the button of the room you wish to communicate with. You can do so hands-free by just pressing the speakerphone button. You can also speak to multiple parties by pressing the conference button, which allows you to include up to seventy-five different parties, if you so wish.

"Here at the spot, in your home away from home, you will find an Olympic-sized swimming pool, a sauna, a Jacuzzi, a stand-up shower, plus his and hers individual walk-in closets. Moreover, you will have access to a catalog of over twenty-five thousand movies that you can play on demand in any room in your suite. These can also be scheduled to play in one of the nine movie theaters located on the premises.

"You'll also have access to over a hundred thousand musical selections with our music on-demand entertainment system.

Additionally, you have a choice of golf, tennis, ping-pong, cornhole, horseback riding, and a myriad of water sports including Jet-Skiing, powerboating, or fly-fishing off one of our extended piers. Or if you prefer, you can just party aboard one of our twelve yachts.

"You will also have access to billiards, karaoke, and I can even arrange for you to play as a contestant on your favorite television game show, complete with a look-a-like host and a live studio audience. And by the way, this can be recorded, and you'll be presented with a keepsake DVD of the whole event.

"And as you requested, we also have scheduled a simulated paintball war game. Additionally, you also have on the complex two museums, one dedicated to exotic plant life and the other to extinct animals. Just as an FYI, both those are the passions of Mrs. Conn, our owner and proprietor whom you will meet at a later time.

"Are there any questions? Very well then, you will now be escorted to your rooms, and in approximately one hour and forty-five minutes, the war games that you requested are scheduled to begin, if that meets with your approval. Here at the Spot, your wish is our command. We treat you like gold, because to us, there is nothing more valuable than you." Finally, after a brief pause for ostentatious effect, he concluded, "I sincerely hope that your experience here at the Spot is indeed one that you'll always cherish and never forget."

"Again," he continued, making direct eye contact with each member of the group, "my name is Malcolm. And if I can personally ever be of any service, please do not hesitate to summon me. If you should ever require anything that your valet cannot get for you or do for you, you may always push the big blue manager's button, and I will try my utmost to resolve any issue that may arise." He then turned to leave, but he aborted his departure and turned to the group. "One more thing. Just a word of caution," he said in a spooky sort of tone. "We have a lot of exciting physically demanding activities, plus a lot of thrilling motorized machines, so please be safe. Accordingly, if you ever feel that you are in danger or you are injured, please press the red panic button at the very bottom of the transmitters and help will be on the way immediately."

As Henry was getting dressed, he commented to Hazel, "Man, I hate to say it, but this place is off the chain. I was hoping that it would be just okay, but I never expected anything like this. Boy, I wish old Jonesy had talked this place up a little more. We probably could have helped to get him some of that money that he wanted. You mark my words, once the word gets out about this place, people will pay and pay dearly to be able to come and enjoy what we are about to experience."

Greg was nicely surprised to hear Pam rave about all the available amenities that they could access. "Boo," she called to him in her usual pet name. "I just love that movie *Love and Basketball*. Can we watch it later on?" Greg smiled and simply nodded in agreement.

He then added, "Only if we can listen to some Barry White baby making music afterward."

She paused and put forward her best attributes as she purposely placed both hands on her coke bottle figure, just at the point where her curvaceous hips met her plentiful thighs.

She stood wide legged enough to straddle a horse and said in her sexiest alto voice, "We can listen to Keith Sweat. Or we can listen to any other baby making music. But remember, we ain't making no babies. None. No time soon." She reiterated, "At least not before you say I do" She pointed to her ring finger, and then to her most private of private parts all in the same gesture.

After about ninety minutes, the group met in the main hall, and they were escorted across the marble floors and out into two waiting limousine golf carts. As they crossed over the laser cut walkways that interlinked every structure on the complex, they could not help but notice that each side of the pavement was adorned with pearl white sand. The kind one might only expect to find in the Caribbean. Upon reaching the war games structure, the group was given a set of brief instructions as to how to play the game.

First, they would have to choose two sides of four, and if they so choose, their valets could join in to create a bigger game. The group chose not to include the valets, and they also decided to exchange partners. Greg and Milton, together with Beverley and Mysty, made up group 1, and they would compete against Henry and LJ, plus Hazel and Pam.

"The second part of the instructions were simple, although you are on teams," bellowed the instructor. "This game is every man or woman for himself or herself. After you as a team have collectively defeated your opponents, you will then turn on each other. Lastly, ladies and gentlemen, may the best soldier win," said the portly man as he disappeared into the other room. His voice then came over a loudspeaker and announced that he and his team were conducting video surveillance, and they would be enforcing the kill rules. Rules state that you cannot shoot from cover, but you must be exposed in order to execute a good kill.

"Now," he said in his best Vincent Price Michael Jackson "Thriller" imitation, "you have ninety seconds to disperse, starting now!" Everyone hurried off to take cover inside buildings, behind cars, in trenches, on balconies, and even in the tall grass. "Five, four, three, two, one, let the games begin," came the sedate and stern direction.

Anxious as always, LJ got up from the tall grass and shot in the direction of Mysty, just barely missing her. Standing beside a replica of a general store, Henry stepped out to take aim at Milton, seeing that he was the line of fire. Milton immediately stopped, dropped, and rolled about five feet until he was underneath a huge truck and safely away from the laser light.

During the next hour or so, one by one, the contestants heard the dreaded words "good kill" booming over the public address. The deceased were identified and asked to remove themselves from the game floor. Again and again and again, the war games manager shouted out the words "good kill" until finally, there were three— Greg, Pam, and of course, Mr. L "I gotta win" J.

Pam, who was technically LJ's teammate, found herself in the unenviable position of having to double-team her man. However, she knew how this battle would play out even before her teammate LJ. The war games manager never identified who killed who, only that so-and-so was killed and should leave the war floor. So none of Pam's teammates ever knew that she was the guilty culprit behind their untimely demise. And likewise, for Greg's team, the two of them secretly hatched a plot of friendly assassination back in their room.

Both having played the war games before, they decided this was their best course of action. The only thing they left up in the air was which of them would be the ultimate winner. Pam was certain that Greg would allow his sweetheart to taste the thrill of victory in order to make up for the agonizing discomfort that she must have gone through during that earlier highway ordeal. She also knew he'd rather lose to her than sit through a second radical conflict in one day.

Believing this to be the case, she located LJ, who saw her coming but was not alarmed as they were teammates. LJ asked if she'd seen Greg. "Yes, his favorite spot is the tall grass. I'll bet he's there right now," she said with confidence.

"Okay, let's go and force him out," he said as he immediately sought to use this new information to his advantage. Just one step later in the direction of the tall grass, he felt an intense stinging physical pain in the back of his neck. He had been shot at point-blank range with a pretty powerful paint gun. But even worse, he felt the intense sting of betrayal as he at once knew that it was his teammate Pam who had delivered the fatal blow to what he thought was a certain victory. "You got me. You got me good. Now at least go and get him so that in any case, my team will have won. And so I will still have won. Go get him, Pam. If you can get me like that, Greg should be less than easy," he said with a tinge of arrogance.

With her gun lowered and without delay, Pam came out of hiding and called out to Greg, only to have him stand up and abruptly shoot her right in the back of her head. Not only did he kill her, but he put paint in her hair. For this egregious and unpardonable sin, he knew he would have hell to pay, but beating LJ was worth the price of any silly argument he reasoned. So right then and right there, he celebrated. "I am the champion, my friends." He sang the lyrics to the old Queen song from the eighties. "I am the champion, my friends," he repeated. "And I will keep on fighting till the end. I am the champion, I am the champion of the woooorld." He ended with a long out-of-tune crescendo.

As they rode back to the great hall, everyone talked excitedly about the war games and how they had unfolded. They even gave the young couple plenty of praise for their diabolical and very successful win strategy. The talk then turned to how magnificent and luxurious the place was, plus a discussion of all the amenities they had yet to enjoy. To a person, everyone was enamored with the place so far.

After changing and some rest, the group reassembled in the dining hall. They wanted to put the chefs to the test and see how good they really were. They collectively agreed that each would order the most exotic thing that they could think of. Forget the menu. The challenge was issued to see who could come up with a dish that the chefs couldn't fill.

Henry asked quietly so as not to expose the conspiracy, "Is everybody down?" After briefly speaking together with a lot of smiles and nodding, they all agreed to try and stump the chefs by ordering the impossible.

After an orgy of exotic food, with requests for delicacies derived from both Thai and Greek cuisines, Greg stopped the show by ordering some Japanese puffer fish. "This expensive fugu dish was served as oriental delicacy," he said.

"Fugu?" asked LJ.

Greg replied, "Yeah, that's the Japanese word for puffer fish, and it's delicious. When eaten, it numbs the lips and creates an alcohol-like buzz." After several awestruck glares, Greg explained, "The fish contains levels of poison, and only licensed, trained chefs are allowed to prepare it, as it may be deadly to eat if not served just right." He shrugged his shoulders.

At first, there was only a growing chorus of oohs and aahs. Then came a showstopping exclamation blurted out from Mysty: "Oh my god! No way they have that here, and if they do…"

"Greg," she resumed after regaining her train of thought. "How can you sit here and order some poisonous fish? And how do you even know about that stuff in the first place?"

Smiling mostly because he didn't like to be in the spotlight, Greg answered calmly, "Did you forget I was stationed in Japan for over three years? When I first got there, I lived off McDonald's and

Burger King. But as time passed, I slowly began to appreciate the culture and the cuisine. And let me tell you, my first puffer fish experience was the ultimate. The joke over there is that if it doesn't kill you, it will thrill you.

"I have to say they were absolutely right. I was absolutely thrilled to death," he said with a smile. As it turned out, the chefs were able to prepare every meal requested. But moreover, they prepared the meals to perfection. Even Pam paid her reluctant compliments to the chef. Greg didn't get a chance to eat much of his puffer fish because everyone at the table wanted to taste some of it, except for LJ, who did not eat fish.

"Hey, guys, what do you say we all go to the movie theater and catch a show later? That is, if we can decide on something that we all want to watch," said Henry, laughing out loud and rubbing his belly as a tribute to the fine meal he had just devoured. His antics brought out a loud round of laughter as the collective culinary afterglow had everyone in a good mood.

This rare all-around good mood was probably why Henry's suggestion was agreed upon, and shortly thereafter, the group found themselves in the movie theater. Hazel found it delightful that each of the plush chairs, some single and some doubles, were able to fully recline. Her other half, Milton, was most excited about the self-serve buffet table off to the left of the room. Even though he had just eaten, he was not about to pass up the chance to indulge in an all-you-can-eat movie treats orgy.

He was absolutely thrilled that the buffet station had the full moviegoing menu. This included fountains drinks of every kind imaginable, a full complement of chocolate and other candies, individual bags of popcorn, plus an array of finger foods such as hot wings, hot dogs, and burgers of both the beef and turkey variety. Everyone helped themselves to their satisfaction and moved to their seats.

Much to everyone's surprise, the group was quickly able to make a selection from the vast library of choices. More surprising was that within minutes of settling into their comfortable seats, the room grew quiet as the lights were lowered and the movie began to play. Almost before he could place his chair in the fully laid-out position, Pam quietly asked Greg to go over and get her a straw for her drink. As he returned with straw in hand, he removed the wrapper and slid it into her cup. She immediately applied a loving kiss to his left cheek. He loved Pam when she was in this mood, which wasn't too often. This was why he cherished these rare occasions so much.

Greg breathed in a lungful of air and let it out slowly so he could savor this telling moment. *I have my baby girl right next to me, and this place has her in a good mood. Better yet, I even beat LJ at something today. I won at paintball, and even he cannot deny it. Man, oh man,* he thought as if experiencing a eureka moment. *Hot damn! This must be heaven.* And then, as if suddenly saddened, he lamented, if this were heaven, how wonderful it would be to never have to return to hell!

As the credits were rolling and the light came up, Mysty began what would become a chorus of praise for the Bright Spot Villas. "Oh my god, this place is fabulous."

"Oh my damn, I must have died and gone to heaven," Milton chimed in, now rubbing his belly in delight and mocking Henry's earlier playfulness.

"Oh my goodness, I've never been to such a magnificent place in all my life. This place has everything," Beverley said excitedly.

"And just think, we've only scratched the surface," said Henry. "When do we get the grand tour so we can get a better feel for some other group activities?"

"I think the tour is scheduled for early in the morning," said Beverley in support of her husband.

Henry cautioned, "Not too early, I hope. I plan to have a late and long night, if you get my drift."

"I hear you. I hear you," replied Milton. "Me too, man. Me too." Everyone laughed and smiled as they headed toward the exit.

Now pensive and reflecting on his decision not to help secure some operating capital for this place, LJ said matter-of-factly, "Yes, I think I have to agree. I believe we might have missed out on something here, Mr. Matthews." He directed the comment specifically to his business partner.

Henry replied sarcastically, "Ya think!" Then he said seriously, "We are definitely going to have to talk to old Jonesy on a more serious note. If I hear you right, I'm with you all the way. I'm all but sold, partner." He concluded with a broad smile and a handshake.

With that, everyone bid their good nights and began to make their way out the theater and back to their individual suites. Just as they all exited the elegantly trimmed double doors, Malcolm appeared in the hallway.

"I trust you are finding everything to your satisfaction," he asked, almost certain of the answer before it was given. A chorus of yeses, and even one hell yes, erupted from the group, almost before the confident man had completed his question. "Good, good," he responded with a smile and a nod of approval.

"Now just as a reminder," he continued, "there is a full service menu located in the living room of each suite, and you have the option to either call down for room service or to come back down to the grand dining hall, if you so desire, any time day or night." Then he paused as if deep in thought or as if pondering a difficult question to ask. Seconds later, he said what was on his mind.

"I realize because of the lateness of the hour that you are probably going to retire for the evening. But before you do so, I would beg your indulgence. Our proprietors' executive assistant, Clark, would like to have just a word with you about your experience thus far. Would that be okay?" he asked, almost in a pleading manner.

LJ spoke for the group and responded, "Yes, certainly. Where is he?"

"Right this way," came the glad reply from Malcolm as he led them down the hall and into the foyer just outside the grand hall.

As they entered, they saw a well-dressed man who looked to be in his early to midthirties. Standing about five feet eleven inches, he was equal in height to Henry. He was taller than both Greg and Milton but, much to his delight, shorter than LJ. He immediately flashed a smile of unidentified origin. "I am Clark, the executive assistant to the owners of this establishment, and it is indeed a pleasure to meet you. I've heard my employers speak of you often," he said and continued without waiting for a reply. "Which one of you is LJ Matthews?" He finally took a breath.

"I am," LJ spoke up. "And this is my lovely wife, Mysty, my brother and partner, Henry, and his lovely wife, Beverley. And this is my older brother Milton and his lovely wife, Hazel. And bringing up the rear back there is my little brother Greg and Pam, his elegant fiancée," he said after a slight but noticeable strain to utter those words.

"Wonderful, wonderful. Now let me ask you," Clark proceeded cautiously, "what are your initial impressions of our little attempt at paradise on earth here?"

"Well," LJ said as he paused and looked at each member of the group to be certain he had the floor. "I have to say that we are very impressed at this early stage. I do not know what is in store for us for the remainder of our stay, but I've got to give it to you, this was a stroke of genius. Again, nothing but positive impressions thus far.

"Moreover, if Mr. Jones had marketed this place to us in a different manner, you'd already have all the capital you need to really get things going. From a personal perspective," he continued, "I think I can unequivocally state we are all enjoying ourselves immensely. From a business perspective, if the rest of the trip is anything like what we've already experienced, I am certain we can do some business."

"Fabulous," Clark said gleefully. "I will inform my employers, and I am certain that they will be pleased at your initial assessment. I realize the hour is late, and I extend my sincerest apologies for interrupting your evening. I will make my leave now," he said, extending his hand to LJ and then to Henry. After a cacophony of good nights, Clark made his way to the exit and left with a wave, accompanied by that mysterious smile of unknown origin.

Taking expert notice, LJ quietly commented to Mysty, "I know that smile. The smile on that guy reminded me of the smile I use when I'm about to pull a fast one."

Mysty replied, "I know that smile well."

LJ quickly shot back, "I don't pull fast ones on you, honey. That stuff is reserved strictly for work and work only."

She smiled a wicked smile and replied, "Yeah, right." And they both broke out in a fit of laughter just as they reached the outer door to their suite.

Once inside, before LJ entered the bedroom, he swept Mysty off her feet and carried her over the threshold. She said, "You've still got it, honey. This is just like on our honeymoon, broad shoulders and all."

And LJ unwisely said, "Yes, but only you are twenty pounds heavier now." And afterward, he gave a little muffled chuckle.

Caught by surprise, he immediately received a few glancing blows to the back of the head. "You bum, how dare you," she said with bruised ego.

"Oh, you know I'm just joking, honey. I'm just joking," he said reassuringly.

"You better be," she demanded.

"Sweetheart, you know I love you just the way you are," he said with equal amounts of tenderness and conviction. "You are the sexiest woman alive, nice juicy butt and all." And without pause, they embraced in a long, deep, and tender kiss.

"Wow, you haven't kissed me like that for a long time, but I'm not complaining," she said lustfully. He didn't say a word. Instead, he placed a single finger gently to her mouth as if to signal her silence. He just wanted to allow the flow of the moment to guide them. He grabbed her around her curvy waist with brute force and pulled her close. Then he began to caress her exposed arms and back.

As the caressing grew softer and more sensual, she felt a gentle warmth slowly envelop her entire shapely body. And all at once, she sensed an urge to rip the buttons from his shirt, just like she had seen so many times in the movies. Finally, she succumbed to her urges and did just that. Now exposed, she kissed his bare chest. Her tongue probed his entire tasty torso in search of mutual satisfaction. Unable to stand it any longer, he lifted her from the floor, and she wrapped her long legs around his waist. He looked into her brown-eyed soul, and without a word between them, they communicated, one to the other, solemn devotion, love, and most importantly, carnal lust.

SAME AS GOD SPOKE

Meanwhile, there was no romantic interlude to be had by the youngest of the four couples. Initially, Pam sat staring with piercing eyes, not uttering a single word. Just as the tension got to be as thick as partially dried oatmeal, she finally spoke. "Excuse me, Mr. Drag Race Man, Mr. Shoot You in the Head Man, Mr. Take Their Side Man, and let's not forget, Mr. Put Paint in My Hair Man," she said in a very low and seductive voice. "I have a little teeny tiny question for you." And suddenly, as if a switch were flipped, she began yelling at the top of her lungs, "WHAT IN THE HELL DID YOU THINK YOU WERE DOING BACK THERE, RACING DOWN THE MIDDLE OF THE HIGHWAY? YOU COULD HAVE BEEN HURT, OR YOU COULD HAVE KILLED ONE OF US. IT COULD HAVE BEEN WORSE THAN DEAD. WE ALL COULD HAVE BEEN ARRESTED!

"Or," she pressed on, "our bodies could have been mangled up in a twisted pile of metal, and we could have been invalids for the rest of our lives!"

After hearing her out as he knew he had to, Greg responded, "I have to give it to you, Pam. You are the most optimistic person in the whole wild world. The very next time that I need cheering up, I will definitely know to come to you." He said it with as much sarcasm as he could muster.

Switching gears quickly, as he also knew he had to, he pleaded, "Listen, dear heart. Please, baby, please, we are here at a beautiful resort, and up until now you've loved everything. This place is great. No, better than great. It is awesome. Just look at that big cozy king-sized bed." Then with all the sex appeal he could muster, and in his best baritone impersonation, he again pleaded with his fiancée to be reasonable. "Look," he said, "look at all these mirrors, baby girl. I don't want to spend this time fighting with you. I'd rather spend it making love to you."

Assuming that he had made some headway due to her silence, he made haste to use a familiar seduction tactic by removing his shirt to bear his ripped abs. He then tried to close escrow. "I think we should make use of those mirrors."

Without so much as an afterthought, her unexpected reply came. "I think you should leave me alone."

Never one to easily surrender, Greg grabbed her around her waist. He again commanded his sexiest voice and seductively said, "Come here, baby." And he simultaneously kissed her on the upper part of her back, just below the neck.

He clearly knew this was her *spot*, and he also knew that she always responded when he paid the right attention to her *spot*. But tonight was different, and this harsh reality quickly sunk in as she firmly said, "Get your fucking hands off me. Don't touch me, you backstabbing, reckless driving, won't listen to me piece of shit."

Angrily, he responded, "Well, I didn't bring your little ass all this way to fight with you."

Almost conciliatory, she replied, "Well, you know how I am. It's not like we just met. It takes me a little time to calm down when I get upset."

He then shot back with both venom and disgust, "Yeah, I sure do know how you are, but I'm not here to fight with you, so right now, I'm outta here! Later, peace out, see ya, and wouldn't want to be ya." Then he slammed door, serving as an exclamation point to his hurried exit.

Greg walked down the stairs and out of the house where he met the curator. Making an unsuccessful effort to conceal his anger, he asked Malcolm, "What's there to do around here at this time of the night?"

"Around this time of the year, we have lots of activities. You see those four signs out there? Each one of those hangs over a trail that leads to some specific activities. Trail number one will take you to the stables, where there is always someone there to help you saddle and mount a horse to go riding. Trail number two leads down to the lake. There you will find paddleboats, Jet Skis, and motorboats, all gassed up and ready to go. Trail number three takes you to the caves. There you can see both stalactites and stalagmites and otherwise just explore. However, I would strongly recommend that activity not be done at night, and especially not alone! Now then, path number four, my personal favorite, will take you to the bountiful gardens, which rest uniquely under a very large waterfall. The sight is awesome and quite breathtaking, if I do say so myself. Above and beyond all of that, there are lots of nature trails. Anything meets your fantasy, sir?" asked the helpful curator in his now familiar squeaky voice.

Greg solemnly responded, "I don't know. I'll find something. Thanks a whole lot though."

As he made his way outside and into the night air, Malcolm said finitely, "Very good, sir."

As Greg stood trying to equally calm his growing anger and also decide which path to take, he felt like a contestant on the *Price Is Right*, wondering which door to pick. Interrupting his thoughts was an uneasy feeling that he was not alone in the dark night. Although not certain, he thought he could feel someone watching him.

Over to his left and down just over the ridge that protected the villa from the roadway, he believed he saw two men watching him. Then out of the blue, he heard someone clearing their throat. Startled, he swung around to see a lovely young Latina woman standing in front of one of the smaller structures off to the left of the main villa.

Naturally, he said, "Hi."

And she replied, "Como esta?"

He said, "What?"

She explained, "I said how are you, but in Spanish."

He said, "Oh, okay, I see. I'm not too good in Spanish. Anyway, I'm not doing all that good tonight."

"Well, don't feel too bad. I'm not so good either, but that's another story," she said as if wanting to focus the attention back to the rugged-looking young man. "Who are you? I am Sara," she said with an engaging smile.

He replied, "I'm Greg. Como estar?"

She laughed at his not so good Spanish but appreciated the effort and continued to make polite conversation. "You look as though you have things on your mind, Senor Greg," she said with an obvious degree of empathy.

He said matter-of-factly, "I do, but I'm going to get rid of it soon. Very soon." He then paused to consider his words and to be certain that they had come from him. After, nodding as self-reassurance, he said good night to this lovely Latina stranger in the night.

Smiling but uncertain, she said, "Good night to you too, Senor Greg."

As he turned to walk away, he looked over his shoulder and said, "Easy for you to say." He continued down path number two, which led toward the lake.

CHAPTER 3

SEVEN DOWN, ONE TO GO

As he peacefully slept, the telltale look that only a romantic afterglow could create was noticeably written all over LJ's face. He thought he was dreaming when he heard someone quietly calling his name.

"LJ, LJ, wake up," came a faint whisper. "LJ, please wake up," came the whisper a second time. "LJ, wake up," came the whisper again, only this time with a bit more authority. Plus, it was accompanied by an intense shake against his shoulder that added an evident sense of urgency to it.

Still half asleep and evidently oblivious to the urgency in his wife's voice, he turned over to Mysty. And in one fluid motion, he pulled her closer to him. He then said with a sheepish smile, "Not again, honey. Let's just cuddle. I thought I did a good—"

But before he could finish his thought, she said with a slightly raised voice, "Not that, you idiot," which was punctuated by a cold hard slap on the back. LJ immediately sat up, now that Mysty had his attention. A good slap on the back, placed just right, tends to have that effect on most. Returning to whisper mode, she again asserted, "I'm not talking about that. I think I hear a commotion going on outside."

Initially irritated, LJ immediately relaxed once he learned of the not-so-earth-shattering news. "Please don't wake me up for that, honey. You know it's only my little brother and his cat woman fiancée', Pam. I'll bet," he said while simultaneously rolling over, "either they are fighting or having some rough makeup sex." He grinned at the thought, if only to himself. He then turned and adjusted his pillow so that the cool side was against his face.

However, before his wife could say anything else, his grin was instantly transformed, first into a look of confusion and then to horror. He, too, had finally heard the commotion that his wife was trying to bring to his attention. In very close proximity, maybe just down the hall, he heard the shout of "Get up! Get your fucking asses up!"

In rapid succession, he also heard bloodcurdling screams from the familiar voice of the sometimes very whiny wife of his brother Henry. Beverley screamed at the top of her lungs, "What are you doing? What are you doing?"

Another shout, but much closer this time, did its part to disturb the previously peaceful and serene night. "Get that room!" Fearing the worst, LJ leaped to his feet. He grabbed an iron poker that was meant to stoke fires in the fireplace. He didn't know who was on the other side of the door, but he did know they had bad intentions. With the poker in his hand poised to decapitate anyone or anything that came through the door, LJ positioned himself behind the door adjacent to the hinges. He motioned to his wife first to be quiet and second to lay back down.

As the bedroom door flung open, two masked men burst into the room. Each of them was carrying a shotgun and shouted the order, "Get the hell up and kneel down!" This angry order was issued from the taller member of the duo. Startled by the sudden intrusion, Mysty sprung up from her place of resting.

With feline-like quickness and bull-like strength, LJ leveled a Herculean blow to the back of the head of the taller gunman. And before he could react, he had leveled a blow of equal measure against the temple region of the second midnight marauder. Both now woozy, LJ moved in and raised his weapon to inflict as much damage as he possibly could on the masked duo.

In retrospect, he probably should have armed himself and his wife for that matter with the two readily available firearms that were lying on the ground adjacent to their semi-conscious owners.

However, he did not, much to his dismay, because just as he leveled his second semi-lethal blow to the head of the first of the two would-be assailants, he heard the familiar click that only a shotgun at the ready could make when it was armed and at its deadliest.

Just mere feet behind him, a low, slow, steady voice calmly said, "Drop it or breathe your last."

At the same instance, Mysty screamed, "My god, LJ! Put it down! He's got a gun!"

After only a minute of pause, LJ dropped his weapon and slowly turned around to face his attacker.

Adrenaline still rushing through his veins, LJ bravely or foolishly retorted, "What the fuck is this, man?"

The gunman—still calm, cool, and collected—ordered LJ to back up and go to the other side of the bed next to his wife. Being who he was, someone not usually accustomed to taking orders, LJ initially hesitated, but the sheer look of horror in his wife's eyes caused him to eventually capitulate and do as he was told. The short, stocky, barrel-chested man then moved over to check on his two cohorts that were sprawled out in the middle of the floor.

Extending his foot, he reached out to shake first one, and then the other, of the two disarmed men lying helplessly on the floor. With his gun still trained on LJ, he unsympathetically instructed the two men to get to their feet. Slowly regaining their wits about them, each man struggled to get to his own feet. Once erect, each began to examine the severity of his own injuries. Both were bleeding profusely, but the taller of the two sustained injuries that were much more severe in nature. The third gunman instructed the shorter of the first two gunmen to go and retrieve the nurse.

Shortly thereafter, Hazel was brought into the room, whimpering as if she were a child about to get a severe beating. "Calm down! And I do mean now," said the calm, collected leader of the masked group. A stern look followed this command. Immediately thereafter, he countered with a gesture of disarmament. He first made intimate eye contact with Hazel, then lowered his gun and demanded the others follow suit.

"Listen to me, and listen to me closely as I will only say this once. I know that you are a nurse by profession, and I would like for you to bandage the wounds of these two men. I know that you know how to do it, so please don't insult my intelligence or I will be forced to treat you with the same disrespect and disregard."

In order to reinforce his assertions, he again paused to make more eye contact with the seemingly unwilling practitioner. He then walked over to a nearby closet and retrieved a first aid kit. He quickly handed the kit to Hazel and stood back, impatiently waiting for her to comply. In short order, and with an expert touch, Hazel completed her task.

Growing impatient at the sight of all that he had witnessed, LJ again demanded to know what the fuck was going on. He imagined in his mind that this was some kind of sick game. To think that you'd be held at gunpoint at an upscale resort in the United States of America in the twenty-first century was preposterous.

The same tall man that LJ had beaten about the head replied to LJ's demand for answers with an answer that was both unwanted and unexpected. The tall man struck a thunderous blow with the butt of his gun to LJ's mouth. Both lips immediately split wide open. The gashes were so great that massive amounts of pulp and deep tissue were exposed.

LJ instantly fell to his knees under the weight of the vicious blow and under the searing pain that had just exploded into his now throbbing face. His attacker then sarcastically replied, "It's checkout time, that's what the fuck it is." With that he repeated the previously issued order, "Now I said get up and kneel down." Then he sarcastically said, "Oh, I see you're already down…now stay there." Then turning to Mysty, he instructed, "Now you join him." Mysty was not moving fast enough for him, so he shouted, "Let's do this! I don't have all goddamn day!"

"On second thought," said the tall gunman, "get to your feet, boy."

His vision blurred, with blood streaming from his mouth, and his terrified wife screaming at the top of her lungs in his ear, not to mention, sobbing uncontrollably, LJ struggled to stand. Once erect, he was instantly knocked back to his knees with a second gut-wrenching blow to the abdomen. This blow, much more potent than its predecessor, caused him pain like he'd never felt at any other time in his life. The impact was so intense that it forced the undigested remains of LJ's late-night dinner from his now excruciating bowels.

The thick reddish-green vomit shot out of his mouth with the speed and force of a finely aged champagne gusher. Much of it landed on the feet and lower pants leg of the tall gunman. He again raised his gun in order to strike LJ for a third time but was cautioned not to do so by the short and stocky leader.

LJ and his wife were summarily bound with their hands behind their backs and then led from their suite, down the stairs. Pushed along at every step of the way, they were led outside to the circular driveway. There they saw the others in their group, each on their knees and each with hands tied behind their back.

One of the masked gunmen said, "Hey, there's only seven of them. Where is the other one?"

The stocky one and obvious group leader replied, "How the hell should I know? Now go look for him. Search the whole villa and check the servant bungalows too." He then strategically continued, "Maybe he is holed up out there with one of them Latino maids." Aiming this filth-laden taunt directly at Pam, he added, "Maybe he's out there fucking one of the maids or something." He then added salt to this open wound when he made the mocking sounds of lovemaking. "Ooh, ah, ooh, baby, ah shit now." And then he laughed a menacing laugh to continue applying the emotional hurt to an already wounded Pam. Unbeknownst to her, this mockery was in fact a cold, calculated strategy. He wanted his painful words to serve as a divide and conquer measure. He wanted her anger to loosen her tongue, if indeed he needed it to waggle.

Although none of the captives found this very amusing, the comment brought loads of laughter from their captors. The second after she had heard those coldhearted words, a chill ran down Pam's back. Just then, her innate jealous streak got the better of her. Despite her present peril, her only thoughts were of consequence and revenge. *If he is out there with one of those whores, if these bastards don't kill his good-looking ass, come tomorrow, I will,* she thought privately.

Groggy and half asleep, Greg walked up the trail from the lake where he had spent an uncomfortable night sleeping on the docks. As he drew near, he heard the screaming of unfamiliar voices, so he quickened his pace. As he drew even nearer, he heard a gunshot, which was followed by a bloodcurdling scream. It was LJ; he was screaming as if he had been shot.

Then a loud voice shouted as if to instill even more fear and even more urgency. "That one just grazed your ear, you little piece of shit. The next one will be in lodged in your fucking brain. And this time it will be at point-blank range."

Summoning all of us his courage, LJ shouted, "Dammit, I don't know where he is! None of us do, so go ahead and—" But before he could finish his sentence, he was again struck in his head by the hardened steel at the base of the gunman's weapon. This blow was as violent as any human being could ever level against another. LJ collapsed like a ragdoll into a pile of unconsciousness as he fell face-first to the ground.

Mysty screamed so hard, her gag fell away. Henry looked on in muffled horror but dared not move. Milton immediately shut his eyes and began to pray at the sight of his crumpled up and severely injured brother that he publicly loathed but secretly admired. Pam was numb. All she could think about was Greg and why he wasn't there to help her. Beverley fainted at the sight of all the blood that gushed from the quarter inch puncture wound now permanently embedded in LJ's skull. Hazel shouted under the limitations of her binding, "Let me help! Let me help him! My god, let me help him!"

Willing herself for LJ's sake, Mysty was able to calm herself enough so that she regained at least a fraction of her usual composure. Nearing hysteric exhaustion, albeit through sobs and heavy breathing, she reassured the stocky man in charge that her husband did not know where his brother was. "I swear to you he doesn't know," she whimpered and moaned while wiping her tear-soaked eyes and cheeks. "How could he?" she implored. "For god's sake, if you have any decency at all, please leave him alone. You're going to kill him."

SAME AS GOD SPOKE

She insisted, "How much can one man take?" With his tormentor standing over her beloved LJ, poised to strike yet another and maybe fatal blow, she continued to plead his case. "I swear to you mister. I swear. I swear he doesn't know. He just doesn't know," she repeated over and over.

"He didn't do anything to you. He didn't do anything to anybody," she said now in full panic mode, sensing that the would-be assailant did not seem to be moved by her impassioned pleas. "You've made your point, mister. For god's sake, you've made your point!" she screamed hysterically while shaking her head violently in one final effort to elicit some measure of mercy from the seemingly merciless man.

By this time, Greg had positioned himself behind a thicket of bushes and trees some four or five hundred yards away from the surreal scene unfolding before his very eyes. A quick analysis of the situation led him to a very practical decision. He knew that he had to hide. He knew that any help he could provide would have to come at a later time, although his every instinct, together with every fiber of his being, told him to go and fight. Told him to go and save the others.

His many years as an elite Army Ranger had taught him how to do two things exceptionally well. How to disarm and how to kill by a variety of means. Although the thought of killing the masked gunmen had crossed his mind several times during the brief period that he watched this unlikely drama play itself out, he knew all too well what was meant by the common wisdom of "discretion is the better part of valor." He knew all too well that his continued freedom was the only way for them to be saved and for them to make it out of this situation alive and okay.

Having resigned himself to this fate in order to save his family, Greg quickly spotted what he thought to be a perfect place of concealment. He ducked underneath a thick patch of midget shrubs and nestled in deep among some high ground moss. His all-black attire, as was his usual which he adopted from LJ, made for great predawn cover. He reasoned that he would hide in the thickets, and out of sight, for the next couple of hours. Then he would find a way to contact help.

After what seemed like an eternity to the captives and the lead captor as well, one by one each of the other seven masked men returned. Each had a similar report, which was not well received by the man in charge.

"Big Walt, we can't find him anywhere. There is no sign of the guy. It's like he just up and disappeared." They went on to report that they had searched the main villa, all the servant's quarters, in addition to all the main grounds.

Big Walt, the barrel-chested stocky boss, said in a slow and low monotone voice, "Okay, okay. First, Chuck and Roscoe, let's get these others in the van. You two boys ain't in no shape to tussle with nobody else." He shamelessly chuckled. Then he pointed to the remaining five henchmen. "You guys, search the grounds again. You might have missed something. And this time, include the four trails and the small wooded areas that lead down to the lake. Oh yeah, one more thing," he said in a very loud and contentious voice. And he paused to be sure that he had captured everyone's attention. Once they had all stopped dead in their tracks to hear this last-minute instruction, Walt took his sweet time to deliver the message. Finally, he said with a wagging finger of warning pointed ominously toward no one in particular, "FIND HIM!" Even without him saying so, each man in the hunting posse knew this to be a veiled threat. "He's got to be here somewhere because both cars are here. I know he didn't decide to walk back to the Big Apple. Apples are good, but not that damn good," he said with a mock laugh and a fake smile. Even if no one else found his dry humor to be all that funny, he always did.

Then, with great calculation, he reiterated his order, "Chuck, Ole Roscoe, and the rest of you boys, everybody is watching on this one. We can't afford to fuck up. Now go down, around, and through to them damn trails one by one and find his punk ass. And don't come back until you do, goddammit." He added with greater emphasis, "Now let's get to!" With that final charge and challenge, everyone was sent scrabbling into action.

One by one, each of the captives was then loaded into a waiting cargo van. The last of which was LJ, as he needed extra assistance, and it would prove easier to lay him nearer to the door. Despite being only semiconscious, bloodied, and badly beaten, once inside the van, LJ still managed to bark threats in a symbolic attempt at defying his captors. "If you harm my wife or any of my family, I'm going to kill you. So help me I will kill you all," he said with strained effort.

"Shut the fuck up," came the tort reply, which was immediately followed by a wicked left fist to the face. "You gonna do what to who? You ain't gonna do shit! Matter of fact, you just watch what we're going to do to your wife." And after a quick pause for dramatic effect, the masked man continued in a slightly elevated voice, "And maybe even you too. You're kinda cute from the back."

At that moment, Chuck must have fancied himself a major headliner at a comedy show who was on his A game. No sooner than he had finished his utterance in response to LJ's benign threat, he laughed as if he had told the funniest joke ever. Ole Roscoe laughed as well, but he cautioned his partner to be quiet for fear of Big Walt's wrath, but to no avail. Hearing the curious laughter from the front of the van, Big Walt moved quickly to the back and around the opened door to identify the source. Without speaking, he laid a wicked backhand slap to the face of the loud jokester, who had begun the apparent comedic atmosphere.

"You see that bandage on your head?" he angrily said. "You've already fucked up as much as any one asshole could. Now to top things off, you want to laugh, play, and joke! This shit is dead serious, and dead is what your dumb ass would have been if I had not come into that room to save both your stupid asses! Now for the first and last time, cut that shit out and get them the fuck out of here." The laughter stopped immediately, and the rear doors of van were slammed shut.

"All right, this is how we'll do this. I will search the grounds right round here. You take trail number one, you take two, you can take three, and you two take four. It's the longest. We will stay in touch over the walkie-talkies. And remember, you can pull your gun, but only to keep shit straight. This guy is not to be shot or killed, unless you want the same from the Good Doctor. Everybody got it? Okay men, let's move."

"Let's do this, guy," came an enthusiastic cry from one of the masked trackers, trying to interject some life in the otherwise subdued group. Each of the masked men cautiously set out to look for their would-be victim. Hiding in plain sight, Greg overheard most of the capture plan. He knew that no one would discover his secure hiding spot, but what he didn't know was almost enough to make him reveal himself.

He had unknowingly taken refuge in a nest of savage red army ants. It seemed the ants took their cue from the masked marauders. As soon as their voices went silent, their attack began. After only a few moments, he had been bitten many hundreds of times. Each bite was more painful than the last.

Pain or not, the well-trained soldier did not make a sound, nor did he move a muscle. At this point, all his military preparation for resistance to high-intensity torture was now paying off. He could hear his drill sergeant's voice in his ear: "No pain, no pain, no pain." He held on to that thought with a mental death grip. He had to; it was all he had.

Eventually, this tactic failed him, and the pain began to get the better of him. Unwilling to abandon the strategy, he focused his thoughts on other vacations. Just the year before, vacation was like heaven, and it did not include guns, kidnapping, and torture. He began to psychologically relive sitting on a sunlit beach in the Caribbean.

He could see the sun lying low just above the horizon and the brilliant reflection it cast upon the warm blue water. He remembered looking on in awe at just as it prepared to set. He also remembered being under a beach umbrella with his feet and legs wrapped in a cool towel. He could almost feel the icy water packs tucked in between. He was comforted by the thought.

He was further calmed and comforted by the thought of Pam, his love, his desire, his princess. He imagined her dripping wet, standing in the distance, and admiring her shapely body. He could see the droplets of water sitting atop a freshly applied layer of suntan oil. He smiled at the thought of the droplets shimmering in the brilliant sunlight as they slid helplessly down her beautiful body.

He continued to focus on similar thoughts, and it worked. He found that unleashing the emotional power of pleasure more than numbed the excruciating pain that he was being subjected to. All except that last bite; it was inside the rim of his nostril. *That one hurt*, he thought!

Meanwhile, it was about to time for the place to get busy and for the team get off the premises. Five times over, as each man returned, each provided the same report. "No sign of him, boss. Nope, no sign of him."

Standing mere feet away from the target of their search, the group engaged in a detailed discussion about their next series of moves. Greg could hear every detail in spite of his lightheaded state of consciousness. The plan was to collect the group's luggage, load it into their cars, and then take both cars to Quick Sand Alley and sink them.

"So that there are no mistakes, listen to me real good," he said, now eyeing each man directly as he spoke. I want you to drive both them cars side by side once you get to the mark. You know that old weeping willow tree with the half-dead branches hanging off it? The big ass one that got struck by lightning a while back. And I know I don't have to tell you how to open the door. Put your foot on the brake, put it in gear, get out, and watch it roll into bye-bye land, but I will anyway.

"That way, Sheriff Darren and his deputies can write it up real nice and neat, no loose ends, nothing to lead back to us. The accident report will say that they took a wrong turn, and because they were driving side by side and not knowing these roads, they both went into the quicksand at the same time.

"When they pull the vehicles out, all their clothes will be there, and it's only right that everyone will believe that they were trying to get out and they just went down further than the vehicles. They tell me those things are bottomless, but I never been down, so I wouldn't know," he said half-jokingly. "Now get these cars out of here." To the remaining man, he issued another directive. "Go get the car, jackass, so we can head back to base."

Inside the van, each of the seven was tormented by his or her own private thoughts, even if some chose to make those thoughts very public. Recounting the brutal beating that her husband had just received, Mysty cried hysterically. She repeatedly sobbed, "Oh, honey...oh, honey, are you okay? Are you okay?" Half for LJ and the other half for fear of their own mortality, Hazel and Beverley also sobbed sheepishly. Pam, however, was another matter altogether.

Even at this time of times to be emotional, she again was devoid of anything close to expressing emotion. Nothing was vocalized, but the others, Hazel in particular, thought she must be even more of a coldhearted bitch than they had first believed. The collective shared thought was how could, even she, not be moved considering all that they had just gone through?

Through the dimly lit darkness, Pam could tell from the expressions etched on the shadowy faces of the others just about what they were thinking. Self-trained to be both private and practical, she considered it a weakness to allow people to read her personal thoughts. If they only knew though, she thought to herself, they would have given her as much comfort as they feverishly worked to give each other. Her thoughts, much like their own, were fixated on what she feared to be her own impending merciless torture and cruel death.

LJ was battered and bloody, not to mention without hearing in one ear. He believed that the explosion of the gun right next to his head had busted his eardrum. He felt as if his ear was on fire. Although quite severe, the burning sensation in his ear was not his greatest source of pain. That dubious distinction was reserved for the spot where his mouth had been split open.

Seated next to the brother he thought most of, Henry was way past angry. He was now hearing firsthand Mysty's up close and personal account of the immense swelling and distortion of LJ's face. Ever the noncombative one, Milton was very afraid, and the evident fear written on his face said exactly that.

After a short distance of mostly silent travel with the exception of Mysty's interludes of hysterics and lucidness, Henry said with great uncertainty, "What are we going to do? What are we gonna do, y'all?" This query was addressed to no one in particular, but everyone knew that it was Henry's way of looking for guidance from his partner.

True to his nature, LJ took the lead. "I don't know exactly what we can do, but I do know that we are not going out without a fight. No way in hell!" he added for good measure.

"Someone try to untie my hands. We need to try and get free so that when we stop, we can rush them," he said.

"No, don't do it. Be easy, man," Milton said in a voice filled with warning. "We can't be too rash. We've got to think about what we are saying and consider the risks involved. Can't you see that?" he begged.

LJ emphatically responded, "Hell no. That's some of the dumbest shit I ever heard in my life. No wonder you—" And he broke off his wording, electing not to finish the thought. Instead, he continued by restating the immediate sense of urgency. "Risk? The only risk is to continue getting our asses bashed and trashed if we don't fight back. That's the motherfucking risk. We've got to rush them and that's it. We got to fight back, man. Fuck that. We just got to fight back. What you say, Henry?"

Without the slightest bit of hesitation, Henry backed LJ up. "Hell to the yeah. I agree," he said with certainty. "These guys gotta know they are at least in a fight. This whole shit has been too one-sided up till now. 'Cause power only knows power," he concluded after a thoughtful but small pause.

Secretly fearful of the coming battle, if left up to his too pampered ass, fucking big shot boss brothers, Milton again made an effort to reassure everyone else that his position was a better option. "No, no, LJ, Henry, listen to me," he pleaded. "They're not gonna hurt us. If they wanted to hurt us, they would have done it already."

LJ immediately shot back, only in a low monotone voice which strongly indicated that he was both agitated and determined. "Listen, Biscuit." It was a nickname that Milton did not particularly care for. "Stop acting like the fucking punk that you've always been and do what we say. 'Cause unless you do as I say, if they don't kill your punk ass, I swear to God almighty I will.

"By the way, do I fucking look like I'm not hurt? Do I look like they didn't want to fucking hurt me," he asked with even more distain. "Now shut the fuck up and untie Henry's hands," he said in unbridled disgust aimed directly at his underachieving older brother. "Where the fuck was you when they busted my face and almost shot my damn ear off?" he continued in full rant. "What the fuck do you mean they're not going to hurt us?" he again asked without expecting or even wanting an answer.

After that overly harsh two-fisted gut check and without a word of rebuttal, Milton summoned the courage to move and sprang into action. He twisted his body around so that his back was to Henry's back, and after some intense effort, Henry's hands were freed. Soon after, he had Milton's hands untied. The two then began the onerous task of freeing the others. The job was made tougher because there was almost no light. Plus, the inside of a pitch-black cargo van without the benefit of seat belts was not the steadiest of rides.

Once they were all freed, LJ urged, "Search around for a weapon of some kind."

"Yeah, search along the walls and on the floor. Maybe there is a jack or a tire iron," Henry said hopefully. Feeling somewhat empowered now, their collective spirits were momentarily lifted. Sadly, that feeling would be short-lived, as there was no weapon to be found. There was not a tire iron, not a jack, not even a screwdriver or a stick of any kind to be found.

Yet determined to pull a rabbit out of the hat, everyone busied themselves and continued with the fruitless search. Suddenly, the fast-moving vehicle came to an abrupt stop. As they each tried to regain their now lost balance, both back doors flung open, and they were immediately struck by bright blinding lights, as it was still not yet six o'clock in the morning. They were again greeted by more masked captors. However, these were not the same as the first group. They had on different uniforms, but like the other group, they had drawn guns of the semiautomatic variety.

And right away, the solemn realization that the well-intentioned but ill-fated plan of attack would have to wait for another time simultaneously overcame each of the seven captives. Though for a brief moment, they each looked to LJ to follow his lead. LJ had just made a gut-wrenching speech about fighting back and about having no option but to fight, so they wondered what he would do now that it was time to show and prove. Above all, Milton hoped that he did nothing.

He knew that LJ did not have a death wish, but he also quickly prayed that he did not have brave-man syndrome either. He sincerely hoped that he did not feel the need to try and prove himself to the rest of the group, especially after all his big talk about fighting back. Collectively, the others shared in this hope; they all knew LJ could be strong-willed when his back was against the wall. However, although momentarily tempted, even if just slightly, LJ was no fool, and he surrendered peacefully, as he knew he must.

* * *

After being bitten countless times, Greg finally summoned the courage to move from his very well-hidden place of concealment. As he stood, he slumped back to his knees. He felt extremely dizzy from the effects of having received ant bites in the tens of thousands. His body felt as if it may be filled with infection, or possibly even poison. His hands, his arms, and his legs, all the way down to his feet, were swollen to the point of disfigurement. His wounds needed some attention. He needed medical treatment, and he needed it now. Above all else, he needed for the intense pain to go away.

Once again, he tried to clear his head; he tried to block out the pain. He had to think clearer now, more than at any other time in his entire life. Hearing the sound of an approaching vehicle, the weary and disfigured spectacle of a man again dropped quickly to his previous hiding place. And instantly, the repeated bites from the angry ants in attack mode against an outside invader resumed.

As he lay motionless, listening for the vehicle, it never materialized. It was just his imagination, he finally figured. He thought, *Oh my god, my mind is playing tricks on me.* He said to himself, in a slow, hushed, deeply focused voice, "Man, you've been in much worse situations than this. You been in firefights, you've had to go one against five, and you came out to the good, so this is nothing."

"You've got to get your shit together," he said again in a focused effort to regain control of his wandering mind. "You are the only one that can save Pam, your brothers, and their wives. Now that's it. Get your shit together," he said in one final effort to compel himself forward.

Recalling his survival training, Greg remembered being taught that small fruit from low-hanging trees, which was green or grape in color, was a good counteragent for poisons and other toxins that one might encounter during field exercises. He remembered being taught that when eaten with the underside of tree bark, that combination was a powerful cleansing agent and detoxing that was always readily available.

At once, he headed for the thick of the woods. He needed something to fight off the thousands of tiny drops of poison slowly taking over his nervous system. He could feel himself begin to twitch and shake uncontrollably. He knew that with so much of it in his bloodstream, it was just a matter of time before he succumbed to the epileptic and then paralyzing effects of it.

Some hundred yards into his journey, he literally stumbled into a wild apple tree. He grabbed a piece of the fruit and bit into it like a ravenous hound. He then dug his nails into the base of the tree and pried away a small chunk of bark. He consumed one and then the other, then he repeated this rotation again and again. After some thirty minutes of eating wild fruit together with the underside of tree bark, Greg began to feel the counteragents take hold.

He noticed some of the swelling had subsided and that he had regained partial feeling in his lower extremities. His mind was immediately comforted, for he knew that it was just a matter of time before he would be back to normal, or at least as near to normal as could be under the circumstances.

As he began to now think with some semblance of clarity, Greg identified two problems that instantly came to mind. The first problem was who could he turn to? Who could he trust that was readily accessible? The people at the villa, Malcolm, and the servants must have seen what went on. Yet no one stopped it. No one said anything, so they must have been in on it, he reasoned.

The next problem, which was even more pressing, was that there were no telephones at the villa. He remembered LJ bragging about the fact that the group would have ten days of solitude and silence.

"Don't know who to trust and can't reach out to anyone that I could trust. Very tricky," he said. "Very tricky indeed. For goodness' sake, if I had only brought my cell phone. God dang it, why did I listen to LJ?" Things began to crystallize as his thoughts became more clearer by the minute now. "Hey," he said aloud in his most vivid moment of clarity. "If I know my Pam, my dear, sweet, set-in-her-ways Pam, I know there is no way she'd come all this way without her cell phone. I know my baby."

The thought continued, *I'll bet she has a cell phone hidden away somewhere. Now where would she or could she put it so that I wouldn't find it too easily and start a fuss about our agreement to leave them behind? Where would she hide it?* He quizzed himself a second time. *In her suitcase? Naw.* He dismissed that thought after only a second. *A couple of my things are in her suitcase, too, so probably not. Think, man, think. For God's sake, think*, he challenged himself.

"Now where would I hide a cell phone? I know," he said aloud. "I'd hide it in plain sight. But where the heck is plain sight?" he quizzed again. Then, as if in a eureka moment, he yelled, "Plain sight has to be the glove compartment! Yeah, that's it exactly. She would hide it in the glove compartment, right in front of her, with full expectation that no one else would sit in her seat.

"Now I heard those guys say they were going to dump the cars in some quicksand someplace nearby. I hope I can find those cars before they sink. This may be my only chance to save everyone, but how? That's like finding a needle in a haystack.

"Oh God, my head hurts," he blurted. "Why me, God?" he asked, looking toward the sky. "Why fucking me?" he asked again, looking to the heavens as if hoping for some divined intervention. "I'm sorry, *God*. I didn't mean that!" He pleaded his case to the most high. Refocusing after his moment of temporary insanity, he said aloud, "Now where in the hell do I find this quicksand?" Then in the following moment, he spazzed out and yelled to no one in particular, "DAMMIT, DAMMIT, DAMMIT!"

CHAPTER 4

SAME AS GOD SPOKE

BROUGHT IN AND lined up, as would any chattel on display, the forced captives watched in both silence and horror as a second group of interested men entered to view them. They were led by a peculiar looking man with a huge cigar clutched tightly between his ultra-thin lips. The new group huddled in a far-off corner, murmuring words that were unintelligible.

She didn't know which, but either the sight of him or the putrid smell of the preparation chamber in which they now found themselves had Mysty extremely nauseous. She compared the smell to the god-awful odor of rotting cat in a Chinatown back alley. She also thought the thin-lipped man looked as if he might be somewhat psychotic. That was because he fit all the stereotypical profiles of the madman characters she had seen in the movies: tight lips, beady eyes, and always with beads of sweat dropping off their foreheads.

Although simultaneously sickened and frightened at this very moment, Mysty was more angry than scared. And even through his bloodstained face, she could tell her beloved husband had all but reached his boiling point as well. She feared for his safety because she knew that he was both brave and sometimes hotheaded, and in this very situation, that could prove to be a recipe for deadly disaster. She said a silent pray, asking God to give him the wisdom to know the difference between being brave and being be-damned. Her next thought was interrupted by the chatter of her captives.

"Okay, Good Doctor, here they are as you ordered," came the haunting words from a well-dressed young man who had previously introduced himself while they were still guests at the villas. Clark was the chief executive assistant to the Good Doctor. Moving front and center of the room, the Good Doctor prepared himself to speak to the group of people whose lives would forever be changed after this day.

Standing before them now was a tall, dapper, and rather refined middle-aged man. His first order of business was to carefully place his unlit cigar in the lower right pocket of his very wrinkled lab coat. With his slightly concealed but very evident German accent, he finally spoke.

"Well, well, well, look what we have here," he stated with a noticeable nasally twang. "If it isn't the high and almighty Matthews brothers, together with their clan," he said with slow and deliberate disgust. LJ and Henry immediately turned to each other in total disbelief as they both simultaneously recognized the very distinct voice of the Good Doctor, who was known to them as Mr. Jones, the resort owner who kept asking them to help get him some funding.

Looking just over his spectacles and tugging tersely on his long but not so white lab coat, he began as if he were a paid guess lecturer. "It is indeed a pleasure to finally meet the two of you," he said with a half-smile, more taunting than friendly. "I do hope the feeling is equally mutual," he said in jest with one slightly raised eyebrow. But he continued with as much malice as he could muster, eyebrow still raised. "By that puzzled look on your face, I can only imagine that you are somewhat befuddled at this precise moment.

"Matthews and Matthews, venture capital specialists. 'You supply the ideas and we'll supply the money.' That is your slogan, isn't it?" he asked rhetorically. Immediately after the comment, he came to stand directly in front of LJ and looked him squarely in the eye, as if to demonstrate his superior position, even if for the moment. His position was indeed superior, because LJ was barely able to see through the slow but steady stream of blood and pulp trickling down his forehead and over his eyelids. Looking through dual streams of blood, as if two side-by-side waterfalls, LJ stared intently at the man that was undoubtedly the precipitating cause of this hellish daytime nightmare.

After a purposefully long pause, the Good Doctor continued, "Please allow me to bring some clarification to this matter. Although we've never met—well, at least not in person—we have talked on the phone on more than one occasion, as you may well know by now." Then with a sudden overt display of anger, combined with a venomous tone that had not been evident before, he began to yell, "That is on those rare, and I do mean rare occasions, when I was able to get either of you hotshots on the phone!"

Abruptly taking notice that he had utterly lost his composure, he took two giant steps back, as if playing the childhood game of Mother May I, and summoned his chief executive assistant to stand at his side. "Clark," he said in a calm, complete about-face. "Would you please be so kind as to formally introduce me to these two fine upstanding gentlemen? After all, in my circles, it is quite rude to introduce yourself, because it's a known fact that men of standing are always introduced by others. So, my good man Clark, without further delay, please do the honors."

"Mr. J. Matthews, please meet Dr. Jones. Dr. Jones, Mr. J. Matthews." The Good Doctor nodded and then added a silent cordial smile. It was a greeting that would have definitely been better suited for a medical convention. Clark continued, "Mr. H. Matthews, Dr. Jones. Dr. Jones, Mr. H. Matthews." Again, the Good Doctor afforded Henry the same cordial smile and friendly nod. Both LJ and Henry experienced the same spontaneous thought: *This guy is nuts.*

Still in psycho mode, the Good Doctor then proceeded, "I do say it is most regrettable that we meet under these circumstances. From what I have read about you and your firm in my research reports, you are quite the entrepreneurs. So much so that most of the time, you wouldn't even bother to return my fucking phone calls!" He returned to a scream level that taxed the total capacity of his air-filled lungs.

Now completely reverting back to the overt psychotic, the Good Doctor absolutely let loose and showed his wild side. "Just who the fuck do you think you are?" he continued, still yelling his loudest. "Do you know who I am?" he said in a surprisingly low whisper, which served for greater dramatic effect. Adding more drama to the tension-filled room, he continued in his low monotone whisper, "I said, do you know who the dammit-to-hell I am?"

Not sure of what to say to this man who was obviously deranged, to put it mildly, neither Matthews uttered a word in response for fear of an irrational reprisal.

"I, sir, am the Good Doctor," he said with all the authority that he could muster. "And please know this. Although I'm sworn by my Hippocratic oath to preserve life, I am sworn to a much higher oath of loyalty to myself. And if there ever comes a time to choose my allegiance between my oath to preserve life and my oath to preserve my honor, you can be positively certain that I will always choose honor.

"In life, gentlemen, we all have choices to make. Many, many choices. You, my friends," he stated flatly, "have chosen to fuck with me. You've unfortunately chosen to minimize me and to unnecessarily relegate me to a stature of insignificance. And finally, my dear, dear friends," he said in a fit of full-throated anger, "you've chosen to dismiss me in the same manner as you would some common trailer park trash from West Bubblefuck village right on the outskirts of hick-city USA!

"Those were your choices. Regrettable choices, I would bet, if I were a betting man," he said succinctly. Then after a quick pause, he added, "Which I'm not. I kind of like sure things myself." It was obvious that this extra added commentary was meant to be a smiling insult. Despite its transparent intentions, it definitely hit its mark, as both of its intended targets had immediate reactions. Although neither man spoke, the temporal lobes of each man twitched uncontrollably, LJ even more so than his younger, much calmer brother.

"And now, as a practical matter, right now it is my turn to choose, gentlemen. And I choose to own your sorry asses for the rest of your worthless fucking lives. You would not meet my needs when given the chance!" he shouted. "You would not respond to me before now, but after today and forever more," he said in a quiet and deliberately venomous tone, "you will follow my every salacious and whimsical command. And dammit to hell!" He again shouted as he returned to his high-pitched oration, "You best goddammit well believe I have the power to make it happen!

"What you did to me was egregious!" he said, staring the two men down with unabashed indignation. Pausing from his diatribe, the Good Doctor walked over and again stood directly in front of LJ, having noticed his animated state. This was evidenced by the only sign of displeasure that LJ could not conceal, his rapid temporal lobe movement, and it was on full display. Moving ever closer to the target of his taunts, the Good Doctor said, "Why, Mr. Matthews, it looks as though you want to say something."

As LJ continued his epic internal struggle to hold his tongue, the Good Doctor was unrelenting in his effort to taunt. "It really does look as though you want to talk to me. I would love to hear what you have to say for yourself, and your little fucking brother too. But you know as I do that if you dare, I might be forced to remove a body part or two. I might even be forced to do some unspeakable things to the missus." He looked at Mysty, certain that he had just pushed LJ's nuclear button.

However, he had not. LJ showed remarkable restraint, given his propensity for active self-preservation. Not one of the others in his group, especially his little brother Henry, could imagine that another human being could speak this way to LJ and that he would do nothing. Then to top it off, the Good Doctor had done the unthinkable; he had dared to speak ill of Mrs. LJ Matthews, and still no LJ outburst. To the group, this was unbelievable. But to Mysty, this was a godsend, an answered prayer. She knew that LJ was being tested, and she was glad that he was wise enough to know that as well. She said a prayer of thanks that her first prayer had been answered.

Not missing a beat, the Good Doctor continued, "I know you both wish you had taken a meeting with me now, don't you?" He did not expect a response, and none was given. "Well, too fucking bad!" he said without a shred of remorse. "I gave you over fifteen months to talk to me, and you chose not to. Now it's too fucking late!" he said again, with much more emphasis on the *too* and *late* parts of the statement, drawing each word out.

He continued in his taunting manner, now standing almost eye to eye with Henry. "Ever played that game I spy? Well, right now, I spy the look of horror in your eyes," he said, trying to arouse Henry. "I also spy the look of fear, and I do declare, is that also anger I see there?" he asked almost playfully. "Well, it really doesn't matter. Any look that you or your pitiful comrades may have now will soon turn into blank stares.

"And would you like to know the best part of this whole fucking thing?" he asked again in a rhetorical and mocking fashion. "You probably do," he answered for Henry. "So I will tell you. The best part is this: I know that I will sleep well tonight, comforted that I put that blank stare there." He then concluded with a grandiose and climactic statement, "Because no one, and I do dammit-to-hell mean no one, ever disrespects the Good Doctor and gets away with it!" He ended his diatribe with a confident menacing smile and turned to walk away, but he paused.

Still not completely content that he had impressed upon his captives the severe ramifications for their untoward transgressions, he pivoted in order to continue. "First, I will rob you of your will. Then I'll take your dignity. And finally, I may even take your sorry ass life or what's left of it."

Again, noticing LJ's visibly raised stress levels, the Good Doctor again mocked him directly. "Ooh, ooh, I'm scared. I see the fire in your eyes, Mr. J. Matthews. I do. I do indeed see the fire. But be careful," he warned. "Even that may tempt me to extinguish that fire, and that would be very unpleasant, I can assure you.

"You see, here in Coulditbe, I am all that there is, and my word is law," he stated with certainty. "So there is nothing that you can do. There is nothing that your little brother can do. There is nothing that any of you can do," he bragged with the conviction that only someone in charge could. "Here, right here, in this place and as far as the eye can see, my word is the same as God spoke. Can you imagine God giving an order and it not be followed? I think not.

SAME AS GOD SPOKE

"And so it is, when I speak, it's the same as if God spoke, just like the drug that will render you powerless to act unless commanded. It's just the same as when God himself spoke so many eons ago. So let it be written. So let it be done. The Good Doctor has spoken." He then broke out into almost hysterical laughter, pausing only briefly to see the reaction of his captives. "Ha, ha, ha." He laughed again in a mocking fashion, but this time it was much more sinister, more callous, and more deliberate.

He gathered himself from his overindulgence. "While you will retain the ability to think private thoughts, you can never again act on them. And while trapped alone with your own private thoughts for the rest of your natural lives, you will assuredly take comfort in knowing that you were bested, as many have before you and many will after you, by the Good Doctor. Now won't you excuse me, Mr. Matthews and young Mr. Matthews. I have pressing matters to attend to," he said with a greater degree of finality.

Pivoting quickly, the Good Doctor now turned his poisonous acrimony on to one of his subordinates. "Now to you, Walter," he began. "I thought there were eight of them. Unless my math is bad, I only count seven—four females and three males. Three plus four equals seven. Do I have that right, Walter?"

"Yes, yes," stammered Walter.

"Well, if there are seven here, that means one is missing. Would you agree?" he asked in cynical fashion.

But before Walter could formulate a coherent response, the Good Doctor continued his mocking ways. "What did you do, kill one of the males this time? What did he do, challenge your authority? No, don't tell me. Let me guess. Did he look at you without fear in his eyes? Was he recklessly eyeballing you, or did he try to make a run for it? Just what did he do, Walter? What did he do, pray tell?"

Not fully realizing that the Good Doctor was finished with his impromptu rant and was really expecting an answer now, Walter said nothing. His silence only elicited more of the Good Doctor's wrath. "Well, what the fuck is wrong with you, man? Cat got your tongue? Speak up, you fucking idiot. For the last time, what in the dammit-to-hell happened?"

"Sorry, sorry, Good Doctor. I didn't want to interrupt you. But like I told you before, since the last time, I do it just like you instructed me, to the letter. I mean, I am calm but forceful, silent for the most part, talking only as much as is needed and using gestures when possible. And most importantly, I pick out the leader or the most vocal, and I provide a visual persuasion for the others in the form of blood. That's what I always do, and that's all I did this time," he concluded with a reassuring tone. His voice noticeably lowered in deference to his unforgiving boss.

After pausing to somewhat gage his hard-to-read boss's reaction, he continued. "When we hit the villas just before daybreak this morning, everything went just like clockwork. We went in, rounded everybody up, and we were out on the driveway in about ten minutes or so. Only there was one tiny glitch," he said with a cautious reserve.

"I know that, you damn idiot. Now what was it?" the Good Doctor interrupted. Startled, Walter lost his place in the story line. Annoyed by the pause and with feline quickness, the Good Doctor pounced on him for his ineptness. "Well, what in the dammit-to-hell was it?" he shouted and took a giant step in Walter's direction to apply even more in-your-face pressure on the already nervous man. "Don't stand there acting like the sexually repressed undercover cross-dressing coward that you are. Finish the story, you idiot!" he shouted again.

"Okay, Doc. I'm getting to that part of the story," Walter said in a subservient tone.

Without mercy, the Good Doctor immediately shot back, "You fucking moron! How many times have I told you not to call me Doc? What is my name?" He expected to get a satisfactory answer.

More than just a bit humiliated, Walter answered the question, "The Good Doctor."

Yelling, he carried the humiliation to the next level. "PLEASE REPEAT THAT SO I'M CERTAIN THAT YOU SHALL NOT MAKE THE SAME MISTAKE AGAIN!"

The portly but hulking man shamefacedly repeated, "The Good Doctor."

"The rest, you stay here. And, Walter, you come with me. No, on second thought, we can settle this matter right here. I am the supreme commander of this operation, and I will not tolerate insubordination of any kind. Walter, stand here directly in front of me. Now take three steps back."

With no viable alternatives, Walter complied as ordered.

"Now slap yourself in the face as punishment for your dereliction of duty."

Now mortified, Walter pleaded with his tormentor in a desperate attempt to halt the unfolding public embarrassment. "Good Doctor," he said with pleading eyes and a pitiful tone. "I…I'm sorry. Please don't do this. Please don't do this in front of the men," he asked politely, now in full submissive mode.

"Walter, I will not repeat my order," came the hot-tempered reply. "If you cannot carry it out, then I will get someone else to do so, but with much more force than I'm sure you yourself would use. Now do it, goddammit! Do it or else!"

Realizing that he was out of options, Walter extended his own hand and executed the swift motion associated with a self-induced slap to the face. The splat of the slap echoed throughout the room. "Harder," demanded the Good Doctor. This time, Walter executed a brutal slap to the side of his reddening face. Once again, the harsh sound of violent skin-to-skin contact reverberated throughout the room. With each contact, the sound made all the others cringe.

"Now once more," came the unwelcomed and merciless command. "Do it again, just like that, so that next time you will know." Walter extended his own hand for a third time and again inflicted yet another vicious blow to his own person. After doing so, he glared conspicuously at the Good Doctor, as if to tell him, "What more can you do to me? It don't get no worse than this." Little did he know that it was indeed about to get worse. Much worse.

Seeing that the little man before him had reached his near-breaking point, the Good Doctor made the choice to leave him well enough alone. He didn't like Walter very much, but he loved how he conducted business on his behalf. "Very good," he said, shifting gears. "Now that should teach you that there is a purpose for law and order and discipline and respect. Let us not repeat this teaching, as the lesson can and will intensify the next time around. Now I ask you, for about the one fucking hundredth time, where is the other male from the Bright Spot Villas?"

"Yes, sir. Yes, sir, I'm sorry, and I'm getting to that, Good Doctor," Walter said hurriedly. "Well, according to this cute little, I mean, this female here, the male that is missing left late last night after they had an argument. From all the information that I was able to gather, after I conducted interviews with everyone on the facility, after he left his room, he walked outside and maybe down by the lake area. We conducted a really thorough search of the grounds, the entire property in fact, all the way down to the water's edge. Only, ain't nobody find him yet. But not to worry. We done notified our good friend Sheriff James Darren. We got a story on him."

"Well, what is that four-foot piece of shit waste of life doing about finding this escapee? Before you answer that, wasn't there supposed to be two of your men watching the place to ensure that no one left the premises?"

"Well, yes. Yes, there was," Walter said, now confident that the focus of this unbearable heat was about to be transferred to someone other than himself. "I left ole Roscoe and *good ole* Chuck over there since about ten o'clock last night, and they was right there when the rest of us got there this morning."

"Well, ole Roscoe and *good ole* Chuck, what do you have to say for yourselves, gentlemen?"

Roscoe was the first to speak, hoping to make himself look a little better than his partner, Chuck, would have. "Let's see. *Me and Chuck* was only told not to let anyone leave the premises, and we didn't. So we didn't think that meant they couldn't leave the villa, did it?"

"Well, now that we have this little situation that could spell disaster for all of us, what in Sam blazes do you think you should have done?"

"I don't exactly know, Good Doctor," Roscoe said, gulping in an effort to swallow the large pool of saliva that had instantly built up in his throat. He then continued with as much deference as he could muster, "Sir, maybe we should have got him and tied him up or followed him to know where he was."

"To say the least, you should have done something other than what you did do, and for your injudiciousness, you must pay a price. And I think that you need to pay a severe price, don't you agree?" Roscoe opened his mouth to give a response in the affirmative, but before he could formulate the words, the Good Doctor stopped him dead in the act. "That's rhetorical. Do not answer," he said and demonstrated the same message by placing a single finger to his lips as a visual request for silence. "Walter, give me your belt."

Complying with all the swiftness of a broken-in slave, Walter responded, "Yes, sir, Good Doctor. Here it is."

"Now order your men to remove their shirts. I want them bareback."

Again, complying on demand, Walter repeated the order, "You two, you heard the doctor. Now remove those shirts before I rip them off you, buttons and all." That last comment seemed to be offered to curry favor with the Good Doctor. "Hurry up," he said as the two men removed the last vestiges of the clothing that once covered their torsos. Now barebacked, with their shirts on the floor beside them, Walter pronounced Roscoe and Chuck ready for their punishment. He stepped back and said, "Okay, Good Doctor, they are all yours."

"No, Walter," came the reply, much to his surprise, as was evidenced by his puzzled look. "They are not mine," the Good Doctor explained. "In fact, quite the contrary, they are both yours, and as punishment for their high crimes and misdemeanors, I will punish their superior.

"You see, shit rolls downhill." He then explained further, "Employees are only as good as the leadership under which they fall, and because they have failed, you, my underachieving spineless bonehead, have also failed.

"Now remove your shirt, leader," he said mockingly. "You have failed your men, Walter. You should have spoken up for them when you had the chance. Any good leader would have, yet you stood here, ready to offer them up without so much as a whimper. You said nothing in their defense, even if I didn't agree, which I probably wouldn't have. You were wrong to say nothing. Now bare your back to me, you four-foot-high mound of nothingness. Bend your fucking knees. Bow down this very instant.

"You men, sound off and count as I strike, and do not make the mistake of feeling sorry for this man or you will join in his misery. His perceived pain will be your real pain. He was willing to offer you up as sacrificial lambs, but today, at least for now, the meek shall inherit the earth. Now sound off, goddammit."

"One."

"That first lick echoed real nice. That was a good one, wasn't it? Sound off…"

"Two."

"Sound off…"

"Three."

"Sound off…"

"Four."

"Sound off…"

"Five."

"Six."

"Seven."

"What, no blood…if I've taught you anything about visual persuasion, it's that the sight of blood is a very powerful motivator. Let me turn this belt around. Let's have some double up belt-buckle action. Now sound off."

"Eight…nine."

"Sound off…"

"Ten, eleven…"

"Blood, yes, blood… Sound off…"

"Twelve, thirteen."

"Sound off…"

"Fourteen, fifteen."

"That's right, big boy. Suffer in silence, because if you dare yell, cry, or scream, we will all know you for the true coward that you really are. Real men don't allow pain to break them down. Suffer, boy. Suffer real good. Suffer in silence. Now sound off…"

"Thirty-two, thirty-three."

SAME AS GOD SPOKE

"The blood flows, and it flows like the River Jordan. Thirty-three lashes, the same as for the king of kings. Now act like a prince and clean yourself up. The sight of blood only makes me want to see more. The rest of you, prepare the ones that didn't get away for their initial injection. It's about time for the Godspoke. I want them to be fit for work within four hours. We have a large harvest to sow, as well as lots of cash to reap. Gentlemen, what you have witnessed here today need not have been. Need I remind you that we have billions, not millions, but billions at stake here. That's nine zeros for those who like to count. So please know we cannot afford the luxury of any more fucking miscues. Do I make myself abundantly clear?"

After a chorus of yeses, he continued his instruction. "Now prepare them as I have instructed. And as for you, Walter, after you have cleaned yourself up, I want you to send ole Roscoe and good ole Chuck over here to go out and find that male escapee. And gentlemen, if you should fail, run. Run far and run fast, but don't even think of setting foot in this place again.

"And by the way, and I think you may enjoy this bit of additional incentive, as if the bloody visuals were not enough. If you are not back within ninety minutes or at least to have phoned to inform Clark that you are on the way with him in custody, I will send Mrs. Conn's personal hit squad to take your lives. *And if,*" he said with great authority and a pause for dramatic effect. "And if by some slim chance of momentary stupidness on your part that there is any ambiguity in what take your lives means, let me be clear."

Placing his hands behind his back and standing spread-eagle, reminiscent of a field commander before his troops, he said in no uncertain terms, "My good men, I simply and explicitly mean *murder you*. That's right. This is very serious business." And for good measure, he added a note of finality to their collective consciousnesses. "Whether you know it or not, all of you have sold your souls to the devil. And as far as any of you are concerned, he and I are one and the same." After a pause to look into the eyes of each man, he repeated the haunting remark, "Yes, indeed. He and I are one and the same.

"And now, as I grow weary of the loathsome company here, I will take my leave of you. Walter, you will be so good as to summon Clark once these captives have been prepped and each has received their initial Godspoke injection dosage. It's been a while since we've had some new help around here, but you do know it's not the same as the maintenance dosage, right?" he said rhetorically as he turned and made his way to the exit.

After the Good Doctor and his entourage had taken their leave, the remaining men gathered nervously around Walter. "Oh, hell, no, Big Walt, why you let him treat you like that?" Chuck began mockingly.

"Why didn't you backhand slap him in the mouth like you always doing to us?" said another.

"Why you didn't bust his shit to the white meat like you do each time we try to have sex with some of the spellbound?" asked Roscoe.

"What the fuck is up, Big Walt? Or should I say Walter?" Chuck again mocked.

"Ha, ha, ha," came the spontaneous laughter from the half-curious, half-taunting group of men, now surrounding their diminished leader.

"Listen, Chuck, and the rest of you fucking faggots too. I'm only gonna say this once." He grabbed Chuck forcefully by the collar and pulled him close so that the two men were physically eye to eye. "If you ever call me anything other than Big Walt again, I will kick the living shit out of you. Do you get me, boy? Do you get me?"

Keenly aware of Walter's violent temper and his known propensity to fight, Chuck capitulated. "Yeah, man," he said in a very low voice that was almost inaudible. "Yeah, I got you." But then as if he had regained some of his lost spine, he asked in a semi-loud voice, "But why you single me out? That shit ain't cool, Big Walt. That ain't cool at all. We was all just having a little fun, trying to make the best of a bad situation for us all."

"Whatever! I ain't the one," said the angry man. "You feel me? I ain't the fucking one. Now ole doc Conn may be protected by all of his hoodlum assed girlfriend's money and her goons, but none of you assholes have that kind of good fortune, so don't get fucking stupid.

Cool it or I will do the cooling for your fucking ass. You get me? I got this. I will handle ole Doc Conn when the time comes. I will get my revenge. I just need some time to see what my next move is. When have you ever known me to let it go down like that?" he asked rhetorically. "Sometimes you just gotta know when to hold 'em and when to fold 'em, but my day will come and come soon. I guarantee it!"

In the midst of all the madness, and while Walter and his goons were transfixed on their difficult situation, LJ could see the terrified looks on everyone's face. He knew that the others had seen and heard just what he had. The leader of this ill-begotten motley crew was a wicked little bastard, to say the least. Moreover, if he would go so far as to threaten the ultimate punishment of death in order to motivate his men, then this whole thing was a lot more serious than he had imagined.

He thought, *What the hell have we stumbled into?* Was this some sort of scare tactic by Mr. Jones, a.k.a. the Good Doctor or Doc Conn? Was this supposed to convince him to find some investment capital for the man, or something even more sinister? His mind raced over a hundred scenarios and outcomes. He finally concluded that he and the rest were not there to be killed, at least not yet. That was a welcomed source of comfort. Although he now wondered and worried just as much about what the final play would be.

Just as he turned to look at Mysty, his jaw dropped, and his thoughts froze in place. Her expression was one of absolute sheer horror. Her eyes were bloodshot red and damn near swollen shut. The mascara ran freely down her cheeks, and the veins on her forehead, just above the bridge of her nose, were swelled to almost bursting. He knew her blood pressure must be extremely elevated.

The look on her face made his heart hurt and his head ache in ways that he had not ever imagined possible. His sweetheart, his darling, and the one true love of his life was in pain and needed him, but he could do nothing. He felt more than helpless. At this precise moment, he felt impotent. He knew that he couldn't speak, but he wanted so badly to do something. He needed to at least assure his horrified wife that all would turn out okay, no matter how grim things might look presently.

Just at that moment, he remembered something that his father, BJ, used to do when he was very young, and it always seemed to assure him that everything would be okay. He remembered that BJ, with only his eyes, would silently and slowly command his son's attention. He recalled that his father's eyes would take on a life of their own and that they would actually speak to him. After his father's eyes would speak, his own eyes would always answer back.

Then at the height of this brief exchange of unspoken communication, BJ would simply wink and follow the wink with a simple nod. At that very instant, LJ would know that things, no matter how awful they seemed, would eventually turn out for the good. It was then that he could feel his father's will, and he knew that his father would make it all right. And somehow, it seemed that he always did.

Taking a page from his father's playbook, LJ looked over at Mysty, and right away her eyes seemed to plead with him to do something, anything, but something. He then summoned all the courage that he could muster and stared her directly into his consciousness. With a prolonged squinting stare, he first tried to communicate his love and his fervent desire to make sure she was okay. Then after a slight pause, he winked, and that was quickly followed by a deliberate and calming nod.

Mysty did not exactly know what the wink and nod combination specifically meant, but somehow, she felt comforted by it nonetheless. It wasn't much, but it was all she had at that moment. So for now, it would have to do. For now it was good enough. She held on to the comfort of the gesture, and her imagination gave it even more power than it had originally.

Henry caught this exchange, and it seemed to bring a sense of calm over him as well, which he immediately wanted to pass on to the others, or at a minimum, to his wife, Beverley. He turned to see tears streaming down both her cheeks. He imagined that all the talk of killing and getting prepped for some injection was enough to send Beverley into this free-flowing teary state of fear. After all, she was not the hard-edged type like Pam, or even tough like Mysty to some degree. She was a quiet and gentle spirit, which was above all what made her so attractive to him.

He forced his silent will onto her, and she was compelled to look him in his eyes. He silently told her with his glare that some way, somehow, things would turn out okay. And then he gave her his father's wink and subsequent nod of assurance. But as was mentioned, Beverley was not the brave type. The nod and wink must have had the opposite effect on her as she sobbed and cried even harder and much louder.

So much so that she got the attention of Big Walt, who was already in a foul mood for obvious reasons. "Shut up. Shut the fuck up before I give you something to cry about." He immediately started toward her in a rush, raising his infamous left hand in the backhand slap position, but Little John grabbed him before he could strike.

"Hey, man, we got enough worries without this crap. Take it easy! Besides, you know that the stuff don't work as well when they are all emotional and shit. You heard the doc. We have to prep them, and let's not forget that the dumb duo over here, fat man and boy blunder, have to find the one that got away."

"Well, shut her the hell up. I can't think."

"Okay, okay. Miss, please be quiet for your own good. Please." Sensing the urgency in the stranger's voice, she had no choice. Almost instantly, her crying diminished into the kind of sobs and whimpers often heard from fearful children, afraid of another round of intense corporal punishment if they were not immediately silent.

However valiant her effort to hush herself quickly, the slightest of whimpers, together with the occasional heavy sigh, could still be heard. These gave Big Walt just enough reason to give her more threatening looks, but he did not act on them. This made Henry very thankful, but for what, he did not know.

However, he felt helpless. Here he was tied up like some wild animal or some deranged criminal, and to top it off, so was his wife. He could do nothing to help her. Right now was a very confusing time, and his emotions were running wild. He wanted very much to yell out, even though, like all the others, he was bound and intimidated into silence.

Milton seemed to simply stare into space, just zoned out. It was as if he were pretending that he wasn't even there. Hazel kept trying to get his attention. She needed to share her moment of terror with her husband, but she was forced to share this experience with the most unlikely of all people, *Pam*.

As they all stood in a straight line, her husband, glazed eyes and all, was to her left, and her archrival, Pam, was to her right. Fearful of leaning forward in order to try and make eye contact with anyone else, she was forced to seek comfort, at this gravest of times, from the one person that she would vote most likely to go to hell in gasoline bloomers.

"Okay, people, let's move. Take the women that way and bring the men over here. Okay, Claris, you and Becky get them showered, deliced, and into their uniforms. When you're done, bring them back here and get them strapped into the panic chairs. Then we ought to be able to see a good show."

"Okay, you heard the man, ladies. Let's get to it. Right this way, if you would. Not that you have a choice, ha, ha, ha."

Seeing the tremendous amount of fear etched into the expressions of the terrified four, Becky spoke gently to the group, trying to bring a minimum amount of calm to the situation. "Listen, ladies, forgive my coworker. I realize that this is a very bad situation, but I won't make it worse on you by pretending that this is not really fucked up or that I like my job. However, it is a job and a good-paying job, so I must do it, 'cause truthfully, any one of us that crosses the bosses could be working next to you tomorrow.

"Now if you would, please remove your clothing, all of it, and place it in a pile right here. Becky, stop talking to them like you better than me or something. I don't give a rat's ass about these people. They just some city scum from high-falutin New York City. They is the kind of folks that don't give a damn about our kind, and if you'd take your titty out of your mouth for one hot second, you'd know that."

"Listen, Claris, this is not the time or the place for this conversation. In a matter of minutes, these people will be living zombies, and I can't help but feel for them."

"Well, feel free, 'cause as for me, I don't give one rat's ass about 'em. Better them than me, that's what I say. Okay, gals, into the showers."

Standing naked before their captors, each of the women endured this torment in their own private way. Unable to communicate, except with fear-ridden eyes and frowning expressions on their pale faces, each suffered in silence. Mysty wanted to attack them and try to overpower them, but then what?

She had no idea where they were. A dozen or more armed men were just in the next room less than two hundred yards away. And worse, she did not know where her beloved LJ was. Pam had similar thoughts, but she resigned herself to believe that even if she initiated the rebellion, the others would leave her hanging, and she would surely be killed as a result.

A loud shout disturbed both their mental wonderings. "Okay, you bitches step out of the water so I can douse you with this good-smelling shit here."

"Claris, please stop it. What is the matter with you? Isn't it enough that they are all but dead to the world? Do you have to rub it in?"

"Whatever!" came the terse reply. "Whatever! Okay, step up and get the good stuff. Next, next, and now last but not least. I don't know about you, Becky, but I like sprinkling this delicing powder all over them. It kind of feels like throwing rice at a wedding."

"My god, Claris, sometimes I'd swear that you are the devil himself."

"No," she said devilishly. "That's Good Doctor. Said so himself." They both then shared a brief laugh.

"Okay, you nappy headed heifers and hoes, back into the shower. Ain't that how y'all say it up there in good ole New York City?"

"No mind, ladies. No mind," said the kinder of the two women. "Now please take a towel, dry yourselves off, and then be so kind as to get into one of those uniforms. They all have name tags on them, but the sizes may have to be altered."

Pam thought to herself that she'd like to punch this little half-breed trailer park trash right in her big-assed mouth. But after only a minute, she thought better of it. Mysty caught a glimpse of the raw emotion that was overtly imprinted on Pam's face. Fearing that she would let her emotions get the better of her, she gave her semi-friend a comforting look.

    She gave Pam the same sort of look that she had gotten from her husband. It was a look to assure her that no matter how awful things seemed at the present moment, that tomorrow, or the next day, or the day after, the warm rays of the sun would shine down on them again.

CHAPTER 5

SEEING DOUBLE

AFTER BEING ESCORTED back to the large reception room, the female captives were lined up for inspection beside their male counterparts. Outfitted in matching dark gray khaki jumpsuits, Walter gave each a good looking over. He knew that Clark and the Good Doctor would double-check his efforts more carefully than ever with this particular group. The two of them always checked after him but almost never found anything to bitch about.

However, he knew that would not be the case today. Not this time around, not with this group. These folks were not only more forced free labor, but this was also revenge. This was something personal for the Good Doctor. Not trusting even his own inspection, he repeated the process. He examined them all a second time from head to toe.

He knew from experience that when the Good Doctor had a hard-on for someone, no matter who that someone was or for whatever reason, it was always best not to be in the line of fire. For that reason, this inspection had to be flawless.

When Walter finally reached Pam for the second time, he gave a sudden and noticeable pause. Nearing a dry sweat, he stood and stared in disbelief. Caught up in the moment, he allowed himself to see what he did not want to see before. He allowed himself to see double. In fact, he could only imagine that he was seeing a ghost. The ghost of someone that he knew, someone that he secretly desired, someone that haunted his dreams, both day and night.

Pam was the spitting image of Ms. Diane. She was standing there with her long jet-black hair, hanging on to her head like a vine to a grape. It flowed straight down to the middle of her back and stopped just above her picture-perfect hind parts. She represented the picture of perfection, if only in Walter's starstruck eyes. Her beautiful hair was no longer in the usual bun, and the sight of it stimulated Walter to no end. It stimulated him to the point of overt nervousness. He was instantly overcome with the simultaneous raw emotions of lust and panic.

Ms. Diane was Walter's dream girl come true in every way imaginable. Just the thought of her made him ultra-nervous and super lustful. She had it all. She was the total package, particularly, if Walter was telling the tale. She was sexy, she was sassy, plus she was funny and sweet too. She was everything that he was not: tall, good-looking, and well-built.

But above all else, Walter sadly knew that she was off-limits, at least to someone like him. Even if she would give him the time of day, and he knew that she wouldn't, he could never travel down that path. After all, Ms. Diane was the Good Doctor's stepdaughter.

But there she was in the flesh, a real-life version of Ms. Diane, with the same hair, same face, same body, same everything. As he stood in awe, a manly urge overcame him, and he wished to God that he could save her from the horrible ordeal that she was about to undergo. He wanted so badly to protect her, to take care of her in her time of greatest need, and he knew why. Maybe, just maybe, she would be grateful enough so as to see him differently than most women do.

An immediate mental tug-of-war ensued within the confines of Walter's overstimulated and confused mind. He struggled greatly with his contradictory and competing thoughts. On the one hand, he reasoned Pam to be a godsend. His first thought was that the gods must have smiled down on him, and this was justified by the evidence. *Why else would I be standing here just two feet from my dream girl, or at least her long-lost separated-at-birth twin*, he thought.

On the contrary, he considered the possibility that this apparent stroke of good fortune just might lead to his own demise. He could just imagine the stinging rebuke, or worse, hand delivered by the Good Doctor. If he would resort to religious-like buckle beatings for poor leadership, what would he do about a significant protocol violation for nonfraternization? Walter shuddered at the thought. Nevertheless, he quickly dismissed it. *Chances like this don't come around very often for people like me,* he thought.

After only a moment, Walter's mental pendulum had swung for good. Right then and there, he decided he was taking his shot, no matter the odds or the consequence. *God himself must have done this for me, being that I am a good, just, and upright man,* he further reasoned. *I mean, why else would she be here, right here, right now?* he pondered deeply. He allowed his train of thought to continue, now unchallenged.

After another elongated pause, and the complete mental dismissal of the severe penalties that he might face if discovered, he directed Pam to follow him to his office. The other staff in the room dared not say a word, because they all knew what was on Walter's mind, and they knew all too well how he would react if they said anything.

Walter also knew that LJ and the others could only watch, wait, and pray for Pam. Once inside the safe confines of his private domain, Walter again took a deep-breathed pause to gather both his thoughts and his nerves. As he stared into the eyes of what he thought to be heaven on earth, he searched the recesses of his scrambled mind to find just the right words to say.

He flashed an "ice cream with warm pie on top" kind of smile and stood back. He wanted to thoroughly savor the beauty of his godsent piece of heaven on earth. Seeing the noticeable discomfort in her facial expression on full display, the portly man asked Pam to relax. "I just want to talk to you," he said calmly, trying his best to put her at ease.

Growing up in a super tough neighborhood, Pam knew that it was now best to relax her expression. Although she stayed silent, she remained on guard. Always trying to gain the mental edge, as she was trained, she strategically allowed him to do all the talking. She knew very well how to lead from behind. That was her best asset growing up. Moreover, in her adult life, it had become her specialty. In fact, she'd had lots of practice with her now missing fiancé.

Cautiously, Big Walt began by asking the most obvious question. "You want to know why I have chosen you to come to be alone with me, don't you?" Unmoved and sticking to her initial game plan, Pam silently nodded in the affirmative. She already had a pretty good idea what was on the mind of the loser that stood before her, but she innocently played along. "You don't know this, there is no way you could, but you are my dream girl come true," he said without emotion.

Pam offered a quizzical look in response to the intriguingly bizarre statement, but again she said nothing. "Just look," he said as he confidently pulled out his wallet and showed his beautiful captive guest a photo of a strikingly beautiful young woman. It was a woman that anyone, other than Pam herself, would have sworn was, in fact, Pam. If she had not known better, she would have sworn the same. She could readily see that the resemblance was an almost unquestioned perfect match.

"So you see, this is you, only not you. And you are her, only not her. So for me, you are the one, because she is the one. I mean, the one, the one for me," he stammered. "You might think I'm half nuts or something, but I love her even though she doesn't know it. Without even doing anything, she makes me feel all sweet inside. When I see her and I am close to her, she makes me sweat and my heart beat fast. She has this effect on me that I cannot explain, and I know it's for no good reason, but I absolutely adore this woman."

Continuing after a moment of reassuring reflection, the brutish looking man stated unequivocally, "I can honestly say that I worship the ground she walks on." He continued with a bright smiling face, "And I would do anything within my power to make her happy. I love her with all my heart and soul. I would do anything and give anything to make her mine."

His once bright face then turned sour as he added, "But there is one huge problem for me. As far as I am concerned, she is poison, at least for me. She is poison. Ms. Diane, that's her name, is the Good Doctor's stepdaughter, and to me she is absolutely hands off. That is, unless I want my hands to be sawed off. And believe me, that sick fucker would do just that. You saw the way he beat me earlier. You saw the way he spoke to me, like I was less than human or something. Even though I don't show it much, I got feelings too, damn it!"

Seizing on an opportunity to exploit a perceived weakness on the part of her adversary, Pam acted quickly but cautiously. When she finally spoke for the first time, her words were expected, considering the circumstance, but both her tone and delivery were much to his great surprise. "I did see him beat you, and I felt bad for you," she said softly with an air of pity. "Honestly, I closed my eyes and prayed that he would stop." Her sympathetic words hit home and landed on his heart, just as she had calculated. Walter was not accustomed to kind words from any woman, especially one that was drop-dead gorgeous.

In full control of his attention, she shifted her stance so as to accentuate her generous hips and small waist. The shift was combined with a slight swivel on her heels in order to provide her would-be lover a better view of her ample bottom, plus a glimpse of the rest of the total package. As a finishing touch, she folded her hands and dropped them seductively in front of her, causing his hungry eyes to follow them to their convenient resting place.

As a social outcast and relationship rookie, he could not anticipate what she was about to unleash upon his unprepared mind. No woman had ever spoken nice to him, never, so he was now in uncharted territory. Her revelation really shocked the romantic misfit, but he felt good just hearing those words, even if they were pretend, as he deep down somewhat suspected. And though he was unsure of her motives, he chose not to question them. Truthfully, he really did not want to know if they were disingenuous.

The now starry-eyed man continued, "I have been here for over ten years, and I watched that young lady get prettier and prettier by the day. I have grown to love her in ways that you cannot imagine. I am going to tell you something that no one else on this planet knows. This may shock you, but here goes.

"I have kept myself pure for her since the day I first laid eyes on her," he said sheepishly. "You might think that is silly," he said with almost no confidence, "but I believe in the one-man, one-woman way of doing things. I mean, who needs all them different women when you got one perfect one? I have always believed in happy endings, and I have always believed that me and Ms. Diane would hook up someday and that I would be able to give her the gift of my purity. You think it's silly and foolish, don't you?"

Thinking fast on her feet, Pam replied with what she thought was the perfect answer. "To answer you truthfully, I don't think that what you said is silly. Not at all," she said shyly and added a gentle smile. "In fact," she said with as much tenderness as the situation called for, "I actually kind of admire you for what you did. And to be even more real with you, I would love for a man to love only me and not have to chase all them other women out there." Her intentional use of substandard language was to further put her mark at ease.

"I swear," she said with both pleading and passion, "I don't know why men do that, especially when they don't like it when it's the other way around." Then she paused to see his reaction.

"Yeah, that's what I'm talking about," he said in full agreement. "I would never want my women playing me for a chump, so why would I want to do it to her? I love how you see things just like I see things," he said, full of genuine naivety.

"Now I know I said I loved her," he said almost apologetically. "And that I would never play her dirty, but I can't have her, and that's some hurtin' ass truth. That's why this situation is so good. It can work out great for us both. That's why I brought you in here to talk to you," he said as if to ask for permission to continue, which he was given, if only by his guest's silence.

"If I could have you, it would be just like having her, and that might not make much sense to you, but I ain't bring you in here to pump you fulla lies. I know I'm not a good-looking man like that handsome some-ma-ma-bitch Clark or maybe yo boyfriend. I ain't seen him," he readily conceded. "But looking at you, I can tell he ought to be a good-looking sumthin' nother. I see it like this," he added, still making his case. "I been here ten years with the Good

Doctor. Now he can be crazy as hell, but he is a businessman first. Plus, he can also be sort of an all right guy at times," he said, almost thinking aloud with his practical voice of balance.

"I figures it like this. I can have him give you to me, or I will buy you or replace you. As I said, he is a businessman first, and I don't think he got it in for you personal, not like he does those two Matthews characters. You and the others just got caught up, is all," he said with a hint of pity. "And if all that fails, I will just have to steal you away from here in the middle of the night. That is if you'll agree to come to live with me.

"Before you answer, hear me out. Nighttime around here is my time," he said loudly and boastfully. "At night, this shit belongs to me." Walter immediately realized his poor choice of words and instantly apologized for his use of profanity. This was an overt and obvious effort to impress his prospective live-in lover. That is if he had his way.

"I promise on the good man upstairs, with my right hand raised to God Almighty himself, I will take care of you real good. I get paid a damn good salary here, and I ain't hardly got no bills. My house is paid for. It ain't as big and fancy as these people here, but it is nice. It is pretty roomy, and it would be all yours, and you can have all the money you want to decorate it and stuff like that. I am a plain man, so all that stuff don't much matter to me. I just eat and sleep there and watch TV, but only sometimes. I don't hardly get no visitors, so no one would come there to bother you and stuff like that.

"I would give you money to go shopping whenever you feel like and even get you a maid to clean up and cook for you and stuff like that. I got over eight hundred and fifty thousand dollars saved up 'cause I don't spend my money on nothing. Hardly got any food bill 'cause I eat here all the time. Almost no light bill 'cause I sleep here most of the time. Plus, I barely go home. Here so much, some of 'em don't even know I have a house, but I do. Honest and true, I do.

"All what I'm saying is, I think I can get you out of here if you would agree to some terms."

But before he could continue, Pam made her play, beginning her declaration in her most temptress of voices. "Before you go on," she said in a soft, low, and slow voice, "let me say this. I am no fool. Not by anybody's measure. Have never been and don't intend to start anything new on that front." She then added a sharp piercing glare, with both hands firmly placed on her full hips to emphasize her point.

"I know what lies ahead for me and my friends out there," she said in a matter-of-fact fashion, now apparently resigned to her fate. "In fact," she said with the covert intention of distancing herself even further from the others, "they are not much my friends, just my boyfriend's family. And as for him…" There was an open hint of sadness. "He is probably dead by now or he soon will be, at least to me, especially if they inject him with that stuff that they've been talking about so much.

"I am young, and I've only just begun to live my life. And I really don't want to walk around like some sideshow freak with a blank stare on my face for the rest of it," she said without emotion. "And as for taking orders and working my ass off in some field, as what can only be compared to a slave, it is not my idea of a good career choice. So I am open to almost any option. But like I said, I am nobody's fool, and I refuse to be.

"I mean, I know my fate if something drastic does not happen, so trust me when I say I am open to almost anything right now. I mean, I might marry a donkey or a mule if it would keep me from being one of the Godspoke workers. Not that I am comparing you to a donkey or anything like that. I'm just saying how desperate the situation is, if you get me.

"So that said," she softly spoke, now transitioning back to her softer side. "Let me say this. I can see that you are a good God-fearing man, and you say you would treat me good. However, if I take you at your word, how can I be sure that once I give myself to you that you will keep your end of the bargain?" she asked with a brooding look on her face.

"That is what you want right now, isn't it? For me to give myself to you," she continued without pause. "Give myself to you before any marriage, before any arrangement with the Good Doctor, before I really and truly know my fate, before I know whether or not I will walk around like a hypnotized robot for the rest of my life, or if I will get to be Mrs. Walter…hmm." She paused. "I don't know your last name. What is it?"

"Lildevil. Walter Lildevil," he said sheepishly, as if purely mesmerized by the vixen standing before him.

"Mrs. Lildevil," she continued without missing a beat. "What guarantees do I have? I would feel just like a fool, a complete and utter fool, if I was to be tricked," she repeated as reinforcement. "A dumb blond bimbo without the blond hair. I would feel just like you had raped me, or worse. Like you had taken a part of my spirit that wasn't meant for anyone to touch without my unequivocal consent. How cruel that would be. How very, very cruel… Are you such a cruel man? And how can I be sure that you aren't?" She finished her flurry of verbal jabs with what she thought was a knockout blow straight to the chin of her unworthy opponent.

Walter began slowly, unsure of how to convince his stand-in dream girl of his good and honorable intentions. She stood quietly, awaiting his response. "Ms. Pam, I…I…I…" he stammered. "I am not what you think I am. At least not with women, and not when I am away from this place and away from my men. I learned a long time ago in my outside life to be hard 'cause people used to pick on me when I was coming up. I am short now but was a lot shorter back then.

"From the time I was born, I had cradle cap and only got a full head of hair when I turned twenty-one years old, so people always got on me for that. Plus, I'm built like a Mack truck, square at the top and round at the bottom, so me and the girls never did see eye to eye. Mostly 'cause I was always shorter than them at whatever age I was," he said with a nervous self-deprecating chuckle. "Truthfully, I have never been with a woman in my whole life, at least not for real. I ain't never paid a woman to sleep with me either. I only watch them nasty movies or look at them nudie books sometimes. But never did I see a live naked woman, except my two sisters, and they always told Momma when I peeked at them, you know what I mean.

"So I ain't about to sit here and blow smoke up your ass for no quickie roll in the hay. I got plenty of money, and there are plenty of women around this broke ass town that I could pay just to have sex with me, if that's all I wanted. Hell, the way I see it, you and me got a chance to be a couple. I know you wouldn't ever choose me under no other conditions. I ain't no stupid man by far, but I do know that I can save your life right now, and for that you ought to be very grateful. At least for a while, that is. And if I can squeeze myself a little bit of happiness out of this coldhearted situation, then dammit, I ain't gonna be bashful and not do it.

"I ain't never been happy my whole life, between getting picked on at school and in my neighborhood, plus getting treated like a misfit in my own damn house. Who could blame me for any way I turned out when I growed up? But I ain't so bad. The one thing I do know is that I keep my word. I live by that, Ms. Pam. I keep my word. When you don't have much else to fall on or to rely on, you got to make a name for yourself somehow, and my way was keeping my word.

"One time, my buddy got this job driving trucks, and he had to be at work at three o'clock in the morning. And when his car broke down, he asked a couple guys in our little circle to take him to work so he don't lose his job and all. Everybody said yes, but nobody came through. He asked me, and for two months straight, I got up every morning at one forty-five and got in my car, drove over to his house, and took him to work and didn't miss a day.

"I did that not even because I liked the guy so much. I did that because I gave my word. You can ask anybody about Big Walter Lildevil, and they will tell you to a man that he is an ugly little dumpy piece of shit, can't dress for nothing, and has breath like cheese, but goddammit, he keeps his word.

"Yeah, that's me. I keep my word. So when I say I will do what it takes to get you out of here, I will do just that. And when I say I will give you a very good life, I will do just that. And when I say I will never play you dirty, I will absolutely do just that."

Pam gave Big Walt a good "head to toe and back again" looking over. She said at last, "Somehow, I believe you. I probably shouldn't, but I do." She moved in closer to him and asked him point-blank,

SAME AS GOD SPOKE

"What do you want me to do first?" She kissed him gingerly on the side of his short thick neck.

Feeling very disconcerted, Walter did not say a word. He did not know what to say, and he readily admitted the same. "I told you, I don't know how this is supposed to go. I sometimes watch some of them movies, but my mind is blank right now, so do whatever you normally do. Do whatever you want to do."

Pam stood back from her would-be lover and ordered him to get down on his knees and kiss her feet. He obeyed as commanded and kissed her feet. He kissed them greedily but with unbridled passion, and all without removing her newly issued flip-flops. "Now take your shirt off, you naughty boy, and be quick about it," she snapped. Like an excited child, Walter again complied with this resolute request.

Bare chested, Walter asked, "What next, my queen?"

"Lick my fingers, and by god you'd better do it right or you will displease me."

Walter hurriedly grabbed her left hand and began to suck her fingers as ordered, but she quickly rebuffed him. "Slowly," she said. "Do it very slowly." Now taking his time, Walter licked and sucked each finger on his dream girl's hands. First her left and then her right. He thought while performing this exotic act that he had never before felt so good, for so long, in his entire miserable life. This was as close to sex as he had ever been, except for when he was alone at home with his blow-up doll. And to think, this very first time would be with a close second to his dream girl.

Suddenly, he felt very flush inside. He could feel a fast-moving warmth begin to envelope his entire body. Walter moaned and groaned and almost purred like a kitten while sucking Pam's tasty fingers. He thought her fingers tasted like two pounds of good-as-hell. He also believed that this feeling was oh-my-god good. The more he tasted the sweetness of her fingers in his mouth, the more intense the flushed feeling became.

His body began to gyrate and move back and forth in a seemingly uncontrollable fashion. Before an eye could blink, Walter was in full launch mode. He yelled out, 'Oooh, ooooh, Diane. I love you, Diane. Oooh!" Again came the loud erotic moan, and before he could do anything to avert an unintended inevitability, he had reached his climax and released a fully loaded discharge right in his pants.

"Walter, Walter, snap out of it, man. Walter, what's wrong with you, dude?" This very familiar voice came from Liljohn, who was Walter's friend, confidant, and right-hand man. "Are you okay, man?" he said quietly. "Man, Walter, you was doing some strange stuff. It was as if you was in a trance or something," the younger man said with genuine concern.

"I didn't know what to do," he said remorsefully. "Hey, man." He leaned over and whispered, "You need to go get cleaned up. You got a big wet spot on the front of your pants. You need to go and get cleaned up now. You know the doc and Clark will be here in a minute. We already put the call in," he said with a sense of concerned urgency.

Once Walter fully regained his bearings, he found himself standing right behind Pam. He also found himself shirtless and covered in sweat. More than that, he did indeed have a huge wet spot on the front of his pants. He felt a sense of shame and embarrassment that he had not known before. This, he thought silently, was worse than any of the picking and insults that he had suffered as a child or the everyday adulthood torment of not being able to meet a woman that would actually take him seriously.

This was worse than all those things combined. Walter's mind raced at warp speed. He needed to do some damage control. What would his staff say to him? Would they still have respect him? Would there be quiet laughter every time he would enter or leave a room? *Too much to think about. I got to get outta here so I can regroup*, he thought.

His private thoughts were again interrupted by the voice of Liljohn. "Hey, man," he said with as much assurance as he could muster. "You go ahead and I will cover for you for a few. That is if they get here before you get back. Go ahead, man. Hurry up." Liljohn had a discernable amount of sympathy for his friend of many years. Walter felt very ashamed. He was almost paralyzed in his tracks. He looked around to see who had seen him in this humiliated state.

SAME AS GOD SPOKE

Just as he gave notice, every eye in the place that was trained on him and his semen-stained pants quickly turned away. So everyone knew, everyone except the spellbound Godspoke workers as they were under the spell of the stuff as everyone causally referred to the Godspoke serum. They had not been given an order to look, so they remained looking forward the whole time.

For Walter, this was one point of solace, because it meant that his dream girl hadn't seen him in his embarrassment of a lifetime. Which further meant that he still had a chance to make his daydream a reality. He knew that he would never get to be anywhere near the real Diane, but he could get next to good ole Ms. Pam if he played his cards right. He just needed an angle and the right opportunity, he thought with a confident grin.

He simply needed a good solid plan, and he could finally get what he wanted most from his sorry excuse of a life up until now. He could finally get to be with a woman, a real woman—a woman that could talk back to him and no plastic involved. Walter was now a man with a purpose; he was a man on mission. And that mission was to get to Pam by any means necessary.

As Walter walked away, he could feel the penetrating stares of those behind him. And before he turned the corner to retreat to his office, he yelled over his shoulder without looking back, "What the hell are you looking at? Get them ready. Never mind me, you fucking morons. When I get back, if I find one thing out of place, someone will answer, but good!" This fiery order sent his staff into an animated frenzy, most of them more concerned with the appearance of looking busy rather than actually doing anything substantial.

Once inside his office, Walter quickly grabbed a change of pants. He then wiped the remainder of the mostly dried sweat from his face, neck, and torso. "How fucked up can you be?" he said aloud while looking at his reflection in the bathroom mirror. "How goddamn fucked up can one person be? I came on myself in front of a roomful of people, all because of a stupid ass daydream. A sweet daydream, but a daydream nonetheless. Well, I guess it coulda been worse. She coulda saw me and seen what a fucking perverted degenerate I am, and that woulda killed any chance I have at snagging her for myself.

"Okay, Big Walt, stop fantasizing about the shit. It happened, so now what?" he said aloud, trying to provide a self-pep talk in clear and lucid tones. "Okay, okay," he said, pointing his finger at the image in the mirror. "Okay, here is what we do. Go back out there and act like it didn't happen. You are in charge of these clowns, and you can make their lives miserable if they get out of line, so use your power and this will blow over real soon.

"Besides, Liljohn has my back, and he will keep a lid on any real slick talk about me behind my back. He's my boy. We been through a bunch of shit together, so I know I got some eyes and ears out there so I can put pressure on whoever it is that wants to keep this little story alive. Okay, that's what we will do. Ignore it and squash it." Now with a half-confident smile, he said finally to the image in the mirror, "Okay, now get your horny ass back out there, Mr. Big Walt. You got work to do."

Before Walter could return, he had been betrayed by one or more members of the team that he supervised. The Good Doctor and his trusted assistant, Clark, had been fully briefed about Walter's erotic episode, and they were waiting to pounce on him.

"So, Walter." Not wasting any time, the Good Doctor began his lecture once Walter returned to the scene of the crime. "I hear that you have taken an inappropriate interest in one of my new Godspoke workers."

"How do you figure that?" Walter blurted out without thinking about the gigantic can of ridicule that he had just opened himself up to.

"I figure that, my good man, by virtue of your lewd and lascivious pornographic episode that you put on in full display of everyone in this room, with the exception of myself and Clark. I'm even told you wish to take undue liberties with her. Is that right?" he asked as if he didn't already know the answer.

Walter's panicked response was "No, sir, Good Doctor. I don't know what came over me."

"One minute I am looking 'em over for the inspection, and the next someone is yelling my name. It was like I was hypnotized," he said in a pleading fashion. "It was just like I was under the Godspoke spell. I don't know what happened. Maybe this one is a witch or something. Maybe we should get rid of her.

"You know them witches got powers. They can make people do strange things. If she has got any powers, she could use it on me or one of the men, and it could be very bad for us all. She might need to get dealt with. She might need to be disposed of. You know the stuff don't work too well on everybody. So I'm saying, well, I mean…" He continued after a pause to gage how his delivery was being received, "I could get rid of her for you, if you just give me the say-so.

"I'm just saying, Good Doctor. I mean, just look at her. She don't even look like the rest of 'em. I think she is what they call one of them mulattos or something like that. They all half-breeds mixed with a little of everything, come from down New Orleans way and practice voodoo and that Shango stuff from the Yoruba people in West Africa. I seen it on the History Channel. They is some dangerous folks, and I suspect she is one of 'em. Just look, her hair is different, her skin color is different, and them eyes is the eyes of the devil. A she-devil, I tell you, Good Doctor. She is bad news. We should do something before it's too late. She had me here doing things that I had no control over. Bad things, nasty things. It couldn't be no clearer that she is a devil. Now we got to act before it's too late."

"Say no more," the Good Doctor demanded. "Shut your weak little pathetic mouth up right this instant," he said with all the harshness of a subzero degree day. "It is painstakingly obvious that this woman looks just like my beloved Diane, albeit in a down-to-earth from the other side of the tracks ghetto-fabulous kind of way. And we all know how you secretly feel about my precious Diane. And for the record," he enunciated with great care, "the secret better stay secret, because if I even hear an utterance that you have approached my daughter, so help me you will have hell to pay.

"Your lack of prowess with the ladies is well-documented, Walter," lambasted the Good Doctor, now in full attack mode. "It would take an utter fool not to realize what happened here, if what your team tells is a hundred percent accurate. You had an erotic fantasy and consequently released on yourself right here in the middle of the floor.

"First and foremost, this act was rather disgusting. But moreover, it was unprofessional. However, we will deal with that small issue at a later time. I have much more pressing business to attend to at this time. But remember, I never forget," he said with a threatening hint. "I never forget.

"Now back to the matter at hand. I don't think she, mulatto or mudaddo or putatto, has any devilish ways about her. Do you?" he said mockingly as he stood directly behind her and patted her on her bottom for good measure. "No, no, you don't. But you, sir, Lildevil, you do have devilish ways. I know that now, and I've known that since you came to work for me those many years ago," he said almost with glee.

"But damn-it-to-hell, that's what I liked about you then and still do. You see, it takes a devilish mind to get ahead. All bleeding-heart liberals want to do is save the world and help everybody. They want to discuss their feelings and such. That is the cause of mediocrity. I need soldiers who don't give a rat's ass about anyone but themselves. That means they will tend to my business, because helping me helps them, and that's how it ought to be," he said with one triumphant finger pointed to the ceiling.

After a long silent pause, much longer than his usual pauses that were built into his long speeches for dramatic effect, he continued, "I don't know what you exactly have on your little pea brain, my good man, but do us all a favor and get that thought out of there. You really could use the room for more constructive things like getting my fucking work done. Even you, as dumb as you are, should know that you don't have the luxury of holding too many thoughts in such a small place now, do you?"

When Walter did not respond, he repeated the question as a demand for an answer. "Do you?" he shouted.

Realizing the Good Doctor's familiar need to exercise and demonstrate his absolute control by demoralizing others, Walter replied, "Yes."

Although the response was in a very weak and almost unintelligible voice, so Walter's oppressor refused to go away. "What was that? I didn't quite get that," he taunted.

"Yes! Yes, Good Doctor!" he blurted out in a mix of frustration and anger. Unrelenting, the Good Doctor could not resist having the last word. "Walter, my dear Walter, I detect a note of anger. So you do have a spine. I'm glad to know it, but don't let it get you into trouble." He then gave Walter a stern look to remind him that the fine line between the two men that should never be crossed nearly was.

Having completely and utterly humiliated Walter, the Good Doctor transitioned his attention to more pressing matters. He declared, "Now let's get these fine folks into the fields while there is still some daylight left." Then he added insult to injury. "Looks like you Matthews boys will help me make some money after all."

Stepping to the side, he summoned Clark. "I must go prepare for our meeting. I will expect you shortly. However, please see to it that these workers get the proper command instructions. Additionally," he declared in what initially appeared to be a very serious tone, "see if you can do it without staining yourself." With that comment, he let out a huge chuckle. He turned on his heels military style and exited the room.

"Okay, Walter, that's your job. You don't need me for that. Please tell me that you at least gave them command response instructions."

"I did. I did, Clark. Just test them. Call out some commands and see if they don't respond."

"Okay, I will do just that because I am not going to take any heat because you and your little group of misfits didn't do as you are paid to do."

Before Clark could finish his insulting remarks, Walter quietly asked Liljohn, "We did train them with the commands, didn't we?"

"Yeah, Walt, we did. We did," replied Liljohn. Walter sighed a big sigh of relief.

CHAPTER 6

THE SETUP

AT MIDDAY, JUST like every other day, Carmen slowly made her way along the concrete sidewalk that lead to Back-Lane 3. Back-Lane 3 was the only way to access the living quarters that housed the Bright Spot staff. Each entrance, in the long row of bungalow-styled microapartments, was intentionally designed to face the woods so that the servants were kept out of sight as much as was possible.

Tired and now hungry, she was glad that the first part of her day was over. Starting work at six thirty in the morning was not easy, but her daily ninety-minute noon break always helped to revive her. She came to her door, the last one on the long bottom row, and stuck her key in the knob that led to ninety minutes of heaven. Just as she turned the key and pushed open the door, a large hand came from nowhere to cover her mouth. at the same time, its owner pushed her into the small darkened unit. Frightened, she tried to scream, but her assailant applied even more pressure and warned her to be quiet.

Weighing her options, she quickly decided to comply and wait for her chance to make a move. The owner of the hand began to spin her slowly so that they were now face-to-face. She tried her best to make out the figure of her captor, even in the absence of light, but this only proved to be an exercise in futility. She could not make out who it was.

Then after what seemed to be an eternity, he spoke. "Don't be afraid, Carmen. It is me, Greg. I met you last night," he said as he flipped on a nearby light switch. "You gave me directions. Do you remember?" She nodded an affirmative as his heavy and rough hand still covered her petite mouth. It also covered at least one of her nostrils, so much so her breathing was very staggered and labored. However, she did not protest. Instead she conserved her energy, staying as still as possible so that her insufficient oxygen intake would not exacerbate matters.

"I am not going to hurt you, but I do need to talk to you. I need your help, and I need it in the worst way. Do you understand?" She provided a second nod, this time with an added benefit of maternally concerned eyes. The eyes must have done the trick because his next words were the most welcomed of her life to that point.

"Now I'm going to remove my hand from your mouth. Please don't scream. Please don't yell! I am not here to hurt you. I don't want anything you have. I just need your help. Now are you sure you are not going to scream?" Looking directly into his searching stare, she provided a third nod in the affirmative.

Greg slowly removed his hand from his frightened hostess's mouth but kept it mere inches from her face. Just in case she had a sudden change of heart or had altogether tried to deceive him and was just looking for an opportunity to alert others of his presence. She knew she was at a great disadvantage and felt that she needed to find out what his true motives were before she made her next move, so she gave him no reason to doubt her loyalty. In all truth, she provided the absolute impression of being genuinely interested and thoroughly concerned about his plight and his troubles.

"Senor Greg, you are frightening me. What are you doing here? What is the matter? Please tell me what it is. You really are frightening me."

"Carmen, I am really sorry, but you have to be very quiet. I really need to stay out of sight right now, and if anyone was to hear you talking, that might not be so good for me. So please do not be alarmed when I ask that you stay very quiet. It's only because my life depends on it.

"As I said, I really need to lay low for a little while, so I'm gonna need to stay here for the time being. I don't know if that is okay with you or not, but I don't have much of a choice, so truthfully, you don't have a choice either. I know that sounds kinda harsh, but it's just so I can think things through, just so I can figure out how to make a phone call."

"I do not know if that is such a good idea, Senior Greg. I'm not supposed to let anyone in my room, especially one of the guests, and especially not a man. I could be fired for this. I need my job. My family back home depends on me to send money. I am pretty much all they have."

"While I am truly sorry for this inconvenience, as I said, neither of us has much of a choice right now. I'm really, really sorry, but I got no place else to go."

His terse words and resolute demeanor confirmed what she already knew—that she had a desperate man in front of her. She did not know exactly what was going on, but she knew that she did not like the feeling of being held captive; the very thought was overwhelming. Privately, she thought she had it together, lucid thoughts, coupled with a calm demeanor. But without realizing it, she was actually in a near state of panic. Quite suddenly, Carmen became almost hysterical. As evidence, she tried to scream.

Greg quickly placed his over her mouth again. Right then, he knew that he had to act fast, or this potential ally could soon turn into a potent enemy. "Listen, Carmen, please pull yourself together!" he said sharply but peppered his words with a tone of understanding. "I know what you must be thinking just now. A million thoughts must be running through your head, and about 999,999 of them are bad. Please give me five minutes to explain. I will tell you everything, but I need for you to please calm down.

"Once I know that you are calm, like I said, I will tell you everything. I'm asking, no, I'm begging you to please just relax and let me relax for a few minutes. After that, after I've had my say, if you still do not want me here, I will go. Deal?" After an uncertain nod, he slowly removed his hand.

"Okay, Senor Greg. We have a deal, but you only have a few minutes, so please talk fast." She took full advantage of her newfound freedom and moved to the center of the room. Both to sit, so that she could calm down, plus to put some distance, no matter how small, between her and her captor. "Come sit here," she said as she motioned for him to take a seat on a chair while she sat feet away on the edge of her bed.

At that moment, she quickly decided to pivot from innocent protestor to concerned ally. "Please tell me what is going on," she said softly. "I am so confused. Please, Senor Greg, please explain." Her soft-spoken words were comforting, but her troubled look spoke volumes over her calm words. "Ay dios mio. I hope no one saw you come in here. I do not know what I would do if anyone saw you."

"No one saw me. Now please calm down. You said I only have a few minutes, so here goes. Okay, I'm in real trouble, and I need your help. Some dangerous men are looking for me. I think they abducted the rest of my family, and unless it's some sick game that I don't know anything about, they are in real trouble too. That's why I need a place where I can be out of sight for a little while. They are searching for me as we speak, so time is of the essence."

"But, Senor Greg, why would they search for you here? We all were told that your party checked out early in the morning. They said there was a problem and that you do not like the place and that you left suddenly."

"No," he quickly interrupted. "That's not true at all. In fact, it's a great big lie. Now I wonder why they would have told you that great big lie." He then paused to consider the answer to his rhetorical question.

"What do you mean great big lie?" she asked, wanting him to continue with his story.

"You mean you don't know what really happened?" he asked suspiciously.

"No, Senor Greg. Whatever do you mean? They tell us you leave, and I did not expect to see you again."

"Well, I didn't expect to see you again either. That would have been especially true if those goons had anything to do with it."

"What goons? What do you mean?" she asked, half frightened.

"I mean it's some freaky shit going on around here, and I haven't figured it out yet, but you can bet your sweet ass that I will. No disrespect intended. That's just a figure of speech where I come from."

"That is no problem. I understand," she said. She continued to speak softly and calmly so as to put the much larger and much stronger man at ease. "Okay, but I still do not understand. Now please tell me everything that happened, and I will try to help you if I can."

"Okay," he began slowly. "You remember last night when I came out late. I saw you and we exchanged names and you gave me directions. Yes. After I left you, I went down and slept on the dock. I was in the military for six years, so I'm used to sleeping outdoors. I had a lot of training for that kind of thing.

"Anyway, I woke up very early in the morning and started to head back. I was on my way down the Path of Destiny, and I see this white van pull up, which was nothing by itself. But then I see a bunch of masked men get out with guns, so I hit the deck and I hid myself. Look at my arms, my legs, my face, and my neck. I have the ant bites to prove it.

"I guess it was the luck of the draw, but from my vantage point, I could see everything that happened. One by one, they brought the entire party out of the house and ordered all seven of them to get down on their knees at gunpoint. They were all bound by their hands, and after, they questioned them about me for a good while before they loaded them up and drove away. I was just close enough to overhear some of the conversation.

"They must have known how many of us there were, 'cause they went looking for me. I mean looking everywhere. First, they all ran into the house, all except one. He just kept on asking questions. Then they came back out and came over here to bungalow row and searched. After that, they searched all the grounds and the Paths of Destiny. Lucky for me, I found a good hiding spot, but not so lucky it was right on top of an ant's nest. Army ants. As I said, look at me. I have the bites and the swelling to prove it.

"Anyway, they loaded the whole group into the back of the white van and drove off. But before that, a short chunky one hit my brother

LJ in the mouth with his gun. I think he got hurt bad. I wasn't that close, but from where I was, his injury looked bad. Real bad. Out of the group, he has the biggest mouth, and he always thinks he is the boss of everyone, so even with his hands bound and looking down the barrel of a gun, he was probably still giving orders and ultimatums. LJ thinks he can sell snow to Eskimos. He is a smooth talker all right, but not that time.

"Anyway, two of 'em got in the van and drove away with my family tied up and tucked away in the back. The other five guys in the hunting party stayed behind to look for me, but as I said, I hid myself really well. They walked right past me several times, and one guy almost saw me when he bent down to scratch his leg.

"He was only three feet from me and looking directly at the pile of summer moss that I was lying in. But I guess the good Lord or something or somebody was on my side, 'cause he scratched his itch and never saw me at all. After a while, they all loaded up. And they took my car and my brother's car with them.

"Now I've told you my side of things, and I swear to you that what I said is the absolute truth. Not one word is false, fabricated, or fiction. Those men mean to do me and my family some harm, and I am the only thing standing in the way of their plans. And you are the only thing, except not having a phone, that is standing in the way of me helping them and saving them. So what is the verdict? You believe me, or do you still want me to leave?"

"I do not think that you can make up such a fantastic story just like that, Senor Greg. I do believe you. Of course, I believe you! And let me say this. That must have been terrible to see your family go through such a thing and not be able to help and only able to watch. I wish I could help in some way. What can I do to help you? Anything, you just name it."

"First, let me say thank you. I was beginning to sweat over here. What a relief. I don't know what I would have done if you had not believed me and had asked me to leave. Man, what a relief. I'm glad to know that somebody is on my side. I was beginning to feel as though everyone here was in on it," he said with a smile. Carmen returned Greg's brilliant smile with one that rivaled his own.

But inexplicably, as he continued to speak and analyze the situation, his smile turned upside down. "I'm trying to make some sense of it all. I mean, if not everyone, I was thinking at least some of y'all had to see what was going on. I mean, how could not one of the many, many sets of eyes that live and work in this place, how could they all not see what went on this morning?

"I mean, I couldn't hear what they were exactly saying from where I was. As I said, they were too far away. But I know everyone had to hear my brother scream, or at least someone. I mean, even as far away as I was, I heard it. I heard it clear as day. I mean, it was god-awful, and it lasted a little while, so somebody had to hear it. Maybe not everybody, but at least somebody. And if they didn't hear his scream, they should have at least heard the gunshot that the short fat guy fired at my brother's ear."

Growing ever more agitated by the second, he continued to speculate and parse together a total and collective conspiracy. He now reasoned that every man and woman that worked at the place must be involved to some degree. "I can't believe that no one heard all that commotion, not even the people at the front desk, not even the overnight or early morning kitchen staff, not even the groundskeepers.

"This shit is crazy. I know in my heart of hearts that someone had to hear something. Everything in me tells me that someone, anyone somewhere out of all these folks up in here saw or heard something. So now, one and one always equals two. If everyone heard it and said nothing, I can only conclude." He then stopped abruptly in midsentence to carefully measure the facial expression of the very attractive woman sitting just inches away. If they heard it and no one said anything, then they must be in on it.

Turning his focus from general to specific, he asked Carmen in a tough sounding manner, no longer peppered with the sweet convincing tone of just a moment ago, "Are you in on it, Carmen? Are you in on it too?"

In the briefest of instants, Greg had turned hostile. However, Carmen's horror-stricken look all but convinced him that she, if nobody else, was not in on the obvious conspiracy. Regaining his composure, he immediately apologized for his accusation-laced rant.

"I am sorry, Carmen. I am under a tremendous amount of pressure right now, so you must overlook my wild speculation. Right now, I don't know what to believe. So once again, please forgive me. This is all hard to believe. I kinda wish I would just wake up from a bad dream, but if I can't have that, I really could use a friend right now, and I could also really use a phone."

"No apology needed, Senor Greg. I completely understand. But as I tell you, I am sorry, but I do not have a phone. There are no phones here that I have ever seen, not even at the front desk. Only intercoms and walkie-talkies.

"Yeah, I've heard! One of the marketing strategies that the Bright Spot Villas uses is that you won't be able to communicate with the outside world. They say that no one will have access to you, no phones, no faxes, and no e-mails. I wonder who thought up that great idea.

"Okay, so let's start again. I understand that you do not have a phone, but there must be phones here, or else how do you all communicate with the outside world?"

"As I have told you, we have to go into town to use the phone."

"I know, I know, but I cannot do that right now. I told you, there are some bad men looking for me, men with guns. Men who want to do me harm. The same men who have my family and would have me, too, if not for a dumb fight over nothing. Do you understand?"

"I understand, but I do not know what else to tell you."

"Okay, okay, let's just chill for a sec. I just need to sit here and think this thing through for a few. I know if I give it enough thought, I can figure this whole thing out. How do I do it? I need to call my father in the worst way. He will know what to do about this whole thing. He is in the agency."

"What is he, Senor Greg? A police officer?"

"No, something better than that. He's an FBI agent. Although he is retired now, he still has some serious connections and some seriously badass friends."

As Greg spoke, pus dripped freely from the wounds on his body that had now swelled to bursting after hours of neglect. The brownish green liquid oozed slowly down his face, and the sight of it made

Carmen's stomach quiver with nervous revulsion. She promptly offered him some much-needed first aid.

"Senor Greg, you have many wounds. Let me dress them for you. Take off your shirt and roll up your pants and I will help you." He shook his head no, but she persisted. "Please, take off your shoes. I will get a clean cloth and some peroxide to clean your wounds. You need your head clear so you can think. And you will be here for a little while, no?"

"Yes, and thank you. Thank you very much. But right now, I'd rather you tell me how to get to a phone. There must be a phone in one of those buildings. There must be a phone somewhere on these premises. How do they order food, supplies, and other materials from outside vendors? How do they send faxes or e-mails?"

"Senor Greg, I told you, I go into town. I don't know all the details about all the buildings in this facility. I only started to work here a couple of months ago. But wait, there is a room with the word *communications* in the lower level of the main building."

"There is?"

"Yes, I have seen it many times, but I never gave it any thought before now. I just mind my business."

"Great. Just tell me where it is."

"Senor Greg, I must take you there. First, it is tricky to get to. And second, even though I have been in the building many, many times, I have never been in that room because it's very secret and very secure. It is always locked, but I do believe that Malcolm, our manager, has the keys to that room. Also, if it is as you say, it will be very dangerous for you to leave here and go back up to the main building. They may be waiting for you there, or they may be looking for you there."

"Don't I know it, but I desperately need to make that call. So when it gets dark, I'm just gonna have to take my chances."

"Okay, Senor Greg, if that is your plan, that is your plan. But we have some time until then. Now will you please relax and allow me? I will clean your wounds before they become even more infected." Before he could speak again, she disappeared into the bathroom and returned with two clean washcloths and a bottle of liquid that looked nothing like peroxide.

"I am very sorry, but I was mistaken. I do not have peroxide. The good news is," she said with a devilish smile, "I have something much better. I have this green rubbing alcohol. It will sting a little at first, but it will keep your wounds from getting infected, which is the most important thing. Right?"

She then extended her hand to him, which he gladly took, and she slowly guided him to the head of her bed. After helping her one-time captor to remove his shoes and shirt, Carmen knelt down to roll up his sweatpants. She rolled them as high as his upper thighs, exposing the many, many wounds that he endured in the name of continued freedom. In doing so, she took careful notice of his muscular build and rugged features.

"Okay now, I need for you to lie right here on the bed." Her voice now call girl seductive. "Wait, let me pull the covers back so that we will not soil the comforter." As he stretched out across the bed, she again took painstaking notice of his chiseled physique. "If you do not mind me saying so, Senor Greg, you must be a very strong and brave man to lay there on top of all those ants and take all those bites. How strong…how very, very strong. How I so admire you for that."

"Thank you," came his curt reply.

"Take this cloth," she said as she handed him the larger of the two that she held. "Place it between your teeth and bite down hard. I need for you to lie still and focus so that you do not make noise and alert anyone that you are here. This will sting some, but I know you can do it for this small pain. After all, you did it this morning for the ants."

As she liberally applied the most common household disinfectant, she made several off-the-cuff remarks, much to Greg's surprise. Intentionally avoiding any eye contact and looking down, she boldly stated, "I've always pictured myself the wife of a strong and brave man. In my country, as far as the women in my culture are concerned, machismo, as we call it, is the sexiest quality a man could have."

Greg did not reply. He did not want to spoil the moment or to put too much stock into what he had just heard. Although his every instinct told him that his woman was making a pass at him. "Oooh, aaah, aaah, ooooh, oh, ooh ooooh."

"I'm sorry. I'm sorry, Senor Greg. I know that must hurt, but that means it is killing the germs."

"No, no, Carmen, it's okay. Don't stop. It actually feels kinda good."

After the briefest of pauses to smile at Greg's last statement, she applied another dose of the green burning antiseptic. "Oooh, aaah, ooooh, ooooh." Tickled in schoolgirl fashion, Carmen laughed at her patient's reaction to the stinging sensation that he was obviously experiencing.

"Senor Greg, if I were on the other side of the wall listening, I would think you were doing something other than having your wounds cleaned."

"Yea, I know. I sound like a half a sissy, don't I? Let me man up. Man up, G. Man up."

"I wasn't talking about it like that. I meant something else."

"Oh, *oooh*," he said rather loudly after catching on. "I have to be quiet then. First, wouldn't want anybody to hear me. And second, wouldn't want them to hear anything like that if they did," he said with a half-smile.

"Okay, there. Just one or two more. Now may I do your face and your neck?" she asked ever so softly. Without waiting for a reply, she continued to speak. "First, I will need another cloth for your face. I never use the same cloth for my face as I do for the rest of my body. I will also need to heat this one so that it can help take down the swelling in your face," she said as she turned on the faucet in the bathroom sink.

Laying on his back, hands behind his head and half clothed, Greg called out to Carmen to continue their interesting dialogue. "You seem to know a lot about taking care of someone. Where did you learn?"

"Well, back in my country, I was a nurse. And before that, I was the doctor in my house," she said jokingly. "My two little brothers, who were always cutting, burning, or scraping something of theirs, were my best patients."

"A nurse, but…but," he stuttered.

"But," she said, taking him off the awkward hook, "my credentials are not recognized here in this country. That is why I work here, but only for the time being. That is until I can straighten my papers out. I either need to have someone sponsor me as an exchange student or to marry someone. Then I can transfer my college credits and apply for my citizenship. Either way, once I go back to school, it will be a breeze to get my nursing credentials. I love this profession. I was an RN in my country. Plus, I honestly know almost everything there is to know about nursing."

Before either of them was ready for their close contact to end, Carmen had cleaned every wound on Greg's face and even cleaned some places that didn't have wounds. Ceasing on the moment, she quickly said, "Senor Greg, would you like me to now to put some lotion on you? Alcohol can make your skin very dry." Forgetting his troubles for the minute, Greg played along with his gracious hostess.

"My skin is beginning to feel tight, so yes, that would be awfully nice of you, Carmen. Ordinarily, I would insist on doing it myself, but right now everything on my whole body hurts. So if you really don't mind, I think I would like that."

"Mind? I do not mind at all. I told you, I love to serve people and to heal the sick. And you, Senor Greg, you look like you can use a lot of healing," she said in between giggles and polite laughter.

As she began to apply the soothing cream to his skin, Greg closed his eyes and tried to shut out the misery that was waiting just beyond the safe confines of Carmen's room. After a deep sigh, eyes still shut, he said, "I hope this will help me relax and help me to think better. My mind is so scrambled, so cluttered, and so utterly jacked up that I can't think straight. I really need to get my head together."

"You just relax, Senor Greg. I will take good care of you."

"I bet you will, Carmen. I just bet you will," he said with a smile. "You know, Carmen, this reminds me of my room when I was thirteen years old, only I had everything on the floor."

"Senor Greg, this is not good. I am a devout Catholic, and I believe cleanliness is next to godliness. I hope you have outgrown that thirteen-year-old clutter-making boy."

"Oh yeah! Yes, indeed. Many years ago. Many, many years ago! When I went into the military, they taught me how to be a lean, mean, fighting machine, and rule number one was a place for everything and everything in its place. Right now, I'm so neat, I'm almost anal retentive, but not quite," he said with a chuckle.

"Although, my fiancée, Pam, wouldn't share that opinion," he said, reflecting. "She'd probably say the exact opposite, knowing her bougie ass. That feels good, Carmen. That feels very, very nice. Uuuum, seems like you know what you're doing down there. Wow. That feels very nice. If you don't mind me saying so, wow and wow again. That would be like wow to the second power, wouldn't it?" he added with a second chuckle.

"Senor Greg, you are kidding me. Do not kid with me."

"You think I'm kidding, but I'm not."

"In that case, thank you, Senor Greg. Now roll over so that I can do your back."

"Nice, nice, very nice. This feels good enough to be a sin."

"Oh my gosh, why you say that?"

"I'm just kidding now. But, Carmen, seriously, are you married?"

"Oh, no, Senor Greg."

"Why not? a beautiful woman like you, a professional woman at that, you should have men lined up at the door."

"Well, right now, I live for my family, my mother, my father, my four sisters, and my two little brothers. My family works hard, but as fishermen, they don't earn very much. What I send them every week, they do not even earn every month. So right now, I don't have time for me. I only have time for my family."

"So you've never been with a man?" he said.

"Senor Greg, that is very personal," she replied.

Greg said, "You're right! I am sorry, Carmen. I did not mean to go too far."

"Oh no, it is okay. I will answer your question," she said, looking down. "I do not have anything to hide. I am proud to say I have never been with a man. I came close, but just one time. However, that was a long time ago."

"How long ago?" he said in animated fashion, now very excited by the thought. "You don't have to answer that. But wow, how can you stand it?"

She replied, "Well, you know what people say? You cannot miss what you have never had. It does not really bother me. Only sometimes."

"Sometimes?" he asked.

"Yeah, like when the other girls that work here tell me their romance stories. I like their stories, and sometimes I do get aroused by the them."

"Yeah? What do they say?"

"They tell me about some steamy stuff with some of the guests that come here. Very, very hot stuff."

"Stop playing. For real?"

"Oh yes! Goodness, yes. They talk about it when a bunch of us are sitting around having lunch or in the laundry room. They have very good stories to tell. Very good stories. Sometimes I wish I had my own story to tell, but my family comes first."

"You have no stories? Not one? I see that smile. Tell me about your story. I know you must have at least one. You are very beautiful. You gotta have one story."

"No stories for me! There are just no stories to tell. Me, I just have dreams. Many, many dreams, and sometimes daydreams."

"Okay, tell me about your dreams," he said, almost panting now.

"No, Senor, you don't really want to hear about any of my silly dreams. I know you do not really want to hear about my simple fantasies."

"Yes, yes, I do, and I'm not going to move or say another word until you tell me one of your daydreams."

"Okay, but you must promise not to laugh."

"Here's my right hand, and I cross my heart on a stack of dirty magazines."

"Oh, Senor," she protested playfully.

"Oh, that's just a joke, but I promise."

"Okay, well, as I said, machismo is very important to the women of my culture. Sometimes when I sit here in my room, I close my eyes and lay on my bed like this," she said as she demonstrated by laying down next to him, eyes closed.

"Then I imagine that one day, a strong man with lots of machismo would come to the resort, and as soon as he walks in, he would look at me in such a way that I instantly know he greatly desires me, and my eyes will tell him the same. Then I imagine that he will come to me in the middle of the night, that he will take me up in his arms. He will kiss me deeply and passionately, all over my quivering body. Then he will slowly undress me," she said now, almost in a whisper. Greg leaned closer so that he was almost touching her lips with his own. "He will touch all my tender places, like here and like there," she said while again demonstrating. "He will love me as no other woman has been loved before. He will make me a woman for the first time, and we will be in love eternally. He will decide that he cannot live without me, and he will take me from this place to begin a new life together."

She then went silent. "Wow, that was very raw with emotion. How could I even think of laughing at that? I only wish I could be that man. I am sorry. I did not mean to say that, but you are a very beautiful, sexy, and intelligent woman. I would have to be made of stone not to notice or desire you."

"But, Senor Greg, did you not tell me that you have a fiancée, Pam?"

"Yes, yes, I did, but that does not stop me from seeing what I see or feeling what I feel."

"Senor Greg, you lie down to rest now," she said as she planted a soft kiss on his lips. "I am going to the bathroom to freshen up, and when I get back, who knows, maybe you can be that man, even if it's just for a little while. Now let me go. I will be right back."

Lust now dominating his mind, Greg not only encouraged her to go but also to take her time. "I will be right here. I am not going anywhere," he said with an expectant grin. After about ten minutes, Greg noticed that the usual sounds from the bathroom had ceased. "Hey, Carmen, are you okay?" he said softly. In a loud whisper, he called to his woman in waiting a second time. "Carmen, Carmen, can you hear me? Are you okay in there? Carmen? Carmen?"

Half concerned and half horny, he decided to take a look inside. "Let me see what is going on here. I am coming in. Peekaboo." Much to his shock, the small space was now abandoned, and he instantly knew that he had been betrayed.

Now in instant panic mode, he murmured aloud, "Goddammit, where the hell is she? Why you little bitch. Ain't this a motherfucking shame. Everybody is in on it!"

As he quickly transitioned from fight mode to flight mode, he rightly reasoned aloud, "Let me get the fuck out of here!" And he fled, full speed toward the safety of the nearby woods.

CHAPTER 7

Don't Come Back without 'Em

Once inside the van, Chuck and Ole Roscoe sat quietly for the first few minutes of what seemed like the longest twenty-minute ride of their lives. Each man was totally absorbed in his own thoughts about what the future held. Finally, one of them broke the awkward silence.

"What are we going to do, man?" asked Chuck. "What are we going to do?" he repeated.

"You know this man is psycho," he stated matter-of-factly. He continued after a brief pause to see if he had his partner's attention, "And you know, just like I know, that he will make good on his promise to hunt us down and kill us if we don't find this little piece of shit and bring him back."

"And," he continued again after a second exaggerated pause, "on top of that, you know his wife has every goddamn body in this town under her thumb, so there is no place to go, no place to run, and no place to hide." The troubled reality of what he had just said made him quiver. The very thought of being hunted down and killed sent a numbing chill down his back.

Now almost hysterical after truly contemplating the full meaning of the words he had just uttered, Chuck forcefully repeated his question. Only this time in a very slow and staggered manner, as if talking to someone intellectually inferior. Using a very condescending tone, he screamed at the top of his lungs, "WHAT THE HELL ARE WE

SAME AS GOD SPOKE

GOING TO DO, MAN!" Chuck's over-the-top dramatics aside, Roscoe shared his great sense of urgency, but he said nothing in reply.

In fact, all Chuck got in return for his over-the-top outburst was more of the same silence and uninterested demeanor that his partner had displayed since their departure from the Conn estate only brief moments ago. Shocked and confused by this silence, Chuck paused during an intense moment of disbelief. Making no headway through animated urgings, he decided to try a quieter approach but could not decide on what exactly to do. Meanwhile, he stared compellingly for minutes on end at the driver with the sandy brown hair.

Simultaneously, his mind raced as his thoughts took him back to a hundred plus times that the two had been in tight situations. Then like a sudden flash, it hit him, and he smiled while looking at the tall slender man just to his left, driving along as if he did not have a care in the world. He thought he knew why ole Roscoe was so calm, so cool, and collected when he should be shitting bricks right about now. He had seen Roscoe in action too many times not to recognize this play. He thought he knew exactly what was going on.

At that very minute, his mind was filled with admiration, but also with an abundance of wonderment. How could his buddy of almost fifteen15 years be so calm and so serene at a time, if ever there was one, that literally screamed out for panic? It could only be only one thing, he reasoned to himself. Ole Roscoe must have something up his sleeve. *His lack of emotion almost gives it away too easy*, he thought.

Now, almost in a hushed and calm whisper, he spoke again in an effort to elicit some kind of feedback from the driver of the vehicle. "I am talking to you, Roscoe. Don't you hear me? Don't you care about this whole mess we in, man? Don't you care? Ain't you scared, man? Ain't you scared?"

"Listen, Chuck, we have to handle this thing the right way," Roscoe uttered his first words since leaving the estate. Chuck smiled instantly, certain that he was about to hear a master plan from the master himself, *Ole Roscoe*!

"We have a couple of options on the table, and none of them are to our advantage if we go and fall all apart," Roscoe continued calmly. "Since we left, I have been sitting over here thinking this whole thing through," he said matter-of-factly.

"I knowed it. I knowed it," Chuck interrupted. "What you got? What you got?" he repeated.

"Calm yo ass down is the first thing I got. I need yo head in this with me. Stop acting all excited like a schoolgirl on her first date. This is serious business. Now act like it, goddammit."

Chuck did not reply because he knew that Roscoe was right. He had been acting erratically and compulsively. Confident that he had gotten his harsh but necessary message across, Roscoe continued, this time uninterrupted. "Now the way I see it, we can go back over to the Bright Spot Villas and find this maggot, or we can use the time to stop by our house, pack up some stuff, and get the hell out of dodge.

"If we take the chance of trying to find this guy and we don't, we've blown our only chance to make a run for it. Now we both know that we make pretty good money, and I have quite a few thousands in the stash, and I know that you should too. I hope you do at least, because if you don't, you are damned fool. And more than that, you are on your own. I can't carry you, and I wouldn't do that even if I could. My father always said, a fool and his money will soon depart, so if you have no money, that makes you a fool. Furthermore, if you are a fool I'm getting as far away from you as possible, as quick as I can."

"I got as much or even more than you, so that's not an issue. Now keep going. Let's hear the rest of this idea," Chuck urged.

After a brief pause, but without breaking stride, Roscoe picked up right where he left off. He continued with the solemn choices that lay before the two men. "So we can pack of a few things and get the hell of here, or we can try and find this guy and not interrupt our lives. Either way, we would take it a big gamble. If you look at this thing real deep, we are working for some real, real, real bad folks. I mean, I've never seen the Good Doctor come down so hard on somebody the way he did Big Walt this morning. That was downright crazy, man.

"Since they got control of that biosphere and started that whole drug thing and the whole Godspoke thing, this shit is getting way,

way, out of hand. I mean, who knows what will be next. Who knows who will be beat down, stomped out, or even worse, next time around. I'm telling you, man, if you really weigh it all up, this shit is for the birds.

"As a matter of fact, I have a good mind to not to even pack any clothes but just to get on the road and make a mad dash. That would save some more time, which means more time to run further. I don't even know if this is all worth it anymore," he said with some obvious doubt.

"We used to be big time around this town and no one could touch us," he said with a small bit of reflective happiness. "Now we got all these new people with all these specialized skills coming in on this organization, and we getting pushed down lower and lower on the totem pole. I wonder if we will ever get back to those days and those times when we really was important to the bosses, 'cause right now we seem like less than half a pile of old horse dung.

"We used to go into the diner or any store in town and not take a dime out of our pockets. Hell, we still can most places. But is that worth putting your life on the line? Every single day knowing that the people you work for are ruthless and coldhearted. And not just that way against any so-called enemies but against us.

"I mean it. They could take us out any day. Any time they want us dead, they could kill us. What kind of life is that, Chuck?" He asked the question, not fully expecting an answer. "Really, what kind of pathetic fucking life is that?

"Looka here, Chuck. Everything in me is telling me that we should run. We can go to a small town somewhere in North Carolina or in Ohio or something like that. Somewhere where nobody would ever think to look for us, a real small-town USA. What do you think?"

"Man, fuckin aye. I'm totally with you on that! I'm not trying to get beat down like Walter did. I'm not trying to get slapped around and humiliated. And I don't want anybody threatening me, because I ain't no goddamn fucking punk," he said with authority. "I wish that son of a bitch, the Good Doctor, would try and put his fucking hands on me like he did Walter. I would beat his punk ass to a pulp.

"That shit was foul! Real foul, and ain't no way it shoulda gone down like that. That was some straight bullshit that happened this morning, and I can only think that it will happen again because he got away with that shit. Them rich bitches think they can get away with anything!

"If he can take down Big Walt like that and treat him like that, what the hell can the rest of us expect? So I'm thinking just like you. I say we hit the stashes, we gas this motherfucker up, and we burn up as much highway as we can between now and when they start looking for us. I think we still have about eighty or eighty-five minutes before check-in." His comments delivered with a childlike anticipation only experienced with the thought of a new and exciting adventure.

"Hey, man, I'm sitting here listening to you, and trust me when I tell you that shit sounds real good. I mean real, real, and I mean real good. Me and my boy starting all over again in a new town, in a new city, in a new place. That shit would be so freakin' cool." Still in fantasy mode, he continued, "That would be some of the best shit that I could think of. I mean man oh man, that would be something to tell the grandkids about."

Roscoe then took another moment to really savor and enjoy his thoughts. He smiled to himself and visualized his words coming true. However, he had very mixed emotions running through him. Then, all at once, reality set in, and his smile was gone.

"Who do we work for, Chuck?" he asked solemnly, breaking away from his temporary moment of make believe. He paused to wait for a reply from his friend. Chuck responded in a low monotone voice, "Some crazy motherfuckers, that's who we work for. Some very crazy motherfuckers."

"That's right. Some crazy and murdering motherfuckers. So let's quit beating our dicks and start fucking getting back to reality. That kind of shit only happens in the movies and shit like that." The very thought caused Roscoe to seethe with anger. His anger was in full evidence as he hit the steering wheel violently with the palm of his hand several times and cursed aloud at no one in particular. "Fuck!"

After a moment to regain his composure, Roscoe began to systematically reason aloud. "These people are into some really crooked shit now, even more than before. I do not think they would like it too much knowing that we were out there somewhere and capable of bringing down their whole shit if we so decided. So on the real side, my man, as much as I'd like to, and as tempting as it is, we can't run," he said in a quiet voice. "We just can't.'

Even more solemn now, he continued, "They're not gonna let us run. They will hunt us down, they will find us, and they will kill us. We will always be a threat as long as we are unaccounted for. So the way I see it, the Good Doctor was right. We have sold ourselves to the devil, and now it's time to pay up.

"So I say let's go find this stankin' bitch and bring his ass back. And from now on, we will just watch our asses and make sure this kind of dumb shit don't happen again."

Confronted with his new reality, no longer revitalized by the thought of a new adventure, Chuck's shoulders slumped. Saddened, he said, "You know what, man, you are right. We can't go nowhere. We know too much, and if it were me, I wouldn't let us go either."

The two men rode in silence for the remainder of their short trip, each man deeply tormented by his own thoughts. Each beleaguered by a lack of options. Each fearful of what might happen if they proved unsuccessful. The fear of imminent death, coupled with the challenge of finding someone who desperately did not want to be found, was a recipe for anxiety at its highest level.

Saner men might have gone over the edge, given the grave circumstances under which these two were forced to operate. However, despite the extreme situation, the daring duo maintained a state of relative calm. When they pulled onto the grounds, they were immediately greeted by several excited and overly animated staff.

There was genuine concern. The word around the complex was that there was a rapist on the loose. An armed and dangerous rapist. Clark and Malcolm's disinformation campaign was in full effect, and the two men took full advantage. Under the guise of locating the predator, they immediately went to work. They wanted any news or information about the matter.

The dissemination of this story was a thing of beauty, as far as they were concerned. It made their jobs so much easier. As Roscoe began to question those present, his partner had Malcolm summon the rest. The two men were determined that they would not be the victims but instead the victors on this day.

In a very serious and intensely urgent voice, Roscoe asked if anyone had seen the eighth member of the group. Carlos, a well-spoken male valet, spoke up. "Senor Roscoe, Carmen, one of the chambermaids, encountered a guest last night who identified himself as Greg. She told me so early this morning," he offered.

Once Carmen was front and center, Chuck took over the questioning, although he was not so skilled at it. "Now, Carmen," he said in a slow and deliberate voice. "What can you tell me about this guy Greg?" Sensing the seriousness of the situation, she nervously began to speak.

"Well, Mr. Chuck," she said in her nervous thick Spanish dialect. "There is no much I can tella to you."

"Hold on there, senorita. I can't understand shit you saying. Ain't no need to be nervous. I ain't the bad guy here, so calm yo-self down and speak some good English so's I can understand you and make some good sense outta all this."

Carmen tried her best to conceal her anger and contempt for the man's condescending and patronizing remarks. She began again with the hope that her much slower pace would satisfy her brash and smug questioner.

She pointed toward her sleeping quarters and explained, "I was standing outside of my room, and this man, he walking up to me and say to me questions. He tella to me that he want to get away from he room 'cause he fight with he girlfriend.

"I remember he say he want to get a Jet ski. He say he want to cool off. I tella to him, as best I can, where to go. I point to the path. He say if it still open. I tella to him everything is open all night. Then he walk off to the lake."

"What happened after that?"

"He say good night and he walk away. And that's it," she concluded.

"That's it?" asked Chuck, still searching the woman's eyes for signs of dishonesty.

"Yes, senor, that's it. I don't know nothing else to tella to you."

"You don't know or you won't say, hmmm?" His comments were said aloud in typical bullying fashion, not fully expecting an answer. After more brief interviews, the two men realized that they were no better off than before they had arrived. They had no new leads.

Standing in the middle of the grounds to discuss their unenviable circumstance, each man seemed weighed down by the overwhelming pressure of it all. After some time had elapsed, they agreed on their next best move. They instructed the staff to spread out and conduct another search of the complex and grounds. Walkie-talkies would be used to report any sighting of the wanted predator.

Just twenty minutes later, a sighting was reported. A strange man was seen tampering with the door to the communications room. The two men became instantly frantic. They knew that room had everything in it to make contact with the outside world, so the two goons for hire immediately jumped into action.

They raced on foot toward the operations center. The room they sought was located at the end of a long corridor, better known as the underground railroad. Situated two stories below ground level, that corridor housed most of the facility's unseen operations.

"If he gets in that room, the jig is up. He can blow this whole circus wide open," Chuck said, panting and half out of breath from running at top speed. "Move it, man. Move it," he urged.

"Move it? What the hell do you think I'm doing over here? Hell, I'm in front of you. Bring yo slow ass on," Roscoe said, obviously annoyed.

"Shit," came the reply. "I outweigh you by fifty pounds or more, so you should be way ahead. That's my point. I'm wide open, but it seems like you should be way ahead of me, not just a step or two considering the weight."

"Cut the bullshit, Chuck. You know I got bad knees. And besides that, I ain't built for this shit. I'm a lover, not a sprinter," said Roscoe.

"Well, I don't know what you are, but I do know that if that asshole gets in that room, I know what you will be, Roscoe."

"Yeah? What's that?"

"Up shit's creek…just like the rest of us. That's what you'll be, right up shit's creek! And deep in too!" touted Chuck.

"I know that's right, so you shut up and let's both keep it trucking," replied Roscoe.

They sprinted down the three flights of stairs and only slowed once they came to the landing at the bottom of the final flight. In front of them was a long dimly lit bending corridor that led to the communications room. Initially, they moved cautiously and checked every door along the way. They did not want to outsmart themselves by walking right past their intended target. Just then, a loud thud could be heard, and each man froze in his tracks.

Roscoe said, "Did you hear that?"

"Of course I did," Chuck whispered. "What do you think it was?"

"I don't know. There is a bunch of shit down here. The laundry room, the supply room, and some more shit. Could be any one of 'em. But I do know that the only room down here with a metal door is the communications room. It was fortified by order of the Good Doctor, so no one could get in who wasn't supposed to and shit," replied Roscoe.

"See that's what I mean about you. How do you know that? How do you know so much about this place? I don't know almost none of that stuff you saying, including what rooms is down here," Chuck said.

"Hey, keep it down. You make more noise than an old man with dentures trying to chew nuts. I know 'cause I know. If you'd listen more and stop walking around with that noise in your stupid ass ears all the time, you would know some shit too. Keep it up. One day you'll be deaf and that'll learn ya. Just keep it up," whispered Roscoe.

"Hey, man, I do listen. Just that most of that shit don't concern me. As for my music, ain't nobody can take my comfort. My music is my comfort. Until the day I die, it will be my comfort," he replied.

"Well, if you don't shut up and get your head in the game, today might be the day you die, so focus and please shut the hell up. All this nervous chatter is making me more nervous. And hell, why should we be nervous? It's two of us and just one of him," touted Roscoe.

The conversation continued undaunted as they moved closer to toward the source of the sound. "I know that and you know that, but does he know that? I hope he doesn't put up much of a fight. You know we can't use our guns on this guy. We got to overpower him and bring him back alive. A little bruised and beaten, but alive."

"Okay, okay, now shut the fuck up please."

As they arrived at the destination door, they heard a voice from inside. The voice was pleading with the operator to place the call without an authorization code because it was an emergency. "Please, miss, why can't you understand? You have to make this one exception. I am begging you please, please, please."

After a short pause, while still getting up the nerve to face their adversary, the dynamic duo overheard the voice shout, "*Yes!*" This celebratory exclamation was enough to move them into action.

Without any further thought, the two burst through the door. "Put the phone down and do it right fucking now!" This forceful command came from Roscoe. Greg spun around on his heels to face his two would-be captors. As he spun, he intentionally dropped the phone so that the line was still open. He hoped BJ or Big Momma had answered the phone by now and could hear what was going on.

"What have you done with my family and my fiancée? Where are they?" he insisted.

"Never mind you worry about them. It's you that you should be worried about. We came to take you to them, and we mean to do so, buddy. We got guns, but we can't use them, so don't make us lose our jobs."

"Chuck, you fucking dummy, why did you go and tell him that for?"

"I just want to cut to the chase 'cause we ain't got much time. "Now you listen, fella. We ain't letting you outta this room. We already called the others who will use their guns, and none of us want that. Do we? They will be here in a minute, so if you will surrender peacefully, we will make this nice and easy for you."

"Tell you what," Greg defiantly responded. "Tell me what's going on first and I will come along peacefully. I give you my word."

"You swear?" said Chuck.

"Yeah, I swear. Just tell me what's going on. I am not armed, and I won't fight you or try to run. Just tell me, is my family okay? Is my fiancée okay? Just what the hell is going on? Why were they taken hostage? What do they want, money or something? Just tell me and I'll let you take me where you have them. You're not going to hurt me, are you?"

"Listen, dude, if we wanted to hurt you, you'd be dead now. We both got guns and you don't. Make sense?" replied Roscoe.

"Yeah, makes good sense, so what is it then? Where you taking me, and where are they? I know this is Coulditbe, Pennsylvania, and Dr. Jones invited all of us down here to his resort, the Bright Spot Villas, and Malcolm is the resort manager and Clark is like the…like some executive guy or something. Who are you guys? Do you guys work at Big Luke's dinner where we stopped to get instructions on how to come down here to the Bright Spot Villas here in Coulditbe, Pennsylvania? What's the name of that diner? Luke, big tall sandy blond guy works there, right? He owns it, right?"

"Hey, Roscoe, why does he keep repeating all that stuff, man? Is he cracked or something? Is he that scared or something?"

"I don't…hey, Chuck, he's got the phone off the hook. He's trying to give clues to whoever is listening."

Both men rushed over to subdue their mortal adversary. As they got into punching distance, Greg swung first at the larger of the two men. However, hitting Chuck turned out to be a grave miscalculation. Just as he delivered a thunderous right-handed blow squarely on the jaw of his intended target, he received a much harder blow. Roscoe used the butt of his gun to land a shocking blow to Greg's exposed left temple and rendered him semiconscious. His knees buckled and down he went.

This gave Roscoe enough time to remove a pair of handcuffs and place a bracelet on each wrist of his nearly comatose victim. Wrists that were still sore and swollen after suffering several thousand ant bites earlier. As the bracelets were squeezed tight, Greg was immediately returned to his senses. This was evidenced by several loud agonizing screams of pain as he pleaded for mercy. "Goddammit, man, please loosen them up some! I can't take it. I can't take it!"

Now semi-recovered from the jaw-splitting blow he had just received, Chuck took the liberty to retaliate. He let loose with his own version of a jaw-breaking blow on his now defenseless opponent. Greg withstood Chuck's blow much better than did his nemesis, as he hardly flinched.

Chuck was impressed, so much so that he pleaded Greg's case for Roscoe to loosen the handcuffs. "We can't take him out of here like this, man. You know we can't take him out of here yelling and screaming like that. Take them a loose, man. Please take them a loose."

"No fucking way, man! No fucking way. This dude is real badassed. He knows that shit. I saw the way he hit you, and I saw the way he took your hit. Regular people don't hit like that or take hits like that. I don't know if you know, but I'm certain that dude can whip both of our asses if he got loose."

"Listen, I didn't say take them off. I said loosen them just a little bit. He ain't gonna try no funny business. He knows we got him now. Tell him, buddy. Tell him."

"Yeah, like he said, you got me. You got me dead to rights. Just loosen the cuffs up a little and I will be as calm as a kitten."

"You heard him, Roscoe. You heard him. Just loosen them up some."

"Okay, man. It's like this. If you so much as move the wrong way, I will put a bullet through your brain and suffer whatever consequences I have to because of it. Do I have your attention? And do I make myself clear?"

"You are the man. I get you and I got you," came the sullen reply from the strong and rugged handcuffed prisoner.

"Here, Chuck. You take the key and loosen the cuffs some. I'm going to stand way over here. And look here, big boy. Look here. Do you see this nine-millimeter? Hey, Chuck, wait a fucking minute. Give me a second to put this guy straight. I don't rightly trust him. Now you listen to me, boy. I suspect you have some kind of military training. Well, so do I. So I know what I'm looking at, and I know what you're capable of. I was in the army for six years before they kicked me out on some bullshit trumped-up charges. So I got some or most of the same training that you got. Now my blabbermouth friend over there done told you that we was not supposed to use our guns. Well, let me set the record straight. He done told you wrong, 'cause so help me, if you even twitch wrong, the good Lord will be singing you bedtime stories tonight. All right, boy, now I'm only going to say this one more time. You listen to me and you listen good. I got sixteen bullets, and here's my right hand to God. I will use all sixteen to make my point. I might die tonight or tomorrow night, but I swear you won't be the one to kill me.

"Now I don't like repeating myself, but I did because I really don't want to kill you, but I will just as sure there is a sun up in the sky. If you fuck around, my pretty face will be the last face you'll ever see, soldier boy. Better a dead you than a dead me. Do you get me, black boy?"

"Damn, how many times do I have to tell you that I got you? Any smart man knows when to give up. Ain't no coming back or getting loose from these handcuffs. Do you see me? I laid down in a nest of angry army ants hiding from you fuckers. I've been bit so many times I can count. My body is swollen, my mind is racing, I am near starvation, and I just want to see my family. So do what you gonna do and get me out here. I ain't trying to go nowhere. Satisfied now?"

"I guess so."

"Now quit bitching and loosen the cuffs, but just a little. You sound like it was hurting you more than him." Chuck, now salty, complied and did in fact loosen the cuffs so that they were snug yet not unbearable.

"All done. Now let's move out."

"Okay, Chuck. You two walk about ten to fifteen yards ahead of me, so if he does try any funny business, I can keep my promise and send him to meet his maker. I don't know if it's heaven or hell that made him, but whoever it is, if he makes the wrong move, he will get his return to sender notice."

Chuck grabbed Greg tightly by the back of his shirt with one hand and strategically placed the other on the chain links between the cuffs so that he would have full control over his prisoner. Roscoe waited until they were a good way's in front before he moved out into the long corridor. This strategic error would prove to be their undoing. Roscoe's gun was now lodged in its holster, but he kept his hand on it just in case. As they walked the long dimly lit corridor, the two guns for hire moved particularly cautious and extremely slow.

It was as if they were somehow overly frightened of the man that they had in custody. Frightened to the point of sheer nervousness, as if all hell could break loose at any minute and that they would end up on the bad side of hell. Neither man could precisely put his finger on the source of his fear, but knowing the little that they did about this man was enough to put them ill at ease. In less than eight hours, he had compiled an impressive list of accomplishments.

Since dawn, he had eluded their intensive search, had endured thousands of ant bites in order to keep his place of concealment, had gained the trust of one or more of the facility staff, and made his way into the locked communications room which required getting past a dead-bolted steel door. To add ice cream to this cake list, he had obvious military training and mercenary instincts. Even this dull-witted pair acutely recognized that this was not someone to take lightly. Not at all.

Roscoe was so intent on watching Chuck's back that he forgot to watch his own. After only a few short steps, he felt his body get hot, instantly hot, like he was on fire. At the time, he didn't know it, but he had just been hit with fifty-thousand volts of electricity. The power of this awesome jolt silently took him to his knees, fists clinched in unmodified agony. The job incomplete, he was hit with a second jolt of the handheld lightning, which then rendered him down for the count. He now lay unconscious on the thick carpeted floor.

Chuck was so far ahead and so engrossed in nervous chatter with his captive that he never noticed his fallen partner. And before he knew what had hit him, he, too, became the victim of the fifty thousand volts of manufactured stun. Chuck did not drop to his knees after the first jolt, so the silent deliverer of the handheld lightning applied a second and then a third jolt to the thick neck of the somewhat obese man. After this almost lethal application, he, too, was reduced to an incapacitated fallen lump.

Startled, Greg began to run, but before he could get very far, the masked assailant shouted at him to stop. Surprised by the voice that he immediately recognized, he stopped in his tracks at once. Scarcely able to believe with his mind what his ears had already confirmed, he waited to hear more. "It is okay. You do not have to run now."

He slowly began to smile, now even more certain that he knew the identity of his small-framed masked guardian. Fast approaching with the keys to free him, the familiar voice issued a quiet and polite command. "Ay, Senor Greg, please, we do not have much time. Please turn around so that I can free your hands." He quickly complied.

She continued to talk while she worked to remove the restraints from the man that she helped to capture with her report no more than a few hours earlier. She then removed her mask, and the newly freed man recognized that it was Carmen, the maid he had met only a night ago. Greg was now somewhat puzzled because this was also the same maid who had tried to seduce him, lull him into a false sense of security, and then turn him in for a reward. "What's going on? Why did you save me, Carmen?"

"I am so sorry, but they tell me that you do something very bad. They tell me you tried to rape one of the other maids, and they tell me that you are a very, very bad man."

"Let me get this straight. They said I tried to rape another staff member and that's why they were after me?"

"Yes, that is so."

"So what changed, Carmen? How did you know that I wasn't? I don't understand. I mean, I'm very glad, don't get me wrong, but I am also very confused. Why did you decide to help me?"

"I help you because Sonya tell me this is not true. She is the one who they say you rape. Just now, she tella me these people are bad. She tella me everything. How they take you family in the night and how they drown you nice car. Such a nice car too. She tella me how they use the drug to control you and to make you work like a slave."

"Okay, but how did you know what was going on down here?"

"I hear the call over this. They give me. I feel so bad for what I do to you earlier, I just knew I had to helpa to you."

"Thank you! Thank you! I can't tell you how much this means to me. I probably wouldn't have lived past today without you, 'cause there no way I was letting the likes of those two take me to see Dr. Jekyll and Mr. Hyde, or whoever the hell those people are. I was just waiting to get to higher ground before I made my break. That means one back there probably would have made good on his promise to shoot me. So thank you again.

"Now what drug? And where is my family?"

"Senor Greg, we have no time. I do not know any more than I have tella to you. Now we must hurry. We are in danger."

"Okay, Carmen, but one more thing. They pulled the phone cord out of the wall and poured water into the computer, so I'll need to get out of here to make a call. Do you know of anywhere else I can make a call?"

"No, senor, only in town. But they call the sheriff to you with the same story, and everybody is trying to collect the money. There is a twenty-five thousand-dollar reward for you, Senor Greg. In my country, that is the same as a million dollars in this country. Many people are trying to collect, so you need to go."

"I'm curious. Why didn't you collect it? It was you who told them I was still on the compound, right?"

She hesitated at first, then shamefully admitted her guilt. "Si, Senor Greg, but now I must go, and you must go too. That way out is no good, so follow me. I will show to you a better way. The back way."

"Okay, lead the way. But answer me. Why didn't you just keep quiet and collect the reward? I'm really curious about that."

Sensing his determination to have an answer, she gave him one, but one that was unexpected. "I really like you, Senor Greg, and I was glad when I find out the truth. After I know the whole truth, I could not enjoy the money, even if I get a hundred thousand dollars. My spirit would not rest knowing that I send you to be like a slave. Besides, I already tella to you, I really like you. You are so easy to talk to. It's like I know you all my life."

"So you weren't just faking me out back there. That's good to know. And it's also good to know that you have a conscience and trust me. You will be rewarded. The Matthews family will not forget you. And I will never forget you," he added with a hint of tenderness.

However well-intentioned, his words were tempered by the urgency of the situation, so they did not have the sweet piercing effect that he had intended them to have. Nonetheless, he refocused.

"All right, thank you again, but I need another favor. Please hand me that taser. I want to make sure these two are out for a good while so that I can have time to find another way to contact my folks." He then proceeded over to each of the unconscious men. After he turned the voltage up to full power, he applied two more jolts of nervous system paralysis.

The 110 thousand volts that were twice passed through each man's body caused instantaneous and considerable damage. Having just administered what could amount to lethal doses of life-altering current, he did not know if they were dead or alive. And frankly, he didn't care. He just wanted them to be neutralized.

Carmen led the way through a small tunnel and up two hundred circular steps. The tight staircase was not easy to maneuver, especially in Greg's dizzied state. Only through great effort did he make it to the top. She then pointed the way to a nearby tree line. She also told him that it would take him down to quicksand alley, where they were supposed to sink the vehicles. She further advised him that they sometimes wait a day or two before they sink them. They routinely wait so they can search them for any valuables and other stuff.

Without any notice, Greg grabbed Carmen by the shoulders and, with no hesitation, kissed her deeply. She swooned and blushed like a schoolgirl, her cheeks a rosy shade of red. She did not, however, forget that both their lives were in imminent peril at this very minute, so she hurried him on his way. "Go, Greg, go," she urged, dropping the Senor for the first time.

"You will be caught, and I will get into some serious trouble, too, if anyone sees us together. Now go, go," she said. sending her romantic man off on his mission to get help. He flashed a brilliant smile that only a Matthews knew how and ran off, newly energized by the courageous act of a stranger.

CHAPTER 8

The Roundtable

"Gentlemen, I hope that your ride from the airport was not as unsettling as I imagine I would have been if put in the same position. The surprise of blackened windows and a sealed limousine compartment must have been somewhat of a shock to some of you. And I do dare say that each of you looks both marvelous and magnificent in your caricature masks.

"After we have had an in-depth discussion and you each fully know why you have been summoned here today, I hope that you will appreciate the absolute and total irony in us depicting some of this country's most noted historical figures as we simultaneously scheme and plan the greatest underworld criminal syndicate in American history.

"Welcome, Presidents Roosevelt, Lincoln, Jefferson, Bush, and Clinton. Welcome, General George Washington. Welcome, General Custer, General Lee, General Ulysses S. Grant, and to you as well old hickory, General Andrew Jackson. Welcome to all of you.

"Forgive me for that small indulgence. In all honesty, I do apologize for all of the I spy theatrics, but it was and remains, in any case, quite necessary. As advertised in our telephone conversations, keeping this location, as well as each of your identities and mine, a secret is truly for your own protection, not to mention that of this organization. Everything that you will learn about this group is on a need-to-know basis. What you don't need, you will not know.

"So again, the masks are an essential means to that end. So is the need for your continued silence. Like it or not, know it or not, some of you may be readily identified by your voices. That is why you were instructed to communicate any comments or questions that you may have throughout your visit here today in writing. And by the way, my heartfelt apologies for those of you who are not the only person wearing a particular mask. Unfortunately, they only replicate so many historical figures.

"Moving right along, each of you have been uniquely identified and invited here today. Invited because of what each of you individually brings to the table and what we can accomplish through our collective efforts if we all play our cards right. The table, of course, being the table of success. Success at what, you ask. I will reveal that momentarily.

"Seated next to you, across from you, and down the table from you are an assembly of the best and worst that this great country of ours has to offer. Underneath those masks that you see before you are some exceptionally intriguing individuals, to say to the least. In this room right now, although you would be hard-pressed to tell, there are CEOs of major corporations, which shall of course remain nameless.

"There are also some high-ranking government officials, and they are not alone. Also representing our illustrious government are five undercover agents with alphabet law enforcement credentials. FBI, CIA, DEA, it doesn't really matter…let's just say they are all deeply involved in the information awareness arenas.

"Additionally, I'm happy to report that there are also several captains of industry who lead, shall we say, companies best described as blue-collar professions. And finally, there are a few of you who are heavily invested in the underworld pharmaceutical industry, as well as other black-market enterprises. In another day and time, most of us would be at odds. The remainder would be investigating the others of us. However, today is not that day. Today, we have a common goal, a unifying cause, and a shared hunger. Today we need each other, but more on that in a minute.

"For now, allow me to put your minds at ease. I can sense some of you looking around to see if any of the others recognizes you or if you can recognize any of them. Rest easy, my dear friends. Rest easy. Let me assure you of the following two things. First, the good news is that no one in or outside this room knows your identity except me and the driver that picked you up. Second, the better news is that within twenty-four hours, I will be the lone person who can truly attest to the fact that you were ever in this room, other than yourself, of course.

"Let us just say that by then, each of your drivers will become a casualty of war. A small price to pay for the ultimate success of this enormous venture. Wouldn't you say, gentlemen?" he asked rhetorically, fully aware of the no-talking policy in effect. "And if you don't, my guess is that you would, if you knew what the venture was." Greeted with multiple looks of impatient expectancy, the speaker acknowledged his slow pace in lifting the veil of secrecy that he had previously promised to soon uncover.

"Aaaah, yes, why are we here? We are getting to that just now. Well then, to that very issue. The issue of why we are all gathered here today. My good men, without further ado, I would like to introduce you to the future of big business. Our collective future is based on the grand-scaled enterprise theory of business.

"Gentlemen, I give you the God Spoke Syndicate!"

With a single dramatic click of a handheld remote, he unveiled a huge blank screen hidden behind a sheer black velvet curtain. One dramatic click later, he stepped to the side, and the room went black. On the screen was an ultra large image of a stunning marquise diamond. Suspended inside its inner prism was an emblazoned number 4.

Over the eerie silence that enveloped the room, another click could be heard as the scene on the screen changed once again. With the aid of a laser pointer, the man concealed behind a Teddy Roosevelt mask directed everyone's attention to another diagram, this one depicting a smaller diamond attached to each of the four points of the larger diamond. "This is how we will operate as a cohesive group," he coldly stated.

"What you see represents the GSS 4 points of perfection. Besides being really cool to say, the God Spoke Syndicate, with its four points of perfection, is, for all intents and purposes, a multilayered money-making machine. GSS will operate in the same manner as these four inextricably bound pillars. On these, we shall build a new way of doing business, a new way to take control of our chosen enterprise, a new way to seize power, a new way to usurp the system, a new way to have our cake and eat it too, god-dammit!" he said triumphantly.

"And the best part of it all is that we will all get rich in the process. And when I say rich, I'm not talking about filthy rich. I mean downright ungodly and unseemly wealth. I'm talking about rich, so rich that your money makes more money than all of those in your employ. I speak of so much money that it would take you months on end to count it all by hand. Now that's a lot of money by any standard.

"I now trust that I have your full interest. All right then, pay close attention as I explain exactly how we will usher in this new era of opulence and wealth. I know that name God Spoke Syndicate elicits all sorts of nasty and nice thoughts. So I believe you must all be hungry for more details, but…again, you must wait.

"Be patient, my friends. Beeeee patient," he said, dragging his words for the dramatic effect that he so loved to create and utilize at every possible occasion that presented itself. "I shall not reveal the truth about the exact nature and origins of the name until a bit later. So for now, feel free to imagine as you might. In fact, for right now, let your imaginations churn with wonderment."

Sensing the serious disgruntlement settling over the room, the Good Doctor capitulated. "Okay, okay, we will get to that just now. However, much more important than its name is its multifaceted mission. Quite simply, GSS will corner the illicit drug market on this entire continent. We will do this by soon making obsolete the need to ever again import any form of illegal narcotic.

"Now I can only imagine that those two words, *illegal* and *narcotic*, together in the same sentence has at least some of you squirming in fear right now. I can also imagine that right about now, some of you may be extremely tempted to speak. However, I both urge and caution you to remember your need for silence. And by the way, just as a little reminder, this policy is for your own protection."

Injecting a small measure of philosophical wisdom into the equation, the Good Doctor then offered the group a tiny morsel of food for thought. "A little discomfort can be a good thing," he said quite bluntly. "It keeps you on your toes and may well serve as a magnificent source of motivation.

"However, I assure you there is nothing to worry about. Nothing here should cause you any discomfort. Before long, I will explain away all your fears," he said as he perused the semi-darkened room to gage who was most bothered by his previous statements. Perceiving a significant amount of discomfort, he tried a second time to calm any fears.

"Believe me, in due time, my friends, in due time. I promise to answer each and every question that will eventually pop into your head. As they come, so shall the questions go as I continue to speak, so just be patient.

"Let us now look at each of the four points of perfection, and without a word to any individual, you should immediately recognize what your role will be in our exciting new venture. We have in this corner production. And in this corner, we have logistics. Next to that, we have finance. And finally, rounding out the squared circle, we have intelligence. Nice and neat and very complete, and that's what we will be as a group.

"As I have just articulated, each of us will be associated with one of these four points. Equally, each of us will play a significant role in the team's ultimate success. Please take that to mean that the rest of us are counting on you to excel in your respective area of expertise. And, my friends, if we are all counting on you and you are also counting on us, that can only mean one thing—we sink or swim together.

"So look, learn, and listen well. Our success and your very life may well depend on it. Take that as a literal and not figurative statement. After today, you will have enemies that you could never have imagined when you awoke this morning.

"Just for general principle, I will provide a brief overview for each point. Production, of course, is growing and packaging the product we intend to sell. Real simple! Logistics will encompass not only the transport of our product to the various markets but also the distribution and sales end of things. Even simpler.

"The finance folks will take care of collecting and cleansing all of our ill-gotten gains and thereafter creating very ingenious ways for both you and I to show how we have legitimately earned the ungodly sums of money that will now be ours. And finally, our intelligence operations will make sure we are always one step ahead of whoever is looking to do us harm, either as a unit or as individuals. By the way, that includes law enforcement as well as competitive underworld rivals.

"With regard to the transportation aspect of logistics, we have enlisted the aid of the four trucking company executives present today. As a group, they will handle the four time zones of the United States, Mexico, and Canada. At present, one of you holds the title of company president, one of vice president, and the others hold unnamed high-ranking positions. As a matter of record, each of you will soon be elevated to the position of company president. Don't ask me how I know, gentlemen. I just do," he said. He executed his signature dramatic spin and repeated, "I just do! And don't worry, gentlemen. You all are spread so far apart that the news coverage of your promotion will never reach any of the others.

"Now where were we? Oh yeah, we have co-opted the trucking companies, which will take care of transportation to the four corners of this great continent of ours. The United States of fucking America and its subsidiaries, Mexico, and Canada, you gotta fucking love it. The actual drugs will be shipped in large containers which we shall not identify just now but that can move freely about without creating much notice or suspicion. In each city, we will have a drop-off location that will only be made known to the driver mere seconds before he or she is to arrive at the location.

"Each truck will be outfitted with a specialized Global Positioning System. These GPS units will serve as the only guidance that the driver has to provide direction. Drivers will only be provided with turn-by-turn directions. The unit will not, and cannot, display any future destination points or the final destination before it is time to do so. As I said, the final destination will not be revealed until the vehicle is within thirty seconds from its programmed destination.

"By the way, programming can be only be done remotely, so even when trucks are to come here for a pickup, the driver will not know his exact or even relative destination. And for those of you that are thinking it, no, the units do not provide the amount of time needed to travel to the programmed destination point.

"I will also elaborate on that aspect of transportation a bit further once we reconvene. But overall, let me summarize by saying that the drivers will not know the true nature of their cargo, and drop-off locations will never be the same for two consecutive shipments. Drivers will never come here more than once. Drivers may also be required to drop a truck off in one location where another driver will take over and continue the journey.

"The next area of consideration will be local distribution. There are twenty-five of you present today that have thriving drug distribution operations currently existing in the various cities that you represent. Make no mistake about it, we have done our homework. We know who you are, we know what you do, and most importantly, we know how well you do it.

"That said, you have all been chosen because each of you possesses, well, let's just say certain intangible qualities that are required in order to be a member of this now elite organization. Each of you is charged with the distribution and sale of our various products. And as I said, we know how good you are at what you do, but now you will have to be even better than before.

"As mentioned earlier, we will have the best product on the market, but only if you rule with an iron fist. The old ways of doing business are forever gone. Street dealers and everyone else up the distribution chain should not be permitted to tamper with the product. It is our goal to establish a reputation of having a product of the finest quality on the market.

"If we are successful in doing that, and that solely hinges on whether or not you are successful at controlling your people, we will take over the entire drug market in the USA, and thereafter, who knows. Tell me, how do you think one company outsells the other? Better product and better services. It's as simple as that, gentlemen.

"As it relates to the market price, we will set our price to undercut everyone else by twenty-five percent, depending on the location. Gentlemen, remember this simple fact: if it's cheaper, they will buy it. If it's cheaper and better, they will buy it again and again and again. Enough said.

"With regard to the movement of money, we will use scrambled communicators and speak only in codes. The codes will be changed weekly, and you will receive your updated copy by hand delivery. At that time, you will have to validate the authenticity of what you have been delivered by making a phone call to the secret number that will be affixed to the communiqué.

"If you are a James Bond kind of guy, as I am, I hope you will find the whole idea of coded messages intriguing, not to mention kind of cool. We will discuss those details in much greater depth later.

"Now then, I know there must be at least two burning questions, not in the back but in the front of each of your minds. The first question, if I am the fortune teller that I profess to be, will hinge on how we cut so much cost from our pricing equation.

"The second question, if I am as good as I think I am, should have something to do with where on earth, no, correction, where in the United States is there an environment that is suitable to grow not only the cocoa plants needed to produce cocaine and not only the poppy seeds needed to produce heroine, but at the same time grow marijuana? And did I mention and not get caught by the authorities? Now you tell me, am I good or am I good?"

Mr. 3, seated at the roundtable, raised his communication card and waved a pad in front of him to get the Good Doctor's attention.

Clark immediately moved in to get the note and read it aloud at the behest of his employer.

"Okay, Mr. Roosevelt, you have us all curious. Now please do us a favor and quickly put us out of our misery. You are exactly right about your assumptions. Now would you please be so kind as to answer the burning questions that you have accurately supposed we want answered."

"My apologies to you all," said the Good Doctor with a hint of guarded contempt. "I get carried away with myself sometimes. Now back to the presentation. The drugs will be grown in a very large and very secure biosphere. For those of you who may be in the dark about what a biosphere is exactly, it is a man-made enclosure designed to replicate any desired environmental climate, including that of the tropical persuasion, if you get my point.

"This biosphere is huge, comprised of tens of thousands of acres. It is necessarily manned by hundreds of workers, but get this, none of which do we have to pay. Our workforce is totally comprised of those who have been reported as either dead or missing. We are certain of this, as we have law enforcement declarations and death certificates to prove it. In most cases, we have either abducted them by luring them to a nice hideaway or simply by visiting highly populated urban areas and scooping up a few runaways and other such undesirables.

"After twenty-four hours with no solid food, each of them is then injected with a doping agent that renders them in a state of absolute submission. In fact, they become spellbound. It's as if they were sleepwalking. However, they retain the ability to follow commands. Moreover, after a short specialized programming session, they only follow commands from their handlers. So when they are instructed to cultivate the crops, that's exactly what they do. It rings kindred to the glory days of the antebellum South, don't you think?

"Now I know what you must be thinking, but generally, they retain the complete spectrum of their mental faculties. They can do anything that any other person can do, except they cannot do it of their own free will. They are able to eat, sleep, drink, and solve problems that prevent them from completing a task, such as walking around obstacles in their path or picking up a tool that they have dropped.

"Additionally, we have a medical staff on hand to ensure that they are healthy and disease-free so that they may put in many, many hours of free labor and for many, many years to come.

"Quite remarkably, and of particular note, once the spellbound are given instructions, they will not stop until they have completed the given task. Additionally, unless they have been given a series of instructions ahead of time, they will in fact stay at the very spot of a completed task until they receive further instructions. Isn't science fantastic? Isn't it just fucking wonderful?

"So as you can see, gentlemen, we have at our disposal an independent will-numbing secret weapon. Our stealthy advantage has been aptly coined the *Same as God Spoke*. When you speak to those spellbound by its power, it is the same as if God himself had spoken to them. As stated, they cannot refuse any order and will obey any command, so when we speak, it is like I said, the *same as God spoke*.

"SAGS, same as God spoke. Beautiful, don't you think? Now then, why is SAGS so important to us? I'll tell you why. It is unquestionably the very foundation of our very enterprise. Through the power of SAGS, we have amassed a small army of free labor, and we intend to grow this workforce exponentially, both here at this facility and in the hometowns where many of you live. More on that later.

"I know this sounds too good to be true, but it does get even better. Imagine the upside to this whole thing. They will never, ever be in a position to cause us any problems because they don't know anything. Don't know who we are, don't know where they are, or even what we are really doing.

"And get this, the only costs associated with them are food and clothing, which are modest at best. The food is not what we would describe as top-shelf. It is merely sustenance. We work them hard, so we feed them well. But let's just say they don't eat steak every day." After a brief pause, he spoke his private thoughts aloud. "Or any day, for that matter." He then chuckled, if only to himself.

"With that as our foundation, gentlemen, the God Spoke Syndicate will be able to undercut the price of any other drug distribution outfit in the world. I will, of course, provide you with a both powerful and compelling demonstration of the all-consuming authority of SAGS. But that will take place just after we have completed a facility tour."

Then he added what seemed to most as an afterthought. "But can you just imagine that kind of raw power in your hands?" he said with purposeful excitement in his voice. "Can you really? Do this! Do that! Do the other! And just like that, with no hesitation, absent any questions and no need to ever repeat, it gets done! Just think of it. It's the same as God spoke, only you get to play God. And thus, you have the name of our merry band of Robin Hoods here today, the God Spoke Syndicate."

After that moment of solemn self-indulgence, the Good Doctor returned to his presentation. "To reiterate," he flatly stated, "there are three main reasons that will foster our collective success. First, the overwhelming majority of our labor is free. Second, there are no burdensome transportation costs associated with importing our product, which in the past has originated from foreign shores. Finally, there will be no need for adding impurities, as many of our competitors do, in order to quote unquote, stretch the product.

"The production and transportation costs associated with our products, the Godspoke, will be so insignificant that we will insist on product purity. Our Godspoke will continually call to the users so that we will eventually garner almost a hundred percent of the market. Everyone will buy from us because we have the best product in terms of purity, quantity, and more importantly, we have it at the best price. What could be better? I ask you, what could be any fucking better?

"Now in order to make this venture the huge success that it is eventually going to be, the need arises for several areas of expertise. In case I did not mention it earlier, we do not want there to be ever a time when one of us, in a time of desperation, decides to point the finger at the remainder of us. Therefore, we will not ever use names, but instead we will use numbers.

"As you will notice on the table, in front of you is a number in the form of a place card. You will also notice that there are accompanying name tags with the same number. Please place the name tag on your clothing so that when we leave this area to begin the facility tour, if anyone needs to be recognized, we can recognize them by their number—Mr. 34, Mr. 23, and so on.

"Now then, in a matter of a few minutes, you as a group will be taken on a tour of the entire facility. You will also have the luxury of an aerial vantage point wherein you will see that it would be almost impossible for you to return to this place without direction from me or one of my staff. And finally, you see that not only is the God Spoke Biosphere run in a first-class manner, but more importantly, you will know it as the birthplace of a multibillion-dollar conglomerate, which we will formalize today right after the facility tour.

"That's right, men. I said b*illion*, and that's with nine zeros, especially if you're counting. And who wouldn't with that much money at stake? But let's not get ahead of ourselves. First, allow me to formally introduce myself. I am…well, you may call me the Good Doctor, and I can assure you I have earned that name. I have taken a Hippocratic oath in the cause to save lives, but I have taken an even higher oath in the cause to make me extremely wealthy.

"That means, in very plain terms, that I can bring both pleasure and pain. I can heal or I can euthanize. But in either case, please take my word for it. I will do whatever is necessary to get the job done. All the money that you will soon have the opportunity to make in this newly formed coalition will no doubt bring all of you great pleasure. It will save some of you from bankruptcy and others. It will allow you to become legitimate businessmen, at least on the surface. So in that sense, I have lived up to my oath to save lives.

"But on the other hand, as I said, if you cross me, I will not hesitate to reveal my darker side. I will not think twice about applying pain of a horrific nature. And make no mistake about it. The pain I so casually speak of is both physical and, in particular, mental. My senses tell me what some of you must be thinking.

"Even in the absence of words, I can only imagine some of you may be thinking at this very minute that this guy is up there making idle threats." Just as he uttered those words, two very different and distinct people cleared their throats respectively. The Good Doctor took this as sign of blatant disrespect.

"I know who you are, gentlemen!" he said, shouting in the midst of what appeared to be instant but boiling anger. "I handpicked you," he said, shaking both of his balled-up fists at those seated at the roundtable. Both fists were tightly held, but his pose looked awkward instead of scary, because of an extended pinky finger that will no longer bend as the result of an experiment gone wrong.

Realizing his awkward look, he immediately tried to calm himself by lowering his balled-up fists of fury. "Well, gentlemen," he said matter-of-factly, "allow me make it absolutely clear." Then again, he paused during this critical juncture of his speech, as he was accustomed to doing merely for the theatrics of it all. "I do *not* make idle threats or threats at all for that matter!

"I merely reveal my intentions, which I will always see to a satisfactory conclusion. A conclusion that best serves me," he said as he turned sharply on his heels so that his back was to the group. His now slightly elevated voice gave off an eerie kind of moan as he strained not to engage his usual soprano-like crescendo when he was upset. He did not want to sound weak or foolish, and he equally did not want to make a bad first impression in front of his new partners in crime.

Moving ever so slowly to find his words while also taking elongated pauses, the Good Doctor succeeded in his quest as his antics served to build up quite a bit of nervous anxiety. "Why does Mohamed have to go to the mountain when the mountain is already in Mohamed's biosphere?" A lot of nervous shifting and anxious movements further demonstrated that he had his audience captivated, if not just plain ole frightened or freaked out, at this point. "Again, I have teased you with something of interest, but again you will have to be patient. I guarantee that your wait will be worth far more than you can even imagine.

"My area of expertise," he continued after regaining a grip on his ever-rising voice, "lies in biotechnology and engineering. It was I that singlehandedly gave this government the technology to reproduce any atmospheric conditions on earth. I oversaw the building of the world's largest biosphere, albeit right in plain sight. It was completely inconspicuous to the naked eye.

"This invention could replicate any of the conditions that might be found in any of the barren desserts on the globe, the subzero life-threatening temperatures of either pole and or the tropical-like temperatures found in the most plant-friendly climates known to man.

"All of that, and what do they do with it? What do they, in their infinite wisdom, do with the eighth wonder of the world? Something so colossal, something so awe-inspiring, something so magnanimous that words do not begin to do it justice/ What do they do with such an awesome piece of perfect technology? They use it to grow diseases that they intended to use in biological warfare. What a bunch of imbecilic morons. This was something that was truly designed to give life or at least make it better. This was the eighth wonder of the world, and they treated it like it was a laboratory of death.

"I was having no part of it, and being the 'get it done, take the bull by the horns' kind of guy, I did something. I stole it. How? Ah ha," he mocked evilly, which was immediately followed by an even more cynical bout of uncontrolled laughter. The Good Doctor stood in front of his would-be cohorts and laughed as if he had absolutely lost it. And just as suddenly as the laughter had begun, it stopped.

"Since I will never have to worry about any of you ever revealing what I am about to say, I will feel free to say it. In short, I killed every single person who knew where the biosphere was located. We had a top-secret project. I mean the clearance level for this project started at the joint chiefs of staff level, with the exception of the small group of scientists that built the thing. Once I found out their intentions, I systematically took the life of every individual involved on the project.

"Oh, yes, it was quite *Godfather*ish. Each of them died on the same day at the same hour and in the same fashion. We then blew up a smaller scale prototype so that this place would never be discovered. Sounds incredible, I know, but that's precisely why I shared that story with you. I want you to know the incredible lengths that I will go to make this a success and also the incredible lengths I will go not to allow any of you to make this anything otherwise.

"That notwithstanding, the stated purpose of this group of both reputable and nefarious characters is plain and simple. The reason we are gathered together into one room is to corner the drug market, and," he said with greater emphasis, "to get rich, very rich, in the process.

"As was mentioned, the name of this newly formed arpeggio shall be called the God Spoke Syndicate. Forgive me for my pretentious indulgence. For those of you who may not be familiar with that strange sounding word *arpeggio*, it simply means a combination of three or more notes that blend harmoniously to make beautiful music, just like the beautiful noise we will make as a group."

CHAPTER 9

THE LONGEST NIGHT

"Listen up, all Godspoke workers. Get in your bed and go to sleep." The loud and gruff shout reverberated across the large sleeping quarters that housed fifty spellbound Godspoke workers. There were ten such sleeping quarters on the premises, and each amounted to nothing more than its intended use. The hastily constructed tin buildings were rectangular in shape, measuring only ninety by eighty, or roughly seven thousand square feet. These were modest accommodations at best, with not a lot of space, to say the least.

Each unit contained the same simple layout and the same meager furnishings: fifty metal-framed twin-sized beds and fifty sheet metal thin mattresses, replete with a single pull-out drawer beneath each bed to store a single change of clothing. The nearly six foot by two and half foot beds were arranged as if they were plants in a garden: each laid exactly three feet apart, in five rows of ten, with a cramped two-foot-wide passage between each row.

It was a good thing these structures, designed with only one window and just two air vents, were located in the protected environment of the biosphere. Otherwise, they would have less than a snowball's chance in hell of withstanding any harsh extremes of any wind, rain, or snow. To say that any face-off with the elements, combined with the intentional lack of ventilation, would prove inhospitable to the workforce is an understatement. The toilets in the multi-occupancy bathrooms were without dividers and so closely bunched together that it was nearly impossible not to touch, in some way, any person next to you, either standing or sitting.

The tightly arranged beds, which measured exactly five feet and ten inches in length, made it next to impossible for the taller captives not to have their feet hang over the end of the bed. Any overhanging feet proved a mischief magnet, as the overnight guards would never miss the opportunity to play tickle feet as they made their head counts twice nightly.

Since the spellbound could not respond except for natural bodily reactions of jerking and twitching, which they found hilarious, the guards would share reaction stories with one another. They would detail how they got one or the other of the spellbound to react, especially in an intense fashion. The more intense the reaction, the better the story. The better the story, the more laughter that was had.

A report of a very intense reaction would inspire the next tour to try and recreate the experience or enhance the reaction, and thereafter, more stories would be shared. This was a daily ritual fueled almost entirely by the testosterone-driven game of one-upmanship. This simply meant the next story would have to top the prior, which also meant the guards would take that much more liberty to elicit a desired reaction in order to get a story worthy of being told and retold.

Laying awake, each in the newly captured Matthews clan could scarcely believe the astonishing events of the past twenty-four hours. The entire mind-numbing experience was surreal at best.

This first night was the same for each of them. Lucid thoughts accompanied by ridged determination competing with clouded, heart-pounding delusions. Absolute resolve morphing into anxiety without notice. Hopes of a miracle rescue stilled by the sense of impending doom. All the while these contradictory emotions were compounded by the mental struggle to comprehend what was happening, and more importantly, why it was happening.

Each mind of the Matthews 7 was filled with thoughts of self-control, escape, and revenge. But overall, a deep sense of panic was in full function, and it spared no one from its ugly rampage.

The mental anguish of being forced at gunpoint into the bowels of captivity was no different than the experiences of the newly enslaved so many decades ago. This was even more true for those, like the Matthews, who had previously enjoyed a very high quality of life.

Even without the benefit of free will, the transition from upper-crust socialites to spellbound captives was the equivalent of going from state governor to maximum security prisoner. Only this was worse than any twenty-four-hour lockdown rules. To each, this was like a bad game. A very, very bad game that they would love to stop playing, but they were forced to continue without regard to their feelings, wishes, or desires.

LJ followed the command to go to bed, as did the other forty-nine captives, including his two brothers. They did so not because they chose to but instead because they had no other option. They were each compelled by a force unknown to them but very intimate with them all at once. The Godspoke was now free-flowing through their veins, now having had time to take full effect.

Although in his bed as instructed, LJ was not asleep. He could not sleep. Tormented, his mind would not allow him the luxury of sleep and the promise of temporary freedom that comes with it. He, like all the others in his group, was reliving their collective daytime nightmare. However, being the quintessential problem solver that he was, LJ struggled to remain transfixed on solving this dilemma. The one thing he prided himself on was finding that elusive missing piece to the almost unsolvable puzzle. If there was a way out of this, he was confident that he would find it.

Now almost uncontrollably, his mind raced. Initially, he focused on blaming himself for getting his family involved in their present predicament. Yet he fought that thought. Next, he blamed himself for being so badly duped by the likes of the Good Doctor or Mr. Jones or whoever the sick fuck that abducted him was. He then became enraged at the very thought of being injected full of some evil sick shit that could render him powerless and devoid of his own will.

That in itself was torment enough. However, his mind raced on. Over and over, he thought about the events that had brought him to this point, laying helplessly inside a body owned and controlled by someone else. Ever the man in charge, he tried to remain in control of his thoughts. At least the Godspoke had not taken his mind away.

He realized that he could think anything he wanted, but he could only act on instructions from others. He tried repeatedly with his all to direct his thoughts to some useful purpose, but this was a fight that even LJ would not win. Try as he might, his efforts were a mere exercise in futility.

Unable to seriously focus on solutions, LJ allowed his mind to go where it damn well pleased. Unfortunately for him, his thoughts headed straight for his personal highway of horror. Against his better judgment, he again allowed himself to further analyze how his will had been systematically robbed, little by little, since being injected some hours ago.

After some deep analysis, he accurately concluded that the Godspoke total control process was a gradual occurrence. The first thing to go was his ability to control his legs. Almost instantly, he could not move them on his own. It was as if they had been planted in a ton of quick drying cement.

Seconds later, a sudden warm sensation overcame him. and he immediately lost the free use of his most vital body parts,—his hands and arms. As he lay motionless, as if hog-tied with restraints, he relived the frightening and fiendishly strange feelings of going under the Godspoke spell. He also recounted the horrifying sounds let out by his family members as they, too, fought to fend off those same strange feelings. His closed eyes twitched violently, reminiscent of the rapid eye movement associated with the REM stage of deep sleep.

In his mind's eye, he could hear the deafening noise as it played over and over in his head like a never-ending rerun. There were endless random shouts, swears, and threats, as if they each suffered from a severe form of Tourette's syndrome. Then all of a sudden, silence.

Lastly, the Godspoke took over the ability to control even your own speech. After that greatest of the free will functions is taken, the Godspoke spell is complete. Thereafter, you become one of the spellbound.

Mysty was also in bed, having received the very same command that was given in the living quarters of their male counterparts. She, too, law awake with rapidly changing thoughts and impulses. She first wished that she would wake up from this satanic nightmare. She tried several times to open her eyes but found that she could not. Even the simple task of opening and closing her eyes was no longer her choice, and she began to sob involuntarily.

As she lay sobbing hysterically, she wondered how evil someone must be to ever imagine creating such a horrific drug. The thought of not even being able to go to the restroom without instruction—and for that matter, permission—was overwhelming and made her cry even more.

She then thought and asked the ultimate unanswered question, one in which she was better off not having the answer to. *Will I ever get to leave this place? Will things ever be the same again? Will somebody, anybody, save us? Is this my life forever and ever until I die? Is this what God had in store for me when he put me on this earth? What did I do so wrong to deserve this as my fate? I have children to take care of. Who will love them like I do? Who will care for them?*

After some time to ponder it all, she was sickened by her next thought. *I am only thirty-two years old. I have so much living to do. Forty or fifty more years of life expectancy, and this, this is what I have to look forward to. This is what I have to deal with day in and day out. I would rather die first.* Then after several minutes of feeling very much the victim and very much like her spirit had been killed along with her will, quite abruptly, her sobbing came to an end. It instantly turned to anger.

What kind of evil mind would even think of something as wretched as the Godspoke? What kind of twisted, sick individual would want to impose such a heinous, diabolical, mean-spirited subjugation on another human being? Why would one person want to rule and have power over another? The thought of one person wanting to enslave another was just the tonic to make Mysty's blood boil, and boil it did.

Instantly enraged, she turned her newly formed anger into thoughts of revenge. Her thoughts raced so fast, they tripped over one another. These people were mad, as mad as any psychotic you'd find in a mental institution. She thought it simply ironic that they were allowed to roam around unmolested while she lay in the drunken stupor of a bad dream that she could not awake from. *I wish LJ could fix this*, she thought, *like he always fixes everything else.*

When I get out of here, if I get out of here, jail won't be good enough for these people. I am going to hire some of BJ's secret friends to come back here and do some unspeakable damage. I want these crazies to suffer. I want them to hurt bad, as bad as I do right now. I want brains spilled. I want arms and other body parts chopped off. I want flesh to be burned. And I want it all videotaped so I can enjoy it. God forgive me, but I do. I swear I do.

* * *

Henry tried his best to remember if he had locked the door to the safe in his office. If he had, he reasoned that it would be hell to retrieve any of his level 1 documents. Always the pragmatist, he kept all his life in the safe at work: personal pass codes, security keys, insurance policies, and bank statements. And no one but LJ knew how to gain access to it. So how, he thought, would his kids get all those millions of dollars owed to them if no one could gain access to those documents? Hell, only one or two people even knew he had a walk-in safe in his office. and if no one could reach him or LJ, what would happen to his kids?

All his money would go into state run escrow, and by the time everything was settled, his kids would be almost grown. Sure, he thought, BJ and Big Momma would care for them, but they lived on retirement pensions and were only as comfortable as they were because of the monthly commission checks from the investments that he and LJ had set up for them some years back. BJ's agency did not bring in a lot of income. They did it mostly for the thrill.

His thoughts then turned to his children. He thought of little Duck, his seven-year-old who was his spitting image. The spitting image in more ways than one. He smiled at the thought of his first child wanting to emulate him in every possible manner. He only dressed in suits, complete with a bow tie, to go to school and almost anywhere else he went. The only exception was to play. This thought made Henry smile inside.

He then turned his happy thoughts to the little princess who stole his heart the moment he first laid eyes on her in the delivery room. Young Ms. Virginia, who was wise well beyond her four years and named after her maternal grandmother, was the light of Henry's life. How he adored this exceptionally bright and gifted child. She was able to both read and write at the tender age of two.

He recalled the many times that she sat on his lap and amazed both he and his wife with a quick wit and yet unexplained high level of intelligence. He remembered the time when she asked if she could go to where Mickey Mouse lives so that she could ask Donald Duck to stop talking like that because it was hard for her to understand him sometimes.

How he loved for her to ask him question after question in her unending quest to better understand life and the curious things around her. How do birds fly? How do they know where to go? How do they get married? And on and on.

These heartwarming thoughts of Duck and Virginia brought him pure unadulterated joy that could be felt in the deepest recesses of his soul. At first, his inside smile got wider, then that same inside smile quickly dissipated. The thought of his two precious children living below the means that he was able to provide for them was unbearable. No one could get to his money. He had it planned that way. His pragmatism all but ensured it.

What have I done to my poor children? he bemoaned. I never thought it would end like this. *I thought I would have time to better prepare. Why me, God? Why me? I do all the right things, and look at this. I give to charity. I volunteered for the Big Brother program. I even help my little assigned brother's family out and do it without shaming them. I go to church every chance I get. I am faithful to my wife, not like LJ. I don't smoke, drink, and hardly curse. Why me?*

Man oh man, live a good clean life, love your kids, cherish your wife, treat your employees with respect, do your level best for your clients, and don't even knock your competitors down when you could, and this is what you get for living a squeaky-clean life like that. I don't get it. Maybe I'm missing something.

This is what I get, and Ted Kaczynski, the Unabomber, lived free for sixteen years after all the destruction and mayhem that he caused? His thoughts saddened him deeply. He wished with all his might for a miracle, but he resigned himself to the fact that none would be forthcoming, sadly enough.

* * *

Beverley lay on her back and stared blankly at the ceiling. She did not want to close her eyes. In fact, she refused to close her eyes. Her obstinate side had reared its unpredictable but useful head, and it was in full effect. When she wanted to, or just couldn't help herself, she could be as stubborn as any of the mules in any of those stories we've all hear about that has it as its star. A stubborn mule.

At times, she had a will as strong as the strongest of metals. She would outwait LJ until he apologized. She would outlast her closest and best friend Misty when they had their girl-to-girl disagreements. And she could even outlast the kids as they whined relentlessly to get their way. Her well-known ironclad stubborn will was the only explanation as to why she could override the instruction to go to sleep and the customary practice of closing one's eyes to do so.

While she continued to stare at the ceiling, she wished for the return of her free will, if only for a brief moment. She wanted to accomplish just one simple thing. She wanted to whip some ass. That ass belonged to Claris, the matron who had chided her unmercifully as she and the other women were being prepped for the Godspoke injections. Oh yeah, she thought. She had a personalized good ole-fashioned backhand slap for that mis-raised, no-manners heifer.

Beverley knew that this brand of Wild, Wild West gunslinger, fight-to-the-death kind of thinking was way out of character for her. It was for that reason, and that reason alone, that made it all the more appealing. The thought of being naughty, the thought of just letting go and breaking the rules for once, the thought of being fearless and unafraid like Mysty. All of those thoughts combined to make her smile.

She smiled at the thought of facing off with Claris's punk ass. She smiled at the thought of initiating the first punch to the bridge of Claris's nose and her shocked look when she saw the blood run freely down her now not-so-white smock. She relished the thought of her doubling over after a hard and sharp gut punch. She smiled even more at the thought of standing over Claris's ragged body after being laid on the floor by a stiff leg sweep and a subsequent mule kick to the back of the head.

However, the smile was quickly interrupted and short-lived as the lights in the great chamber were abruptly cut off. Instantly, the room got pitch-black, and the absence of light was as numbing as was the Godspoke injection site on her upper left arm. The wide smile was now gone as reality set back in with all the subtleness of a thud.

* * *

Milton thought to himself, *I guess we're all even now. Look at my two rich ass brothers. Look at them now, looking like beat-up zombies. I'll bet they don't think they're better than me right now. Neither one of them has on any of them fancy ass thousand-dollar suits they always wearing or none of those five-hundred-dollar shoes. What? No bling-bling today, fellas? Where is all of them diamonds, fellas? What is that? Yo hair out of place, what? Man oh man, I wonder what's going through their heads right now.*

And just look at man-pretty LJ, all beat up and swollen about the face. Look at the pretty boy now. Look at the one who used to get all the pretty girls. Wonder which pretty girl would have him now with that swole up mug. Just look at pretty boy LJ. You not so pretty now, huh? Where's your pretty at now, Mr. LJ Matthews? The only real Matthews, as you like to think. Look at you, you rich son of a bitch. I can't stand yo fucking ass. Look at you now.

What I wouldn't give to know either of their private thoughts. I've never been rich and powerful, so this is not much of the step down for me. I know hardship, I know pain, I know what it is to live check to check. I know what it is to not have shit and to be told what to do and when to do it. I know what it is to get up at four thirty every goddamn morning and go open that shitty ass diner. On top of that, I bust my ass from the time I get there till I can finally go home at God knows what hour. I work hard all day, every day. These two clowns, all they do is get manicures and pedicures and buy fancy suits and expensive watches and rings and silk ties and all the shit I don't have.

What I do is so much more valuable than what they do. Yet they make ungodly sums of money doing it and never once thought to include me in any of it. They could have me doing something and making some of that good money. So what, I don't have no college in me. So what, I had to go to rehab a couple of times. Shit, they ain't perfect neither. So what, I went in for some shit I didn't do. That shit can happen to anybody. So what, they gave me the money to buy that shitty ass restaurant. That shit is way too hard.

I work too fucking hard, and they know it but don't do nothing to help. What would they know about hardship, all up in that big ass penthouse? Get in at ten and leave by three. what a fucking joke. Mildred, can you get my brother Milton on the line for me? Mildred, can you get my father on the phone, please?

Can't even make their own phone calls, especially that punk ass LJ. All they do is give orders all day. Sounds like such hard work. I feel so bad for them. Good for they fucking ass. I can handle this shit. I just hope they can!

* * *

With a controlled and servitude body but an alert and free mind, Hazel's thoughts ran as wild as any wild Mustang on the open prairie. Like all the rest, her thoughts took her to her zone of priority. Her immediate thoughts focused on better times. She thought about her senior prom night in high school and how that night was filled with so much promise and opportunity. She thought about her choices, those that were distant and those that were recent, and concluded that choices count.

She wondered what her life would have been like if she had chosen money over love. At the time, she reasoned to herself, "We're both young and we will have the opportunity to make as much money as anybody else." She believed that love conquered all, and she had high hopes for the future.

She had it all planned out. She would ride the incredible journey of life side by side with her first true love, Milton, and they would set the world on fire. Little did she ever think that Milton would take that term literally and set someone's car on fire.

Although, in his defense, he has always maintained that it wasn't him. Too bad the jury didn't see it that way, even after LJ and Henry got him one of the better criminal lawyers around. She thought vividly about her fateful decision to choose Milton, whom she fell in love with during that magical initial encounter on their first day of high school.

It was during lunch in front of the school's main entrance. For so many, it was the best hangout spot on campus. It was after fighting the daily heavyweight bout with the cafeteria ladies and their mysterious presentation of something that looked like food. She recalled exactly how they met.

She was catching a few rays after eating some unrecognizable cafeteria food. With ten minutes left before the bell would ring and this high school version of the midday rat race, escape would be over. He came out of nowhere. Standing there looking all tough and rugged, he confidently walked over and asked her name.

That was it. That was all it took to spark the fast burning flames of puppy love. That puppy love eventually blossomed into full-grown bloodhound love. They could sniff each other out a mile away. After that, for a good little while, they became inseparable.

Although easy at first, this choice was made harder later on. Refusing the repeated offers of Russell Smooth became a hill-high challenge. Russell had wooed Hazel for nearly all their high school years. He tried every way imaginable to get her attention, to win her heart, and steal her way from Milton.

SAME AS GOD SPOKE

He failed at love, although he was an honor student, class president, and the all-around Mr. Popularity. Plus, it didn't hurt that his parents had won the lotto during the final month of their senior year.

In all truth, he really never had a chance. First, he lacked that ruggedness that she fancied so much. But moreover, Russell did not possess the one intangible that Milton had to his sole credit. Simply put, Milton could make her laugh.

He had the uncanny ability to make Hazel laugh at will and laugh hysterically. The thought of life with no more of the shared laughter with Milton was enough make her sad. So sad that she sought her first night of spellbound sleep in order to escape the growing and vexing sadness.

* * *

From the outset, Pam was angry. She was angry at everyone and everything, but she was especially angry with Greg for not saving her. *How could he leave me when I most needed him? How could he be off somewhere, doing whatever, and I'm stuck here like a robot to do this, do that? He better get here quick or else his ass is mine when I ever get to it.*

She was mad at LJ for coming up with the stupid idea to accept this wack-ass vacation from the paradise suites of hell. She was mad at Hazel for being a bitch and for being a pain in her bottom and for having hair longer than hers. She was mad at Mysty and Beverley for always taking Hazel's side. And she was mad at Milton for marrying Hazel and for being so weak when it came to Hazel. She was mad at Henry for agreeing with LJ to accept this wack-assed vacation, afforded only to those who wish to serve a master.

She was also mad at the two ladies that dosed her with that god-awful stuff that they had put on her and for making her put on a god-awful jumpsuit. Pam was angry at the world at this very moment, and she began to cry. She cried not because she was afraid, not because she wanted someone to come and save the day. She cried because she knew that at that moment, she was powerless to improve her situation.

She cried because she could do nothing, and that, to her, was unforgivable. She always prided herself in always having the wherewithal to make her situation better. When she had crooked teeth in junior high, which she hated and refused to live with and her mother could not afford braces, she sought out to find a way.

That way came in the form of her counselor at school, who directed her into a free dental program for left-handed people of all things. When she did not have the money to go to cosmetology school, she got three of her high school teachers to sponsor her tuition. At every turn of her life, Pam knew how to make things happen.

Pam knew in her heart that she was a force to be reckoned with, but this was different. This was so much different. *What is this Godspoke stuff?* she thought. *God did not give any special orders like this for us to follow, so why are we spellbound? God would not do that to his children, so why are we going through this?*

She thought of a thousand things to do, yet none of them seemed realistic. None of them seemed possible, not under these conditions. Ultimately, all that she came up with was that there was nothing that she could do to change her circumstance or her state of mind; they were both utterly helpless, at least for right now.

* * *

Each of the seven lay awake under the watchful eye of a unit guard. Each had a stampede of thoughts run through their minds, no less chaotic than a runaway locomotive. This rich cacophony of thoughts had almost nothing in common, as each individual struggled through this night of misery in their own unique way, with their own unique set of life experiences and beliefs to guide them. But each kept coming back to one simple question.

Why us? Why me?

CHAPTER 10

THE FORBIDDEN TOUCH

BIG WALT STOOD peering through the window of the housing unit in which the newly obtainable object of his affection was assigned. He stood there as watchful as any predator, at the ready, about to devour some unsuspecting prey. Pam was his intended entrée, but Justin, the guard on duty, would necessarily be his appetizer.

If Walter knew anything, he knew he did not think much of the man he was glaring at. Plain truth was, he thought Justin was as simple as a one-way street and about as dim as a ten-watt light bulb. Be that as it may, Walter knew math. So he knew that it would take more than one to accomplish what he had in mind, and Justin fit the bill perfectly.

First, it did not take much to manipulate him. Second, he was a kiss ass. And finally, but more importantly, he suffered from a severe case of naivety. After another moment to reconsider the ninety-nine things that could go wrong and blow up in his face, Walter gathered himself and stepped inside the unit.

Immediately asserting his authority, he called for Justin to come. His harsh tone was designed to throw his feeble-minded prey off-balance. Startled, his unsuspecting prey came near. The grave look of concern on the young man's face told Walter that he had accomplished his goal. However, he promptly put his gullible subordinate at ease.

"Take it easy, young fella. I just wanna chew the fat a little. You know, good ole boy style." Walter grabbed him by the arm and pulled him close. He wanted his prey at ease. After looking around to be sure the coast was clear, he began quietly, almost in whisper mode, "Justin, is it me or is that new gal Pam just the spitting image of Ms. Diane?"

Relieved that this visit was not work related, Justin gladly replied in his Creole-based broken English dialect. "Ya knows, Big Walt, tanite was my furst time seeing har. Seent har when I did my furst count, ya know. Ba, as soon as I seent har, I thunk that same thang right away.

"I tell ya what else, boi. She show is purdy. Ain't she? I mean, she real easy to peep at. Real easy. Yes sir-reee," he said excitedly.

"Man, shut yo mouf. What you talking bout?" came Walter's dumbed-down country hick reply.

"She bout the prettiest thing I ever did lay my eyes on," he said, smiling, still trying to make a good ole boy connection with a man he felt beneath him in all aspects imaginable. "You know, Jus, I might just ask Lady Sara if Ms. Diane was half of a set of twins, 'cause ain't no way this here gal and Ms. Diane ain't twins."

"Hey, Big Walt, I'll bet you a wet dollar to a dry donut that you won't to tare into her like a windmill in a tornada? Don't cha, boi? Don't cha now, huh, huh? What you say, Big Walt? What you say?" he repeated between the most irritating of cackles.

"Well, now, little Jus," he said, cozying up to his newfound friend while simultaneously surveying the area to make sure no one was within earshot. "That is the very hush-hush. Keep it on the low. Reason why I called you over here.

"First, I gotta ask you sumpin' gud, buddy," he said, now pouring it on thick.

"What that be?" Justin asked simply.

"Now you can keep some thangs to yaself, can't you, boi?"

"Show nuff, Big Walt, show nuff. Anythang you's gone leave wit me is wit for all time. My pappy always did say, a mane ain't a mane if a mane ain't got his word to him friends. Now you go head. You can tell me anythang."

SAME AS GOD SPOKE

"'All right then, here goes," he said, now ready to pounce. "Now you know that ever since I furst laid eyes on Ms. Diane that I wanted to jump her bones, but you know as well as I do that both the Good Doctor and Lady Sara would skin me alive."

"Can't say they wuldn't. Probly wuld do mor'an dat, ask me," replied the dull-witted prey as he was being slowly devoured with every word he spoke.

"Man, don't I knows it, so that's out. But back in my day, there was an old song that says that if yous can't be with the one you love, then you ought to love the one yous with. I ain't know bout you, but I'm sho is a definite a believer in that there."

"Go on way from here, Big Walt. You crazy as all hell," he said with his all too familiar cackle.

"Now to me, it looks like we have ourselves quite a little dilemma here. I would love nothing more than to fuck the shit out of Miss Diane, but seeing as that ain't never gonna happen, I gotta do the next best thang. Next best thang is right inside that door in one of them thar yonder beds. And good part bout it all is she can't tell me no. She can't do nothing but what I say or you say.

"Look, my friend, right in yonder, least ways as I see it, seem to me we have the next best thing—Ms. Diane's long-lost twin. She is ripe just like some sweet grapes on the vine and ready to be made into some mighty tasty wine. Some wine that I would love to drink to the very last drop.

"Only problem is the fact that she is under the Godspoke spell. And if I was to have sex with her, she would come out from under the spell. And right after I finish cumin', I would be going. Going to hell, that is, because the Good Doctor would kill me and send me there."

"You can bet yo sweet ass on dat, Big Walt, special since she look so much alike Ms. Diane."

"That is true, lil Jus, if he ever found out about it. But that won't ever happen, will it, good buddy?" he asked rhetorically and moved right to his next point. "So in order for me to satisfy my sincere desire for carnal knowledge with this little half-red heifer, ole Good Doctor would have to be kept in the dark."

Justin's puzzled look made him rephrase his previous statement. "I mean, if I wanna hit it, we gotta stay hush-hush."

"You know it, mane, but how we gon do it?" the younger man asked of his older and wiser coconspirator.

"Well, first thang is that no one, specially the Good one, or Clark, the bad one, or no one, not no one can ever know what we doing har tanight." His urgently stated message was delivered using more of his impromptu country grammar. "Now hares what we does to pull this off. Fact, I got two ideas. Listen ta tha furst and tell me what'cha think. Then if'n ya don't like that'un, I'll tells ya bout idea number two.

"Number one is real sweet. Just listen ta it. Y'all know I keeps two syringes in my desk draw. Each of 'em is full of a dose of Godspoke, just in case of emergencies. I could get myself a little bit, and after I was finished, I could hit her with it again. Yeah, that thar jus might work. What'cha think, lil buddy?"

"Well, Big Walt, I dun'no much bout that stuff, but I does know ya had'na oughta mess round wit it. Ya knows that stuff is mighty powful. Mighty, mighty powful. Clark is always going on and on bout how they is only posed ta get xact mounts, and they posed ta get it at xact times. I don seen'em both, the Good Doctor and Clark, go crazy if somebody done, done it even a lil ways off fom what them wanted. Crazy, I tell ya.

"If'n you was me and If'n I was you, I'd most be scuured, real scuured. 'Cause, boi, looka har. If'n yous mess up har injection times and they stick har when it time again, she might get too much or it could be badder. She cooud get onea dem thar overdose, and that wooud be real bad fo you n me. Hell, um nervos bout it jes thankin bout it, Big Walt. We could kill har, and then ya know the rule. One'na us gotta take har place. End dat probly be me. My vary best vice ta ya is to let me hur idea nember two, 'cause I ain't wont no partsa idea nember one."

"Okay, okay, don't start actin' soft on me now. I got you, buddy. Gi'me a minute. I did not get to be manager around here cause of my good looks. Although that mighta helped some." He then burst into a very controlled laugh. "Ha, ha, ha. Let me think here. Jus gimme a sec 'cause I know there is more than one way to skin a cat, or in this case, to trim some pussy, ha, ha, ha." Again came the manufactured laughter.

"Sometimes I crack myself up. Go ahead and laugh, Jus. You know you like that little play on words. Cat and pussy, huh, huh, cat and pussy. You get it?"

"No, Big Walt, can't say I rightly do. What you mean cat and pussy? I really ain't get it."

"Boy, you amaze me. Sometimes you can say very smart things, like tellin' me bout the overdose, and then you go…well, you go and can't get a little joke like that. Boi, you got some special set of brains on you. Real special, I tell ya. But, Jus."

"Huh?" came the one-word reply.

"That was a very funny joke. Don't worry though. I'll explain it ta ya one day. Anyway, okay, okay, listen to this then. What if I was to take her over to my quarters and have her get naked and maybe touch herself a little bit? You know, I could maybe make her do one of them there stripteases. 'Cause it ain't like she could refuse anything that I tell her to, and maybe that would be enough for me."

"Big Walt, Big Walt, that is TMI."

"TMI…TMI…what the hell is TMI?"

"Too much in fo ma tion. Way, way too much info! I heared the Good Doctor say that. He smart, and I'm trying to get smart like 'em. But wat I wanna know is how you gone sit up here and tell me that you wanna jerk yaself to a naked woman who ain't even know she naked? Dat is sick, man. That is so fucking sick."

"Okay, Mr. Holier Than Thou. Now you can just shut the hell up? I just happen to know that you jerk off all the time to those nasty girl magazines. That's right, the ones that you bring in yo lunch box and keep in the top right-hand desk draw at your station. I know all about all them late night, long ass trips to the bathroom.

"I also know bout you stopping by the bedsides of them Godspoke women to pull the covers back so you can *get a good long stare* before you go in there too. Didn't think I knew about that, huh? Now tell me I'm wrong." He crossed his arms over his barrel-shaped chest and waited for a response that would never come. "I didn't think so."

The humiliated man quickly lowered his head in shame and meekly asked, "Who told ya bout my magazines? Who ya bann talkin ta, Big Walt? Who is it dat gi'me way liken dat?"

"Take it easy, kid. Nobody gave you away. I just make my rounds at night, is all. I seen you go through your routine a dozen or more times. I can even tell you what time you usually go in and how long it usually takes you get done. But don't worry. All of that don't matter, kid. Yo secret is safe wit me as long as my secret is safe wit you. We clear?"

"Yeah, yeah, we's cleear."

Looking to retrain the focus of his embarrassed comrade in arms, Walter tried the partner-in-need approach. "Now listen heaya, lil Jus. The old man need yo halp," he said, reverting back to his manufactured "make Justin comfortable" language. Now, in whispers, he continued, "God knows that I have been wanting to have my way with Ms. Diane for years and years. Everybody know dis. An now I have finally have a chance to have her, at least if'n only in my mind. So suck it up, mane, and quit bein a little bitchin baby. Now I need yo goddamn help, and I knows ya ain't gonna let me down. What ya say, kid?"

"Well, old man, if'n I's ta help ya, what I get outta the deal?"

"Let me see," he said sharply, his anger on full display. "For one, you get to keep your fucking job. And for two, you get to keep from having me kick the living shit out of you. And for three, I won't tell everybody around here that you are the nighttime creepy crawler that you are. How bout them three for starters, Jus, and I can think of some more if I need to. But for right now, that's what you get. How's that work for you, lil buddy?"

"In that case, um in! What ya wont me ta do?"

"What time tonight do you get duty relief to have ya lunch?"

"Probly bout one in the morn, and I gets a haaf hour."

"That's real good timing 'cause… well, let me see now…okay, let's say about two o'clock after you are alone again. I want you to quietly order my Ms. Diane to get up and report to the manager's sleeping quarters."

"I kin do dat, but how she posed to know where the manager's sleeping quarters are?"

Growing more impatient by the minute with his dim-witted accomplice, Big Walt barked sharply at his sensitive second. "Listen, shit for brains. The manager's sleeping quarters is less than a hundred yards away. Just point it out, you fucking imbecile."

"Okay, I got'cha, but ya ain't hada go dat hard on me. Damn, mane!"

"My bad, my bad. I just a little nervous bout the whole thing. You know how it is. But I didn't mean nothing."

At precisely 2:00 a.m., Justin did as he was instructed. "Workforce Pam, wake up," came the soft-spoken command with a highly noticeable Southern drawl. "Workforce Pam, wake up," he repeated a second time. Once Pam's eyes were open and alert, he gave her the next command.

"Workforce Pam, you r'ta report ta tha manager's sleepin quorters. Workforce Pam, folla me so's I can point out tha building fo ya." Once he was outside the door, he gave her the next command. "Workforce Pam, dere is a small green building rat ova dere," he said, pointing. "Big Walt, tha manager, is in dat dere building waitin fo ya. Report ta him now."

Pam was eagerly greeted at the door by Big Walt, who could barely contain himself. "Come in Workforce Pam, come in," he said devilishly, and he wasted no time in getting to the thick of things. "Workforce Pam, please take this washcloth and towel and go in the bathroom and take a shower and use that good-smelling soap I put there on the soap dish. I bought that just for you," he added as she began acting on his commands.

"I also bought a nice big pink bottle of hair shampoo, and it's on the shelf inside the shower. Use some of that too. I usually buy the ninety-nine-cent brand, but this time I spared no expense. That bottle cost me almost two and half dollars.

"After you shower and dry yourself off, please put on the lingerie and robe that I have placed in there on the sink for you. Oh yeah,

Workforce Pam, I also left some perfume in there too. I picked it out myself. It smells damn good. After you put on that pretty red and black little number, I hope it's just your size, please spray some of that nice smelling perfume on you.

"As a matter of fact, spray a lot. I like my women to smell good. Real, real good. I want you to spray so much that my nostrils are on flames or something close to it. Hot damn, Ms. Diane is here. *Hot damn!*" he said, almost shouting from excitement.

Against her will, she went about the business of preparing herself to be raped or worse. It hurt her deeply that she was totally powerless to stop the madness. She watched herself, third-party style, only from inside her own body, following the instructions of her demented and perverted soon-to-be lover.

Unable to follow her own thoughts, which included the bludgeoning and decapitation of this man, Pam steadfastly wished for a miracle. All the while, she struggled mightily to stop herself. However, the Godspoke had other plans. It was in full control. And ultimately, no matter her level of resistance, it would force her to follow Big Walt's instructions to the letter. The thought sickened her.

Oh my god, what is about to happen to me? she thought. *What is this sick, ugly fucking man about to do to me? God, please let me wake up from this nightmare. This has to be a nightmare. Oh my fucking god. Why is this happening to me?*

What have I done so bad to deserve this fate? God, if you are God, please don't let this sick little twisted, insane, deranged, demented, imitation of a man touch me or do me any harm! I have no idea what it is that they gave us, but I can't refuse their instructions.

If you are the God of mercy, the God of love, the God of compassion that I been taught that you are, and that I have come to believe that you are, please reveal yourself to me. Please, God! Reveal yourself to me right now, oh God. Right now, God. Right now in my greatest hour of need. My God, my God, please. Do not forsake me. Do not leave me at this man's mercy. He has no mercy. He has no compassion. He has no love. He only has carnal lust.

Resigned that she had done enough begging and that she had done enough to be heard by God if there was a God, she now returned to more familiar forums. *I know he's going to do some unspeakable and ungodly things to me.* And in an unfamiliar moment of female acquiescence, usually reserved for those Pam considered weak and dependent, she wished with all her heart for Greg to come and save her.

I want Greg. I want my Greg to come through that door right now. I just know he would rip out this guy's tongue and force-feed it to him. I know that he would beat that ass ten ways to Sunday and then do it all over again 'cause I would ask him to. I also know that he would tell me to dry my tears and to hush because everything is going to be all right.

Then I know he would hold that bastard down and let me just whoop his ass. I mean, whoop his nasty ass till I'm good and tired of whooping his nasty ass. Oh, Greg, why can't you, for one time, surprise the hell out of me and surprise the shit out of his nasty ass too when you come through the door or through the window or something? Where are you, my love? Where are you when I need you most?

If ever there was a time when I would allow myself to be subservient to man, this would be it. I would definitely be like yes, Greg. Okay, Greg. Whatever you say, Greg. We will do it your way, Greg. Just please, Greg, LJ, Henry, somebody. Hell, I'd even take that bitch Hazel right now. Somebody please come and save me.

Thoughts of a miraculous rescue all but dissipated once she began to dry herself. As she liberally applied the awful smelling perfume, she became more nauseous by the minute. Although the perfume was cheap, gaudy, and smelled to high hell, that was not the source of her nausea. She knew that she was almost done following all the instructions given to her and that she was now nearing the time of her play date with Mr. Nasty, her date with destiny.

If he touches me, so help me, she thought as she exited the safety of the bathroom, which was quite spacious. *I hope his nasty ass rots in hell!* Walking slowly across the room to whatever fate awaited her, her mind raced with random thoughts. Many of those thoughts were filled with the most hateful and vicious of rhetoric, while still others bordered on some pitiful submissive groveling.

And I hope his mother dies a slow torturous death at the hands of twelve sex-craved bandits. And I hope they make him watch! And I hope that after they've finished raping her repeatedly for many agonizing minutes, they turn around and rape him, too, but only worst.

Oh my god, what am I saying? I don't mean any of that, God. I really, really don't mean any of that! It's just that I'm nervous, I'm scared, and worst of all, I'm powerless with no control of my own will and at the mercy of a madman. Please, oh God of mercy, please show me some mercy right now. I'm sorry for every bad thing I ever did in my whole life, and I promise to be a much better person from now on. Oh, please, God, don't let this filthy man touch me like that.

"Hey, Workforce Pam, stop right there and let me look at you. I've been waiting for this for a very, very, very long time, and I am absolutely going to enjoy it. Now, Workforce Pam, hurry up and drop that sheer lace robe. I want to see all of your little hidden goodies!

"Oh my god, you look heavenly. If you weren't a woman, I'd swear you could walk on water. Come closer so I can take a little look-see, up close and personal. I know a girl has to have her privacy, but I'm a private investigator, and I spy a little pussy tonight.

"Good gracious alive, you are killing me! Lady, you are as hot as a firecracker, and you got my blood on instant boil. I can't take it any longer. Where is my super-sized jar of grease? Yes, ma'am, this is one experience that I am going to thoroughly enjoy.

"Tonight I will have my one night to enjoy, to remember, and to brag about, even if I decide to stretch the truth a little. Don't think I wanna tell nobody bout the super-sized jar of grease, but I will tell them all bout this fine, fine specimen of a woman I see right before my very eyes.

"Oh no, I forgot to take my manhood pill! Calm down, Walt. Calm down, big fella. You in control here," he said aloud as he teetered somewhere between all-out nervous panic and restrained composure. "Aw, what the hell," he said in a moment of revelation. "I'm not really going to touch her, so I won't need it. Ooh wee, spin around there, Workforce Pam. Spin around, hot to the damn!

"My, my, my, it's just about showtime. Okay, little fella, time to stand up and get in the game. Standup, little fella! Stand up! Don't go acting all shy on me now. Don't you see what your eyes is beholding? Even if you only got one eye, I know you can see what I see. I know what you want, little fella. We just need to set the mood in this place. We can start with it being a little less bright, so let's turn the lights down low. Not too much though. I need to see all the details on the flesh on that body that I can see.

"Oh my god, you are so beautiful! You look soooo heavenly. I almost feel bad for doing this to you, but I'm going to do it anyway. Oh yeah, mood music. Lets me and you put on some of this sweet slow music to better set the mood up. Maestro, if you will.

"Workforce Pam, dance very slow and very sexy to this music. Oh, yes, baby, oh, yes. Do it just like that. Move those hips. Swing that perfect lil tight ass of yours. Oh my god, Lord to the have mercy. I can't stand it. Lord, what I wouldn't do to make this a physical thing.

"Unt, unt, unt, God you have got a body on you. Ooh yeah, oh yeah, baby. I do declare you have the sexiest frame that these old eyes have ever seen. My god, my god, I would truly like you to really be mine. Workforce Pam, move your hands slowly over your upper body, your shoulders, your neck, and your breasts. Oh yeah, baby, take your time, baby. You are making my little fella feel real good right about now.

"Workforce Pam, now take off your bra while you continue dancing slow and sexy to the music. Oh yes, baby. Oh yes. Oh yes, baby, oh yes. Oooooooh, damn-it-to-hell. I've done made a mess here."

Even before she could completely remove her bra, Walt had reached his climax. His ejaculation was way premature, even for him. And in a fit of shame, he ordered his voluptuous guess to go away. "Workforce Pam, return to the bathroom and put back on your work clothes."

She was again forced to follow his instructions, but these instructions she welcomed. Now alone with her thoughts, she felt an immediate sense of shame for having to perform like some hoochie in a burlesque show. Her initial response was the desire to cry, but somehow she did not.

She could not fully reconcile with this need to cry. Besides, crying was not her style. She was not about to play the role of some little victim. She knew that she didn't do the victim role very well. She was a problem solver, so her pride would not allow her the indulgence of a therapeutic cry.

As she sat to remove the tawdry getup, which she thought showed remarkably poor taste in lingerie even for a man, something inside her felt very different.

Thank you, God, that you didn't allow that man to touch me. Thank you, God. Thank you. Oh my god, all that slow dancing made me feel. It made me feel funny. I feel real funny. What is it? Why do I feel so strange? I feel so shaky. Oh my goodness, my hands are trembling. That freak didn't give me anything, so why do I feel so, so strange? Oh boy, what now? What other misery and indignation can these people pile on us?

"Workforce Pam, hurry up in there!" At his command, she immediately stood up and hurried herself. Then after another moment to reconsider, she disobeyed the order. *Hurry up, my ass. You go to hell, Mr. Nasty. I'm going to sit here and take my time.*

She immediately recognized her disobedience. *Hey, wait a minute. That was my decision, not his instruction. Yeah, that really was my decision.* Confused as to how this could be happening, she asked herself aloud, "What is happening to me?" The mere fact that she could speak aloud told her that something was very, very different.

After some intense thought and some quick deliberative analysis, it came to her. "Oh yeah, now I remember. When we first got here, I believe I overheard them talking about sexual arousal and how that was forbidden. Okay, now I get it. Being sexually aroused is the antidote for this Same as God Spoke drug that they've given us.

"In order to remain in control over our will, we cannot be allowed to get aroused, and who could get horny around this place, under these conditions? And they say I am the dumb one 'cause I don't own my own business. Huh, I guess you really don't need a college degree to figure some things out!

"Okay, now let me hurry up so that he won't suspect anything. I can feel it now. I can feel it now. My will is coming back to me. I can't wait to get out of here, because when I do, I'm coming back to kill this old stinky fat bloated motherfucker."

"Workforce Pam, come out of the bathroom now. My god, you look beautiful, just like the spitting image of Ms. Diane. Ms. Lady, if I thought there was any way I could go ahead and make love to you for real and then hit you up with that Godspoke I got in my draw over there without anybody knowing, girl, you'd be good and naked right now. You better thank your lucky stars that I don't want to overdose you, 'cause I damn sure ain't taking your place. I got a real life to live here.

"Enough of this shit, Workforce Pam. Return to your sleeping quarters. I should've asked for a kiss, but I don't want to get her aroused. Kissing these sweet juicy lips would get any woman riled up. Ha, ha, ha, ha. This I know. This I do know," he said with an obvious hint of delight, feeling the afterglow effects that could only be had with the romantic pleasure derived from a sexual encounter.

As she passed by her pathetic host, she silently thought, *I know that you are a fat disgusting pig who looks like the remains of afterbirth*. Remembering her need for stealth, she cleared her mind of such thoughts for fear of a facial expression that would render her new secret transparent. *Okay, let me straighten up right now so that I don't act any differently*.

She left Big Walt's quarters, acting as if nothing had changed and walked deliberately back to her housing unit and her bunk. On the way, her thoughts raced faster and faster with each step that she took. "Let me think," she said over and over. "Let me think.

"First, how did I become aroused? I would hate to think that I was turned on by that little ugly fucking degenerate of a man. That man couldn't turn me on with a switch, let alone by the looks of him. What the hell happened then? 'Cause I sure don't know.

"Let's see, what could it have been? Maybe it was the scented candles, which did not smell all that bad. Maybe it was the dimly lit room, full of the slow baby-making music. I do love me some Barry White, but I'd never tell Greg or any of his family that. I can't figure it out just now, but so what? Somehow I was aroused, and if that's the price I have to pay to get me out of here, then so be it."

During those first few minutes of her regained mental freedom, she wrestled with the difficult task to admit that it had actually happened. Although mortified at the thought of being aroused by the likes of Big Walt, she was simultaneously extremely glad that it had happened. *I am very glad about it,* she thought over and over. However much she tried to instill that comforting thought in her mind, the thought that it was supposed to replace still made her sick to her core.

After some time had elapsed, she eventually made the transition to pondering a decision on what she should do now with her new-found mental freedom. "It would be hard for me to try and escape from the biosphere because there's no way out," she reasoned first. "The only two ways out of here that I know about are the glass elevator and the secret loading dock. Don't really know where the loading dock is since none of us never got to go to it, but I've heard them talk about it too many times not to be able to find out. But how?

"Okay, loading dock, loading dock, bad idea. I could never get out through the loading dock because it is always guarded. What else? What else… I could try to seduce that perverted degenerate Big Walt and ask him to release me on the promise that I would not tell anyone about this place once I get back to my life. I know he's horny and stupid, but I don't believe he's that stupid.

"I could try to sexually arouse either Henry or LJ and get them to help me, but knowing them, that might not be such a great idea either. What with all the humiliation that they've been subjected to, their heads might not be in a good place. Just think. The Matthews brothers being forced to do manual labor, plus having to take orders from all these rednecks that they despise so much.

"Huh, never thought I'd see the day that LJ would be taking orders. Ha, ha, ha. In any case, they are both hotheads, and they would just probably get us all killed. No, I think I have to do this myself. What to do, what to do?

"Hey, I have a great idea, but I have to think it through. First, I have been sitting up too long. I need to lay my butt down in here and pretend like I'm asleep. Now if I play it just right and I timed it just right, I think that I could just walk straight through the front door and no one would say a word. I would save the day, and even that heifer Hazel would lick my boots in thanks, and all the rest of those Matthews clowns would have to give me my respect too.

"Oh yeah, this is going to be good. I might be young and all, and I might not have all their education or money, but who's got the juice now? Don't listen to her, Greg... Really? Really, people? I'll show all of y'all. Now let's see who Mr. Gregory Eric Matthews listens to after this."

CHAPTER 11

The Offer You Shouldn't Refuse

"Gentlemen, please follow me. As promised, we will now take a tour of this magnificent moneymaking machine. In just a short time, you will indeed see that SAGS is all that we have boasted and bragged. We can grow and produce a premium product right here. Plus, and most importantly, we can do so quite inexpensively. This tour should answer the burning question of how. Once we return here, there should be no doubt that we can, in fact, deliver as advertised.

"Right this way, if you would. Okay, gentlemen, as we exit this structure, I ask that you take very careful notice of everything that you see. Please scrutinize everything. As you may have already guessed, my request has an ulterior motive.

"I want you to identify anything out of the ordinary and everything that would cause you pause. Look for anything that might make you want to take a second look. Also, make note of things that may motivate some rambunctious law enforcement officer to conduct a closer inspection.

"These are rear grounds of my personal estate. All that you see is included. You'd be hard-pressed to find a backyard of any good mansion more traditional. The outdoor centerpiece of our lovely home is our Olympic-sized swimming pool. Very impressive, wouldn't you say?" Not waiting for or expecting any response, the Good Doctor proceeded.

"Pass the pool and a few hundred yards to your left are the tennis courts. The whole area is quite spacious and replete with shaded viewing stands. Of course, we host tournaments here from time to time. My daughter is an exceptional player," he said with an air of pride.

The guests were then led to the horse stables some several hundred feet past the tennis courts. "Here," he said confidently, "we have our equestrian stables replete with the finest European thoroughbreds that money can buy. Now there are also a couple of stallions in there with a bona fide Kentucky bluegrass bloodline, but only a couple." He chuckled arrogantly.

"You see, they cost far more than their European stablemates," he said, bragging. "My ponies are my indulgence. They are undeniably my weakness. And believe you me," he added as a side bar, "I will definitely be adding to my stable once our little venture is up and running at full production."

The silent group was then led to the next visible structure situated some four to five hundred yards away and to the right. "We have here an aboveground walk-in wine cellar," he stated flatly then redirected everyone's attention.

Before entering, the temporary tour guide paused to point out some of the more appealing features of the landscape. "Quite striking, do you not agree?" he said, pointing to the picturesque scenery that flowed seamlessly before them. Everything fit perfectly in the grand scheme of an intentional design.

The pool was surrounded on three sides by a glass wall, three feet wide and four feet tall. This structure appeared to be a hand-built outdoor aquarium. Inside was the bluest water, with thousands of tropical fish of all sorts and variety, gleefully playing. It was set back about fifteen yards from the pool itself.

Beyond that were tennis courts as polished and professional as any in existence, only with smaller scale seating. Just beyond that were the horses' stables, a beautiful black onyx structure that resembled an expensive dollhouse. And finally, the coup de grâce was a breathtaking tree line that rivaled any panoramic scenery in any Hollywood movie ever made.

The tree line all but surrounded the huge mansion and the spacious yard that lay at its borders. With the place seemingly in the middle of nowhere but with such amenities at one's disposal, who would care or even notice, for that matter?

"As you will notice, the wine cellar sits very near the edge of the property. From this vantage point, you can also see our riding trails. Each of the trails is lined only with the most majestic of plant life. The trees are mostly weeping willow trees. They are my personal favorite. In any event, they go back for miles and miles.

"So, gentlemen, tell me honestly. Do you notice anything out of the ordinary? I mean, take a very good hard discriminating look around, and please scrutinize all that your eyes, and any of your other senses for that matter, are able to survey. After you have done so, please tell me truthfully, do you see or feel that anything is out of the ordinary?"

There was unanimous head shaking in the negative sense, which actually affirmed the Good Doctor's boast of an invisible biosphere hidden in plain sight. "Well then, let us all step inside the wine cellar and choose a bottle of Chardonnay for lunch. What do you say?"

"Right this way, gentlemen. Right this way. Allow me to give you all some light," he stated, still exhibiting an ever-present coy demeanor. "Quite a collection, wouldn't you say?" he asked as he individually pointed out fourteen glass-encased sections around the spacious room. "Yes, yes, indeed. We have worked very hard to compile this collection.

"Each of the fourteen sections raises independent of the others. Each glass casing can only be accessed with a specific code. We must always protect our investments. You can never be too careful. Don't you agree, gentlemen?" he said with an intentionally hideous laugh.

His laughter stopped abruptly. Then he continued, "This is a very large structure by design, large enough to hold our entire party, as you can see. The size was a major factor when it was constructed because we planned for our collection to have selections from all of the major producers of the world. I think we have over two thousand five hundred different selections. I know, for a fact, quite a few bottles date back to the late 1800s. I am extremely proud that some are more than a hundred years old.

"If you like your wine white, we have sauvignon blanc, pinot gris, White Zinfandel, and Chardonnay. If, on the other hand, you like your wine red, we have Pinot Noir, Hermitage, and Cabernet Sauvignon. And finally, for those of a more discriminating palate, we did not forget about the champagne. In addition, we have some very nice sparkling wine choices.

"Now, as for the growers, that list is even more impressive." Just as he was about to continue with the next segment of the braggadocios name-dropping session in progress, a note was passed to him. The hastily written note came from the man sporting the President Jefferson mask and the badge that read Mr. 28. He first read it silently, then he read it aloud. His delivery was as if he were vying for the Academy Award for best dramatic performance.

As he read it, he expressed quite an unusual look, somewhere between solemn and perturbed. "Excuse me, my good man, but I thought we were supposed to be here to take a look at your brilliant operation. Didn't know a beginner's course for wine connoisseur wannabes was also on the agenda. While I appreciate your collection, I cannot see how it would make me any money.

"Well said, and you are absolutely right! We are, and that is precisely why we are at this very spot. I first wanted you to see that you were blind," he said to his perplexed audience. Then he simply offered, "I will explain in a moment, but first things first.

"Gentlemen, has any of you been able to discern anything out of the ordinary?" After a prolonged pause to give them time to scribble a note if anyone so desired, the Good Doctor made two surprise declarations.

"First, gentlemen, let me assure you that you could look and search until doomsday, but either exercise would prove to be utterly fruitless. My engineers and I have worked long and hard to do the unthinkable. We have made something into nothing. A very large something, in fact.

"While you were outside, you were standing just feet from the largest man-made structure in this state. In fact, that statement is also true for any of the surrounding states, if I wanted to be technical, and leave no doubt, I do.

"How large, you ask? Larger than fifty football stadiums. And yes, you heard me right. I said stadiums, not fields. Not even one of you was aware! Not even one of you had any inkling that you were looking at it, or should I say right through it, all the while you were touring my estate. And that, my dear friends, was the ultimate goal when we set out to accomplish this, never been done before David Copperfield illusion.

"You didn't know it, but you were looking at the biosphere all the time. The next thing that you could not have known is that at this very moment, you are standing in its entrance. That's right. *Believe it or not*," he said in a very low and slow baritone voice. He did so in order to create more of the manufactured dramatics with which he was so enamored.

"No, no," he said, lifting a single finger of rebuke. "I can almost hear your internal murmurs of disbelief. A good dose of skepticism is healthy. However, *seeing is believing*…at least most of the time." His voice was noticeably tailing off. "Very well then, gentlemen. I give to you the land of make believe come true."

And with one dramatic push of a button that he secretly held in the palm of his hand, he instantly made them believers, one and all! The cellar door closed abruptly, the room went pitch-black, and a bright reddish light suddenly flooded the enclosure. The floor, which originally looked to be textured stone, now revealed itself to be textured glass, as the lights beneath it were now visible.

Much to the shock and near panic of everyone inside, the room began to move. Most of the occupants immediately experienced what may best be described as a sinking feeling. In truth, they were actually sinking. Apparently, this sudden descent proved to be very unnerving. Even though they had been warned, they seemed to be caught off guard.

The glass that protected the wine bottles did not stop at the floor, as they all imagined. It kept going down and down and down.

Before anyone had time to react to the shock of the hidden-in-plain-sight elevator, with the dramatic closing of the doors and the sudden floor movement, the occupants of the wine cellar now found themselves lowered to a subground floor.

Once the doors of this very well-concealed entrance opened, the occupants cautiously moved out. They then found themselves in a glass-enclosed walkway that spanned approximately 150 yards. To the left and to the right, there were a series of structures, some much larger than the others.

"Gentlemen, if you would be so kind as to follow me, I will take you to the promised land," he said as he led the way. "We call this place Persephone, after the Greek goddess of spring's bounty. Here it is always spring, and the bounty is always flourishing.

"The structures to your left are the sleeping quarters for our spellbound workforce, which currently stands at just over five hundred. We do, however, plan to expand that number to well five thousand. That plan is in place, and it should, no, scratch that. It will be completed within the next six months.

"That's right. We will help decrease the homeless and runaway populations in the nearby big cities by putting them to work. They won't get paid obviously, but they won't be wards of the state either, so we are doing our little part to give back to the community," he stated brazenly.

"Over there, to the right, we house a variety of supplies and materials needed to keep this place running, and that largest structure is the dining hall. Anybody hungry?" he asked jokingly. "As mentioned earlier, each member of our workforce is a living breathing human being who has entirely been robbed of their personal will to act and is now, and forevermore, spellbound. And although spellbound, like all human beings, they must eat, sleep, and even bathe once in a while. Ha, ha, ha.

"Now walk with me and allow me to fulfill my promise. You will now witness a demonstration of the awesome power of our synthetic drug called Godspoke. Workforce, what is your name?"

"My name is Roy," came the simple answer. "Workforce Roy, kneel down and kiss my feet. Notice, I said feet and not foot. And as you can see, he is kissing both of them. Now you will also notice that since I gave him an open-ended instruction, he will remain in the new position undertaking the given task until I instruct him to do otherwise."

After several minutes, the Good Doctor gave the cease and desist order. "Workforce Roy, stand up. Workforce Roy, slap yourself repeatedly, and do so with all your might." Guttural grimaces were uttered by some, but not a spoken word as they witnessed the man willingly and mercilessly self-inflict several painful blows to his own face.

"As you can see, he is doing some very extensive damage to himself, and if I do not stop him, he will continue to do so until he is so badly injured that he cannot physically continue. Workforce Roy, stop slapping yourself now. Workforce Roy, please remove all your clothing. As you can see, there is no command that I can give him that he will not obey fully and explicitly."

"Workforce Roy, do ten jumping jacks while you bite the blood out of each your ten fingers, and then you may stop." The spellbound man did as he was instructed, and the sight of his bloody hands made at least half in the group sick to the stomach. That notwithstanding, the Good Doctor pressed on. "In fact, if I were to give him a gun and instruct him to... Well, you can imagine the rest."

As the Good Doctor was about to transition to the next demonstration, a second note was passed to him by his assistant, Clark. He read it to the group after he first read it silently. The note originated from the same source, Mr. 28. "Thank you for your sterling observation and your keen insight, President Jefferson, or Mr. 28, if you prefer. Let's share this with the others. Then we will see if we can provide you with the demonstration you so desire.

"'Dear, sir, how do we know that this man is not an actor paid by you to do exactly as you have instructed?' Superb question. I love a skeptic. Gentlemen, follow me into our Godspoke prep facility. This is where we prepare subjects to become one of our spellbound. There is a three-step process that each must go through.

"Step one is to sanitize them so that they are free of any bacteria that may be present at the injection site. Step two is to administer the injection and wait for it to take effect. Step three is to provide them with special command response training.

"Step two is the trickiest though. We can't explain exactly why, but in some cases, even after the decontamination procedure, an injection can cause illness or even instant death. The occurrence is quite rare, but it does happen every so often. We call that a hot shot," he said, laughing. "Most that get the hot shot become violently ill, although only for a short time. Most do not die, but if so, we simply incinerate them and move on to the next subject.

"Admittedly, we have a couple of kinks that we are still trying to work out, but ninety-eight percent of the time, we are successful in putting them under. Now who wants to volunteer? Don't worry. We will bring you back out after a short while. There is an instant antidote." There were numerous looks to the left and right to see if there were any takers, but none would step forward.

"Not to worry, gentlemen. That was just a bit of humor. We have a subject that has undergone step one and is now ready for the Godspoke injection. Bring him in, Clark."

A young man in his late twenties was led in from another room. Initially, he was gagged and bound by the hands and shackled at the feet. He was a fighter. No longer gagged, he hurled curse after curse after curse. On top of that were a bunch of swears, plus multiple threats of what he would do, followed by who he would do it to if not released at once.

He resisted even more as he was forced to sit in a chair equipped with both arm and leg restraints. Mr. 28 was invited to come and administer the injection. He readily complied. After jabbing the needle in as hard as he could, he emptied the stem and quickly stepped back to enjoy the show.

Almost immediately, the subject began an even more fierce verbal tirade. In summary, he promised in great detail to kill everyone present, even if he had to do it from his grave. "Watch closely, gentlemen," Clark declared as he spoke his first words directly to the group.

"The Godspoke takes over in three phases," he explained in a matter-of-fact fashion. "About two minutes in, we can remove his leg restraints. Control of the legs is always the first bit of willpower to surrender. Start to finish takes less than five minutes total."

Clark then warned the subject, "Do not panic. You will now experience a sudden and all-encompassing burning sensation that feels just like fire in your bones. The feeling will pass quickly," he said in a calming voice. When it hit him, he screamed out in foul-mouthed fashion, just like someone with Tourette's syndrome. "This is usual, gentlemen," Clark proclaimed in an effort to ease the tension of the nervous onlookers.

"Once the Godspoke has made two complete bodily circulations, shortly thereafter, he will lose the free use of all limbs. At that point, his mouth is all that's left in his control." Indeed it was, and he used it to scare the living daylights out of everyone in the room, except those who had witnessed this spectacle before.

After an endless amount of screams, threats, and swears, there was sudden silence. Power over his speech was the last insult to an already long and cruel list of injury. It was very evident that the Godspoke had finally conquered his will! The subject was now rendered spellbound.

With all imminent danger behind them, the Good Doctor immediately reassumed his lead position. "As you can now see, gentlemen, after that greatest of the freewill functions is taken, the Godspoke spell is complete. Thereafter and forevermore, he is one of the spellbound. That is as long as we keep him full of this," he said while holding up a syringe full of the spellbinding magic in a bottle.

"He is now powerless to do anything other than follow instructions. Later on, he will be given a special set of coded instructions so that thereafter, he will obey only a select few. This training is very specific and quite secret. So of course, we will not reveal that particular trade secret. As I have forcefully stated, most of what we do is revealed strictly on a need-to-know basis.

"However, back to the matter at hand. This subject is raw, and he can take instructions from anyone. So it works out better that we have not as yet given him the special training. Now let's demonstrate the highly effective nature of my invention. Paid actor indeed," he said sarcastically in the direction of Mr. 28.

SAME AS GOD SPOKE

"To that end, and just for a brief moment, we will suspend the rules we established earlier. As a part of this demonstration, I will now allow just one of you to speak. And since this was mostly your doing, why don't you, Mr. 28, come forward and do the honors? Why don't you come and instruct Workforce Gary here to do something? He'll do anything your little heart or great big imagination desires. And by all means, please make it something interesting. I bore easily."

Mr. 28 had an accent of some kind, and it was very evident when he initially spoke. After some hesitation, he gave his first instruction. On the surface, it seemed gentle and mild. At first, it seemed he would take it easy on the subject, but the second command quickly turned vicious and cruel.

"Workforce Gary, remove your shoe and kick this chair with as much force as you can muster." The spellbound subject immediately, and without any consideration for his own well-being, did as he was told. There were several nods of approval from the group. Then Mr. 28 gave his next command.

"Workforce Gary, bite a chunk of your forearm then chew it and swallow it." Amazingly, at least for the onlookers, the spellbound subject, again, did as he was directed. However, he fainted as he was chewing his own flesh. "Bravo. Well done, Mr. 28," came the sarcastic critique from the Good Doctor, which was accompanied by an insincere round of applause.

"I may have failed to mention that even though they cannot control their actions, they do control their own minds. Which is why they are able to carry out instructions, even complex and sophisticated ones. What you see here, gentlemen, is the same result as you'd expect to get from anyone who had undergone some very traumatic experience, such as being forced to eat your own flesh.

"My earlier instruction to bite a finger was at the edge of what we can push them to do, as far as self-inflicted injury. It is much easier to get people to injure others without any adverse reaction than it is to get them to hurt themselves. That is a horse of a much different color, gentlemen, as you have just witnessed. And for future reference, we must proceed with caution when traveling down that exceedingly murky boulevard.

"The good news for us is that all we need them to do is to work for us and do so for free. Less room and board, that is. You know, do things like plant the cannabis, the hemp, and the coca seeds. Like harvest them and cure them and package them and simple stuff like that. A bitten finger should quickly heal, but swallowing one's own flesh…that…well, that was simply brilliant. But in any event, is everyone satisfied that the promise of a spellbound workforce has been delivered? Well then, with no objection, we will now complete our tour of this place."

As the group walked and observed the many Godspoke workers busy executing their given instructions, the Good Doctor tried once more to shed a better light of understanding with regard to the awesome power of the Godspoke drug.

"Some of you may be wondering how the Godspoke works and what causes the spellbound effect. I know we said it robs the subject of all independent will, but *how* is the question I'm sure some of you have.

"Technically, after five minutes, the Godspoke attaches itself to the base of the brain stem. It then has the uncanny ability to block all the neurotransmitters that allow the process of free will. I know that sounds very complex, but in real simple terms, it works like this.

"All humans have a command center in their brain. It tells all the other parts what to do. The Godspoke locks the command center down so no messages can go out. No messages equals no action, so the person has to wait for external instructions. That's where we come in. Wish we could restructure it to control the female complaining," he said with a loud chuckle.

"Kidding aside," he said, directing everyone's attention to the vast expansion that lay before them. "This, my fellow entrepreneurs, is the fertile ground that will supply America and the world beyond with all the feel-good that they shall ever need. You gentlemen have stepped inside of our little piece of man-made paradise.

"As warm as the tropics, sunshine every day, and never a day with rain but plenty of irrigation. And if you look up, you will see what you'd swear to be the brilliant sun. Up there just shining down to warm this place, as if it were indeed a tropical island, even though it is very late autumn at present. How, you ask?

"Gentleman, you are inside what you know to be a biosphere. Although I must say that this fine piece of work is deserving of much more complex description. As previously mentioned, the technology on which this place is built, was, and still is mine. The financing, however, was sponsored by, shall we say, a few friends with the right government connections. Thank you again, gentlemen. You know who you are.

"With that said, I will let well enough alone, as you are aware some secrets are necessary. I am a firm believer in the theory that you cannot repeat what you don't know. Suffice it to say, this is an artificial world, the mad-happy world of make believe come true. Not only do we have absolute control over the workforce, we also have absolute control over the weather, so to speak.

"In here, we can recreate any atmospheric conditions on this or any other planet that we so desire. But that's not all we can do. No, no, gentlemen, we have taken man-made atmospheric conditions to the next level. We have actually found a way to speed up time itself. This science is called biogenics.

"Biogenics is the exact opposite of cryogenics, which is the science of slowing down molecules to the point that they do not age. This science, on the other hand, a breakthrough that rivals going to the moon, affects molecules in such a manner that it speeds up their growth. So in essence, it ultimately allows plant life to reproduce and grow at a much faster rate.

"Unfortunately, it does not have the same effect of humans, but we are working on that. With that science marvel, we could take some of these useless and throwaway kids, only to turn them into productive Godspoke workers. It would be wonderful for society and for us as well.

"Wishful thinking aside, in another setting, somewhere in the outside world, it would take a cannabis plant used to produce marijuana approximately six months to grow from a seedling into a mature plant. That means it would be ready for processing. In other words, ready to be turned into something prepared for human consumption.

"Now let's examine the facts. First, the cannabis or any other plant can grow no faster than the rate that its leaves can produce energy for new growth. When we began this project, our most important goal was to understand how to influence plant growth. We discovered that it all boils down to the daily number of hours of light versus dark a plant is exposed to, better known as the photoperiod.

"Under ideal growing conditions in nature, these plants are known to grow six inches a day, although, universally, the usual rate is one to two inches. We have successfully increased the daily photoperiod, and now our plants grow at least twelve inches a day, and they mature in only forty-five days.

"Well, just think of it, gentlemen, in this atmosphere, the same plants that everyone else must grow takes one-third of the time to grow, which no one else in the whole wide world can match. And even better, we have found that the faster growth creates much larger and healthier plants, which ultimately means more profits. The same is true for the hemp plant and the coca plant, which are used to produce heroin and cocaine, respectively. Are we getting impressed yet?" he asked devilishly.

"This is why our supply will be so plentiful. This is why there will never be a need to dilute our product and cut down on its potency. There will be no need to stretch it so as to increase profits. Which is also why we will all but corner the market. Which is, most importantly, why we will all be very, very rich come this time next year. Hell, even before then, if things go exceptionally well, which they should.

"To reiterate, we can create any atmospheric conditions on the planet and even beyond, if we so choose, by simply moving a few dials. This place is constantly monitored so that the temperature remains a constant ninety-two degrees Fahrenheit, and the humidity a modest fifteen percent or less so that it's very warm but at the same time not at all unpleasant.

"Again for security reasons, I will not mention the exact square footage of this sphere, but as mentioned before, right now, we have the capacity to produce enough feel-good," he said with both passion and vigor, "to supply the entire US and then some. Gentlemen, we shall now go to the heliport and take an aerial view of what you have just witnessed."

The group left the underworld compound in the same fashion as they had arrived, through the remarkable glass walkway, into the secret incognito elevator, and out of the walk-in wine cellar. On the west lawn of the estate was a helipad with five idling choppers, each ready to take flight. As instructed, the group split up and boarded. Once he had conducted a validation check to be certain of two-way communication between the aerial vehicles, the Good Doctor gave the command for liftoff.

"Okay, Charlie, let's get these things in the air. All right then, now that we have a clear aerial view of the place, I would say the layout is quite impressive, wouldn't you agree, gentlemen? Now then, as you can see from this very meaningful vantage point, the estate and the grounds for miles behind it is clearly visible. You should also take notice of the pool, the tennis court, the stables, and the wine cellar.

"If you will now direct your attention to the riding trails and the area behind the property line so that you may survey and scrutinize once again? What do you see? Well, I will tell you what you see. You see a bunch of weeping willow trees, and that is all you see. Is there anyone of you that sees anything out of the ordinary?" There was another symphony of silently shaking heads in response to this question.

Then without warning, and at the top of his lungs, the Good Doctor yelled out to no one in particular, "Dammit-to-hell! My headset is giving me feedback!" After a long concerted pause, the Good Doctor excused himself for the out-of-character outburst. And then, in a surreal and monotone voice, which was always an indicative sign that his sub-surface anger was about to boil over, he continued, "I hate it when things malfunction, because that usually, and I do stress usually, spells incompetence, and I will not tolerate incompetence in my organization." Although he sought to control his growing anger at least temporarily, his emotions were extremely evident. "Charlie, who is in charge of aerial communications?" he asked calmly.

"Gus," came the one-word reply.

"Very well then. Give me your headset. Hey, Gus, as you heard, my headset was out. Did you receive my previous transmission in that chopper?" Without waiting for a response, he proceeded to repeat his previous statements about the estate and the view below. "Very well then, pilots, let's get these babies back on the ground. You really would not believe it. As much as I fly, I really detest it," he said, looking directly at Mr. 28 who could only who offer a fake smile.

Now back on the ground, the Good Doctor could barely contain himself, even though it was in his best interest to do so in front of his guest. He was seething. "Gus, did you check and test the communications equipment on this machine earlier today?"

"Why, yes, Good Doctor. I did."

"Then why did it fail?"

"I don't know, Good Doctor."

"I don't know is not sufficient, Gus. Do you have a better answer?"

"No, Good Doctor."

"Charlie, give me your belt. Gus, remove your shirt."

"Yes, sir."

"Now hold on to this belt and stand right there until I get back, and do not make the mistake of moving even one inch."

And without another word on the subject, he led the group back to the roundtable. "Gentlemen, right this way please. We shall reconvene back in the boardroom where I am certain they have something for us to nibble on, as well as some contracts for us to sign.

"However, first things first. Gentleman, one quick announcement. When you first entered this room, my audio techs released a plutonium pulse, which in fact neutralized any recording devices and white noised any video surveillance transmitters that you may have opted to bring with you.

"That was some two hours ago, and you must be warned that any neutralized device that was affected by the pulse will in fact become radioactive and thereafter fatally lethal within the next thirty minutes. Therefore, I am going to afford you the opportunity to remove any such devices from your person, large or small, so that you, nor any of us, will be adversely affected by their continued presence.

"I will, in fact, step out of the room momentarily, but moreover, I will also darken the room. You will have the opportunity to anonymously remove the aforementioned audiovisual devices and place them in one of these two very large baskets. As I leave the room, and I will be gone for approximately ninety-nine seconds, I want all of you to get out of your seats and move about the room so that the cloak of anonymity will remain constant.

"When I return, I will ask everyone to be seated, and at that time the baskets will be removed. You have absolutely nothing to fear in the way of reprisal, because as I see it, before you got here, you did not know what you were walking into. And if I were in your shoes, I certainly would have been tempted to do likewise."

The room went completely black. The sound of objects dropping into both baskets could be heard above the faint whispers of the room's occupants. "Now that we have taken care of that nasty little matter, we can move on to much more pleasant things, namely the money.

"Again, first things first though. The contract being placed before you, as we speak, is a limited partnership agreement. Each partnership agreement is unique in that no two are alike, because each of you is a limited partner for a different reason, providing a different service or a distinctive asset. Your signature is required so that we can ensure your loyalty to this organization. Anyone that does not wish to sign this agreement may stand up now so that you may leave.

"I see there is no one. Very good then. You have all made a very prudent and sagacious choice, because in the end, all of you will be greatly rewarded for that same said prudence. We all know that people want to get high. We know they want to escape. And they want to get away from it all. And to be truthful, some just want to have a good time. In any case, they will spend lots of money to achieve these ends.

"In any event, our job, from this day forward, will be to help them meet their needs. So here is to drugs, power, and money! But most of all, here is to you being rich. Very, very rich. In fact, the

SAGS accountants have estimated that our first fiscal year of operation should net us approximately five billion dollars in profits. Let me repeat that, gentlemen. The SAGS accountants have estimated that the first fiscal year of operation should net us approximately five billion dollars. That is nine zeros, gentlemen. Nine sweet zeros.

"As stated in your partnership agreement, you are a shareholder in this corporation and as such are entitled to five percent of the net profits. Now I do not know how many of you are mathematicians or even good at math, but five percent of five billion equals 250 million. That would be US dollars. That is the low-end figure, and that number could get quite higher. Now again, I do not know about you gentlemen, but to me 250 million dollars is a whole lot of money. In no uncertain terms, that is a whole lot of fucking money. And to think; it could be substantially more.

"A few years of this and we can all retire to a beach in Tahiti or somewhere. Somewhere with warm tropical breezes, cool refreshing drinks in the day, and hot sizzling women in the night. Gentlemen, lift your drinks if you are in agreement. Here, here. Here, here. I think I speak for us all when I say it really, and I mean really, really does not get any better than this.

"Now as mentioned, we have a vast network to create. Some of you will be responsible for the transportation of our very profitable product. Some of you will be responsible for the sale and the collection of the proceeds from our very profitable product. Still others of you will be responsible for laundering the proceeds from our very profitable product. While still others of you will be responsible for monitoring the work of your partners. And yes, there will be monitors to monitor the monitors.

"That may sound somewhat troubling to some, but consider this small bit of logic. I would only care if I am monitored if I have something to hide from my partners. Think about it, gentlemen. I would only be concerned about being monitored if that monitoring would reveal something that I wanted to remain hidden and in the dark. Makes real good sense, huh? In any event, and after all is said and done, each of you will have a numbered account, which will contain a monthly payment toward your annual earnings in excess of 250 million dollars.

"Please, print and sign your full name. And by all means, do not forget to date it. My assistant will be around shortly to collect them from you. The instructions' detailing your responsibilities is yours to keep. Additionally, before you is what appears to be a regular telephone. However, it is not.

"It is a two-way communications device, but it only transmits to any one of the other units. It sends a scrambled signal, which allows us to be in direct contact without the fear of being compromised in any fashion.

"Please remember that you must keep it with you at all times. It is impervious to moisture, water, or physical damage from repeated dropping. Short of you taking a hammer and beating the damn thing, it will serve you for many years to come. Please be advised that each time it is activated, this device emits the same plutonium pulse of which I spoke earlier. The pulse is continuous until such time as there is no communication for at least thirty seconds.

"The pulse will not harm you in any fashion unless you have on your person or are in close proximity of a listening device of any kind. If there is such a listening device in your immediate presence, without your knowledge, of course, the pulse will detect it. It will immediately interrupt the transmission, and a low beep will emit from your communications device, thus making you aware. After you hear these low beeps, you must remove yourself from your present locale and thereafter reset the device. That is accomplished by depressing this button on top, which then allows you to reinitiate transmission."

"Good Doctor. Good Doctor, is it?"

"Yes, Mr. Lincoln? But did you forget the rules?"

"I think I have heard enough. I did not sign on for any pulses or devices that can kill me or spy on me. I think it is now time for us to part company. I no longer wish to be a part of this great opportunity. In parting, however, I wish to thank you for considering me, and let me assure you now that anything I have heard here today shall never part my lips. I am a true man of honor. I respect the code, and I would not betray your trust under any circumstances."

"Mr. Lincoln, I am very disappointed in your decision, but nonetheless, you may take your leave. Right this way, sir. My assistant will show you the out to your limo." The man wearing the Lincoln mask exited through a side door. Instantaneously, the room went dark, and a section of the wall rose to reveal a two-way mirror.

As Mr. Lincoln was waiting for a second door to open, a man previously identified as Workforce LJ shot him in the back of the head at point-blank range. The occupants of the room gasped at the execution-style murder that they had just witnessed. The raised section of the wall was then lowered, and the lights came up.

"Gentlemen, as you can now clearly see, ours is an offer that you should not refuse. You have been carefully chosen, and our ultimate success depends on you. As we speak, dossiers are being placed in front of you. In it are all the intimate details of your life, beginning with your childhood. We know all about you. We know all about your family and your friends. We know your preferences, and we even know your little dirty secrets.

"So again, please know that this is not an offer that can or should be refused. You did not choose us. We chose you. This offer is the same as if God spoke!" After pausing to look into the eyes and possibly the souls of each man seated at the roundtable, the Good Doctor asked with certainty, "Now does anyone have anything that they want to say?"

No one dared move a muscle. Seeing their collective total submission, the Good Doctor flashed the smile of a conqueror and concluded, "Well then, welcome to our little happy family."

CHAPTER 12

Almost Caught

Tired and out of breath, the last best hope for the Mathews 7 stopped to take a breather. At this very moment, the entire weight of the world seemed to rest squarely on his weakened shoulders. As far as he knew, he was the only one in a position to save the others, so he rebuked himself for acknowledging the tired, near-exhaustion feeling that was in full command of him at that very minute.

"A good solider never leaves his comrades on the battlefield," he said through staggered breaths. He sucked in all the air he could force into his sore lungs, and he heard his heart pounding through his expanded chest. He knew he could not give up or give in. He knew he had to keep going no matter what measure of physical or psychological pain he was forced to endure.

The close call of nearly being captured brought a new sense of urgency to him. The thought of them all held hostage and God only knows what else made him all the more resolved to complete his mission. He began this day wanting to get in touch with his father so that he could enlist his aid, and he was determined that he would not fail no matter what!

As he continued on his run for dear life, he could not help but think about his savior turned captor turned savior. "Carmen told me that I needed to cross the road just a little ways past the road sign that reads thirteen miles to town. I wonder about her though. Can I really trust her? And why did she really set me up only to save me?

"Maybe she saved me to set me up another way. Naw, that makes no sense. But let's see. First she acts like she's into me and on my side, then she sells me out. Then she turns around and saves me. Wow! This shit reads about like some double agent spy thriller stuff. I don't know, but I do know she's one very hot babe. Beautiful women can confuse you. Just look at how Pam makes me crazy."

A passing car caused the wounded warrior to stop, drop, crawl, and roll to avoid detection. As he crawled on his belly toward safety, he was pierced repeatedly by what felt like the sharp prickly thorns that can only be found in the midst of a very dry and mature briar patch. The intense stinging pain was concentrated on his lower abdomen and only served to compound the painful stings that he received earlier from his small buddies, the red army ants. He wanted quite badly to scream out so as to alleviate some of the searing pain, but he knew that he could not afford that luxury as it could well cost him his freedom.

Instead, he grimaced in silence like the exceptional solider that he was, and he made his way to cover. As he rolled and reached the edge of the ditch by the side of the road, he expertly tumbled to its shallow bottom. Although submerged in what seemed like a foot of muddy water, he did not mind at all. The coolness that was found at the bottom of the shallow water soothed his aching belly, if only temporarily.

After soothing his wounds momentarily, he peeked above the ridge of the ditch to see if all was clear. It was, and with all of the swiftness of a big jungle cat, he sprang to his feet and dashed across the highway. He stealthily moved down the same path used by the carload of gunmen who had helped to kidnap his brothers and his beloved Pam.

About half a mile into his mad dash, he thought to himself, *I wish Pam could see me now, trying to save everyone. She would be so proud and loving to me.* Then an alternate reality flashed before him as he pictured Pam saying, "Well, it's about time. What took you so long?" He could only smile as he continued at a frantic pace.

Just then, another loud noise captured his attention, and he immediately dropped to the hard ground. As he settled into his hiding spot of the moment, he heard what he thought to be bubbling noises. It sounded as if there was something being filled with air or air being let out of something.

His first instinct was to run first and ask questions later, but something stilled him this time. This time, this noise did not seem so eminently dangerous. So he overruled his natural instinct to run in the opposite direction and instead headed, albeit cautiously, toward the source of the noise.

Again, he found himself in a familiar scene as he crept cautiously on his belly. About fifty yards into this snail-paced crawl, his eyes could not believe what they thought they saw. LJ's Escalade was nose deep in the middle of what looked to be a big puddle of mud. However, Greg knew better. He knew instantly and for certain that his brother's car was slowly sinking in quicksand.

And just as he was wrapping his mind around the fact that the Escalade was sinking, something just to the left of this scene caught his attention. It was his Lexus. It was cleverly, albeit lazily, concealed underneath some brush about fifty or sixty feet away from the quicksand.

After checking to ensure that the coast was still clear, Greg cautiously approached the abandoned vehicle. As he did, he could not help but think of how much he loved this car. He brushed some of the dust off with his hands and shook his head in disgust. *Look what they've done to my baby. I would never let you get this dirty, girl. Never,* he vowed.

"Hey, I might be able to use this," he said as he removed two long bungee cords from the bike rack in the rear of the car. Pam just had to bring her own personal bike, stating that no other bike fit her just right.

He smiled to himself as he remembered the very day he drove it off the showroom floor with Pam watching close by, generating her brightest smile of approval. This was, after all, his first brand-new car, and it was a top-of-the-line Lexus. Not his ideal choice, but it was a luxury that he had to have; especially if he wanted to keep Pam quiet.

She always complained about his sporty Nissan Maxima because his brothers drove better cars.

Thoughts of those days and all of the fighting with Pam made his head ache. Without much effort, he shook away those thoughts and refocused on the matter at hand.

"Now let's see how lucky I am. Hopefully, those assholes didn't lock the doors. I mean, who's going to come out here to steal it?"

"Aw dammit, who in the hell locks the door of a stolen car out in the middle of nowhere? Now how do I get in the car without sounding the alarm? Man, I wish I had a Lincoln Navigator. They have those handy keypads on both front doors. Press a four-digit number and bam, you're in the car."

Frustrated after pulling and tugging each of the doors to not avail, he slumped down beside his beloved automobile. A million thoughts raced through his mind about how he could solve his dilemma, and all he got was a million rejections as counter thoughts. Then out of the blue, it hit him.

"Aw man, I think I have that little valet credit card-style key that they gave me in my wallet." As he reached for his wallet, half hoping and half praying that it was there, he tried to use every distraction imaginable in order to forget about the fear that presently engulfed his entire psyche. He did not, at all, like this totally foreign feeling of being deathly afraid. He then pretended to mock his tormenters by cheering himself on in cadence style. "Go, Greg, it's your birthday. Go, Greg, it's your birthday. Go ahead, go ahead, they stupid, not me, they stupid, not me."

He momentarily held his breath as he opened his wallet, only to exhale in a sigh of great relief when he found the key just where he had put it. He then stood up confidently, forgetting for the moment where he was and why he was there. Then he said aloud, "A bunch of redneck porch monkeys can't stop the kid."

Right then and there, he felt a little bit better. Finding that key was a real confidence booster. Along with his newly found small bit of confidence, he even had some hope that his current situation was about to improve. However, all that momentary confidence would soon abandon him.

SAME AS GOD SPOKE

Carefully, he slid the fragile valet's key in the passenger side door and turned it, but nothing happened. The door did not unlock. He tried several more times, but to no avail, until frustration began to set in. He returned to his previous position of being hopelessly slumped next to his beloved vehicle.

"Now I know that *this is the right fucking key!*" he yelled out in frustration. Realizing that he had done so, he sat up to look around to be sure that no had heard him. "Shit," he said in anger, only this time not so loud. "I only have one car and one valet key. Why won't this stupid thing work?" Again and again he tried, but to no avail.

He was entirely mystified as to why the key didn't work. He suddenly felt sick. "Now I know that I have never used this thing before, but it still should work. Maybe I had to call Lexus in order to activate it or something. No, that can't be it," he reasoned. "Why wouldn't they activate at the dealership when I picked it up? That would just be stupid on so many levels.

"What is it then?" he continued to think a loud. "Maybe they gave me the wrong key at the dealership. Oh hell no, that can't be it either. It must be something else. I know that I'm just missing something. Think, Greg, think. Come on, get your shit together now and stop acting like a brain-dead blond."

Before his next thought could reach maturity, it's development was suspended by a new round of fear. A white van was noisily making its way back down the pathway to where he sat crouched next to his car. It was the same white van that had carried his family away.

He quickly scrabbled to the surrounding brush and assumed the all-too familiar position of hiding from someone that wanted to do him harm. *Boy, is this getting old,* he thought as he stilled himself as the van came to a halt.

"Hey, that first one is done. Let's get this other one in there too."

"Okay. Help me move all these stupid ass branches and shit. You got the key?"

"Hell naw. I ain't got it. You was the one that drove it over here. You should have it. You had it last."

"I didn't have it last, 'cause when I got out of the car, I handed you the key, and you hung it on the mirror in the van so we wouldn't lose it. See, you dummy? Told ya I didn't have the key, and I didn't. Least ways that's how it all turned out."

"Now get the stupid key and drive this fucker in there and please stop giving me so much shit about everything I ask you to do. I'm already on edge. You know we got this huge dark cloud over our head, and we got to make some serious moves or we gonna be fish food tonight."

As instructed, he backed the vehicle up and drove it to the edge of the quicksand. He held the brake, opened the driver side door, and quickly exited the running vehicle. It rolled slowly two feet forward and plopped into the quicksand where the nose began its long awkward and painstakingly slow decent into the abyss. The lesser of the partners in crime had a sudden thought. "Hey, I wonder," he said inquisitively.

"You wonder what?" came the terse reply.

"I wonder how far down they go. I mean with quicksand. It's like stuff goes in and never stops going down. Least that what it seem to me. We been putting cars in here for a good lil while now. I wonder when they will pile up so high that they reach back up to the edge."

"You see that what's wrong with people like you. Why you gotta think about dumb shit? How high they pile up? Who gives a rat's ass if they pile up or when they pile up. We got a job to do, and it don't include much wondering bout that dumb shit. What you gotta be worried about is whether you will be living or dead come tomorrow."

Greg watched in horror as the two men carried on like an old married couple who were tired of each other but could not stand the thought of being without the other—a classic love-hate relationship. However, their asinine conversation was not the true source of his horror. That dubious distinction went to the sight of his beloved top-of-the-line Lexus slowly sinking in the quicksand.

"Should we wait while it goes down? What do ya think?"

"I think you are as dumb as you look. Hell no. And anyway, I do not know why you insisted that we come back here in the first place. We could have sunk that shit anytime. That jackass who escaped does not even know about this place. Even if he did, why would he want to come back over here?

"First he ain't got no keys to the car. We took that. Besides that, hell, everybody in town is looking for him, including the sheriff and both of his deputies. Everybody thinks he is a rapist. Plus they are on the lookout for the car. So even if he got back here and hotwired it, he could not drive it far without being stopped. Duh!

"But the biggest reason of all why we should not be here is because we have someplace else to be. You heard what the Good Doctor said. Time is running out, and if we don't find him again and soon, our ass is grass! Cut grass!" he said as an emphatic exclamation point.

"Well, for your information, just so's you know, if we don't find him soon, I am catching the first thing smoking. I know what we said earlier, but personally, boat, plane, train or automobile, I don't give a fuck. When the time comes, I'm gettin' on it."

"Will you shut the fuck up and stop whining? Hey, hold up a minute. I think I heard something."

"What?"

"Shush, be quiet. I really do think I heard something."

"What did you hear?"

"If you would shut the fuck up, I could hear what I heard."

Greg's heart began to pound at a furious pace. Ge wondered if he had moved to cause some small crackle or create some slight noise. He always enjoyed sharing the riddle about the tree falling in the woods and nobody being around and if it makes a sound. He argued the answer many times, but this was the real thing, and only now this was no riddle. Moreover, he was the tree, and somebody was around.

He froze every other body part, but he obviously could not stop his heart from beating. Although he did try. It seemed to beat so hard, he surely thought his two hide-and-seek buddies would hear it. As still as the very earth beneath him, he gathered himself and engaged in a very focused effort to control both his pounding heart as well as his exaggerated breathing.

"Oh damn, whatever it was, I don't hear it anymore. Whatever it was, your big ass mouth probably ran it away. Shit, you done messed up my supper," he said jokingly. "It was probably one of them great big old elk or a fat juicy deer. We coulda been eatin' good tonight," he said with a gleeful pat on his partner's back.

"Well, now it's gone. Now get your stupid ass back in the van and let's go. 'Cause, boy, if our goddamn luck don't change for the much better in the next few hours, I am heading straight south, and I ain't looking back." As he climbed in and slammed the door behind him, that last words Greg heard him say were, "If we do not find his guy, I will tell ya what. I'll be right with ya."

Greg remained still until he could no longer hear the noisy white van that brought him so much misery in such a short period. Then like a bolt of lightning, it hit him. He remembered that the valet key only worked in the driver's side door and the ignition. But his vehicle was in the quicksand. Though it was not very far along, and the rear wheels were still on the solid earth behind the quicksand plot.

He quickly scoured the surrounding area and grabbed two handful of vines. He had learned to make extremely strong rope out of common dead plants with no tools. He decided the dogbane close by had to do, but he preferred the milkweed he passed a good ways up the path. It would take several minutes using the reverse wrap technique, which can turn any decent fiber into a sturdy cord.

As he just about to begin the arduous task of executing this water-to-wine miracle, he had a eureka moment. "What the hell do I need to make a rope for when I have bungee cords?" He sprinted back to his hiding spot and hastily picked up the cords that he had thrown there. "I sure am glad Pam insisted on bringing that bike!" he said, smiling.

He first tied one to the other using the strongest knot he knew how to tie—the double figure-eight loop, most commonly used by rock climbers. He then tied one end to a nearby tree and attached the other to his waist. He did not want to risk being caught in the quicksand if his added weight speeded up the vehicle's descent to the bottom, wherever that was. He nervously chuckled, thinking back to the dumb comment made by one of his dim-witted pursuers.

Easing his way up to the driver's door, he entered the unlocked cockpit. It saddened him that he was about to lose the best car he ever had. He thought, if only for a minute, that he could save the car. He imagined he could put it in reverse and hopefully back it out of harm's way. The pleasant thought quickly turned bad when he pictured himself being chased or pulled over by the local authorities. After all, rightly or wrongly, the fact was he was a wanted man in these parts.

Once inside, he removed the ignition key and opened the glove compartment, and underneath some of those courtesy napkins that everyone hordes from fast-food restaurants, he found what he was looking for. With Pam's cleverly hidden cell phone in hand, he was just about to exit the doomed vehicle when something in the rear-view mirror caught his attention.

The white van had suddenly come back. He was trapped. He didn't have time to jump out of the car and make a run for it. The nose of the car was now submerged, and he would have to navigate the quicksand to get back to safety. By the time he would pull himself out, he knew they would already be on him. He would just have to wait inside the tinted vehicle and hope that they were not back to watch it go completely under.

"Help me look," came the loud, obnoxious, and now familiar voice of Chuck. "I knowed I lost it right around here somewhere. I had it when we got here. Goddamnit, I hope I dint leave it in that goddamn stankin' ass car. It done damn near sunk, and I couldn't get to it even if I wanted to. Come on, Ole Roscoe, help me look, goddammit. This shit ain't funny. You standing over there laughing and snickering. This shit ain't funny at all. Come on, Roscoe. Now don't do me thisa way. Help me out here."

"It is too funny. Boy, this ain't yo day. First, we get threatened with a killing. Next we almost get killed with them damn tasers. And now this. Boy, I know yo momma give you that phone, and I'd hate to be the one that gotta tell her you done lost it. Man oh man, she gone set fire to yo ass. Hot damn, boy. This is some funny shit all right. Funny as hell. Hey, did you look over there by the bushes? Look there where we put the car at first."

"Naw, I didn't, but while you giving orders, goddammit, you coulda been looking ya damn self. It ain't over here."

"Well, ole boy, I hate to say it, but that phone of yourn is going down to the bottom of quicksand alley with that there pretty ass Lexus. Unless yo gonna hop on back and try to get it? I say forget it so we can get going."

Peeping over the seat, Greg could make out most of what the two men were saying. His only problem was that he wished with all his might that they would finish saying whatever it was that they were saying, very soon. He really wanted to avoid his third shot at death in one day. "Yeah, yeah, get going. His stupid ass phone ain't in here. If you wasn't trying to kill me, I'd tell you that," he said sarcastically.

As he listened to the now recognizable bubbling sounds of air escaping, he felt his Lexus slowly sinking beneath him. He thought it strangely ironic that two cell phones might ultimately decide how things would turn out. The one in his hand had the potential to save him, and his family, for that matter. Ironically, another cell phone, the one that Bevis and Butt-Head were searching for could well seal his fate to a muddy death and God knows what to his family.

Again, his mind raced as he considered his options. He first considered jumping out and taking his chances in a two-on-one fight to the death. Those odds were not too appealing, even though he did not think much of the two against him in a fair hand-to-hand combat situation. The only problem was they had guns. And as stupid as they were and as scared as they were of their own fate, they would probably shoot first and ask questions later. *If they were to let me get away three times in one day, they would be definitely killed if they botched this up!*

"Two on one...*not!*" He then thought about sitting tight and getting out after they had gone. "This car is very well-made. I only hope there is no pressure to burst the windows once I go under. I don't think I heard the windows break on LJ's car when it went under. I know a Lexus is better made than Cadillac.

"I may have a chance," he reasoned some more. "I'm inside a large roomy compartment, and there should be plenty of air for me to last ten or fifteen minutes after I go under. If they left in time, I may still be able to get out. Plus my bungee cord still has some slack."

"Hey, let's go, Chuck. It ain't here, so let's go."

"Hell naw, Roscoe. I needs my phone! You got yourn, so hold ya damn horses."

"You said a minute and a minute is all you got. Now hurry the fuck up."

"Man, I needs my damn phone. This is some bullshit."

"Hey, Chuck, you dipshit. Look at what I got in my hand."

"Hot damn, Roscoe, you found it."

"I know I did, but yo dumb ass shoulda found it. It was right here in the wedge of the seat. All I did was dial the number and it rang." The lost phone now found, the two men climbed in the van and quickly made a U-turn.

Having witnessed the departure of those hot in pursuit of him, Greg tried unsuccessfully to open the driver's side door, which was all but submerged at this time. He stretched out across the seat and pushed with all he was worth, but to no avail. He was barely able to crack the door, but that actually made things worse. The sticky mud began to ooze into the cabin.

"What do I do now? What do I do now?" he asked himself over and over. A million burning questions crept slowly into his mind, but rapid-fire answers filled his head in response. He immediately set about putting those thoughts to good use.

First, he took off his bungee cord and climbed into the back seat, and then again over the seat into the rear compartment. He then pushed the button on his keys that signaled the lift gate, and it popped open. The back of the vehicle was not yet fully submerged, but because the nose of the car was submerged, the vehicle was vertical. He would have to make a four-foot jump for it, and he would have to do it soon.

The downward descent of the car was hastened by its now totally vertical position. It seemed like an easy jump of just four feet, but there was some major risk involved. If he misjudged his jump, he could land in the river of slow death and die an agonizing inch-by-inch death. Everyone knew that it was almost impossible to escape the clutches of quicksand without some assistance.

He decided to risk it and jump and threw caution to the wind, but something threw it right back and he paused. He wanted to think this thing through just once more and be sure he had no other option. Although the longer he waited, the higher the quicksand got and the less of a height advantage he would have when he did finally jump, as he knew he would eventually be forced to do. Then another eureka moment. What happened to his bungee cord, his safety rope? If he could grab it, he would have a much better chance.

He looked to the side of the car, and there it was, lying on top of the murky mess. But it was just out of his outstretched arms. He quickly scanned the back of his car and found a mascot cane that he used at an alma mater party hosted by his alumni chapter. With the aid of the cane, he was able to grab the cord, secure it around his waist, and jump to safety.

Turns out he didn't need the cord after all, but he always believed in his training, which mandated an ounce of prevention over a pound of cure. It was a good thing the sun had all but set and dusk had settled in over the thick wooded area. The dynamic duo had not noticed the cord at all. Things could have been very different if they had.

Glad to be safe on solid ground again, he was tempted to bend down and salute the earth with a great big kiss, but he thought better of it and refocused on getting help. "Thank *God* for cell phones! I just knew my little prima donna would not travel outside the city limits without her constant ear companion. She stays on the phone more than most operators. Ha, ha, ha." He laughed to himself. He powered up the phone and laughed aloud some more as he saw it come to life. "I got a full clip baby. I got a full clip, hot damn!

"I knew if anybody would have a fully charged battery, it would be my sweet talkative Pamela! Man oh man, that anal retentive little heifer is so predictable. God, I love her! Now, let me call Dad so we can put an end to this fucking nightmare. I got a few rednecks I want to stomp a mudhole in. The signal is weak. I only got one bar. Let's see, if I move around a little. How bout here? No good. Well, how bout here? No better. And over this way? No, no, no. Shit, this is getting worse. Why won't anything go my way?

"Please, God, if you care even just a little, please let this thing work. No, no, no! I said please. Now let it work, damn it! That's worse. Okay, God, I'm sorry I said damn it. Okay, okay, don't panic. Every time something was wrong, all you had to do was figure it out calmly and coolly. Now think. What makes cell phone work or not work? I know. It's all of this brush and trees and these woods. I know. I'll go back closer to the road.

"Okay, ditch, where are you? Closer, closer. Come on, baby. Work for Daddy. Come on, baby. Come on. Oh yeah, two bars. Oh yeah, two and a half. Now three bars. That's it. Okay, three bars. I won't be greedy, so I am not moving. This is good enough.

"Aw damn, the voice mail. Any other time his give-orders-all-the-time ass would have answered the stupid phone. Hello, Dad, this is Greg. Listen to this message very carefully, as I may not be able to repeat it any time soon. I have a very weak signal out here so you may not be able to get me back. Me and Pam and LJ and Henry and Milton and Beverley and Hazel and Misty came down here to *Coulditbe*, Pennsylvania, a small resort town about three odd miles on the other side of Hershey, somewhere near the Pocono Mountains.

"We checked into this villa that is owned by some guys that wanted LJ's company to get some investors for them. They gave us all a free stay so that LJ and Henry could decide better about helping them raise some investment money. Okay, okay, I know I'm rambling, but I'm tired, I'm hurt, I'm being chased by the police and a bunch of men with guns, and did I mention that I have been accused of a rape that I did not commit?

"And one more thing, did I forget to say that LJ and all the rest have been abducted and that they have the whole town looking for me? I think I said that. But anyway, Dad, I can't explain it all now, but I need you to come and get me and to help me get the others. I don't know where they are, but I can tell you where I am. Almost.

"I am hold up at the bottom of the ditch on route 1. I think the mile marker said 17.9. And I think I've told you that we are in Pennsylvania. Hurry, Dad. Hurry. We need you, and bring lots of help. We are going to need it. The police are even in on this thing. I know I'm supposed to be the bad boy of the family, but right now I am powerless to really do much on my own. As I said, the whole town is looking for me on a phony rape charge.

"I don't have any weapons, and even if I did, I'd be greater outnumbered. I don't think I can take out twenty or thirty guys by myself like they do in the movies. Oh yeah, did I tell you that they hit LJ in the mouth with a shotgun? I think he was hurt bad. Really bad. So please come. Please come soon. We need you.

"I'll tell you everything about how I got away and everything else when I see you. You can try to call me, but I don't know if the call will get through because I can't stay where I'm standing right now. Someone may see me. Right now, it's about six in the afternoon. I will call you back exactly at seven o'clock, so hope you answer the phone. I love you, Dad."

Without much notice, the white van reappeared, and all Greg had time to do was duck right where he was. His fear factor was immediately elevated because he thought the hunting party of two would realize that he was in the car because the cargo gate was raised. But he quickly dismissed that thought because the pressure could have done that as well. "I would feel a lot better if I had been able to get across the street. But what the fuck, I think I'm pretty safe right here.

"Oh, God, please help me now! What did I do to deserve this?" he said in another temporary moment of panic. "I didn't get no pussy last night, my family has been abducted, I have been accused of raping that maid and I did not so much as smell the pussy, and now here comes some crazy redneck fuckers that are going to kill me. Okay, God, whatever I did, I am extremely, and I mean very, and I mean really, really, very, very sorry for it. Please forgive me!"

The white van passed his well-concealed hiding spot and turned down the dirt road to head toward the quicksand. From his hiding vantage point, Greg observed both the passenger together with the driver exit the vehicle, slap hands in satisfaction, and return to their vehicle. Greg's heart slowed its fast-paced beating. After taking a moment to gather himself, he waited for the van to pass again and road to be clear and crossed to the other side and on to what he deemed to be safety, at least for now.

CHAPTER 13

DEAD ON THE CASE

"Sara, please hold all my calls and cancel all of my appointments. I have to leave town right away. I have an emergency. Greg called and left me an urgent distress message. So drop whatever you were doing and get my guys on the line. I have a situation that calls for a Black Ivory solution, if any ever did.

"I know my son. The way he sounded…I know this must be real serious. First off, I am going to need all the intelligence that I can get. So hit all your inside contacts. I'm gonna need you to call in any and all favors that you've got out there. Let's leave no stone unturned on this one, Sara.

"I'm really worried. And worse of all, I am mostly in the dark. His message was altogether scattered but overall very clear. He is in danger. They all are. Truthfully, I'm scared for them, and I don't like feeling like this. Now let's get moving here. Do something, *please!*"

Sensing his internal struggle to keep it together, Sara finally interrupted her employer of the last twelve plus years. She offered him a much-needed word of counsel. "Mr. Matthews, no matter how serious it is, you have many years of training and experience in these types of situations. And there is nobody under the sun, moon, or stars that can put together and execute a plan like you and the Black Ivory team. So no matter the situation, now that you are on the case, it is all but taken care of.

"Who does it better, Mr. Matthews? You tell me. Who does it better?" she asked a second time. Only before he could answer, she did so herself. "Nobody, with a capital *N*. That's who. Nobody! Now gather your thoughts like you always do! Think of all the angles like you always do! See the situation from the bad guys' side like you always do! Then give the bad guys some irresistible bait just like you always do. And before you know it, you will have accomplished another successful mission *just like you always do!*"

Thoughtfully, he said, "I know the best thing to do at a time like is to remain calm, cool, and collected. And I know I'm supposed to remain emotionally detached so that I can maintain my objective perspective. I know all of that, but I gotta tell you, Sara, when it's your kids who are in harm's way, what you know and how you feel are worlds apart. I can't imagine that he would send me such a message if it were not exactly as he describes.

"Anyway, I heard you loud and clear. Sara, you are a treasure to me. How did I ever find you?"

"My father, that's how," she blurted out in reply, and they both shared a needed moment of laughter and tension relief.

"Okay, now that I have my senses about me, let's get to work. I have to get on the road and head up to Coulditbe, Pennsylvania, to see what this is all about. And you have to get me some intelligence by the time I get there. You can phone once you have some specifics. In the meantime, I spent the last half hour extracting any information and clues from his message. It's all here on this pad, so you can work from that for now."

Before leaving, BJ once again conveyed to his assistant the seriousness of the situation. "Sara, I know you are as good as they come as it relates to paying attention to fine details. In most cases, I do not have to even tell you what is needed, and somehow you just instinctively know what will be needed. You always seem to have it available, even before we know to ask for it. Please do not be anything less than that on this one. I feel like my boys have gotten themselves into something a lot bigger than they know, and it is literally up to me and you to save them."

"You can count on me like always," came the reassuring words that the part father, part soldier of fortune team commander needed to hear at that moment.

BJ sat in his Chevrolet Suburban and held the steering wheel with as tight a grip as he could muster. "I am not going to allow my emotions to get the better of me. I am not going to allow my emotions to get the better of me," he repeated several times over.

"Emotions are for the reactive. Deductive reasoning is for the proactive. I am proactive. I don't get emotional. I make the other side get emotional, expose a weak point, then I capitalize by exploiting their weakness. I will not be the weak point that jeopardizes the lives of my boys.

"Okay, let's get rolling. First thing, make mental list. Call Red China to get an ETA on the strike team. Second, call Sara to check on any updates. Third, call Greg just to see if I can get an answer. Fourth, hit the safe house vault to get some goodies. You never know. Better to have it and not need it than to need it and not have it. Fifth, and finally, hit the highway and haul ass down to Coulditbe."

He made a meticulous mental list of things to do, and then he did what he always did—he checked the list twice. Satisfied with his list, he started his car and went about the business of accomplishing his self-defined tasks.

"Yes, hello, can I speak to Red China? Yes, I will hold. Why does anybody put this stupid elevator music on? Red China, hey there, good buddy. It's been a good little while, huh? How the hell are you? Good, good. I am glad to hear that you're holding on with both hands and still scared to let go. You always did use that line. That's classic and funny as hell too. Anyway, I'm glad that everything is all right. I wish I could say the same.

"Fact is, this is a Black Ivory call of the highest urgency. It involves my family. Earlier today, I received a distress call from one of my boys. He tells me that he is down in a small town on the other side of Hershey, Pennsylvania, called Coulditbe. Ever heard of it? Well, I've never heard of the place either, but be that as it may, apparently, he and his brothers went down there and got into some serious trouble. The story is they were invited down so that they could make an assessment of some property that the owners were trying to use as collateral to raise some investment capital.

"To make a long story short, it seems to me that this invitation was given to facilitate an ambush. Greg said he witnessed three of my boys and four of my daughters-in-law get abducted at gunpoint. And then they were taken to an undisclosed location. My youngest boy only got away because he was not with the rest when they got taken.

"And you know they must have search parties out looking for him at this very minute. They have to be deathly afraid that that he will contact the authorities and expose them. If that happens, the whole thing will blow up in their faces. Unless, of course, it's as he says, and the local authorities are in on it. You just never know with these small-town backwoods communities.

"Fast forward, his message said that they checked into a villa and that they were the only ones there. Yeah, I think that sounds strange as well. Why would no other guests be in this place? It may be a front to lure people in, sort of like a feeder. A phony company whose only business is to set people up for these other jokers with the guns.

"Greg said he just happened to be outside when he saw some masked gunmen rush the place. He hid himself. It was the only thing he could have done, with no weapon and overwhelming odds stacked in the other direction. Now, Red, I know this boy. If he could have done anything, he would have. This boy is ex-military, special ops and all that, so he definitely had to be greatly outmanned and outgunned for him to be close enough to witness what took place and not act.

"Anyway, he gave me a landmark where I might start my search. His message said that he was at mile marker 17 something on Route 1 South. I am in my car headed that way now, but I sent a GPS trace to last known location of the phone he called me from. I should be getting that back any time now, but what I need from you is for you to make a few phone calls and quickly assemble all the equipment for the team.

"Pull together as large a team as you can, because if my assumptions are correct, we will need all the firepower and man power we can have at our disposal. Get them together, and then you all get on the road and call me when you're close. I will send you my GPS coordinates once I get stationary. In the meantime, just plug in Coulditbe, Pennsylvania. Yeah, yeah, it should come up. I got a reading on the place in mine. First, I am going to the location on Route 1. And after that, I am going to that place he said they were invited to—the Bright Spot Villas.

"Supposedly, that location was just a mile or two away from the kidnapping, so I will nose around some, conduct some reconnaissance. I will ask them a few questions and hopefully flush some rabbits out of the briar patch. If I do not have any luck, I will find a hotel to check-in by the time you get the team together and get close.

"Oh yeah, don't forget to bring the good stuff, and lots of it. I don't know what we may run into down there. Like always, I am counting on you, Red. I know you'll be there. This one is for my kids. I know. I know that too. Black Ivory forever. Kill or be killed. One more thing. I know it's not necessary, but Red China, thanks, man!

"Sara, it's me. I'm over that now, but thanks anyway. Now listen close and jot this down. Leave nothing out. I want you to go online and get me all the intel that you can find on the Bright Spot Villas in Coulditbe, Pennsylvania. The owners, the investors, the staff, the layout, and any other particulars you can think of. Next, I want you to find out who the town officials are. You know, the mayor, the sheriff, and city council, that sort of thing.

"Finally, pull up the local newspaper or any other periodicals that they might have and find out who is actually calling the shots in that town. If I know one thing, I know newspapers always suck up to small-town big shots. Yeah, yeah, in the big cities too. But mostly in the small towns, because frankly, there is nothing else to write about.

"Get on it yesterday, and get back to me as soon as possible. And by the way, if you have to, you can use my name to even call in a few favors over at the agency. Thanks, darlin'. Now strap 'em up and prove to me one more time that you are indeed the best, as I know you are."

As he approached mile marker 17.9 on Route 1 South, as his son's message had instructed, he slowed to a cruise and perused the nearby tree lines. He made several passes in between mile marker 17 and 18 but saw no sign of his son. He pulled over to the soft shoulder and got out of the car.

He stood looking for a moment, pointing in all directions with his flashlight, and then he yelled out, "Is anyone out here?" He had not heard from his son again since his first message, and to BJ's trained mind, this could logically only mean one of a couple of things.

The absence of a second message could mean that he had no more access to a phone, could have dropped it, lost signal, or lost power. It could also mean that he was on the run and unable to call from his current location. As he pondered and weighed the many options before him, there was one that he wanted to avoid, one he really did not want to even consider.

His mind continued to race. Greg could have been caught after all. He could be with the rest of them. If so, they probably discovered that he had the cell and that he made a call. In that instant, if they were smart, they'd get rid of all the evidence. Although, sadly enough, the evidence, in this case, is Greg and the others. "Damn! The evidence is my kids!" he yelled.

Just as he was contemplating his next move, a car pulled up behind him. With his flashlight, he could make out that it was a police cruiser, the words *Coulditbe County Police* boldly inscribed on the side of the car. He moved to the front of the cruiser and behind his own car so that the officer would not have reason to look inside his car.

This was a simple but effective strategy used by all guns for hire. He put himself on guard and started the secret listening device held in his upper inside pocket by patting his leg in just the right spot.

"Good evening, sir. Are we having car trouble today?"

"No, no, I am just here looking for my sons and my daughters-in-law."

"Your sons? Don't see any other cars here, so what would your sons be doing by the side of the road with no car?"

"No, no, they called and said they had some car trouble and they were having some trouble getting a tow truck."

"Is that right?"

"Yes, they said that the triple-A service that they use did not have a listing for any tow truck company within fifty miles of here, and a tow that far would not be covered. So they called me because I live right up the road, just on the other side of Hershey."

"Do you now?"

"Yes, so have you seen a black Lexus SUV broken down on this road?"

"Well, being that you just told me all about your sons and their car trouble, if I had seen them, wouldn't I just come out and tell you without you having to ask me, mister?" Then, in a most authoritarian manner, the deputy took things a step further. "I'm sorry. I did not get your name."

Angered and suspicious, BJ shot back with even more authority. "That is probably…no, exactly, because I did not tell you my name, Deputy B. Conn, is it?"

"Yes. Deputy Buster Conn. And your name is?"

"Again, I didn't say, and for the record, in case you're keeping score, that's the second time you've asked for my name and the second time that I've informed you that I didn't say. I would sincerely hope that we do not need to go a third round of I didn't say. I would definitely hope that those first two rounds will suffice. Where I come from, that is called redundancy, or is my elocution foreign in some manner? Do I need to speak faster, slower perhaps, or would you prefer a different dialect?"

Without pause, BJ masterfully transitioned away from his eloquent insult. He recognized it was time to do so by the curious look on the deputy's face. His indecisive demeanor revealed that BJ's words did not quite register as the overt insult that he had intended them to be. In any event, he stated matter-of-factly, "Could you direct me to the Bright Spot Villas, as I am looking for some friends in the area?"

"What friends are you looking for?"

"Deputy Buster, I really don't think that is any of your business. But more importantly, as a public servant, you are duly charged with the obligation to serve the public to the best of your ability. If I wanted to identify my friends, in that I know that you are from the area, at least you work in the area, don't you think I would have stated who I was looking for?

"Now as a resident of this great state, and if my political science serves me correctly, I believe that some of my state tax dollars goes to the coffers of your city's municipality to help pay your salary. So in an indirect manner, you actually work for me, *sir*. And in that light, I am asking you, *sir*, to do your fucking job, Deputy Droop Along. Now which way to the Bright Spot Fucking Villas, if you do not mind?"

"There is no need to get upset or be disrespectful, sir. I was just trying to be helpful."

"You mean disrespectful such as being asked about your intimate details by a stranger whose intentions you do not know or completely trust?" The stunned deputy opened his mouth to form a response, but before he could answer, BJ continued, "Well, young man, if you want to be helpful, tell me where I can find the Bright Spot Villas, and stop asking me so many unwelcomed, unwanted, and unneeded questions, okay?"

"Okay," came the sullen response from the young deputy who quickly realized that he had just been severely outmaneuvered and outflanked by a more seasoned and strategic operator! "Well, sir," he said as he swallowed hard, still trying to recover from his verbal lashing. "You are just about a mile and a half away. The Bright Spot Villas," he said, pointing west, "are just up the road here, and it will be on your left."

"Thank you very fucking much, and you have a nice fucking day," BJ said as he returned to his vehicle, made a U-turn, and headed off toward his new destination.

"You, too, sir!" yelled the deputy as he headed back to his car to call headquarters.

At no more than a snail's pace, BJ pulled cautiously up the circle driveway. As if in drive-by mode, inch by inch, he crept toward the villa entrance. As best he could, he took a painstaking visual survey of his surroundings against the backdrop of a dimly lit compound. He casually exited his vehicle, but with some measure of hesitation.

He had hoped to see a passerby or a staff member that he could perhaps catch off guard and extract some straight answers. However, his wait was in vain, as not one soul was visible to the naked eye. While it was true that no one passed by, BJ had the eerie feeling usually associated with being secretly watched. This was not the first time he had experienced the "I'm being watched" feeling.

He took a deep breath in an effort to prepare himself for the evident string of lies that he was about to be told. His only hope was that the liar in question, whomever was chosen to present them, was not very good at the craft. BJ knew all too well how to instantly detect an intentional lie. He knew how to watch the liar's eyes and the body language, together with any hand gestures. All of it meant something to him; he even knew the science of voice pitch and tone when detecting and discerning fact from fiction.

BJ causally strolled into the lobby with a noticeable air of confidence. "Hello there, young lady. And who might you be?"

"I am Carmen."

"Well, good evening, Carmen. Maybe you can help me."

"Me, sir? No, sir. I don't know anything."

"Wait, you don't even know what I am going to ask first. I am just looking for my four sons and their wives. They called me yesterday and told me they checked into this facility."

"Well, as I said, I do not know, sir. I am just a housekeeper. I do not greet guests."

"Well then, Little Ms. Housekeeper, perhaps you could you find me someone who does greet guests and who would know something and who does know whether or not my sons and daughters are still here."

"Good evening, sir. I am Malcolm, general manager of the Bright Spot Villa. How may I be of assistance to you?"

"Well, Malcolm, my good man, you may indeed be of assistance. My four sons, together with their respective wives, checked into this facility last night, and they invited me down to join them."

"Well, sir, I am sorry, but there must have been some miscommunication. You see, that could not at all be possible. The fact is that we do not now nor have we had any guest, that is as of yet. Technically speaking, we, and by that I mean this entire facility, are not yet officially open for business.

"In fact, we are not scheduled to open for another two weeks. You see, we do not have all of our requisite licenses from the state at this point. I am sorry, sir, but I did not get your name."

"The name is Mack. Big Mack."

"Mr. Mack, while I am deeply sorry for your trouble, I do believe that there has been some error in communication."

"You don't say," asked BJ. throwing this particular liar some more usable bait.

"Indeed, I do say. Come to think of, though, a thought just occurred to me. We are just one of many villas here in this region. As you may know, the entire region is a vacation resort area, and we just happen to have a name that's remarkably similar to a rival resort. Instead of Bright Spot Villas, what your sons may have said is Bright Light Villas, and that facility is located approximately eight miles due north of here. I have the exact address, if you are using GPS, of course."

"I am. Doesn't everybody these days? What with all these places looking the same and even some of them almost being named the same. What would any of us do without GPS?" The two men shared a pretend laugh, each eying the other to gage whether or not the other was buying their story. After securing the address, BJ took another opportunity to study the pained expression on the face of the young woman that he had initially encountered.

"And did you say the Bright Light Villas?" he asked, turning his attention to the self-described general manager. "Yes, the Bright Light Villas. It's a common mistake."

"You know what?" BJ asked rhetorically. "I can actually see how that name could easily be mistaken for the Bright Spot Villas. Yes, yes, I do see. I see quite clearly now," BJ stated in a duplicitous manner.

"You take care, Mr. Mack. And do have a most pleasant journey."

Once inside his car, BJ paused to answer his ringing cell phone. After the call, he would plan his next move. It did not, in any form or fashion, include traveling eight miles on a wild-goose chase. "Wonder what they had planned for me once I got back with no wild geese. Hey, Sara, what do you have for me? I see. I see. I see." After several successive I sees, BJ finally uttered something other than "I see."

"Got it. The sheriff's name is James Darren. Were there any write-ups on him? I see, official misconduct, abuse of power, and police brutality. Well, well, this guy is a real saint, huh? Acquitted on all charges, by who? A jury stacked with his cousins and their cousins?

"Forgive me, Sara. I digressed. Go on. I see, the Conn family, huh? They are the top dogs around. They run this town, huh? Well, I guess that explains why Deputy Sheriff Buster Conn just pulled over to assist me as I was stopped on the side of the road. No, no, I'm okay. I was just looking around, trying to find Greg. No, I haven't. Not yet," he solemnly reported.

"Of course not. Do you think after serving the last twenty plus years in Black Ivory that some little punk country bumpkin deputy sheriff could do anything to me? If he had so much as twitched the wrong way, he would've been on his way to heaven or hell. I don't know which one, but he would've been on his way, and in a hurry. The truth is, I was never in danger. On the other hand, he was in some serious danger, and the irony is that he never even knew it.

"Okay, Sara, what else do we have on them? Big party tomorrow night, huh? How do you know? Was it announced? Oh, I see, the catering company made a large order. Sara, you amaze me with how you can peek into people's lives and find out things that no one else can.

"Send me the complete write-up via email to my Blackberry. And just in case I didn't tell you or just in case you don't know, *Sara, you are the best*," he said with an elevated voice for emphasis. "And, yes, ma'am, I will be very careful. No, you didn't mention it, but I was probably out of range, so I'll try giving him a call again. Thanks. Now gotta run."

For fear of not having any reception if he moved, BJ sat in his car waiting for Sara's e-mail. As he sat, a distant silhouette pierced the dark night, and he was immediately put on guard. He calmly reached down for the gun on his ankle and brought it up to rest on his lap. His internal alarm was soon silenced as he recognized the nightwalker as Carmen, the housekeeper that he had just spoken to only moments ago.

She hurriedly walked past his car and discreetly threw a note into the partially opened passenger-side window. The note instructed that BJ wait five minutes, then leave the circle and head back toward the road. He was to stop just over the ridge, which would put him out of sight from the main complex but also quite some distance from the main road.

BJ stopped his car just as instructed, over the ridge and out of sight from the main complex. Before he could get his car in park, his would-be deepthroat came running from a nearby tree line. "Ma'am, you asked me to stop here. I don't know why exactly, but I'm guessing that it has to do with my sons."

"That is right, senor. My name is Carmen, and I know your son Greg. Please do not interrupt me. I have very little time to say what I have to say, then I must go. I might be missed. It is very dangerous for me to be here.

"For obvious reasons, I could not speak to you at the front door because I don't know who is who anymore. Greg came to me last night and told me some terrible things about the people that I work for. He tells me that the rest of his family was abducted at gunpoint before dawn earlier in the day and that he only managed to get away because he had a fight with his fiancée and was not in his room when everything took place. Prior to that, my supervisor had informed me that his entire party had checked out because they were being unruly. Senor Greg in particular.

"He went on to tell me that Greg had tried to molest one of the hostesses, so when Greg came to me, he caught me off guard and I was very afraid. He had sustained some injuries, he said from ant bites, so I allowed him to come into my room and I cleaned his wounds. When I had gained his confidence, I went into the bathroom. A bathroom that I share. I asked my next-door neighbor to go and get security so that they could notify the sheriff. I'm so sorry, senor. I am so sorry."

"Did they get him?"

"No, but please do not interrupt. It will only take longer! Later on, I learned that my supervisor told the sheriff that it was me who Greg had molested, and that is not true. I did not know why my supervisor would make up that story, but later on, I overheard him in a conversation, which confirms that he's working with someone named Big Walter, and they want to capture Greg in the worst way. I'm sorry, senor. I am so, so very sorry. But I think I know where Greg may be hiding."

But those words would forevermore be her last. Just as she spoke them, the sound of a very loud and powerful rifle shot pierced the night air. An instant later, a large caliber bullet penetrated her temple, completely shattering her left frontal lobe. She slumped to the ground like a ragdoll, dead before she hit the black mineral-rich farming dirt.

As the thud of Carmen's lifeless body hit the ground, BJ turned toward the direction of the shot. He was just able to see the silhouette of the tall slender gunman as he hustled out of sight back down the other side of the ridge, which gave the compound the illusion of seclusion.

Every instinct in his body told him to go after the gunman and put a bullet in his brain. However, all of his Black Ivory training and agency experience said this hit was a tactical diversion. If it had been anything else, why hadn't they tried to take him out? Why not take him out first? The girl was no real threat without someone to report their crimes to. Everything pointed to a strategic move. They made the first move; now he had to counter.

Moreover, his instincts told him that all his energy and effort would be better spent finding Greg. If he found Greg, he would then be one step closer to finding the others. "'But what was Carmen trying to tell me?" he wondered aloud. Then something she said played back in his mind, and he thought he was on to something.

As he drove off to investigate his hunch, he looked at Carmen's lifeless body once more and shook his head in anguish. It was a bitter pill to swallow, but he knew that this round went to the bad guys.

CHAPTER 14

THE IMPROBABLE SWITCH

AFTER SEVERAL HOURS of not being able to open her eyes because she was commanded not to, Pam found it extremely difficult to keep them closed simply because she wanted to. Lying wide awake in her bunk, she pretended to be asleep for fear of being discovered. She did not have the luxury of a watch, and thus no true sense of time. She wondered over and over, *What can I do? What can I do to get out of here?* Then it struck her as clearly as the brightest of stars of a clear cloudless night.

She knew what she must do, but she also knew what was stopping her from doing it. She had to overcome her deep-seated fear—a fear that she had never known before now. A fear so paralyzing that it prevented her from even thinking about trying to escape. She had never seen a man's blood run from his mouth and drip from his forehead simultaneously. The vision of LJ hurt and bloody was emblazoned into her mind and gave her extreme pause.

These people were in it to win it. They were not playing any games, and if she made just one slip, it would most probably mean instant death. A physical death by violence or a psychological death by way of a decaying spirit. These were the unenviable options that she was presented with, but she knew that she must choose one or the other. Those thoughts tormented her as she tossed and turned while pretending to be asleep.

Finally, she came to a bold conclusion. *No more fear! I have always been able to use my fear to get me ahead. Afraid of not going to beauty school, I convinced my counselor to help me. Afraid of not making the cheerleading squad, I convinced the captain to help me one on one. I can't let this fear, although a life-or-death fear, stop me now. I will use it the same way as I always have, and I will win as I always have.* Right then and there, she mentally celebrated with a triumphant, albeit internal, fist pump.

Fears aside, she concluded that she was as good as dead if she stayed in her current situation. Plus, she further concluded they would soon inject her again. So her window of opportunity to act was modest at best and closing by the hour. She suddenly felt a sense of empowerment now that she had decided to make her move and make it now. It was the move she had been contemplating and planning since Big Walt had unknowingly freed her from the Godspoke spell.

Her plan hinged on an elaborate scheme orchestrated to ensure the timely departure and extended absence of Justin. She needed for him to leave the unit unattended for a few hours. When Justin made his nightly visit to the toilet to do his usual business with his special magazines, she quickly slipped him a handwritten note. The note, supposedly from Big Walt, advised him that he could leave at 12:30 a.m. to go home and that he should return before 6:00 a.m., but not before 5:30 a.m.

She kept a trained ear on the door, listening for any sound indicting that he had gone. She coupled her trained ear with an added occasional impatient peek, just to be sure she didn't miss his departure. It must not have been time yet, because Justin read the note but did not instantly move after he checked his watch.

So she would just have to wait and wait and wait some more. Without the benefit of a watch, it seemed that hours could walk as slowly as old men with canes and minutes could crawl about as slow.

Before even one full day in the life of the Godspoken had elapsed, Pam learned one thing. The work was not at all backbreaking but instead routine and mundane. The simplistic idea was not to break your back but to kill your spirit and slowly your mind. At least, that was her analysis.

Each day began with a head count, followed by fifteen minutes of hygiene time and fifteen minutes of nutrition time. The term *nutrition time* was right and exact, because the food was as tasteless as exposed cleavage at a house of worship.

If the monotony did not kill the spirit of most of the spellbound population, the food may very well do the job. The daily menu consisted of a small ration from each of the four food groups, which the Good Doctor prescribed himself as the recipe for keeping his workforce strong, healthy, and productive.

A glass of powdered milk, which was more akin to white water without the rafting. A slice of dry toast, so dry it had to be consumed with the white water to keep from getting choked. Rounded out by a few dried nuts for protein, together with a small grapefruit as a temptingly delicious dessert. Every meal was the same thing, the same time, the same amount, the same preparation.

The more she thought about the insidious conditions in which the Godspoke were forced to live, the more determined she was not to spend the rest of her life, young life at that, as a spellbound Godspoke slave. She knew that things would not get any better, and to wait on the calvary to come over the hill to rescue her and the others was not her style. She also knew that if she were unable to free herself from this hostile bondage, she would forever be Big Walt's living porno show and masturbation tool.

Her mind moved at a snail's pace, filled with deliberate thoughts of how to best maneuver her way out of this situation and to do so with the help of the men around her. If Pam was good at any one thing, it was manipulating people, but manipulating men was an even stronger attribute. This she prided herself on.

She thought, *Why should men get to have everything their way when we women have the most priceless and sought-after commodity on this entire earth? The female body.* And she knew that she had an exceptionally beautiful body and a not too shabby intellect to go along with it. *So why shouldn't I get what I want if they get what they want—a dime piece, a partner, a lover, and supporter?*

After she had reaffirmed her beliefs by way of a silent geosocial diatribe, she settled on a plan of action. Her initial idea was to instruct the one of the Godspoke women to seduce Justin and to keep him occupied in the bathroom while she set up their escape. She reasoned that once he left his post, she could then sneak out and instruct LJ, Milton, and Henry to take down the workforce guard in their housing unit.

They could then come back and gather the other women in the group. Now complete, the group would then retrieve some weapons, secure a remote, and proceed to the glass elevator. Once out on the lawn, there, they would get to a car and speed away.

Of course, there were several holes in that story line, and she knew it. She also knew that this specific train of thought was just wishful thinking. If it were that simple to break out, she reasoned, someone else would have done it long ago. She had no illusions that she was the only female in the whole camp and whole history of the godforsaken place that has ever been aroused and regained their independent will. Looking around, she noticed several very attractive women, so her theory made perfect sense, and if it did, then her entire initial idea of escape was a bust.

Finally, she heard the door open, and she froze in place but peeked through a slight slit in her left eye. Pam watched as Justin poked his head inside the door to give a last look to be certain that none of the workforce was sleepwalking or otherwise moving. He said aloud, "Okay, you zombies. Be good little boys and girls while I go make Mama very happy. And can't forget about Papa too." Once she could no longer hear his footsteps in the distance, she lifted her head slightly at first, and then she sat up.

She eased out of her bed as quietly as she could, and she made her way over to the door and peeked. The coast was clear, so she left her unit and headed for Big Walt's sleeping quarters. About fifty feet from her destination, she heard the words "Workforce Pam, stop." She was horrorstruck but maintained a calm veneer. "Workforce Pam, what are you doing outside of the workforce sleeping quarters?"

Instinctively, she did not know what to do or how she should behave at that moment, and her mind began to race. She thought hurriedly, *How should a spellbound Godspoke worker act in this situation?* Her nimble mind made what seemed to be over a million calculations in that very instant, but she drew only a blank.

Her first instinct was to run, but run where? Her second intuition was to turn on the charm, but instead she naturally and immediately froze in her tracks. Her heart pounded against her chest so violently that she imagined that it would jump out and into her hand. Right then, she imagined that even the very stillness of the night was interrupted by the pounding of her fast beating heart.

She realized that she was about to expose herself, just like in all of those cop shows that she loved to watch wherein the criminals did all the work for the police by acting erratic and thus marking themselves as the guilty. She refused to replicate this less-than-intellectual act of self-incrimination, so she did what she always did when confronted with seemingly insurmountable odds.

At that moment, she called up a mental picture of her very strong and proud mother. The mother who gave her a backbone of steel, together with an unbreakable will. A mother who never took no for an answer, a mother who, against the odds, always seemed to make it happen.

And with the aid of her mother standing right by her side, if only in her mind, she summoned all the courage that she could muster. And in the blink of an eye, she calmed herself, enough so as to appear to be still under the influence of the Godspoke. She replied, "Big Walter instructed me to come to his sleeping quarters."

As she uttered those words, a great menacing doubt rapidly swept over her entire being, and she could only wonder if the man standing just feet away was convinced by her spellbound impersonation performance.

"Ole Walter, you sly dog you. Now I know why you gave me the night off," he said with revealing glee. "You want another shot at the title, and you didn't want me around to be the referee," he said, looking Pam over from head to toe as if to see what all the obsession from Big Walt was about.

"Well," he said after a moment of pause, which seemed like an eternity to Pam. "Who am I to stand in the way of his freakish love?

Workforce Pam, continue on your way to Big Walter's sleeping quarters." Justin then returned to his post, secured his coffee thermos, and then proceeded to leave the premises. Pam continued to walk slowly toward her destination.

Realizing that she did not have time to panic, exhale, or even think about what might have been, she mentally prepared herself for her next hurdle. Once inside, she fell quietly to her knees. All she needed was for Walter to wake up and see her in his sleeping quarters.

If he wakes up, there's no telling what this half-breed degenerate might do to me this time, she thought. *Knowing his kind, he might think he's irresistible to me and that I came back for more.* This dubious scenario caused her to shake her head at the mere thought as she silently crept and quietly crawled to her final destination.

As swiftly and as stealthily as any member of the big cat family seeking out its prey, she made her way over to Big Walter's desk and cautiously removed three items. She took the remote control needed to operate the glass elevator that doubled as a wine cellar. And she also secured two five-milliliter syringes, each loaded with one very potent dose of Godspoke serum. Then with all the same intensity and focus that she had used to enter into the lion's den, she began to make her way back out.

Just before she was about to stand up to make her speedy exit, she was forced to drop flat to the floor. Big Walt was up. In the darkened room, he stumbled, fumbled, and bumped his way into the bathroom. Once inside, he turned on the light. Pam could see his shadow as he stood to relieve his overflowing bladder.

She did not know what to do. Should she stand, pat, and stay still until he returned to bed? Or should she try to slip out in the middle of his stream in the hopes that he would not notice in his sleeplike state? Whatever decision she made would have to be made in nanoseconds, because time was not on her side. She leaped to her feet and quietly exited the door. She decided that if he came after her, she would turn on the charm.

Now outside, she began to make her way to the glass-encased walkway, which was nestled cozily between the workforce sleeping quarters and the workforce cafeteria. She looked back several times to be sure that her would-be lover was not in hot pursuit.

Inside the walkway, having made it so far, Pam did take that moment to exhale and to equally breathe in a sigh of much-needed relief. After all, this was the walkway that led to the glass elevator, and it was one step closer to her freedom.

She now moved quickly but carefully across the walkway, and as she approached the glass door, she pressed the open button on the remote and passed through the threshold to freedom. As soon as the elevator came to rest inside the wine cellar, she peeked out to be certain that she was alone.

Although it was after 2:00 a.m., she had observed during her short stay that there was always some movement around this place. Quickly, she made her way to the servant's entrance located just yards away. She did not know exactly where she was going or even how to get there, but her astute observation allowed her to make her way to the second floor of the mansion.

As she did, she came to a landing that would have caused most great concern. Straight across from where she stood was the winding stairwell that led to the grand foyer at the entrance of the mansion. To her left as well as to her right were open doors that led to a number of other closed doors. She knew which bedroom she was looking for, but she did not know which bedroom that was.

This was quite a dilemma, trying to find out where her apparent twin, Ms. Diane, slept. "Oh my god, what am I going to do?" she said, clutching her chest and thereafter wringing her hands frantically. "I am not made for this. I have trouble deciding on what color nail polish I want for the week.

"My daddy was strong, and God knows my mama was strong, but that is something they didn't pass enough of on to me. I wish Greg was here. He would know what to do. Hell, I wish anybody was here, because I sure don't know what to do."

Just then, she heard a door opening to her left. She pressed her body hard alongside the wall and slid quickly in the direction of the voices. She made her way to the open door of the west wing and positioned herself behind it.

"Very well, madame. I do hope that the sedative will have you asleep in no time. If you don't mind me saying so, they really do work. I have used them on occasion."

"No, I don't mind, Joshua. Thank you ever so much, and good night," came a soft voice from within the room.

Joshua proceeded down the long hallway toward the servant's access stairway. His heavy footsteps were leading the way. However, just as he was about to take his first step down, he paused. It was as if he had sensed someone watching, or as if he heard something. In either case, his attention was now trained on identifying what it was, or so Pam imagined. Her heart began to race again, only even faster this time.

It was one thing to be caught in the workforce biosphere. That could be readily explained to almost anyone and believably so, but it was quite another to be caught inside the Conn mansion. She wondered if it was her loud heartbeat that had given her way. She thought, *If he comes near me, I will just inject him with the Godspoke.* That very thought comforted her and gave her a sense of power, which promptly replaced her previous feelings of helplessness and fear.

Whatever it was that Joshua paused to think about seemed to have been satisfied, and he proceeded on his way down the stairs. Having overheard the small bit of the conversation between Joshua, the manservant, and the occupant of that room, Pam was convinced that it had to be Ms. Diane.

There were only two women living in the mansion as far as she knew. That voice sounded very young to her. She instinctively presumed that it must be her target. She hoped that her hunch was correct, and the more she thought about what she had heard, the more convinced she was. Finally, she concluded, "At the very worst, I have a fifty-fifty chance."

Pam's better angels cautioned her of a premature move. Her internal radar warned her that now was not the optimal time to enter Ms. Diane's room. If in fact the room in question was the right room at all. She reasoned, *What if Joshua comes back to check on her?*

She also reasoned that her intended target might be bigger or stronger or in better physical condition. *After all, what else do trust fund babies have to do but work out and do Pilates and junk like that?* she reasoned still further.

She wrestled with her reasoning and the conclusions of that reasoning for what seemed like an eternity. However tempted, she did not move from her hiding spot. In her estimation, it just wasn't yet time. Although, she was extremely anxious to get it over with, which was all the more reason that very thought permeated her mind.

The hourly chime from the grandfather clock located somewhere in the foyer rang out. Although it was at the bottom of the winding stairs and a ways down the hall and to the right of her, it seemed much closer. She heard it strike 3:00 a.m., and she again breathed a huge sigh of relief. After what felt like forever, she sensed that now was finally a good time to go.

Although still cautious, she had the realization that she held at her command the potent power of the Godspoke contained in the syringe. Pam now moved with a bit more authority and a bit more confidence. She slowly turned the knob of what she thought to be Ms. Diane's room, and she paused to see it if there would be any reaction from the other side of the closed door.

Having heard nothing, she slowly released the knob, stepped inside the room, slowly turned the knob again, pushed the door close, and slowly released the knob. As she spun around to survey her surroundings, she immediately was overtaken by the opulence of the room that she had just entered.

Silk and lace, together with deep grained mahogany, plus enough gold trim to purchase enough food to feed the population of a small country. *Talk about rich. Oh my god, this is rich. Shit, I might drug this bitch up and take her place for good*, she thought with a devilish smile. *I damn well could get used to this. All right, Pam. All right, Pam. Snap out of it, little girl, and let's get to work here. We do not have much time.*

After stepping out of her momentary fantasy, Pam removed the syringe together with an alcohol swab from her pocket. She took the cap off and gently placed the head of the needle onto the pad, and with one swift motion, she jabbed the needle into an unsuspecting Ms. Diane.

As she forcefully inserted the small needle into the most welcoming insertion point, she emptied its transformative content into her victim's exposed right thigh. Simultaneously, she grabbed the mouth of the sleeping woman with her free hand so that the sudden yell that was sure to come did not disturb the peaceful night.

Ms. Diane awakened in horror to find a sharp stinging sensation in her lower extremity, and that indeed her almost identical twin was muzzling her. Just as Pam had done after her initial injection, the newly injected Ms. Diane struggled mightily to first free herself, but also to shake off the creeping feeling of impending doom that was now racing through her veins.

She tossed and turned violently in an effort to escape while at the same time reigning what she hoped were death blows to Pam's head and body. Undeterred, and not to be denied, Pam withstood the few blows that did find their target. However, fortunately for her, the great majority did not land where they were intended but instead found only her upper arms and shoulders, for the most part. Ms. Diane had never thrown a blow in anger over her entire life, so her death blows were not even close to deadly.

After what seemed like an endless struggle, the Godspoke did what it always does, which was take complete control. Ms. Diane was now a powerless slave subject to the whims and desires of those around her. For someone who was born into power, this was not a pretty picture. Her mind free but her will stolen, she could only cry mentally. She did not, after all, understand any of what was going on and still less about what was to come.

"Workforce Diane, from this point forward, you will answer to Workforce Pam. Do you understand?"

"Yes."

"Workforce Pam, remove all of your clothes. Workforce Pam, put on these clothes."

Thinking quickly, Pam went to the bathroom and drew water into the syringe to replace the colorless liquid that she used to subdue a captive of her own.

She then ordered her new subject to provide her with her remote control for the glass elevator. Moving swiftly, she gave the order for the workforce to follow her. On the way to place her replacement, she gave her new spellbound captive all the same instructions that she was given not so long ago.

"Okay, Workforce Pam, follow me." Pam and her submissive double moved into the hallway, down the servant stairway, and out the servant's entrance without incident. They then quickly entered into the wine cellar and lowered themselves. Once inside the glass-enclosed walkway. they traversed the passageway in what seemed like only an instant.

It was now 5:00 a.m., and Justin would soon return, so she had to move quickly. With no one on duty, Pam escorted Ms. Diane inside the workforce sleeping quarters. But before doing so, she again repeated her instruction that she only answer to Workforce Pam.

She then gave her replacement instructions to follow her once again, and she led her to the bunk where she used to sleep. Pam then gave her distant twin the order to lie down and go to sleep. As Pam turned to leave, feeling secure that she had almost accomplish her goal, Hazel opened her eyes and looked directly into hers. Panicked, she stopped in her tracks, frozen with fear.

Then in an instant, she remembered that she had her will back. She realized that she was no longer Pam but in fact Ms. Diane. Confidently but quietly, she instructed Workforce Hazel to go back to sleep. She thought she should have paused to tell her the plan, but she knew she didn't have time. And beside, she secretly liked the idea of having Hazel suffer just a little while longer.

Having successfully placed Ms. Diane in her workforce role, it was time to assume the identity of Ms. Diane. Her new identity intact, Pam walked confidently over to Big Walters's sleeping quarters and entered unnoticed by the sleeping giant. She made her way over to his desk and returned both the remote as well as one syringe. It felt good to do so standing up this time, she thought with a smile.

Then, without a blink, she walked over to Big Walter who was sound asleep, and she paused. She thought to herself that before it was over, she must exact some sort of revenge on this man who had sought to humiliate her or worse. She did not want to fathom the details of the worse, so she immediately shook the thought. Tapping him gently on the leg, she called out to him, "Walter, Big Walter, wake up."

"What…what the hell?" he said, still startled. Pulling the covers snugly up to his chin, Big Walter was not quite sure what was happening as yet. He spoke in a very low and uncertain voice. "Ms. Diane, Ms. Diane, is that you?"

"Who do you think it is, Walter?" she replied in a whisper.

"Well, I know that it's you, but what…what are you doing here?"

"I came to see you. That is okay, isn't it?"

"Why, sure. But what do you want?"

"Well, I want two things," she said, flashing her best smile.

"First, I want you to take me for a nice long drive tomorrow night during my parents' big party. I can't stand those things. And second, I want you to take my virginity. You don't think I notice how you look at me all the time, do you, Big Walter?"

He said nothing, but his bulging eyes told the tale of guilt. "You don't think that I know that you want me, do you? You don't think I know? I may be young, but I'm not stupid."

"I…I don't think you're stupid," he said. "I think you're one of the smartest, finest, most intelligent, prettiest, best dressed, most sexy women I know."

"I know, Walter. I know, and I think the same of you, although we will work on those clothes of yours. Also, we will do something about that filthy mouth of yours. Although I kinda like it some time. I like bad boys, you know. I never said anything before now because you know, well, because of my mother and her husband, the Good Doctor. If they knew I was here, they would beat me silly, and they would do worse to you, so they better never find out. In fact, no one had better know that I was here. If they do, I'll swear that you got me here under false pretenses and then you forced yourself on me. Are we clear on that? If you don't tell, I won't.

"I want you to keep this strictly between me and you. And tomorrow night, when I give you the signal, I'll meet you out front and you'll take me. You take me for a ride, and after that I will let you just take me. From the front, from the back, and front the side, from on top, and from the bottom, you can just take, take, take, and take me some more. I'm hot, and I want you to cool me off. As I said, you are a badass, and I like the badass type, most of the time. What do you say, Walter? Do we have a date?"

"I…I…I don't know what to say. Are you serious?"

"Why would I be here, Walter, if I was not dead serious? You do want me, don't you? You do want to be my first and only, don't you?"

"Yes, yes!"

"Well then, this is our secret. And tomorrow, we will have our night. I can't wait. Now shush and go back to sleep. I will see you tomorrow evening," she said as she sealed the deal with a long enduring kiss on his frontal lobe.

And just as she had entered, she quickly exited his room, leaving him spellbound and wondering. Once she got back to her room, she sprawled herself out on the luxurious bed and smiled deeply. She had done it. She had done the unthinkable.

Not only had Pam made an improbable switch, but she had also set up a way for her to get to freedom, and hopefully get some help to save the rest, if she could. There was more to do, much more, but she was glad about what she had done so far. She had made the improbable seem quite possible.

CHAPTER 15

The Great Escape

Unable to sleep, Pam sat up, picked up a picture frame from the nightstand, and moved some thirty feet away. She positioned herself in front of the full-length mirrored wall in the palatial-sized bathroom. As she looked, she could not help but be absolutely astonished at the striking resemblance between herself and the woman who must now be trapped in a horrified state of suspended disbelief.

Pam could only imagine what she must be going through. One minute the heiress to a vast fortune and living a life of opulence and luxury, and the next forced into the role of a spellbound abductee. And to think, her very own perverted family created the shit that put her there. *That's worse than what happened to us. Damn! How bad can someone's luck be?*

Troubled by the vision of the poor girl, she shivered and shook her head in pity. However, any pity she felt for Ms. Diane was soon forgotten. Right now, she was more concerned with her own misfortune and present state of peril.

She looked carefully at her profile and examined every inch and aspect of her face against the photograph that she held tightly in her hand, taking every precaution to prevent it from falling. Drawing any attention to herself right now was the last thing she wanted or intended to do. After a long, cold, and calculating look, she decided that she really could not discern any distinguishable difference between her features and those of the new Godspoke Pam locked away in housing unit B.

She carefully replaced the pricy crystal-encased photo and busied herself trying to mimic her look-alike's voice. Although they appeared to be exact physical doubles, their voices differed greatly. An awful lot was riding on her ability to master mimicking Ms. Diane. Hanging in the balance was her chance to escape the confines of her forced enslavement. But equally, if she pulled this off, she would forever more be the heroine in the eyes of her not-so equals.

Pam sighed as she mentally looked ahead to what she knew was a monumental task. Somehow, she had to manage to convince all the people who have daily intimate contact with her twin, including her twin's very own mother, that she was indeed her twin.

Scared senseless with the haunting thought that she would be discovered and returned to the Godspoke workforce, she stood in the mirror and looked deep into her own soul. She had to do some soul-searching. She had to do a gut check. She had to dig deep to draw on something way down at the bottom of her being.

Solemnly, she wondered aloud, "Can I really pull this off, or am I just fooling myself? Do I have the intestinal fortitude of my mother, the resolve of my father, the downright good old-fashioned spunk of my grandmother?" She asked herself these very serious questions, which she knew, in her heart of hearts, that she really did need to answer. And do so with some very courageous responses, especially if she was to really save the day as she imagined.

Ever creeping and growing stronger, there was a nervous and sick feeling in the pit of her stomach. It began as a small, harmless, gaseous rumble. Although she felt that at any moment that it had the potential to quickly transform in to a full-blown vomit eruption. She inhaled deeply and shut her eyes tightly, intent on dismissing the vile thought of green vomit all over her feet and on the nice floor.

She then performed some of the visualization techniques that she had learned from watching her motivational DVDs. Several deep breaths later, she believed she had weathered a violent intestinal storm, and she was no worse for the wear.

She emerged unscathed by the brute force of the storm, which reigned down huge pellets of fear and sporadic blasts of panic. Panic was bad enough, albeit very temporary, but fear was far worse. Fear could be wholly debilitating. Pam knew this all too well, as fear had almost cost her many times in her not too distant past.

After a short while of staring at the very uncertain figure in the mirror, and after many disfigured faces later, she finally answered a confident and resounding *yes* to her every self-imposed query and doubt. Simply put, this symbolic exercise was really intended to shake off a serve case of very bad nerves.

Now more focused and determined than ever due to the emancipation from her fear, she called on her limited memory in a genuinely intense effort to mimic the cadence and pitch of a voice that she had only heard utter a sparse few words.

"Good morning," she says in one voice pattern. "Morning," she says in another. "Good mooorning," she says in a not so convincing Southern drawl. "Morning," she said, first raising her pitch, then lowering it a bit, then a bit more. "Morning," she said in a speeded version, then a few other much slower versions.

After quite some time had elapsed, she was near mental exhaustion and physical breakdown, as it was almost dawn. She had now been awake for almost a full twenty-four hours straight. Twenty-four hours of pure unadulterated hellish havoc. To top it off, she felt as though her numerous attempts to emulate the voice of her double were wasted, and that was to put it mildly.

Frustrated and somewhat disheartened, she said with pouted lips, "Oh, who am I fooling? As soon as they hear me speak, they will know that I'm not Ms. Diane. Then they will take me back to the workforce camp and shoot me up again with that crazy shit. Then all of us will be stuck in this hell on earth forever." Her prognostication of doom, peppered with a small measure of distain, was directed at the woman in the mirror. She heaved another of her now familiar prolonged sighs and stuck her tongue out at her mirrored reflection.

Instantly numbed and transfixed by the sobering thought, Pam almost returned to her previous trancelike state as she sadly and miserably lamented, "What the fuck am I going to do? This shit is crazy." Feeling as though she were looking at a stranger in the mirror, she found herself slowly repeating her previous phrase, "This shit is crazy."

Over and over, she said, "This shit is crazy. This shit is crazy. This shit is crazy." At that instant, she felt even more helpless than when she was under the spell of the Godspoke. Back then, she had a good reason as to why she was powerless to act. The damn creeps had robbed her of her free will, so she could do nothing, but what about now?

She felt so close and yet so far from freedom; frustration did not begin to adequately describe her helpless, hopeless, "all is lost" feeling. Surpassing that helpless feeling of being trapped inside the Godspoke body was a monumental task, but what Pam was feeling right now had done it. And how!

Without realizing it, she repeated the "This shit is crazy" phrase so many times, it almost became a chant. At some point, and she didn't know when exactly, she had worked herself into a dizzying frenzy. Now near hysterics, just like that, she realized herself on the brink of losing it. Clenching her fists together, so tightly that her palms turned red from the pressure, she shook her tightly bound hands in defiance. This gesture appeared to symbolize an exorcism of some invisible external force holding her down.

After a long while, she finally calmed herself by reciting aloud the heedful words of her dearly departed grandma, Virginia. She could literally hear the low, slow, and monotonous voice of her grandma saying, "Listen, chile, solutions always solve problems. Don't you ever worry bout no problem. You only got to worry bout the solution."

Staring steadfast into the mirror, Pam was now and again resolved to find a plausible solution. More importantly, for her, was the decision to that she was unwilling to accept the all-but-certain defeat that she now faced, or so it seemed. Although very uncertain, she hoped with her all that a solution would make itself known.

Putting her fears aside, she focused and began to formulate a plan aloud. Her first thought was, "I could use the phone and call the police." But she thought better of it. "For one," she enumerated, "I don't even know where I am, as they had us blindfolded in the back of that damn van coming out here. Second, with all this money that these people obviously have, the police are probably on their side anyway.

"And third, what if there is some kind of monitoring or listening device on this phone? With all this crooked shit going on around here, and knowing these people, I would not put anything past them. So the phone may not be the best idea. Not the best way at all," she said, stalling for time while trying to gather her next thought.

Feeling somewhat let down by her less-than-perfect first try, she retorted in utter frustration, "Okay, Pam, got any more bright ideas?" While a million thoughts raced through her mind, her emotions raged on; they grew even more conflicted and confused. Trying again to shake off that ever reemerging fear, she said aloud and with authority, "Let's see what else I can do. I know there is a solution to every problem."

"Thanks, Grandma!" she said, looking toward the heavens. "I won't worry about the problem, and I will focus on the solution. Only what is it? Talk to me, Momma Virginia. Talk to me. Tell what to do," she said, still looking upward. "What is the solution to all this hostile mess we got ourselves into?

"How am I going to get through this day? One whole entire day of being somebody else, somebody I don't even know? How do I do it? Tell me, Grandma. Tell me," she said with tears beginning to well up in both eyes. Then, like a flash of light that can only be appreciated by someone lost in total darkness, the solution presented itself like a gift from Santa on Christmas Day.

"Oh, I know exactly how to pull this off! I know exactly how to pull this off," she repeated as if in disbelief. "Why didn't I think of this before? Why was I standing here torturing myself all this time, and for nothing? This was so simple all the time," she said, wiping the tears from her red eyes and wet cheeks.

"Whisper. I will just whisper, just like I did with Big Walter. That's it. I will just whisper. He thought I was her, and he bought the whisper bit, so why not everybody else? Last night, Joshua gave Ms. Diane a sedative. She obviously couldn't sleep, probably wondering which outfit to wear to the party," she said, now confidently laughing.

"So," she continued, smiling as her newly formed battle plan was now taking shape, "if I use the excuse that I could not sleep and that I went out on the balcony to sit for a while. Now my throat is raw and extremely sore because I was out in the night air too long. That's it/ I've come down with a touch of laryngitis.

"When Joshua gets here, I will ask for something hot to drink, and I will say to him that I'm staying in the bed to rest up my voice for tonight's big party. I don't know if they'll go for it, but they should. Why wouldn't they? They will. They have to. And besides, that's my plan, and I'm sticking with it.

"It's a good plan, and it should work. It has to," she repeated, giving confidence to her cautiously optimistic reflection in the mirror. Smiling once more at the winner in the mirror, she nodded in a triumphant symbol of approval and turned to head back to bed.

Once she had it locked in her mind that her plan was solid, she decided that she really did need to sleep in today. As she lay back in the plush king-sized bed, confident in her plan, Pam finally allowed herself a moment to relax. She also took the time to reflect on her small victories.

Although, try as she may, a relaxed mind did not come easy. While a tiny celebration was going on inside one part of her head, she simultaneously contemplated the new challenges to come in another. Back and forth from celebration to contemplation, and so it went for a good little while. Eventually, she fell into a restless sleep, but sleep nonetheless. It was sleep that she needed and sleep that was well-earned.

Never fully able to reach deep sleep, she awakened to find the morning sun, and she could hear the chirping of the small birds outside the open balcony door. She watched as they busied themselves with all the activities and duties of a new day, but mostly looking for crumbs of food. A red bird landed just feet away on her bedroom floor. It stared at first, gave her three or four soft but intense chirps, and then took his leave. She thought this to be strange, strange even for rich people, but dismissed it as simply odd.

However, after some further consideration, she took this surreal scene as a sign, an ominous sign. Did it mean that someone would recognize that she was not Ms. Diane? Did it mean that she would forget to whisper and be exposed? What did it mean? Many thoughts ran rampant through her mind, but none made any sense, and not one eased her troubled mind.

The meaning of the peculiar whispering bird was front and center on her consciousness. Pam lay wide awake in bed, waiting for that dreaded knock. She knew that her moment of true reckoning would soon follow that first knock at the door. If she was to make it, that knock would tell the tale.

At about ten o'clock in the morning, Pam heard a faint tap at the door, but the voice was not that of Joshua. She was expecting Joshua to come back. She could handle men—they were her specialty—but that was not a man. No, that was definitely not the voice of a man. That voice from the other side of the door was that of a woman. Again, the voice called out, "Ms. Diane. Ms. Diane, it is Melissa. Are you up?"

In a whisper, just loud enough to be audible by whoever was on the other side of the door, Pam said, "Come in."

"Good morning, Ms. Diane," said the spry small-framed woman of obvious Latin decent. "I will run a bath for you and lay out your bathing suit. Today seems like a fine day for your morning laps in the pool. It is quite warm, and the sun is shining bright, is it not?" she said with a smile and an unintentional flip of the long dark single braid of hair from one side of her back to the other as she turned to look outside toward the brilliant day.

As quietly as she could, Pam uttered the first words that would provide her with a good indication as to whether or not she could pull off this charade. "No, no, not this morning, Melissa. I'm not feeling well," she said as she watched the young girl closely so as to pick up any sign of unnatural ease.

An immediate look of concern came across the face of her attendant, and Pam knew she was home free. "What is it, Ms. Diane? Are you okay?"

Smiling, even if internally, Pam responded in an even quieter whisper, "I couldn't sleep last night, so I took a midnight stroll, and the night air has given me a touch of laryngitis. I just want to stay in bed and rest up for tonight. Tonight is a big night for us." She waited for a reply, secretly trying to gather some much-needed info about what to expect later on.

"Yes, Ms. Diane. Yes, it is a big night indeed." Turning to leave, Melissa said, "Very well. I will bring you breakfast. Would you like it now or maybe later?"

"Bring it now, and then I just want to rest."

"Okay, Ms. Diane, I will be right back, and I will tell Lady Sara that you are not feeling well and that you want to sleep in today." Pam smiled and faked a cough as Melissa exited and pulled the door close behind her.

Pam was still smiling to herself after Melissa had left the room because she knew that she had just cleared one very important hurdle. If she could fool Ms. Diane's personal matron who attended to her every day, she should have no problem with everyone else. After all, she thought, if this family was like any of those she had seen on TV in those lifestyles of the rich and famous type shows, it would be a breeze. On TV, rich parents never had time for their children, so they would hardly interact or notice anything out of the ordinary.

The day passed by slowly, but evening did eventually come. From her vantage point, Pam could see the limousines as they began to arrive, full of guests. She heard instructions from someone in charge that all the cars should be lined up in rows on the east side of the house. Apparently, they were expecting a huge crowd and many more limos to come.

Pam was startled by another knock at the door, but it was only Melissa again. "Come in," she said in her now perfected low whisper.

"Ms. Diane, it is almost time for you to make your grand entrance. I told Lady Sara you were not feeling well and that you would be down a little late to the party, just as you asked."

"Thank you, Melissa."

"Okay, Ms. Diane. After you bathe, I will lay out your gown and the rest of your things that you have planned to wear. Would you also like help with your hair?"

Still in perfect whisper pitch, Pam replied, "No, Melissa. After you have run the bath and laid out the clothes, that will be all."

"Very well then, Ms. Diane. But I bet you are excited that Mr. Clark and Mr. Tyler are both going to be here tonight and that they both will be trying to have all of your attention. Are you not?"

"That will be all, Melissa," she said as she turned toward the freshly prepared bath without giving notice to the strange look on Melissa's face. She knew that she must have done something that was out of the ordinary, but she hoped the young girl would merely attribute it to her not feeling well.

"Now who the hell is Clark and who the hell is Tyler?" she said aloud as she stepped into the lukewarm water. "I should've known someone this fine, as fine as me, would have a lot of men after her. How will I know them? Maybe I should search through Ms. Diane's things to try and find some pictures.

"On second thought, someone this fine, I don't really have to worry about finding them. If I know men, bloodhounds that they are, they will find me. Although, I wish it wasn't two of them I had to deal with at once. Although having two of them here should play to my advantage. It will work out just great, because once I disappear, one will think I'm with the other."

Pam checked herself from head to toe in the full-length mirror and thought that she made a very elegant Ms. Diane. "Man oh man, I really, really could get used to this. Silk and lace definitely suit me just fine," she said aloud as she executed a perfect impromptu ballerina's twirl. Excited by her own performance, she threw her head back and laughed loudly. However, the sound of her own laughter quickly got her attention, as the giddiness of the moment was transformed in the blink of an eye into the fright of being discovered.

She quickly put the thought of a rags-to-riches fairy tale out of her head and focused herself on the task at hand. With one last look into the mirror for both confidence and a little vanity to boot, she turned to exit the room, but she stopped just short of turning the doorknob. With one hand firmly on the knob plus a foot braced against the door to protect against any unwelcome entry, she paused to say a short prayer.

"Dear God, please give me the strength and guidance that I will need in order to save us from these deranged people who believe that they have the right to play God, or I mean play you and have total rule and dominion over other people. God, this is not right what they are doing, and I am asking you to help me to undo it. God, you said just ask and I shall receive. So, God, I am asking. God, I don't ask you for much, but I am asking you now, because we really need this. So please, God, please hear my prayer. Thank you, God. Thank you, God. Amen!"

Turning the knob slowly, she opened the huge mahogany door and headed toward the winding stairway. They led directly down to the most perilous challenge yet of her young life. Fooling a couple of servants like Walter and Melissa, who were not Ms. Diane's equal, was one thing. But fooling her family, her friends, and even a possible suitor or two was altogether a different proposition.

At the top of the stairway, she again paused briefly, but for a different reason this time. This time it was not to pray or even out of fear. This time it was in awe. As she began her graceful and elegant descent, she moved very deliberately as she marveled at the opulence that was ever present. There were symbols of wealth all around. In particular, the life-sized family portrait. Ms. Diane, together with Lady Sara as well as the Good Doctor, made for a picture-perfect family.

"Well, at least now I know what my mother looks like," she said quietly, laughing to herself but still aloud. As she took her first steps of ascension, she smiled in assurance as she again noticed and appreciated the astonishing similarity that she shared with Ms. Diane, but abruptly that appreciative look turned into a look of resolve.

Looking at it all, a troubling thought somehow occurred to her. *These people had so much, and unbelievably, they wanted to deny me, Greg's family, and all the others over there in Godspoke hell even the hope of ever having the same.* The sheer notion of such arrogance and greed made her instantly angry, and thereafter even more determined to succeed in her efforts to escape to freedom.

Her private thoughts became even more resentful, wondering how people who had so much could be so cold and callous. Almost at the bottom of the long winding stairway, one final thought entered her beleaguered mind. "If I," and she paused midsentence to correct her thoughts with a sense of resolve. "No," she said, calling on all of her intestinal fortitude. "When I get out of here, these people are going down, and this I swear on my mother's life!"

Mustering all her nerve as well as her cool, she entered the grand hall wherein she was immediately inundated with a multitude of greetings and salutations from the many people present. Ms. Diane was, after all, the heir apparent to the vast fortune that the Conn family had amassed, and each one of these people knew it and treated her as such. That thought troubled Pam. *A bunch of kiss asses*, she thought, still smiling and nodding all the while. Making her way across the room, she stopped and engaged in several exchanges of pleasantries and each time having to explain her need to whisper, but no sign of trouble so far.

From behind, someone grabbed her, spun her around, and kissed her forcefully but politely on the lips. And before she could speak, one of the men in the small party that had gathered to talk to her extended his hand and greeted Clark with a hello and perfunctory inquiry about his well-being and that of his family. Clark returned the formalities and excused himself, pulling Pam by the hand to a somewhat quiet corner of the very, very large room.

"I called you earlier today, only to hear that you were not feeling well. What happened? Are you okay?"

In a whisper, she replied, "I'm fine. I do, though, have a case of severe laryngitis, so don't expect me to say much tonight."

Clark replied, "As beautiful and as radiant as you are, you don't have to say a word. Just promise me that you won't allow Tyler to have any of your time tonight."

Pam's whispered retort came instantly. "I told you not to expect me to talk much, so I'm just not answering you."

SAME AS GOD SPOKE

Insistent on getting his wish granted, again Clark countered, "Does that mean you won't let Tyler have any of your time?"

With a very stern look of conviction, her response was repeated. "That means I am not answering you."

All but conceding, Clark responded with a whimsical assertion that made the pretend Ms. Diane laugh and smile. "Okay then," he said in a low and forced baritone voice. "If I have to share you, I'll share you." Then with a slight pause for optimal dramatic effect, he continued, "Because half of you is more than the equivalent of any other woman that I know." And with that, he gracefully bowed at the waist and gleefully said in his best Southern aristocrat voice, "Jeremiah Clark Winslow Jackson III at your service, madame."

Pam just shook her head, smiling on the outside and simultaneously thinking on the inside, *What a bunch of crock*. She then motioned his silence with one finger gently pressed against her lips. She followed this symbolic beckoning with a strategic move to separate herself from her apparent parasite. "Shush. Now go and get me something to drink, would you?" she said in a low whisper.

Looking curiously into her eyes as if to discern her true motives, he smiled widely and then complied with her wish. As soon as Clark had taken his leave, Pam spotted Big Walter, who looked as comfortable in a tuxedo as would any walrus. The portly barrel-chested man walked over to Pam after having made eye contact, and she whispered to him, "I'll see you outside in five minutes. Get the limo and wait for me outside the front door." Walter's eyes brightened up, and he nodded in agreement and smiled as he walked away, contemplating the wonderful experience that he imagined soon awaited him.

Just as he stepped away, Pam was once again grabbed by the hand and forcefully pulled to the bosom of the taller and more elegant man than before. She realized that he must have been Tyler. He kissed her politely on the cheek, and in one motion, he pulled her even closer to him than had his predecessor so that they were locked in a very tight embrace.

"I called earlier today," he whispered seductively in her ear. "But they told me that you were not feeling well." Before she could open her mouth to reply, Clark reappeared with a drink in both hands.

He uttered a very salty salutation directed at Tyler, to which Tyler did not reply. The two men glared at each other in what seemed to be some form of male posturing. This standoff seemed fit for some mating ritual in the animal world. Pam seized this opportunity as any good diva would to make a graceful exit so they could settle it in semi-privacy.

She then took her drink from Clark's hand and excused herself to go freshen up. Not waiting for any objection, she made her way across the room. She turned just once to look back over her shoulder so as to be certain that she was not followed by either man. She saw what looked to be the two men locked in a heated version of the blame game, one blaming the other for her uncomfortable departure. They were so focused, they didn't even notice or respond to her eloquent over-the-shoulder wave.

Once outside of the grand ballroom, Pam headed straight for the powder room. She quickly gathered herself after having had her nerves shaken by all the up close and personal attention. Albeit, she thought to herself that she had done a magnificent job of acting. Taking a deep breath to calm her nerves once more, she gave herself one last glance of reassurance in the mirror for confidence and exited quietly.

She looked around to see that the coast was in fact clear, and she made a beeline toward the front door. Two small steps from her destination and almost certain freedom, she was grabbed by the arm. Spinning defiantly to see who would exact such force on the person of the Conn heir apparent, she was startled to see that Clark had interrupted her path.

Chapter 16

Compromised

"Going somewhere?" came a strangely arrogant remark from the man now holding her by the arm with a tight death grip.

Trying her best not to look like someone on the verge of escaping, Pam mustered a very meek, "Who wants to know?"

"Seemingly the only one in this party that you haven't fooled," replied her new captor. "Ms. Diane, or is it Workforce Pam?" he asked mockingly. As she turned to face her latest captor, she tried her best to continue the charade undaunted.

"Why, Clark, what on earth are you talking about?" she asked matter-of-factly, only this time forgetting to whisper.

"That. That is exactly what I'm talking about. Where did you get such a citified voice, Ms. Diane?" he asked rhetorically. Immediately returning to her low whisper, Pam urged Clark to release her as the tremendous pressure that he was applying was seriously hurting her arm.

Clark tightened his grip momentarily and added, "If you don't play along with me, your arm ain't all that will be hurt. I'm going to release you now, but if you so much as make one false move, I will go to the Good Doctor and have him shut down all the exits. We will then have you found, beaten to within an inch of your life as an example, and then returned to the Godspoke workforce to slave your life away until you die an old haggard woman."

"Okay, you got me. So what now? What do you want?" she hesitantly asked in disgust, fearing the worst.

"What I want," he quickly shot back, "is a free meal ticket, and you are it."

"What do you mean free meal ticket?" she said, now puzzled.

"I mean that we have lots to talk about," he said as he looked around the room to be certain that no one was in earshot. "The first thing we are going to do is step in the Good Doctor's library so that we won't be disturbed." Pointing the way, Clark led Pam, no longer incognito, to the library just off the foyer.

Once inside, he did not hesitate to get right to the point. "I knew it was you all along," he said with a certain cockiness. "When I first walked up behind you tonight, I immediately noticed that the mole that was so prominently placed behind your left ear had mysteriously disappeared. I thought that was strange, to say the least, but I wasn't exactly sure, so I tested you.

"When I kissed you on the mouth over no objection, then I knew it was you for certain. Little Ms. Diane just hates public displays of affection, and she would have had a hissy fit if I did that to her. Then just for overkill, I bowed and stated my name as Jeremiah Clark Winslow Jackson. For the record, none of that is correct, except the Clark part. Now that we have that out of the way, and you know that I own you right now, this is the way it's going down," he said with an evil grin.

"Okay, okay, so now what's the rest of the story?" Pam asked impatiently.

Continuing in his somewhat smug demeanor, Clark answered slowly. "Glad you asked. First, as you can tell by the looks of this place, the Good Doctor and the lovely Lady Sara are worth hundreds of millions of dollars.

"Go ahead. Add it all up—the planes, the boats, the helicopters, the offshore bank accounts, this place, and let's not forget the biosphere and the lucrative crop that the workforce tends to. The point is, they are loaded, and that makes you loaded."

"What are you talking about?" she blurted out again impatiently.

"Well, the way I see it is this. If the doctor and his wife, your parents—follow me now?—were to meet with some untimely misfortune that would spell some very good fortune for Little Ms. Diane, and her newlywed husband, of course."

"So this is about money? And that's it?"

"Of course it is. What did you think? That I wanted a skinny spoiled malcontent like Little Ms. fucking Diane or you for that matter? You look just like her."

"Yes, I do, and maybe that's why you really kissed me. Not to see if I was her but because you were really fulfilling some sick secret fantasy since there is nothing actually going on between you two."

"Don't flatter yourself, or her, for that matter. I don't like either of your types. Oh, I forgot, you don't really know that little pretend-to-be woman whose only ambition in life is to buy new clothes on the shopping sprees that her parents send her on twice monthly. I take her away on her very own private jet, which we arrive at by limousine or by helicopter most times. We go to any part of the world that she wishes. And golly gee, I get to go along as a protector and an escort. The punch line is that her rotten-to-the-core parents also send along her matron to ensure that no hanky-panky takes place."

"But of course," she said sarcastically. "Okay, so this is about money. I'm listening. Go on."

"As I was saying, this is my shot, and it could work out exceptionally well for you, too, if you play along. You and I could cash in like nobody's business in just about three months. That's ninety short days from now. I mean, we could get over like the Feds. We simply make a few promises and then sit back and wait to collect."

"Promise what?" she blurted out suspiciously.

"Promise our love for each other and then take our rightful places as heirs to the Conn throne. That's the promise. We could go out there tonight on this grand stage and announce our engagement. Hell, everyone already thinks that we have something going on. Not me and you, of course, but me and Diane.

"In a couple of days, you could tell Lady Sara that you are very much in love and you can't wait to be married. Then when she gives the okay, the very next day, we'll begin to plan a huge wedding that will take place almost right away. Believe me, her parents won't object. Not at all. Shit, they give her little spoiled ass anything she wants with no questions asked. And I mean none. Not a one."

"Not one question?" Pam quizzed.

"Not a one! For real," he said, wide-eyed.

After a few moments of quizzical looks followed by an awkward silence, Pam began a new line of questioning. "You think we can really pull this off?"

"Can we really pull this off?" he asked rhetorically.

"I guarantee we can pull this off if you listen to my coaching and follow my instructions. I'm not bragging here, but I am damn good at what I do."

"And what is that?" she asked curiously.

"I read people, and I learn how to put them in their comfort zone, and that's where they can best serve me. How do you think I have so much power around here? I know exactly what we need to do to pull this off. Trust me," he said excitedly. "Let's examine the situation. So far, even her own dumb ass parents or her personal servants have made you. Now if they are out to lunch on this, then dammit, we are in. In the money, that is. You've already done the hardest part. You've fooled everyone around here. Everybody except me," he added with an air of confidence.

"With a few tips and some coaching from me, we can seriously do this and get over like fat rats. I will teach you how to act like her, walk like her, and even talk like her so you can stop that fake whisper, which will eventually give you away. It's only a matter of time. But with my coaching, I can teach you in a couple of days. Tomorrow is your trip, I mean Diane's trip, to Las Vegas, and we can work on it then. In the meantime, you will still have to use your laryngitis story.

"This is the long and short of it all. I won't force you to be with me intimately, but we will get married. Then when the time is right, a helicopter ride with your benefactors aboard will go bad. Very, very bad. Afterward, you and I can split the cash equally. At the appropriate time, of course."

"But of course," came Pam's suspicion-filled reply. After a long pause to contemplate his offer, she queried further so as to gage his true motives, if she could. She began quite bluntly, "How do I know that you won't do the same to me once you get rid of them? I'm the only thing standing in the way of you and all the cash, as you put it."

"I'm not that greedy, nor am I that stupid. How would it look if my new wife and her parents all died under mysterious circumstances just shortly after I joined the family? Come on. Get real. Do you think I've gotten this far by being nearsighted or obtuse?

"I know when to leave well enough alone. And if that's not good enough for you, we can put it all in writing. Everything that we've done, everything there we're about to do with all the sordid details can all go down in writing, and we can both have copies. That way, I can have my secret notes, signed by you, sent to the proper authorities. That is, if I should meet my untimely demise, and so can you. How does that sound to you?"

Channeling deep from within, Pam began to genuinely reveal some of her innermost thoughts to this stranger, with whom she now felt a strange connection. "To be quite real with you, I was just upstairs planning my escape, but all the while I was seriously thinking to myself about how I could get used to this life if it were at all possible. Besides that, I really don't owe any loyalty to any of the others that I came here with.

"It's not like they are my real family or anything like that. They are my ex-fiancé's family, and I know all too well that they don't much like me. And personally, I sure as hell don't like them all that much either. Especially that bitch Hazel. I hope she stays here forever," she uttered aloud as a sudden afterthought.

"And as I now give it some more serious thought, I really, and I mean really, really could get used to this. I mean shit, who couldn't? I don't have any kids or any real family, so to speak," she said while shrugging her shoulders. Then she continued, "Except my sister, Velma. And she gets on my nerves too!" Finishing up, she said, "And dammit, I really could do without all her drama in my life to boot."

Taking a long time to pause and think, Pam did her best Clark impression by first looking deeply into his eyes in order to discern his true motives. She then leaned over to whisper in his ear and asked intently, "Do you promise? Do you swear to God Almighty that you will not force yourself on me? You said I am not your type, and believe me, buddy, you're not my type either."

"I swear. I swear on everything that I know and love! I do! I do! As I said before, I don't even like your type. I have a hundred girls I see, but only casual stuff on the side. I always knew that being with her would be just like having the keys to the vault. So I always have to keep up the charade of me courting Diane. I couldn't afford to let all of my hard work go for nothing. But that little skinny bitch wasn't really having any part of my plan. I honestly think the bitch is a dyke!"

Now confident that he had Pam's favor, he bragged, "Hell, without me as his second-in-command, the Good Doctor would have none of this. He is an excellent scientist, but not much of an executive at all. Who do you think makes all the administrative decisions around here?" With a broad smile, he asserted, "I do, that's who. I do, and for what? A miserly ninety thousand dollars a year? Hell, when I go off on one of the little princess's shopping junkets, we spend seventy, sometimes eighty, thousand in a week and on bullshit.

"Hell, I was even the one who gave the stuff its name. So—"

And before he could continue, she interrupted his flow, if for nothing else, so as to throw him off his game. She also sought to gain more of his trust, all in one fell swoop, if possible. Sensing that she may have the upper hand, as he was lost in the lust of self-aggrandizement, she stepped in to make a move. In full command of a genuine, although pretense, curiosity, she blurted out, "How did you do that?"

"Do what?" he said.

"How did you give the stuff its name?"

"I...uh...I." Surprised by the question, he stammered, but just as quickly as he was thrown, he regained his composure. Now more certain, he began again, "Well, I was always saying to myself how the Good Doctor acted as if God himself had spoken whenever he gave an order around here. And so when we first tested the stuff and the people would move on a dime after every command, it was exactly as if God had spoken. And one day, I said that out loud, and the name just kind of stuck.

SAME AS GOD SPOKE

"But enough of that," he strategically shifted yet pausing to notice if she was buying his impromptu and very made-up story. "Like I was saying, I practically built this whole enterprise almost from day one, and I want my shot at the title. I want the brass, gold, and platinum rings all at once. I do swear. I do swear to God Almighty himself. And when I tell you this, it really is the same as God spoke. For me, I don't even enjoy sex unless I have some money. On top of that, I have enough basic sense to know that when I get lots of money, I can have all the sex I want. Until then, I can wait.

"Now do we have a deal or not? We don't have all night to be in here." After a measured pause from Pam, he uttered a last word of encouragement. "I promise, you won't be sorry."

Tilting her head to one side, exposing a sheepish grin, and extending her hand to him, she said, "Okay, Mr. Clark. If you truly mean what you say about half the money, and if you absolutely vow to keep your word not to touch me, then we have a deal!" Shifting quickly, she stated, "But there is one loose end." Having his full attention, she continued, "I'm afraid you all have underestimated Walter. He is my accomplice."

"I guess it is all about sex for him."

Discerning his instant concern, she went on, "He is outside right now waiting in a limo to help me escape."

After some intense thought and quickly weighing all the options available to him, Clark asked, "Does he know your true identity?"

Thinking quickly on her feet, Pam answered an emphatic "Yes." She hoped that somehow, this answer could get her out of Clark's sight so that she could then resort to plan B.

In all truth, she knew that she had no plan B. But on the spur of the moment, a desperate thought occurred to her. *If only I can get out of this door, I am going to run like hell and hope to heaven that I'll be all right.* It wasn't much of a plan, but it was all she had. The thought of not really having an alternate plan aside, she struggled to maintain her composure as she continued to string Clark along.

"Yes," she said, clearing her mucus-filled throat. "Walter is a big fan of Ms. Diane, and I promised him that I would fulfill his Ms. Diane fantasy for his help."

"You promised to sleep with him?" he shouted in both surprise and disgust.

Suspicious of his motives, Pam once again attempted to outmaneuver her rival by responding with a shout of her own. "Hell no!" she shouted without so much as a flinch. "As good-looking as you are, or so you think, if I refused to sleep with you against my will, what makes you think I would agree to do that with him, as gruesome as he is? Big Walter is a voyeur. Plus, he has a foot fetish," she continued without pause. "He wants to worship my feet for as long as he likes after having an official date with me, as he puts it. He says it would be just like having it all with the real Ms. Diane.

"He also thought that maybe when he finally rescued the real Ms. Diane from the workforce, she would be indebted to him, or that the Good Doctor and Lady Sara would be indebted to him. Either way, he would make out as the hero. The plan was to blame one of the guards. The same ones who let my fiancé get away in the first place, so it would be an easy sell. Now what should we do?" she asked hurriedly and waited for a response.

After a short pause, Clark was about to respond, but he was interrupted by the Good Doctor. "Why, Clark, just the man I was looking for. This is Mr. Gensky, and this is Mr. Roberts, and finally, this is Mr. Friday. These gentlemen are very interested in our organization, and after a more in-depth presentation, hopefully they will each become financial backers. I'm sorry to interrupt you and my lovely daughter, but as you know, first things first. Gentlemen, this lovely young lady is Ms. Diane, my one and only child. Now if you will excuse us, dear, I will have Clark back to you in no time at all."

Clark moved slowly toward the door as Pam's escort, contemplating his next move. He either had to trust her or expose her. Once she crossed the threshold, she had the freedom of choice to double-cross him. Just before they parted company, each standing on opposite sides of the threshold, Clark squeezed the hand of his would-be partner in crime with as much might as he could muster. He said to her with threatening conviction, accompanied by a piercing glare, "Please don't disappoint me, my dear. I hope to see you when I come out."

Pam, without a blink of hesitation and no acknowledgement of the severe pain that he was applying, returned his glare and upped him one. She looked him dead in the eye and responded with a wink. This was followed by her most convincing statement of their conversation. "I will be here when you get out," she said emphatically. "And there are millions and millions of reasons why." She smiled politely and then took one giant step back as if playing the childhood game of Mother May I. She then twirled on her heels and simultaneously initiated a second wink of assurance, this time over her shoulder, just as the view of her face was replaced by a view of her shimmering long jet-black hair.

Clark watched her stroll elegantly across the foyer and back into the party. Before he could close the door, she turned and yelled out to him, "Do hurry up! Remember our big little problem!" She was referring to her waiting accomplice. He nodded in agreement and smiled a confident smile. He was instantly convinced as he closed the door behind him.

As soon as she heard the library door close behind her, Pam took two additional steps toward the grand ballroom, but she made an abrupt about-face and headed straight for the entrance door. Walter was waiting impatiently just outside the entrance, and she whispered in his ear, "Let's hurry up and get out of here." Big Walter hurriedly sought out the family limousine and entered the rear with Pam in tow. He then ordered the driver to take them to the end of long winding driveway, back to the roadway, and make a left.

"Just drive," he added. "I will tell you where to stop."

After a short drive of less than five miles, Big Walt then directed the limo driver to a secluded spot in the woods and raised the partition. Once the car came to rest, Big Walt began to roughly caress his dream girl's legs and upper thighs. "Hold on, big fella. Hold on."

The large man became immediately suspicious and asked gruffly, "Hey, what the hell is going on here We had a deal, and now you wanna give me hard-to-get moves? I'm not having this shit. You either let me do what I want right now or I'm gonna take you back."

"Just calm down. We are going to do what we came here to do. I promised you, and I am a woman of my word, just as you are a man of your word. I just need a minute, so I'm going to ask that you be a gentleman and turn around and give me a couple few minutes to get undressed and to put on something sexy that I just bought especially for this night. Go ahead. Just turn around, and I promise you that you won't be sorry. I'm going to give you a night that you will never forget."

These words were like sweet music to his ears, so Walter meekly complied. He turned his back to her, and he placed his large hands over his eyes as he had been instructed. Where he was long of cunning and bravado when it came to work, he was undoubtedly short-changed in the socializing with female's department. Barely able to contain himself, Walter grinned and giggled happily in anticipation of what he imagined was to come.

However, he had never considered the drawbacks of being in this most vulnerable of positions. Pam took complete advantage of her superior premeditated position and launched a full-fledged sneak attack from the rear. With lighting speed and laser-like precision, she jabbed him in the back of the neck with as much force as the fast sweeping stroke would allow. Before her victim could react, she squeezed hard and injected him with a syringeful of the Godspoke.

She immediately jumped to another seat in order to put as much distance as possible between herself and the big wounded man. She realized that this big and powerful man could still cause her some serious damage, even in his transforming state. She immediately picked up the heaviest of the Bellini decanters located in the limo's bar to use as a weapon if needed. She also knew that she had to protect the button used to lower the soundproof partition.

Instantly recognizing the futility of a struggle, Walter decided to make a deal instead. He could feel the tingling sensation of the monstrous concoction rushing through his veins, and he knew that he only had about ninety seconds before he was completely under its hypnotic spell. In desperation, he declared that he had not been adequately prepped for the injection. He further insisted that his skin should have been cleansed before being injected. He then cited the warning about the damage commonly found skin bacteria could cause. "I don't want to die!" he pleaded.

In a frantic voice, he pleaded further with Pam to go back to the biosphere so that he could retrieve the Godspoke antibodies which would protect him from the infection. Seeing the look of sheer terror in his big brown eyes, Pam began to feel somewhat sorry for this big brut of a man and momentarily considered his request. Her consideration was all of two seconds, as her initial thought of *no way in hell* returned to her in full force. In the end, all his pleading fell on deaf ears.

After what seemed like hours to Pam but were only mere seconds in reality, Walter was completely subdued. He was now a powerless prisoner of the Godspoke. As a test, Pam ordered him to close his eyes and open his mouth as wide as he could. He willingly complied, and she laughed at the silly sight but quickly gathered herself.

Still uncertain and alert not to be fooled in turn, she ordered him to bite down into his forearm until he tasted blood. The spellbound man again complied. The sight of the thick dripping blood was revolting but gave her confidence that he was totally in her control. She then partially lowered the partition and ordered the driver to head back to the highway.

While making their way back to the highway in darkest of night, Pam grabbed Big Walter's cell phone from his side carrying case. She dialed BJ's cell and hoped to God that he would answer. When she heard his voice on the other end of the line, she calmly said, "Hey there, girlfriend. Do you know who this is? I can't wait to see you."

BJ replied, "Pam, is that you?"

Still calm, cool, and collected, she replied again, "That's right. You got it, pretty momma."

Confused, BJ asked his future daughter-in-law, "What's wrong with you? Are you okay?"

She gently replied, "I will be, sweetie, if you play your cards right."

After finally catching on, BJ said the words that she so desperately wanted and needed to hear: "Okay, I get it. You are under duress, so tell me where you are."

"I can't do that right now, girlfriend. Why don't you do that?" she said in stealth.

"Okay, so I'll assume that you don't know where you are, so can you get to me."

She was as calm as ever, even though she was growing impatient by the second with her meticulous father-in-law. "I can and I will," she said softly. All the while, she hoped that he would just finally give her a location as she noticed the limo driver was very interested in her conversation. She knew that he was probably very curious as to why she and not Walter was now giving him directions. She wished like hell that BJ would stop trying to be so professional and shit and just give her the damn address.

After what seemed like an eternity, BJ finally gave her his location. "I am at the Town and Country Inn just off Route 1 South."

"Isn't there something else that I need?" she asked politely.

"Oh, oh," he said, catching on again. "I am in room 624 on the ground level."

"Okay, girl, we can do that, so put the champagne on ice. We will be right over. And you should be expecting me and my two friends, I hope," she said with emphasis as she returned the driver's stare through the mirror.

"So there are two of them. We got you, honey. Just hurry and get here," BJ said, but Pam did not reply. She just hung up.

Very puzzled yet intrigued by the conversation he had just heard, the driver asked Pam, "Sorry, ma'am, but I couldn't help but to overhear you. What was that about two friends? Are we picking up someone else?" Just as she'd hoped, he easily took the bait. *Who said men don't think with their little heads?* she thought.

"Well," she said softly while seductively sucking on the tip of her longest finger. "We originally wanted to spend a little time under the stars, but a friend who shall remain nameless told me that some of the deputies around here often patrol for parked cars."

"Yeah, that's true," he replied. "They will flash their lights inside of a parked car in an isolated spot in a heartbeat. So what's the deal? Who do you want me to pick up?"

"Well," she continued almost hesitantly, using even more girl bait than before. "With my family name and all, I could not withstand that type of scandal. So after discussing it with my big teddy bear over here, what I did was have a friend book us a room at an out-of-the-way hotel.

"I hope you can keep some things to yourself," she asked and waited for a response.

"Yeah, yeah, I can," answered the man whose eyes and tone were now clearly greedy with lust.

"Um, by the way, what is your name?"

"Mack, ma'am. They call me Limo Mack. Your regular driver was sick tonight, so I took his place."

"Okay, Limo Mack, do you know where the Town and Country Inn is?"

"Yes, ma'am, but there's two of them close by. Do you want the one over on Patricia Boulevard or the one on Route 1 South?"

"I do believe it's the one on Route 1," she said, continuing her seductive ways. "Now don't get pulled over, but the quicker you get there, the quicker I can get out of my clothes. As I said, my girlfriend is waiting for us there, and she was going to share. But with the looks of you, I think that a late night switch might be a better move. You game?

"What I'm saying is," she said after a pause to let the idea fully seep into the disbelieving driver, "you can come in, too, if you like. We have a suite."

"Consider us there. Consider us there, ma'am," the driver said. His was response dipped in unadulterated lust, which he did little to conceal. "If you don't mind me saying so, but I've heard about stuff like this before with you rich socialite types, but I never thought I'd get a chance to join in. *Thank you, God*," he said without even looking back! If he had, he might have well noticed the look of disgust on his passenger's face in response to his wayward remark.

After just a few short minutes, the driver announced their arrival. "The Town and Country Inn Route 1 South. I got us here pretty quick, huh?" he said proudly.

"You sure did, Mack. You sure did. Workforce Walter, follow me," she whispered softly in his ear. "You, too, Mack. Follow me. I know right where our room is, and as soon as we get inside, you are going to get exactly what you deserve." Oblivious to his fate or to the ominous suggestion of her comment, Limo Mack followed his master to the slaughterhouse.

"Man oh man," said the limo driver with the joy of great expectation. "I can't wait." His lust was again on full display.

"I can't wait either," Pam replied, absent the true venom and contempt she truly felt for the man now watching her with lustful eyes. "I can't wait to see you in action, big boy," she said as she quickened her pace. "Six hundred twenty-nine, six hundred twenty-eight, six hundred twenty-seven," she counted down as she neared her final destination—the real doorway to freedom.

"To be honest, Ms. Diane, I never thought a day like this would come, but I always dreamed about it."

"You did?" she said, not really paying the lustful man much attention. "Six hundred twenty-five, six hundred twenty-four, here we are." With Walter held firmly by the hand, she tapped on the door softly and turned to Limo Mack.

"Well, tonight is the night. Your dream is about to come true. Now let's get in here and get this thing started. You said you couldn't wait. Well, wait no more. Come on in, Bad Boy Max," she said with glee in her voice as the door opened slowly to a dimly lit interior. Led by Pam, the trio stepped inside. Before either of them knew what had hit them, BJ; his lieutenant, Red China; and three other Black Ivory team members joined forces to overpower Mack the horny limo driver and the spellbound baby hulk of a man Big Walter. Four other team members rushed in from their hiding spots in the parking lot as the takedown ensued.

To ensure their complete cooperation, each man received a healthy dose of chloroform, which was forcefully placed over the mouth and nose of each man simultaneously. Once unconscious, both men were searched, and a few items of value were removed from them. Together with the keys to the limo and a small caliber handgun, the most important of these items was a second remote, which they would later learn operated the glass elevator inside the wine cellar. This would prove extremely valuable, as that was believed to be the only viable pathway to rescue the others.

Now in the safety of friendly faces, Pam was reduced to tears, both from relief and from worry about her first and only love, Greg. Leaning on her soon-to-be father-in-law's shoulder, she began to tell him about their whole ordeal. However, her once calm and collected demeanor was now reduced to sobs, tears, and a calamity of words spilling one over the other. She was difficult to understand, if not altogether unintelligible.

Allowing her to see his strength, BJ gently stopped her midsentence with a single finger strategically placed in the center of his wide mouth. His tender but firm shush gave her the quiet sign. He looked her forcefully in the eye, and once he had her complete attention, he gave her his signature reassuring wink, followed immediately by a disarming nod. His goal was to help her regain all the calm and cool that she must have had to display to get this far, based on what he could make out so far from her rapid-fire blur of words.

After a moment to release and collect herself, BJ tried again to get some useful information from the obviously shaken young woman. Keeping direct eye contact to provide a much-needed sense of security, he calmly asked her specifically about the health and location of the rest of the group, and more importantly, how best to get to them. She began slowly, and this time around, she displayed the calm, cool, and collected demeanor that she exhibited over the phone. As she spoke and provided some very specific and well thought-out details, BJ looked on and decided that he was very impressed. He had never thought much of the young lady betrothed to his youngest son, but he was not a brooding parent either, so this was a well-guarded secret.

After Pam had given them all information that she was able to, BJ turned to her and announced, "I have a surprise for you."

"Surprise? After this trip, that is one word that I do not want to hear," she said, wiping away more tears, half laughing and half crying.

"I'm sure this surprise will be a pleasant one. Now go through that door and you'll see for yourself. Your safe now. Nothing can hurt you now. You're with me," he said as a last measure of reassurance.

Pam, weary of surprises on the other side of closed doors, walked over to the door, but she hesitated momentarily before turning the doorknob. After her thought-gathering pause, she took a deep breath, turned the knob, and proceeded through the door. She instantly let out a yell of joy. Sleeping on the bed just two feet from where she stood was her beloved Greg. Startled, Greg awakened and let out his own joyous yell. Immediately, BJ came to the door and demanded that they both be quiet so as not to draw any attention. They both immediately composed themselves.

"But when? But how?" asked Pam.

"It was simple," BJ responded. "He called me and told me where he was, according to the GPS coordinates from the cell phone that, thank God, you hid in the glove compartment. I plugged his coordinates in my GPS, and it took me right to him.

"Listen, we will fill you in later with all the details, okay? Right now, and I do mean right now, we have work to do. You two will have time for a reunion later. But now, we have to save your brothers and their wives."

In unison, the two echoed a meek, "Sorry, Dad" as both knew that BJ was not to be played with when it came to work, and more importantly, when it came to his children!

CHAPTER 17

The Game Plan

WITH SOME STANDING and others sitting, Team Black Ivory was at the anxious ready. The adrenaline rush of subduing the playboy posse in the adjoining room had most of them fully charged. The anticipation of going into harm's way was all the excitement elixir the remainder needed to get amped up as well.

Although each member of Black Ivory could perform a wide range of special ops proficiencies, each individual had a specialized skill set. Each could do at least one thing better than anyone else on the team. Although, each took comfort in the fact that any one of the others could step in for them if, and when it became necessary! In addition to BJ, the team leader, and Red China, BJ's longtime second, this particular team consisted of seven additional members.

Danger was an expert reconnaissance man, a spy among spies. Give him a couple of hours and he could tell you almost everything about anywhere, at any time, day or night, and then some. Cowboy could shoot the *d* out of a dime at a thousand yards or more. And Golden Boy had the uncanny ability to not be seen when he didn't want to be seen. He could literally disappear in broad daylight, right in front of your very eyes.

Fancy-pants was a communications master. He could almost make a radio into a TV without any tools. Heat knew everything there was to know about weapons. How fast a bullet could travel and even where best to take a bullet and survive. Blow-em-up was uniquely adept in the art of explosives. He could burn through any structure on earth, and you'd never hear him do it.

Jumper could climb anything and squeeze his way into any tight spot, which was always helpful when the team needed to get close to someone who didn't want to be gotten close to. Everybody had a role to play, and everybody played their role well. This team was built to succeed.

After ten minutes of agonizing quiet, the tense silence in the small room was interrupted. "What's the plan, BJ?" came the baritone voice of Red China. BJ's longtime confidant and number two man was concerned. The Black Ivory Strike Force were all ex-CIA and Special Operations guys. They were well trained and well equipped to get in and safely get out of any tight spot, but this was different. Red China saw a different BJ.

His cold, calculating leader was missing his edge. That intangible something that always allowed him to make the right calls, even when they seemed to defy logic. He thought BJ always made the right call because he cared for his men. Only this time, the package was his family, and it was only natural for him to care for them more.

It was written all over BJ's wrinkled and ragged brow. Red, as he was called by the group, contemplated whether or not to say something to him and the others. He did not want to go into the teeth of the lion with BJ operating on emotion rather than his trademark calm, cool, collected demeanor. It was not fair to allow the others to risk their lives behind a man that was not fit to lead.

This was not the movies where the good guys would always win. This was real, and people could die. Red dug down deep and thought real hard, but after a serious internal debate, he decided against it. He did not want to spook the team. The fear was that he would doom the mission to failure before it even began. He decided he would wait and accept the calculated risk of BJ pulling through. However, he also decided to keep his ace in the hole. He would play this card if, and only if, he saw that BJ was doing things out of the ordinary.

After another prolonged silence, a second voice violated the quiet. "Yeah, what's the deal yo? I'm ready to eat somebody for lunch.

I'm ready to burn some ass, fry some gizzards, and roast some intestines." This animated cadence came from Danger and was met with a disapproving look from Red China, who always said what BJ was thinking. Danger was not only the youngest of the octet but also the most pugnacious and rambunctious.

In fact, Danger was a turbulently active and supercharged character, to say the least. In spite of his shortcomings, he was, however, the best at scouting a location in order to determine its weaknesses and vulnerabilities.

After meticulously conceiving a plan of action inside the private confines of his head, BJ finally spoke. "Bring Big Walt to me. I need some more information, 'cause right now, we got more questions than answers, and that's not good."

Big Walt lay unconscious and needed to be revived and then questioned. Golden Boy and Blow-em-up quickly carried out BJ's request, as they were the most muscular of the team. And plenty of muscles would be needed to carry the limp body of the hulking man some fifty feet across the room.

They both grabbed the seemingly lifeless man underneath his massive arms. On the count of three, they pulled and jerked him to a near standing position. Even while working together, they struggled mightily as they dragged him across the floor. After a hellish twenty-five seconds, they plopped him into a low-sitting chair next to a dining table. The unconscious man promptly fell face forward and nearly hit the floor face-first, but quick reactions from both men preempted that inevitability.

Quickly analyzing the challenge to keep the huge man in the seat, Red China took charge. Unlike the struggling duo, Red China did not assume the near-lifeless man could remain in a seated position without aid. Unsolicited, as always, he held the wide-bodied ape of a man in the erect seated position with a simple strategically placed hand on one of his huge shoulders.

After all the antics of getting the enemy combatant seated, it was BJ's turn to do what he did best—extract information. Although, this interrogation would prove to be not much of a challenge, since his subject was under the hypnotic spell of the Godspoke. Nonetheless, BJ began his mission with the same intensity that he would any other.

His facial expression revealed the ruthless side of this usually softhearted man. The contradiction in persona was striking, and it was almost hard to believe that he was in fact a real-life Dr. Jekyll and Mr. Hyde type of guy. He first leaned over the man who was now at his mercy, which was in short supply once the Black Ivory show started.

The expression on his face made it very evident that he took extreme pleasure in playing his role. Step one was to revive the sleeping giant by shocking his sense of smell. The once comatose man was instantly jolted back to reality after a strong dose of smelling salts was administered. BJ held the odorous concoction at point-blank range, just beneath two flaring nostrils for quite some time.

Once revived, he struggled to catch his breath. BJ had administered the smelling salts liberally and without mercy and for much longer than was necessary to revive anyone. After his uncontrollable coughing attack subsided, BJ began to question him while Danger took careful notes. He would be the one to first scout the location in an effort to verify the subject's account of things and to identify the most suitable points of entry and exit.

"Hey, Pam, come over here. Is he still under the influence of that stuff? What did you call it, Godspoke or something?"

"Yeah, that's what they called it. I call it slave medicine 'cause that what it does, make you a 'yes master" slave." Looking closely to be certain that she recognized the familiar far-off gaze which was so characteristic of the Godspoke spell, Pam nodded in the affirmative. "Yeah, I would definitely say he's still under. One dose of this stuff is supposed to keep you under for between seven to ten days. At least that's what they said."

BJ methodically began to extract the information he needed to save his boys and their wives. "What is your name?"

"Walter Lildevil."

"Where do you work?"

"I work for the Conn Estate."

"Describe for me the security system at the Conn Estate and also how you get in and every way that you can get out."

Big Walter began to give his slow but comprehensive report. He provided every detail imaginable about the palatial Conn Estate, including and especially the workforce biosphere. BJ asked for and received meticulous details about the armed guards who protected it. The report additionally contained crucial information that described how to access the biosphere through a wine cellar in the rear of the mansion. He also provided the group with critical intel pertaining to the remotes that controlled the only entry point into the sphere directly from the ground level. This was the truck entry, he said, to load shipments and receive supply deliveries.

As he continued to extract every necessary detail from his subject, BJ began to both admire and marvel at the amount of painstaking detail that this man had at his command. Near the end of the interrogation, Big Walter provided a detailed account as to how to override the system. One master remote, which Clark had control of, was able to shut down the glass elevator in case someone was trying to escape. As this was the only portal of access from the estate and the only logical means of escape, BJ took careful deliberation in extracting this crucial piece of the logistics puzzle.

At some point during the interrogation, Big Walt even told his questioner the exact bed numbers for each of his family members. Much to BJ's delight, ole Walter was just full of details. So helpful, in fact, that BJ almost hesitated to chloroform him again once he had all the intel that he thought he would need. Almost, but not quite, as he knew that this man was, at best, partially responsible for the kidnapping and confinement of his sons. And for BJ, this was unforgivable.

All the while, Pam was listening intently in the background. As she watched Walter succumb to the powerful sleep agent that he was forced to inhale, she thought, *Now this is poetic justice. There he was giving the orders to render others helpless. Now look at him. I should go over and knock the shit out of him.*

She smiled at the thought but knew that he probably wouldn't even feel the slap or anything else for a while, at least. However, that didn't stop her from exacting just a small measure of revenge in the form of a wicked Billy Blanks Tae Bo kick to the side of the head. BJ looked sharply at her but said nothing as he knew the source of the obvious internal rage that must be inside his usually mild-mannered future daughter-in-law.

She stood back and smiled as her unapologetic assailant crashed mercilessly to the unforgiving floor. However, the next thought to cross her mind instantly wiped her short-lived smile away. As she watched him sprawled out unconscious with a very visible but small trickle of blood running down his now busted lip, she couldn't help but think that this gruesome looking man had nearly seduced her.

He had gotten her hot and bothered to the point of sexual arousal, and he had nearly gotten her undressed. The very thought of him seeing her nakedness, even half clothed, made her sick to the stomach. Walter was a repulsive man in her eyes, and the thought of him giving her all those commands not so long ago caused her to become instantly nauseous.

The mere thought of this terrible ordeal was very disconcerting, but knowing that her thought was private and that none ever need to know gave her the confidence to dismiss it in secret. And just as the eerie thought dissipated, a clandestine smile immediately returned to her face. She had a secret, and she knew this was one that she would carry to her grave. However, before she had time to enjoy her little secretive moment, the husky and gruff voice of her fiancé's father startled her from her momentary fixation.

"Okay, everyone, gather around. Greg, you suit up," barked BJ. Before Greg had even begun to get dressed in his all-black body armor, the group of men of the Black Ivory Strike Team were already knee-deep devising an emergency rescue and extraction plan. Danger and Golden Boy were asked to provide a detailed report of their earlier recon mission.

"Okay, first off, this place is a huge motherfucker. I can't tell you how far it stretches. All I can say is that it goes on forever."

"Come on, Danger, you gotta tell us more than that," insisted Red China in a noticeably frustrated voice, which echoed and mirrored the look on BJ's chiseled face.

"Well," he said carefully, "if I had to estimate, I would say the place was about fifty square miles. It extends about ten miles down and about five miles over. The backside is hilly, and It's covered in nothing but the thickest woods I've ever seen in my entire life. When I first seen it, all I could say is a hot-to-the-damn."

"One thing," added Golden Boy. "We saw a truck pull up and stop by the side of the road. That was nothing by itself, but what happened next really freaked me out. For real, it was some strange ass shit. After he sat there for a minute, the bushes just like sucked him in. It was as if his vehicle started moving sideways. It was the freakiest thing I ever seen."

Immediately, there was a bunch of sidebar chatter, plus several questions attesting to overt disbelief, much to the group leader's surprise and dismay.

"Hey, BJ," Red said loudly so as to quiet the room and immediately put his somewhat spooked team at ease. "I've seen this before. As I am sure, so have some of you.

"Sounds to me like it's simply a horizontal retraction system. It works like this," he continued, now demonstrating as he spoke. "The driver of the vehicle positions himself in a certain spot. That spot, which is identified by infrared markers, which as you know are invisible to the naked eye, will position him on top of a retracting plate.

"Once the vehicle—or truck, in this case—is in place, the system operator, who is viewing the event through a strategically located closed circuit camera system, engages the system. The vehicle is pulled inward, only sideways. It's sort of like it was on a forklift or a conveyor belt in some respect.

"The gates open up, the vehicle is pulled inside, and the camouflaged gate is closed right after. It's just a measure to ensure no unauthorized vehicles can enter the premises. I'm surprised that all of you guys have never seen that," he said, trying to infer that this high-tech security system was commonplace, even though it was not.

"In fact, we all saw that, at least some of us, when we went on that last mission to South America. Brazil, I think it was. But that's right. You two guys weren't with us. Anyway," he nonchalantly concluded, "don't be alarmed. As long as we know what we're up against, we should be able to make it do what it do, no matter what little tricks they got."

"Good report, guys. Now how do we approach this? Let's hear it. The floor is open for suggestions. And, Greg, get on over here. You need to hear this too," BJ said without pause. Greg joined the group, and he listened intently.

"I say we go in from the rear entry and park just like the truck and go in from there. In smooth to grab them and out smooth to get away," offered Blow-em-up and seconded by Fancy-pants.

"Well, I say we go in guns blazing and kill up every fucking thing that moves on the upstairs and then go sublevel and get the boys" was the counteroffer from none other than Danger.

"No, no," came the paternal reply from Red China. "We have to keep causalities to a minimum. Minimum fuss, minimum mess, and minimum confusion. Less chance of one of us or one of the boys or their wives getting hurt." Red watched BJ's reaction to both suggestions carefully. He did not particularly like the guns blazing approach, but they had done it before. He said nothing, but he listened intently.

The debate raged on for several more minutes, but as it did, Greg thought, *They can plan all they want about keeping casualties to a minimum, but I've got a different plan. All I know is that if I get anyone of those guys that did this sick shit to my Pam and my brothers in my sights, they can kiss their sweet assess goodbye. 'Cause they're all going to hell tonight, if I have anything to say about it! And they can say hi to Satan for me in the process.* Then he smiled as a vision of this afterthought flashed in his head.

BJ again quieted his rowdy band of characters and then directed that they proceed in an orderly fashion to put the finishing touches on their plan of action. Pam watched as the men discussed, planned, checked, and rechecked every consideration, calculation, and analysis before them. Although there was some intense debate about the best approach to enter the premises, she thought the planning session went otherwise relatively smooth, considering all the testosterone and male bravado in one room.

She also silently thought, *Wow, if men paid this much attention to the women in their lives, all of the bitching and moaning that goes on due to the lack of attention would be a thing of the past*" As she looked on and observed from afar, her subsequent thoughts continued to wonder about the validity of her recent conclusion. In doing so, a long stare at Greg made her stop and refocus, as that previous train of thought was fast replaced by an even more compelling one.

"Look at my man. Just look at how intense he is. Oh my goodness gracious, he looks so hot right now. Uuum," she said privately while biting gently down on her lower lip. "I think I've been away from him too long. Right now, I would just like to…" And before she could finish her thought, a vision of Walter's dirty hands touching her rushed in again. *Oh my god*, she thought. *What just happened?*

But before she could come up with an answer to her own question, a loud shout from BJ instantaneously aborted her troubled train of thought. "Dammit, man, you're not a savior! You're a hired mercenary, and that's the bottom line, so no more talk about that bullshit. I'll do all the talking from here on out. Now does anyone else have any other brilliant fucking comments?"

After a long pause, highlighted by his unyielding glare into each man's eyes, BJ gathered himself. He took in as much fresh air into his lungs as he possibly could. He then sighed a deep sigh and buried his face in his hand momentarily. It was very evident that the pressure of the situation was getting to him. After the long and turbulent conversation about all the uncertainties involved with their plan for extraction, no one was very certain that any of their final plans would work.

There were a thousand things that needed to break just right in order for them to have the success that they were looking for. If any one of a number of things that could go wrong broke the other way, that would spell almost certain death for his boys, and BJ knew it. He knew it all too well. The boys that he was so proud, the boys that he had devoted his life to.

For all their lives, he was their rock, their hero, and this was the one time he could not afford to fail them. The one time they needed him most, of the many times in their lives, and he was not sure just how he would make good on his promise to always be there for his children.

The room went deafly silent as everyone stared on in disbelief, having never witnessed their autumn cool and rock steady commander lose it in the way in which they were now witnessing. "I understand about the others. Believe me, I do," he continued in a slow and thoughtful way. "But we are going in there to save my family, and when and only when we get them to safety, we will try to help the others. That's why we are here. That's the plan, and we will execute the plan as such," he said in a slightly elevated tone.

However, in a much more conciliatory although steadfastly firm tone, he then offered an olive branch as he concluded, "Listen…once we are clear, we will send the authorities back in to help the others, but I don't trust the lives of my boys and their wives to any goddamn body else. Understood? Just think if it were one of your children or somebody you loved in there.

"Wouldn't you want trained professionals like us to be on the case and not some dumbass deputy do-right or goddamn sheriff showoff? I know you can understand that," he said directly to Red China, who had offered the idea of alerting law enforcement for the expressed purpose of saving the others held with LJ and the others.

"I got you, man, and I'm with you on this. You can always count on me," came the sullen and abbreviated reply from Red China. To solidify their meeting of the minds, and to be sure that there were no hard feelings, BJ placed his hand firmly on Red China's shoulder, looked him squarely in the eye, and gave him a solid pat on the back, plus his signature wink of reassurance. The meaning of this gesture was clear, and the look on Red China's face confirmed that very fact. He smiled but said nothing further. The BJ wink was enough; it said it all. It always did!

Plan in hand, egos intact, the men from Black Ivory, together with Pam and Greg, exited their meeting spot. In stealth, and with catlike precision, they crossed the courtyard, arriving at their vehicles unnoticed. Once inside, they set out to return to the infamous house of horrors where the others were being held captive. At that very point, engrained in each man's mind was a singular but simultaneously collective thought: *We are going to secure the safe return of BJ's sons and their wives, plus do so by any and by all means necessary.*

From his vantage point in the front seat, BJ turned to ask, "Does everyone have a communications headset?"

"I think so," came an uncertain reply from the responsible party. Without so such as a word, the stern look of disapproval was enough of a silent message to move Fancy-pants into action. Disapproving looks and stern talk was not the usual way Black Ivory executed protocol, but then again, this was no ordinary mission and no ordinary circumstance.

"Done," came the one-word reply from Fancy-pants.

"Heat, make sure everyone's got a weapon and enough ammo."

"Got you, BJ. When I got the call earlier, I made sure I brought plenty of clips. I know how this gang likes to shoot first, shoot second, and overall, just plain ole shoot a lot." Thunderous laughter ensued.

"And make sure everyone is on the same channel," came a second but delayed command from the front.

"Roger that," said Fancy-pants. And then he continued, "I am now going to do a two-way call sign confirmation. When you hear your call sign, please respond in the affirmative. Now let the check begin. Number one."

"Affirmative."

"Cowboy?"

"Affirmative."

"Danger?"

"Affirmative."

"Blow-em-up?"

"Affirmative."

"Golden Boy?"

"Affirmative."

"Heat?"

"Affirmative."

"Jumper?"

"Affirmative."

"Red China?"

"Affirmative."

"Okay, everybody can send and receive. But what about Greg? He doesn't have a call sign," came the query from Fancy-pants.

Before BJ could answer, Pam yelled out, "Let his sign be Baby Boy!" To which Greg immediately rebuffed with an emphatic and resounding "Hell no!" Combustible laughter erupted again, and BJ had to remove his headset to regain his composure, as the sound of all the grown folks' laughter, together with his own, was ear-shattering.

Quickly regaining command of his tactical force, BJ countered with the call sign of Prodigal Son, alluding to the good fortune of Greg's sudden departure on the night before the hostage taking and his triumphant return. Having restored order, BJ now restated the plan so that each man on the team was absolutely certain of his role, as well as that of his comrades.

"Gentlemen," he began in a low voice that was filled with the urgency dictated by the situation. "Our initial objective is to get to the catering hall and incapacitate the catering crew and assume their roles. If all goes as planned, we should the arriving at the mansion in approximately forty-five minutes, which would put us right around nine o'clock as scheduled. That's when the caterers are supposed to deliver that special dessert. But, boy, I'll bet you that they all will have indigestion tonight," he said confidently.

Although he was understandably nervous, BJ trusted his team. He knew two things. First, they were professionals. And second, they all cared for him. So he believed in his heart they would go all out and go that extra mile for him. This gave him a measure of quiet assuredness.

"Copy," he said, asking in the stealthy Black Ivory way if everyone understood and if there were any questions or concerns. He smiled to himself as he received nine replies of "Copy." At this point, second-in-command Red took over the airway for a brief time.

"As Number One's daughter-in-law said, the catering cleanup crew is supposed to arrive at nine to serve and commence the cleanup by twelve o'clock, or right after the last guest leaves, whichever happens first. Now from what ole fat boy here has told us, there are only two guards on the gate." He then continued without pause, "But down in the workforce quarters, there will be about six to ten armed guards, depending on the rotation. And as I understand it, only one of them should be on the watch."

Being the master strategist of the group, Red China laid out the scenario for the group. "So what we'll do once we get into the glass-enclosed walkway, you two, Fancy-pants and Golden Boy, will head straight for the workforce sleeping quarters and disarm and restrain the guard on watch. Once you are done, you will call out the names of BJ's boys. Danger, you and Heat do the same for their wives."

Pam quickly interrupted Red China's instructions to remind the men that before anyone under the influence of the Godspoke will respond, the word *workforce* must be used before the name is said. "Okay, did you guys two get that? You must use the word *workforce* before you say their name."

Working in perfect tandem, BJ chimed back in, "Okay then, while you four are securing the release of my boys and their wives, the rest of us will head toward the guards' sleeping quarters and do what is necessary to disarm and restrain them.

"Once we have everybody secured, we will all head toward the glass elevator, and we will go up in two groups, as I believe that all of us at one time may prove to be too much weight." Then in an effort to bring some levity to the situation, he added, "Especially you, Blow-em-up. You look like you been eating some of that stuff you explode since I saw you last."

Again, loud and uncontrollable laughter erupted in the headsets, so much so that almost everyone had to remove theirs in an effort to muffle the deafening cackles from the entire team.

Self-conscious, Blow-em-up immediately made a childlike effort to defend himself. "Hey, wait a minute. I've always weighed this much." And what did he do that for? The laughter, which was beginning to subside, grew to an even higher crescendo. Still pleading his case, he continued, "Don't start in on me, BJ. Don't we have work to do?" His hope was that the sheer gravity of the situation would readily turn the focus away from him and back to the important mission at hand.

Taking the cue, BJ recanted, "Take it easy. Take it easy. I'm just busting your chops."

"Okay, all jokes aside, let's take it from the top," Red China said as he broke his long silence in lieu of the laughter. "Once we all meet at the glass elevator, we will go up in two groups. Group one will stay hidden inside the wine cellar until the second group gets aboveground. Then we will all make our way to the catering trucks and then make our way back to the road.

"Then," he concluded, "we will also place the first set of explosives at the edge of the tree line behind the cellar. That explosion should be strong enough to rip a huge hole in the biosphere. It should also cause our guest a whole bunch of grief and give us some needed cover to get away scot-free."

"Copy!"
"Copy!"
"Copy!"
"Copy!"
"Copy!"
"Copy!"
"Copy!"

Seven times over, a reply in the affirmative rang through the headsets. BJ then added one last thought as a final point. "We will set the timers on the detonators for one minute and fifteen seconds, which should give us ample time to return to the vehicles and get the hell out of Dodge before the earth gets good and scorched around there."

"I know that's right!" Danger shouted in a somewhat now familiar burst of excitement.

"Hopefully, the blast will only be strong enough to disable the elevator and the wine cellar above it and not to hurt any of the workforce members." BJ then returned to his omnipresent parental mode. With a heavy sigh, he stated, "I know there must be lots of other families who are searching for the rest of the unfortunate folks who make up the workforce." Snapping out of that role just as quickly as he had assumed it, he barked, "Any questions?"

"That's a big negatory," came the reply from Red China, speaking for the rest of the team.

"Oh, well, then, BI, let me hear it." And in unison, the team bellowed the Black Ivory code of honor.

They chanted, "BI forever. Kill or be killed! BI forever. Kill or be killed! Black Ivory forever. Kill or be killed!" They repeated the slogan in unison three times over, and thereafter, each man fell silent for a moment of observance in honor of those who had fallen by the wayside during previous missions.

After a moment of intense silence, BJ broke the stillness by reciting his usual prayer before every mission over the past seven plus years. "Gentlemen, I hope to see you all on the other side, and Godspeed."

Peering through the catering hall windows, they observed two men locked in a mini power struggle, and one of them was winning handily.

"The way you do it is not good enough. I am Andre' Francios LeCler', and it's Andre', not Anndre, as you Americans like to pronounce it. The world does not march to the beat of your drum anymore as you all would like to think.

"I am the finest chef in the world. I cater all the major events. I cook for all the A-list celebrities and top dignitaries. Why do you think they fly me in? If the way you do it was good enough, then I would not be here, wi…I mean yes." He accentuated this last statement with a victorious look of glee. He promptly turned his back on his belittled counterpart and proceeded to shout more instructions to those busying themselves with some final touches.

"My exotic shaved ice desserts must be served at 15.55555 degrees Celsius, and for you behind-the-times Americans, that is precisely sixty degrees Fahrenheit, so do not remove them until I say so." Trying to make amends and return to the good graces of his obvious superior, the lesser of the two chefs tried a more subtle approach to make his point.

"Yes, Chef LeClerc. I am acutely aware of the circumstances under which you are here, and I am both humbled and honored to be working with you. But we have less than forty minutes to get there."

The feisty lead chef replied, "But if my memory serves me correctly, the trip is exactly seventeen minutes from start-up to parking, so we are in no rush at this time."

The other man, insistent on making one final point, played what he thought was his ace in the whole. "If you would just allow me to say so, I fully respect your work tonight and your resumé as a whole, both impressive by any measurement. But I know the Conns. They will not tolerate our lateness."

With everyone in place, Red China gave the order to move in. Without warning, team 1 burst into the front door, and team 2 did the same from the rear entrance. A clerk in the chef's office tried frantically to make a quick call. Unfazed, Blow-em-up called out to him, "No need. We already cut the phone lines. So come on out here, buddy. And we know like you know that there's no cell phone signals out this far. So come on out here and join your buddies on their knees.

"That's right. You heard me. On your knees. Assume the goddamn position," he said, striking one older and somewhat defiant looking man with a hard and sharp jab in the thorax. The man clutched his chest as if he were taking his last breath. Although not quite that severe, his look of defiance was all but gone. Hands pressed hard against his aching chest, he sank slowly to his knees, as had all the others who were now watching this surreal drama unfold.

Each man, including Mr. Lead Chef himself, was asked to undress and place their uniforms beside them on the floor. Each complied, some slower than the others, but all compliant. Thereafter, each man was tied up, and the whole group was placed in a slam lock freezer, stripped down to their underwear. All but one poor soul had them on.

"Bad day not to have on underdrawers." Jumper laughed as he slammed the door shut. And the men, bound and gagged, looked on in sheer fright.

"Find you some clothes that fit!" came the shout from BJ. "Let's move. We got a schedule to keep."

SAME AS GOD SPOKE

Once inside the catering truck, the occupants had a good laugh about the experience that they had just had. Blow-em-up began the conversation with a question. "Did the old guy really shit himself?"

Golden Boy replied, "I think he did. I really think he did."

They all burst out in an all-consuming but somewhat nervous laughter. That lasted about all of five seconds, and then silence.

Unexplained silence...

CHAPTER 18

THE TAKEDOWN

WITH THE ENTIRE strike team, plus two, crammed into the back of an extremely uncomfortable catering truck, there was tons of tension in the air. Tension was easy to tell with this group. They were generally a happy-go-lucky bunch. Jokes, lots of jokes, and jokes of all kind were the constant companion of the Black Ivory Strike Team.

However, today was all the way different. For the most part, the jokes were noticeably absent on this mission. The Black Ivory team prided itself on two things: never ever nervous and always devoid of drama. So far, there had been no drama, so their track record for the devoid factor remained intact. The "never ever nervous" mantra was another issue altogether. From the looks of things, these were incredibly nervous times, and "never ever" was indeed presently at risk.

The current members of the strike team had been together for the last three years now. But more importantly, each member had individually earned the trust and respect of the unit as a whole. Once aboard, each man had to prove that they were not only skilled and gifted but also die-hard devoted. Acting in concert, these guys were a seamless get-it-done operation, batting a thousand as far as successful missions go.

However, something about this one was very different. They all loved and respected BJ to the umpteenth power, and because of it, they would never want to let him down. That's why this wasn't just another job. This was personal. This was for Big Joe. There was a lot at stake. There was also quite a lot to lose—the lives of BJ's children. And that was the difference. That was what caused this mission to be weighed down with so much pressure-based tension.

Riding along in deafening silence, if somebody didn't say something soon, the closed quarters would definitely implode for lack of usable oxygen.

"Why is everybody so quiet?" came the outburst that everyone else was waiting for.

"Because your mamma is not here to make fun of!" came the joking reply.

The truck instantly exploded with laughter. It was nervous laughter. And it came across as such, but it was still laughter, and laughter was what they all needed to calm some obvious nerves that were on edge. That joke proved to be the saving grace; it broke the ice. From that point on, joke after joke rolled out and continued for the next thirteen minutes, which was the duration of their short journey.

As the unassuming vehicle neared the Conn mansion, BJ called for calm. He then gave the order for everyone to be on guard and duly charged his men with the ready. As they approached the security checkpoint, right on cue, the team's mood immediately turned very solemn and businesslike. Black Ivory could turn it off and on like a light switch, which was why they believed they were so successful. They thrived on the "keep it loose and then get it done" model of engagement.

The two security guards, sitting side by side in the glass-enclosed booth, easily recognized the very distinguishable black catering truck. Not only did it stand out because of its atypical color, it was also heavily adorned with numerous pastry decals and gold lettering. With no reason to be otherwise suspicious, they opened the gates and gave the okay for the truck to pass through.

With the gates completely drawn back, the vehicle eased forward. Red China was in the driver's seat. At that critical juncture, when he was parallel with the two guards, he waved to them and flashed a bright smile. Then, without any forewarning, he opened fire. He emptied the silencer-adapted semiautomatic .9 millimeter handgun that he had sitting in his lap.

Each of the bullets met their mark. And without wavering, as would any good special ops agent, he immediately reported two confirmed takedowns through his communications headset. Quiet cheers could be heard from the rear of the truck.

"Be still." Again on cue, BJ called for calm and restraint.

As they cautiously proceeded up the driveway, Pam was suddenly overcome by a feeling of rushed anxiety. The thought of returning to the godforsaken place she had fought so mightily to escape sent cold sporadic chills up her spine. The hairs on the back of her neck were literally standing on end, which was a sight in and of itself, but that was doubly compounded by her sweating brow.

Even more telling were her shaking extremities, because try as she might, she could not keep either her hands or legs still. She did everything she could, but to no avail. So she chose to just ignore those facts and hope like hell that no one else noticed. She thought briefly about asking for help but thought better of it, as she did not want anyone to know.

With all the guns and body armor in full view and surrounding her, all her instincts told her this was a very good time, like no other, to be strong. Any signs of weakness on her part, she reasoned inwardly, might distract one of the others—Greg, in particular—from doing their full part to help complete their mission of freeing the others.

A freedom that they must, at some point, attribute mainly to her cunning, courage, and wit. She smiled outwardly at the thought. Although saddled with a board smile, her greatest fear of the moment was being the cause of a failed rescue attempt. The thought that she might end up being the goat instead of the heroine was motivation enough to be strong, or at least enough to put up a good front and pretend. So that was what she did—pretend!

Although concealed behind the driver's compartment and out of sight as they rolled in, she remained somewhat anxious by being back on the grounds. In any event, she was still able to calmly point out which side of the mansion they needed to be on. Red China guided the little food truck around a number of blocked aisles and through other tight squeezes until he finally pulled to a smooth stop at the rear of the house.

Once they came to a complete stop, each man assigned to the recon team took a turn calling out various logistical factors that they had gathered during their slow entrance onto the grounds.

"I count forty-two cars."

"I see three entrances to the main house from the south and east directions."

"I count four parking attendants."

"There. There is the entrance," Pam blurted out, interrupting the seamless flow of material information being provided to the team leaders, BJ and Red China.

Once the vehicle was completely out of sight from the parking attendants, BJ gave the order for the Alpha team, which consisted of Danger, Heat, and Golden Boy, to go and subdue the attendants. At the same time, the Bravo team of Red China, Fancy-pants, and Cowboy made their way over to secure the wine cellar. Following orders, the Alpha team made their way in single file formation over to the corner of the building. And then they walked in plain sight toward the four men seated on folding chairs near a side patio.

They decided that they did not need the cover of stealth. The attendants had no earthly idea that danger was just about to overtake them. The three men simply looked like part of the catering team. Although, they did have on body armor underneath their unassuming uniforms, complete with long-tailed white jackets. How could they know?

How could they know that they would soon be subjected to untold amounts of pain? How could they know that in mere minutes, they would be forced into the most uncomfortable of all positions, hog-tied and gagged? Several stinging blows about the torso and head before being put out of commission for the night only served to up the ante and made the nightmarish experience all the more real.

But how could they have known? To make matters worse, there was some icing on this extremely unhealthy cake. Before the Alpha team actually closed the lid, they never ever imagined that they would end up being stuffed in the dark dank trunk of a limousine. From driver to prisoner, how could they have known?

Alpha Team confirmed the containment of four subjects and were instructed to hustle back to the truck. Now back at three-fourths strength, the Alpha and Delta teams, after collectively checking the perimeter a second time, made haste to the wine cellar to rejoin team Bravo. Also in tow were the betrothed couple, newly reunited.

Although speed was not at all his forte, BJ traversed the distance in lockstep with the rest of his team. He arrived at just about the same time as everyone else. Each were understating how winded they were due to the torrid pace. Pam and Greg brought up the rear, as neither was in the best of condition. Both were practically out of breath after the quick-paced two hundred-yard double-time burst of speed. This spoke volumes and served as ample evidence of being out of shape.

Once inside the sealed compartment of the cellar, BJ pointed and pressed the remote to operate the glass elevator. As the room began to transform and the glass separated itself from the walls, each man stood cautiously back to back with another team member. Everyone with the exception of Number One, who jokingly said aloud, "This high-tech ride is courtesy of my good friend Big Walter." Big Walter, who was also hog-tied and gagged in the trunk of a limousine back at the motel, could only wish he could have taken this ride.

As the short ride neared its end, every available gun was drawn and trained on the opening door. This was standard operating procedure. "When in doubt, shoot it out" is what they lived, eat. and breathed.

"Get ready," BJ said as the doors opened to nothing but an empty walkway. He always expected the unexpected. "If you expect something but get nothing, that's a whole lot better than getting something when you've expected nothing. So look alive and always be ready," he said in conclusion, forever the trainer-in-chief.

Danger placed a bag in the elevator doors to prevent it from operating, and then in single file formation, they exited to make their way to the end of the lengthy glass-enclosed walkway. As she reached the end of the walkway to her once living hell, Pam pointed out the location of the security guards' sleeping quarters.

Delta Team, who were assigned the task of neutralizing the security guards, went off in that direction. The Alpha Team, plus Greg, escorted Pam to rescue LJ and the others. Team Bravo stayed behind to secure the entrance to the walkway, which then became point rendezvous.

Danger, Heat, and Golden Boy were the first to enter the male workforce sleeping quarters where LJ and his brothers were being housed. Once inside, Pam was supposed to seek out each of her in-laws while her escorts, along with Greg, secured the guard on duty. Much to their surprise, once they burst through the door, hoping to utilize the highly rated and supremely effective element of surprise, they themselves were the victims of a surprise. There was no duty guard to subdue.

"He must be in the bathroom," Pam said softly. "It's over there." She pointed hurriedly. They rushed over to the bathroom, but they found that it, too, was vacant, not unlike the duty station for the guards. Curious but unscathed, the team set out to do what they came there to do. At least the other thing, which was to save LJ, Henry, and Milton, was still doable.

Standing in the middle of the unit near to her brothers, Pam gave her spellbound relatives the command, as only she knew how, having heard it so many times before. Pam knew that in their conscious minds, all Godspokes hated hearing commands of any kind. Be that as it may, she was sure that this was one that they wanted to hear. This was the command that they had been waiting to hear.

"LJ," she said nervously. "No, Workforce LJ, report to the unit entrance. Workforce Henry, report to the unit entrance. Workforce Milton, report to the unit entrance." Her three spellbound brothers-in-law in tow, Pam and her escorts, together with her fiancé, made their way to her former housing unit. She did not notice that Ms. Diane was not in her bed where she should have been, or else she could have alerted the others, and her improbable switch and subsequent great escape had been discovered.

"Workforce Beverley, report to the unit entrance. Workforce Mysty, report to the unit entrance." Before repeating this life-saving command to Hazel, the sincere dislike for this woman briefly suppressed Pam's sense of urgency. In her mind, she thought, if only for a moment, she would love to give Hazel an order to kiss her feet.

She wondered if anyone would see or notice or even care. However, she quickly snapped out of her momentary fantasy and gave the order. "Workforce Hazel, report to the unit entrance." The fact that Greg yelled for her to hurry up might have also helped her to make up her mind a little sooner than she planned.

Golden Boy, leader of the Alpha team, provided BJ with a situational report, and it was none too comforting to the Black Ivory leader. "Number One, I don't know what's going on, but there are no guards on duty in these units like Pam and fat boy said they would be."

"Roger that!" came a short reply.

Through his headset, Golden Boy heard BJ also report that there was no one in the guard quarters either. He further stated that the guards might have been pulled or given the night off because of the party. He then went on to say, "I hope that's it and not some other more worrisome explanation."

While making his way back to the rendezvous point, BJ called out to Greg, "Prodigal Son, how are my boys?"

"All right, considering" was the sober short reply. Then after a brief assessment pause, he continued, "They are under that spell right now, but they will be better once they have their will back. I also think we need to get them out from under the spell right now so they can be of some help to us if we need them. Don't you think, Dad?"

"I'm not Dad now. I'm Number One. But no, I don't. They are under, and who knows how long it takes to get back right. It would kill me and Big Momma, too, if something happened to them all because I engaged them while not at full capacity. No, that's a negatory. I don't want them in any danger, at least not in that condition."

"But Number one," Greg chimed in. "All we have to do it is let them kiss their wives and all of them will come from under the spell in only a very few seconds. Pam told me all about it and explained to me how it works. The antidote to this Godspoke stuff is sexual arousal."

"Okay, Prodigal Son," BJ shot back impatiently. "Why are you telling me and not just getting it done? Good soldiers get it done on their own, son! They don't have to be told every move to make. You know that. Or at least you should."

Still not satisfied that he had made his point, BJ carried on, "They assess the situation, they decide what needs to be done, determine how best to do it in that specific situation, and then they just get it done. So be a good soldier! What are you waiting for? Give them the order then."

Greg took his not so subtle cue and went into action. He gave the order for each of the three couples to passionately kiss, touch, and caress each other. Each husband and wife team followed this command to the letter, just as all Godspoke are compelled to do. This was extremely difficult for Pam to watch. It brought back the bad memory of her orders from Walter, but she made very sure that she displayed no visible reaction. As the couples engaged, Milton was the most vocal. His kisses sounded as though he was way past the kissing part of it and on to the next stage of the romance dance.

However uncomfortable this public display of passion made Pam, it made her fiancé equally uncomfortable, but also very curious. Once the couples had commenced to carry out the command, Greg paid close attention. Truth be told, he wanted to see just how much passion had to be present in order to elicit some sexual arousal from someone under the Godspoke spell.

Although they had not discussed it in any great detail, he was left to simply imagine what kind of experience Pam had to have in order for her to become sexually aroused. He knew that it took a lot for her, usually. The thought was really beginning to bother him. In the days to come, that thought would continue to haunt him. However, now was not the time to dwell on it, so he put it out of his mind. But he knew that he would revisit the thought at some point.

One by one, the kissing couples stopped. The dynamic change was now happening, and it was clearly visible as each individual began to tremble. Pam knew this feeling all too well. She remembered having to sit in Walter's bathroom while she underwent the change. She fully knew that in only a matter of seconds, each of them would begin to feel very dizzy. She yelled out to no one in particular, "We have to steady them and hold them up! You get real, real dizzy when you start to come from under." Greg, Pam, and the team members of Alpha and Bravo moved in to steady the shaky seven.

As luck would have it, Pam was paired with Hazel, and again her mischievous side took command of her better angels. She imagined what it would be like to let her constant source of social discomfort fall face-first down to the hard but shiny stone floor. She imagined that Hazel would see herself in its shiny reflection as she neared what was sure to be a bruising impact.

She knew, to her, that would be funny. She further knew the moment was prime, ripe, and rare. She also knew that she may never get another chance to exact some intentional yet unprovable revenge on the woman who had given her so much grief since joining the family some years ago. *What the hell*, she thought as she let her go of her nemesis even in this most vulnerable of states.

Hazel rocked, stumbled, and just as she was on her way down to take what would definitely amount to a very punishing and unforgiving tumble, BJ came to her rescue. He stepped in, grabbed her, and steadied her once again. Team Delta had returned just in time. He could only give Pam a stern look. Right now, he had bigger fish to fry. She smiled sheepishly and moved in to retake control without remark.

No one, she concluded, could ever prove what she had done was intentional. No one, she reasoned, could step inside her head and read her mind. Not even the Godspoke inventors could do that. And as a final seal of approval, she vowed to never tell on herself. She further reasoned that she would, of course, blame it on all the drama, all the tension, and all the stress of the situation at hand. She would swear that she, too, was overcome at that moment.

Approximately two minutes after the kissing had stopped, LJ was the first to regain his independent will. This was very evident by his first words. "Give me a gun so I can kill the motherfucker who busted my mouth!"

Greg replied, "Hold on, big brother. All things in due time. You're not even steady yet."

Pam, however, had other ideas. She wanted the man that had taken advantage of her vulnerability dead or at least beat within an inch of his life. Her intentions were unmistakable when she blurted out to LJ, "That was Big Walter who hit you, and he is in the trunk of the limousine that we have stashed back at the motel."

Greg then quickly retorted, "And like she said, he's not here. So killing him will have to wait."

LJ stubbornly shot back, "Okay then, I don't care who I kill. Because right now, I just want to kill some fucking body. Where's that crazy motherfucker that calls himself the Good Doctor? I'll kill him. Hell, just give me a fucking gun. I'll kill anybody!"

As LJ continued his ranting and raving about wanting to kill somebody, anybody, and everybody one by one, the rest of the wobbly, shaky seven all got their sea legs back. As each came around, they seemed almost instantly back to normal. Although normal, emotionally speaking, would be an extremely long ways away and would take a very, very long time to come, especially after this taxing ordeal.

However, for the moment, each was anxious to speak, and they all talked over each other, first describing and thereafter discussing the experience. Next they, with LJ leading the charge, swiftly transitioned to extolling the virtues of the sweet elixir that was revenge. They, too, wanted to kill somebody, anybody, and everybody!

Finally, BJ stepped in to bring some much-needed order to a growing chaotic situation. "All this talk of killing and of revenge can come later. Let's get all of you and all of us out of here right now. That is our primary goal, and to do it right now," he said with all the authority he could muster, and that was quite a bit. "We need you to take advantage of the independent will that you just got back and use it to keep quiet and follow directions.

"Anything less," he said in a more modest yet still deadly serious tone, "could put us all in the same unenviable position that all of you just got out of. Are we clear?" He asked no one in particular but directly to everyone present. He made this loud unequivocal declaration for all to hear, and they did.

His voice reverberated loudly as they moved through the glass walkway and back toward the elevator to freedom. BJ did not wait for an answer. He knew he did not need one. He knew his point was well made. He simply moved on to the next order of business, which was getting aboveground, then getting off the property, and finally getting out of this part of the state.

As they walked in unison but in a staggered single file formation, BJ took in every bit of info that he could as he planned to relay it to the proper authorities at the most the opportune time. Revenge. His mind replayed the talk of the sweet revenge that LJ and the others had on their minds and in their hearts. Moving meticulously along, scanning slowly, he thought to himself that no one was as angry or as dead set on revenge as he was.

Only now was not the time, because he knew when to hold them and also when to fold them. He knew when to walk away. And above all else, he knew when to run. He lived by those famous words as portrayed in the movie *The Gambler*, as well as immortalized in a song by the same name. It was one of his all-time favorites.

Now back at the entrance to the elevator, his thoughts were interrupted. BJ asked for a status report. Red China reported that all were present and accounted for, no rounds fired, no takedowns needed, and no combatants engaged or in sight. "That's good, but where is all the action?" asked BJ, trying to get a collective assessment. "Does anyone, besides me, find it strange that we haven't seen anyone other than the parking attendants and the two dead checkpoint guards?"

"Yeah, we went into two of the housing units, and they were both unmanned, right, Golden Boy?" urged Danger as confirmation.

"Yeah, that's right. I called it in already though."

"And I know they are always there," LJ chimed in. "It sure sounds very strange," LJ freely added again, now out of his spellbound state and back to his usual talkative self.

One after the other, the team, together with the newly freed, began to question whether or not they had walked into some sort of trap. Sensing a slow boil to worry overkill, Red China made what he hoped to be a reassuring announcement or at least a timely momentary distraction.

"Not to worry, fellas. We just got ourselves three more guns at the ready. BJ's sons know how to handle themselves pretty well," he said with great emphasis and lighthearted enthusiasm. He then added for good measure, "I, for one, know that these boys know how to lock and load with the best of them. Ain't that right, BJ?"

Looking for reinforcements, he passed the manufactured distraction off to Number One in the hopes that the leader could build on the superficial momentum that he had just started. "This is very true. My boys make this already formidable team just that much stronger," he said without much conviction. "Now let's move." The loud and demanding order instantly shocked the Black Ivory Team back to commando mode, and in no time at all, the group, now fourteen strong, was locked and loaded and ready for action. Come what may.

They had already traversed the long narrow pathway, and several seconds later, they found themselves aboard the elevator. Once the doors closed, BJ was privately glad that they had all safely reached the elevator. He actually thought this mission would be a lot more challenging, but nonetheless, all seventeen members of the group were riding up to the doorway to freedom, and not one major challenge yet. He openly questioned it, yet he secretly welcomed it.

Apparently eager to dismiss their growing fears brought on by all the talk of setup and suspicious circumstances, the team began to come alive. Blow-em-up said excitedly, "In about thirty seconds, we should be back on the truck and just about through the gate. In and out before they know what hit 'em."

"Now that's the way to do it. Lights out style," Golden Boy chimed in.

"Hell yeah. I'm sorry, ladies. Dog-gone right," added Danger, who was followed by Heat with his own adlib version of agreement in the form of a "*Woo-ha!*" victory yell.

Right smack in the middle of this impromptu mini-celebration, BJ cautioned them all, "We're not there yet, guys. So everybody look alive and stay alert." In an effort to double down on the stakes, BJ made this one last urgent plea to his team as they ended the short thirty-second ride from the Godspoke dungeon of hell to the aboveground glow of heaven. All the way down to his very core, on two fronts, BJ felt that something was just not right.

He could sense that his team was almost looking past the now, and he knew all too well that was when very bad things could happen. *It's never good*, he thought, *when you think the mission is over before it's actually over*. So with fire in his belly and blood in his eye, he turned to his team and looked each one in the eye and gave them another stark warning, "Please, please believe this is not over yet!" He hoped that he was wrong and he could live with that, but what if he was right?

The elevator doors opened, and before them was an empty wine cellar. So far so good, they all thought. Red China gave the order for Golden Boy to make sure the coast was clear. Golden Boy dropped to the floor and poked his head out for a peek around the corner. All looked clear, and he reported that he saw nothing. Red China gave the order for everyone to move, but BJ raised his right fist and gave the *all stop* sign. Something wasn't right. No guards, no fuss, no mess, this was all going too smoothly. How could these people, who had so much to lose by allowing anyone ever caught up in their treacherous web, to so simply go free? Be this inept?

"Jumper?" said BJ.

"Yeah, BJ?" Jumper replied.

BJ continued, "You got those heat signature goggles? You know, the ones we use to trail people at night."

Somewhat bragging to the civilians present, Jumper stated, "Yeah, those babies can detect trace elements of body heat that they've left behind." He said, now searching his backpack, "So we all know that they can run, but they can't hide."

Amid a bevy of high-fives, Pam whispered to Greg, "Is that for real? Do they have something that can do that?"

"Yes. Now shush," Greg added as a word of caution not to disrupt the surveillance.

SAME AS GOD SPOKE

"All warm-blooded animals," he whispered in her ear, sensing her distain after being shushed and dismissed, "emit body heat, and even if someone is up to fifteen minutes in front of you. We can use these special goggles to follow a heat trail they always leave behind. It's also really good for detecting people hiding behind objects such as cars or buildings or around corners. It can even tell the difference between the heat from a car or a stove from that of a human."

Jumper dug into his backpack and finally handed the heat-seeking glasses to BJ as requested. When he put them up to his eyes to peer through them, he whispered nervously, "Hot damn, boys! We got company. Everybody stay quiet and stay put. They're out there, and there are a lot of 'em, only I can't make out how many exactly."

As he uttered the last word of his statement, the wine cellar was inundated by a hail of bullets. Without exception, everybody hit the mirror-smooth polished floor, some harder than others. The Matthews women, although most would describe as pretty agile, were still not prepared to skillfully perform such lightning-quick maneuvers without getting hurt. Hazel had an especially bad fall, but that was the least of the group's worries.

Golden Boy went down before any else did, but for a different reason. He was hit in what looked to be the shoulder. Team Black Ivory immediately returned fire through the partially opened door. No one was visible, but they fired anyway in the direction of their unseen enemy. Under the cover of automatic gunplay, Red China and BJ went into harm's way, because that was the only means of retrieving Golden Boy, who had fallen forward just outside the door. In a flash, they had successfully pulled their comrade to safety, and he gladly reported that he had been hit, but only in his right arm.

Red China called out to Heat, "Get me the first aid kit! He's hit."

"I'm okay. I'm okay," Golden Boy countered. "It's not that serious."

"Are you sure you're okay?" Red China questioned, solemnly looking at the stream of fresh blood free-flowing from the wounded man's upper right arm. "I think you better let me check it out."

"I'm okay, man," Golden Boy demanded, pushing away all attempts from the second-in-command to administer any medical attention. "I don't think those bullets were meant to kill or I'd be dead right now." After quickly tying a makeshift tourniquet around his muscular right bicep, he concluded at last, "It's only a flesh wound. They had me. They had me dead to rights, and *dead* is the optimal word here. If they were really trying to take me out, I think that in the next couple days, there would have been some low talking and some slow walking on my behalf." Then to accentuate his point, he mustered a broad smile together with a slightly pained laugh. BJ took a brief second away from being trained on pinpointing the whereabouts of the opposition to ask about the wounded warrior.

"Is he really okay, Red?" came the matter-of-fact query from Number One.

"Yeah, it looks okay. Looks like the bullet passed straight through the skin and only grazed the muscle. He should have himself operational in less than two minutes, soon as that tourniquet takes hold. If we have that long," the large red man said almost under his breath and to no one in particular.

"Gentlemen, although you are not on the guest list, you are more than welcome to join my little party. So come out and play. You would really enjoy yourselves, you fucking maggots!" An amplified voice could be heard bellowing over a bullhorn. "Forgive me. I do apologize. Allow me to introduce myself, although some of you may already know me. However, for those of you who do not, I am the Good Doctor, and I own this magnificent place that you just so happen to be intruding upon as we speak.

"And furthermore, because you have chosen to trespass on my property, unfortunately for you, believe it or not, I now own you as well. I am the Good Doctor, and I own every goddamn thing as far as the eye can see. My eye or your eye, take your pick," he said with a devilish smile. "My vision is not so great anymore," he said, removing his spectacles and holding them up to the light to inspect them. "However," he continued after replacing them, "I still see pretty damn far, so you figure it out.

"By the way," he said with obvious delight. "These are the men that are going to take your fucking lives if you don't lay down your weapons and come out into the open. And allow me to assure you that I do mean this instant. Did you hear me?" came a loud, crazed, psychotic scream. "Of course you did," he said, now returning to a more calm and discernable tone. "My voice carries, so you must've heard me.

"Sooooooo," he said again, reverting back to the nearly unintelligible psychotic scream, "what is taking you so fucking long?" Changing yet again to calm, he said, "Oh, I know." Then after a prolonged pause, which was standard for his usual dramatic effect drill, the tall thin man shifted his spectacles once again and calmly said, "I know it really must be a very difficult decision to live forever captive or to instantly die free. But those are your only options. Again, unfortunately for you.

"Believe me, I do understand. And because I am such a sympathetic and giving human being, I will give you some time to think about my offer and your exceedingly limited options. Besides, I like watching people squirm, especially when I am in control of the squirm mechanism. And trust me, I am. Why do you think I allowed you to get this far? I wanted you all to believe that you have gotten away with your improbable escape, just as we allowed Workforce Pam to believe she had gotten away.

"As she walked across the room on the way to powder her nose, Clark, being the observant individual that he is, noticed that Ms. Diane was missing the signature mole behind her left ear. Only," he continued, "it did not occur to him immediately that the young lady at the party masquerading as Ms. Diane was in fact Workforce Pam.

"By the time we had finished discussing the matter, we decided the first priority was to rescue the real Ms. Diane. We still had ample time to stop her from leaving, but we had bigger plans for her. In fact, we thought it better if she brought her accomplices here. This way, we could take you all at once. Then that would put a wrap on any leads that had gotten out. So in a way, we have been expecting you.

"Also, as punishment for subjecting my only child to such a god-awful circumstance, I decided to set a trap and lay in wait for you. The place could use some more good workers. The Black Ivory Strike Force was only able to penetrate the grounds, my grounds, because I allowed you to. Although, I must give, Ms. Pam, kudos on a hand well played. Had it not been for the quick thinking of my right-hand man Clark, you may have gotten away with it.

"I really must check with my wife, Lady Conn, to find out if she had twins that were somehow separated at birth. The resemblance between these two girls is nothing less than striking. But enough of that. I'm sure you have better things to do than listen to me go on about how I've outsmarted you and how I'm going to either own you or kill you.

"So with that, you have exactly five minutes. I am a very impatient man, so I will give you no more than five minutes of freedom or five minutes to live. In either scenario, the choice is entirely up to you. And remember, choices count! FYI, I would prefer that you come work for me. You won't get paid, of course, but at least you'd be alive, so to speak anyway.

"Now for the last dammit-to-hell time, I am the Good Doctor, and if you don't get out here right now, we will come in after you, and it will not be pretty. You stupid motherfuckers! You have to know by now that you are greatly outnumbered, as I happen to know that there are only nine of you, at least with weapons. I am sworn by my Hippocratic oath to preserve life, but I swear by Almighty God, I will take each of your lives, and I won't even blink in the process.

"Now my patience grows weary, but as I said, being a man of my word, I will give you exactly five minutes. Then, if you don't have your asses out here, hands in the air with your backs to me, my innocuous but threatening conversation will immediately turn into a very, very violent reality. Soooooo, three minutes, fifty-nine. Three minutes, fifty-eight. Three minutes, fifty-seven7. The clock is ticking, and I am counting down. If I should reach zero, you will long regret your fateful decision not to heed my warning. In other words, you will wish that you had."

"Really? Really? Is this guy serious? Talk about blowhards. Are you fucking hearing this guy? Who talks like that, from mad to glad and back again in no time at all. If we were in a movie theater, I'd be laughing my ass off right now," said BJ.

"Yeah, he's funny as hell all right. But besides that, this guy is nuts. He is certifiably nuts. He has to be," LJ chimed in, adding to the discussion. "I know this for a true fact."

"Okay, enough of that. We've got less than three minutes. Now let's get focused," BJ demanded.

"Okay, Black Ivory, this is nothing new. It's kick ass time, just like we always do. So let's keep it together, boys," the leader said, directing his attention to his own sons. "Golden Boy," he barked. "About how many do they have out there?"

"I'd say about twenty to twenty-five, BJ."

"Twenty to twenty-five? *Damn!*" Milton blurted out.

"Calm down, son. Calm down" was BJ's very calm, cool, and collected response. "Now listen up, team. Who are they fucking kidding? They're going to probably need about fifty or more of these redneck hillbillies to take on nine Black Ivories."

"Plus four. Don't forget about us, Dad," came Greg's energetic response.

BJ's comment was not intended to inject an additional dose of confidence in his not-yet-worried team. It was, however, intended to ease the frayed nerves of his on-edge family. He very much needed to maintain a resolute demeanor right now. He needed to be strong for his team, as they were closely watching him. And he did, like always.

"First off, does everyone have a gun?"

"We don't, BJ," replied Mysty, speaking for the women in the group, but her response fell on deaf ears. Initially, BJ pretended that he did not hear her, and thus he did not acknowledge her.

"Hey, Dad, what about me, Henry, and Milton?" LJ said anxiously. "You know all of us have taken some paramilitary training."

"And what about us? We know how to shoot too," Mysty said again, this time with more passion and a bit more volume. "All of us know how to shoot, and we shoot pretty well," she said with certainty and emphasis.

"Shooting targets is nothing like shooting at a real person," BJ said quite coolly. "Taking the life of another human being can be really difficult to handle. But," he said, now relenting, "we need all the firepower we can get, so okay." Nonetheless, he cautioned, "Heat, only give them handguns. We don't want any accidental automatic-weapon spray."

"Shit like that could kill up everybody in here," Blow-em-up whispered to Jumper in jest.

Ignoring the unintentionally heard comment and quickly transitioning back to the plan at hand, BJ turned to his resident escape artist. "Danger, you have a laser torch in your backpack, right?"

"Yes, sir!".

"All right then. Cut an escape hole on that side of this building. Once the hole is cut, LJ, you and the other boys get ready to go. And you, too, ladies. On my mark, the Black Ivory Team will open fire. That should give you just enough time to go through the hole and down to the tree lines. Once you get there, I will give you a signal. You all will open fire, and that'll give us some cover to get down there. We will come two by two.

"Blow-em, Jumper, and Heat, on my command, I want you to toss as many remote M80s as you have in the direction of the bad guys. I'm talking everything we've got. Shoot the works. In the meantime, once the hole has been cut, I want you four to go through first and take up a position in the rear of this structure to provide some fire from that vantage point. Meanwhile, under the cover of the M80 explosions once they start, Red China and I will step to the front and hit it from there. Again, LJ and the rest of you guys stay inside until you hear the explosions and you know that we've begun to make our move against them. Then get going. Now I warn you up front, these things create quite a ruckus. The explosions will be both loud and thunderous, so don't get too alarmed. All that noise will be coming from the good guys, okay?"

"Gotcha, Dad!" responded Greg.

"Blow-em-up, once you detonate the first of the remote-controlled pyrotechnics, and I mean immediately after that first explosion, I want everyone to go on the offensive. The group in the rear, you open fire. Our group will open fire, and the group that remains just inside the doorway will also open fire once you've finished blasting the pyrotechnics. Bullets and the sound of gunfire will pierce the quiet still in the night, and the country bumpkins won't know what hit them until after all gunfire has fallen quiet. And we'll be long gone by then. Is that hole done yet?"

"Almost, BJ."

"Good. But hurry it up. Okay, boys, get ready. It's almost show time. And, oh yeah, Blow-em-up, do me a favor."

"What's that, BJ?"

"Make sure that first one hits the Good Doctor right in his big ass bullhorn." Everyone laughed, but they immediately returned to a state of serious readiness.

"The hole is cut!" Golden Boy shouted. "Okay. Everyone move into position. On my mark." But before he could spit out the word *go* and the Alpha team could take their rear positions outside through the escape hole, they were overrun. The Good Doctor's men, ninety in number, had taken up positions just outside the wine cellar. They were surrounded, and yes, they were greatly outnumbered.

The Alpha leader yelled out, "They got us, man! They got us! They're all around us, BJ. It's just too many of them. It's not twenty-five. It looks like a hundred or more, man. What do we do? What do we do? Fight or stand down?"

"Retreat to the biosphere. Quick, press the remote!" LJ instantly shouted.

"Damn. it's not working!" BJ shouted back. "Clark must have the overrode the lock," BJ stated matter-of-factly, his new reality now beginning to sink in.

"What do we do, BJ? It's your call," said Red China solemnly.

"I say we fight to the death," chimed in LJ.

"Me too, me too," several of the others chimed in, indicating their desire and willingness to fight on, including Henry, but not Milton.

However, BJ was not about to sentence his whole family and all his men to certain death. They were all gunned up and ready to take it to the next level come what may, but they were all overruled by the calmer mind and wiser reason of Number One. The leader sternly said, "*No*! No, fellas, no!"

"Let's lay 'em down. I can't ask any of you to engage in a fight that I know we can't win. What would be the point?" BJ he asked in a defeated man's voice to no one in particular. "Whenever and wherever we've gone in, we've always believed that we could get out. More importantly, we've always believed we could win, or at least we had a fighting chance to win.

"This is truly a first. We've never been this pinned down before. I gotta give it to him, that Good Doctor guy, whoever he is, played a smart hand. He outmaneuvered us, and so that's it. Let's lay 'em down. Dead is finished. I left some info out there in the world, and they will find us eventually, just like I found you all. So we just gotta hope they come before these guys can get rid of the evidence that we were ever here. This place is well hidden, but as I said, I'm sure someone will eventually find us."

With that, BJ opened the cellar door, threw out his weapon, and ordered all his men to do the same. In a single file line, hands raised in the traditional symbolic gesture of surrender, the Black Ivory Team and the Matthews 7 plus one all faced the daunting reality of this situation. Things had definitely taken a sharp turn to the left, and for the worse.

"Did you think that you could outsmart me, outmaneuver me, outstrategize me, Mr. Matthews? I knew about you and your merry band of mercenaries long ago. I knew about you even before I took your sorry ass arrogant son over here.

"BJ and LJ, how quaint. I will be certain to have my staff allow you two to sleep side by side as you waste away, spending your days in service to me and your tormented nights wishing that you hadn't. Also wishing that you had never crossed me or crossed paths with me for that matter. I am the Good Doctor, damn it, and now you all know that I reign supreme, goddammit-to-hell."

CHAPTER 19

You'll Never Know

Dammit to hell was right as he spoke those fateful words. All hell broke loose. Helicopters appeared out of the night sky. Bright floodlights pierced the darkness, illuminating the night and turning it instantly into day. The grounds were simultaneously filled to overflow capacity, with law enforcement agents of every kind. A number of the alphabet agencies were present. The letters FBI, ATF, or DEA were hung around most every neck or displayed on some article of clothing. The Good Doctor's men dared not and did not resist. They were put in the like position of being up against overwhelming odds and did what anyone with common sense would have—they surrendered without a fight.

The Good Doctor was none too pleased with this sudden and drastic turn of events, especially when he learned how he had been infiltrated. His tortured and twisted face told the whole story as he watched in suspended disbelief. Clark, who had apparently infiltrated the Good Doctor's inner circle by way of Ms. Diane, was actually an undercover DEA agent.

He was working on a multijurisdictional task force assigned to bring down the God Spoke Syndicate. As the Good Doctor stared on in unqualified astonishment, his daughter's former suitor came to stand with the DEA agent in charge. He immediately began to point out and distinguish the good guys from the bad guys.

While this game of cops and robbers was being played out, LJ had but one wish—a single moment of revenge. For the egregious acts against him and his family, LJ wanted to give the Good Doctor something to remember him by. As his hands were being secured behind his back, LJ walked over and gave the Good Doctor a two-piece.

He hit the frail man with two of the hardest shots to the face that any man could ever be asked to endure and live to tell about. The Good Doctor's bottom lip split instantly into almost two separate pieces. A stream of bright red blood gushed from the deeply separated tender flesh.

Straight away, he dropped to his knees and screamed out in near-death pain. He was momentarily mesmerized, as if he himself were under the Godspoke spell. For quite a few seconds, he could say nothing, and he offered no retaliatory response of any kind.

Looking on intently at his handiwork, two other agents rushed in to prevent LJ from taking a second bite at the apple. The agents obviously understood the former captive's anguish, as they gently and simply pushed him back to arm's length and quietly advised him to step away.

Not entirely satisfied with his one-hit bloody wonder, he considered taking another swing. But after only a few seconds of sagacious thought, discretion won out over valor.

Coming back to his senses, the Good Doctor could not help but shout one more insult. "You are the sniveling coward that I imagined you to be, hitting a defenseless man! I must admit, I am very disappointed, Mr. Matthews. If only I were momentarily rid of these cuffs, I'd like to see how valiant you were under those circumstances."

LJ spun on his heels at the thought of a chance to pulverize this monster, and he gave a pleading look at the agents in charge. Much to his surprise, they took the bait. His pleading eyes won out. "You got two minutes, son," said the agent in charge. "Two minutes exactly."

With the benefit of his handcuffs now removed, the Good Doctor stepped forward to challenge what had proven to be a very formidable opponent in every sense of the word. Without a word, LJ stepped back and simply grabbed something deep within his body. He gathered every bit of anger, every bit of hatred, every thought of revenge and summoned it all into his balled-up right fist and swung with all his power, all his might.

The blow he sent was a jolting shot to his onetime oppressor's left temple. The Good Doctor immediately dropped like a sack of potatoes and landed face-first with a soft thud. In time, he would be extremely thankful for the soft landing, which was courtesy of the very plush manicured lawn. It prevented even more damage to his already badly injured face.

The movies couldn't have written it any better. It was a one-punch knockout. It didn't even take two minutes; it didn't even take thirty seconds. Mysty looked on at her hero and smiled behind a rush of tears. Henry was disappointed that LJ could not have done more to hurt and punish the pernicious demon.

He wanted a deep puncture wound of some sort, something severe and painful yet not life-threatening. Nevertheless, just knowing that the Good Doctor, who really was the bad doctor, would suffer the harsh reality of life imprisonment under maximum security conditions for the rest of his natural born days was comforting.

During the ongoing situational debriefing, it was confirmed that the alphabet agents had 110 of the Good Doctor's gunmen detained and in custody. They also reported two confirmed takedowns, which were courtesy of a little help from Black Ivory. Along with the Good Doctor, thirteen other God Spoke Syndicate staff members were also in custody, including and in particular Lady Sara, plus the real Ms. Diane

As BJ and his group loaded up to leave, three additional carloads of local police arrived. Late to the party as usual, Wilson was heard to say, as he continued to thank the Matthews 8 and the Black Ivory Strike Force for all their help. He walked over to them and gave them a status report, and before long they left the scene.

"I wonder how much they really knew about this whole thing," LJ said. "'Cause if you think about it, as soon as that deputy heard that we were going to the Bright Spot Villas, his whole tune changed. I'm really good at the art of persuasion, but that was way too easy. In hindsight, I think I was the one getting conned. Get it, Conn-ed?" he said to loads of laughter.

"Deputy Do-right, you ole sly dog you. You'll get yours. You will definitely get yours. What do you say, Dad? Are they going to investigate the sheriff's office to see how complicit they were in this whole thing?"

"Well," BJ said, mentally drained and exhausted, "I'll put that in my report, son. But that's all I can do. These things are sometimes very difficult to prove. Real easy to know but still very difficult to prove. I'm just glad that the cavalry rode in when they did. I was starting to get a little worried."

"I never doubted for one minute," LJ said in his usual flamboyant style. "I knew that we would prevail all along," he boasted with the assurance of hindsight.

"No, you didn't! Stop all that bull," came the salty words of distain. Shocked and jaw dropped, LJ could say nothing. Surprisingly, he said nothing for the rest of the trip. His shock came from the very unexpected source of these words. They came from Mysty.

"My god, you all must have been scared out of your heads," came the sweet, loving, and maternal word from Big Momma.

"I know I was," said Milton.

"That goes double for me," replied Mysty.

Hazel chimed in, "Me too."

Each of the eight seemed to have the same sentiment, all except for LJ. "I wasn't scared, and I would have beat the shit out of Big Walt if he hadn't had that big ass gun."

"Yeah, I know what you mean. A man with a gun and a man without a gun. I'm going with the man with the gun," Henry joked.

"Ha, ha, ha." Everyone laughed in unison.

"Yeah, I'll bet you would," said LJ.

"But what I don't understand is how that stuff works," said Greg, trying to get to the bottom of Pam's improbable escape. "They never put me under. But to be real about it, I don't think I would have just done anything they asked me to do. I really can't see how I would just hand over my will and start taking orders from somebody."

"Yes, you can," said LJ angrily. "Weren't you in the fucking armed services? Well, don't you have to take orders and not question the orders that you were given? Don't you have to follow blindly anything that your superiors tell you to do?"

"Yeah, but that's not the same. I still have a choice whether I want to follow the orders or not. But I do see what you mean."

"LJ, watch your mouth."

"Sorry, Momma," he said meekly.

"All I know is, I'm glad that all of you are safe, but I wonder…" And her voice trailed off, leaving everyone to wonder about what she was wondering about.

"Wondering about what, Big Momma?" LJ flatly stated, never one to be shy.

"I wonder…it's just…well, I wonder if there will be any side effects from that stuff they had you on," she said begrudgingly.

"Well," said BJ, "we won't know that for some time to come. But in any event, and in the meantime, I think all of you should go to get a complete checkup on Monday. I'm going to make a phone call tomorrow, and some very good friends of mine are going to make a trip to Coulditbe, Pennsylvania. I will ask them to be certain to give me a call after they have done the lab work and tested the Godspoke potion that you all were given."

LJ answered his phone in the middle of all the family fuss. He stayed on the line only briefly. When asked who it was, he simply said, "Somebody who wanted something that I was not willing to give." He then called BJ to the side to report that the call had been from the Good Doctor himself. Apparently, he skipped the trip to the station altogether.

"What did he say, LJ?"

"He said, 'Well played,' and that we won the battle and not the war, and that he'd see us before long. What should we do?" he asked with copious amounts of concerned impatience.

"Just sit tight. We will discuss it after all of this is over. But for now, don't say anything to anybody else."

Meanwhile, Greg announced to the group, "I think we all owe a ginormous debt of gratitude to my baby girl, Ms. Diane, I mean Ms. Pamela, who saved all of our butts."

"Ginormous?" Pam asked curiously.

"Yeah, you know a hybrid of gigantic and enormous. Ginormous!"

Everyone instantly laughed out loud. Although through thunderous laughter, there was unanimous agreement about the debt. Even Hazel reluctantly agreed.

"I agree!"

"I agree!"

"Me too!"

"Me too!"

"We all do," said many of the voices around the room.

The one absent voice was that of Hazel, who blurted out at an opportune moment of semi-quiet, "But what did you have to do to save us, dear Pam?"

There was an absolute deadly silence in the room. Not even Mysty, who was often Hazel's ally in her verbal sparring exchanges with Pam, could muster a smile. At that exact moment, the tension in the room was as overpowering as any intoxicant. And as unexpected as that very unwelcomed comment was, the follow-up question, which came from an unexpected ally to Hazel, was even more unexpected and unbelievable.

"Yeah, Pam, we all know that sexual arousal is the antidote for the Godspoke. So how much arousal did you get?" Pam looked around to see that all eyes were transfixed on her. She usually loved to be the center of attention, but not for this reason.

"First, let me say that most of you would not be here if I didn't save all of your ungrateful butts, so get off my back, especially you, Hazel. And as for you, Mr. Greg, a wise man once said, 'Never explain. Your friends, your true friends, don't need it. And your enemies, well, your enemies, they won't believe it.' So in either case, why bother? So for those of you who still need an explanation, even after that brilliant piece of philosophy, I have just three words: you'll never know!"

About the Author

Joseph "Prostock Joe" Wactor is the CEO of Smack Talk Promotions. As a writer, broadcaster, and advertiser, communications is his life. Early on, he fancied himself as a lil' Howard Cosell, because as long as anyone can remember, he would tell the story in a unique and original way. He is also an avid Outlaw Grudge racer and fan. Naturally, he married his two loves, drag racing and storytelling. Feeding his desire to be on stage telling the story, he studied communications and became the guy who tells the story. He first used his innate skills as a motivational speaker, then as a reporter after gravitating to the drag race industry. He has authored several nonfiction works in the self-help genre, including *Think & Win: A Teen Perspective in Conflict Resolution*. However, his latest offering delves into the wonderful world of fiction. *Same as God Spoke* (SAGS) is a definite page-turner. You can follow Joseph on social media. Instagram: @SmackTalkTV. Facebook: Prostock Presents. Twitter: @SmackTalkTV. YouTube: SmackTalkTV.

CPSIA information can be obtained
at www.ICGtesting.com
Printed in the USA
LVHW032356090221
678884LV00002B/175